WITHDRAWN
UTSA LIBRARIES

RENEWALS 458-4574

P9-EDW-657

The Garden
of the Hesperides

The Garden
of the Hesperides

Carlos Rojas

Translated from the Spanish
by Diana Glad

Madison • Teaneck
Fairleigh Dickinson University Press
London: Associated University Presses

Library
University of Texas
of San Antonio

© 1999 by Associated University Presses, Inc.

All rights reserved. Authorization to photocopy items for internal or personal use, or the internal or personal use of specific clients, is granted by the copyright owner, provided that a base fee of $10.00, plus eight cents per page, per copy is paid directly to the Copyright Clearance Center, 222 Rosewood Drive, Danvers, Massachusetts 01923. [0-8386-3794-9/99 $10.00 + 8¢ pp, pc.]

Associated University Presses
440 Forsgate Drive
Cranbury, NJ 08512

Associated University Presses
16 Barter Street
London WC1A 2AH, England

Associated University Presses
P.O. Box 338, Port Credit
Mississauga, Ontario
Canada L5G 4L8

The paper used in this publication meets the requirements of the American National Standard for Permanence of Paper for Printed Library Materials Z39.48-1984.

Library of Congress Cataloging-in-Publication Data

Rojas, Carlos, 1928–
    [Jardín de las Hespérides.   English]
    The garden of the Hesperides / Carlos Rojas ; translated from the Spanish by Diana Glad.
      p.   cm.
    Includes bibliographical references.
    ISBN 0-8386-3794-9 (alk. paper)
    I. Glad, Diana, 1945– . II. Title.
PQ6633.O594J3813   1999
863'.64—dc21   98-35809
                                 CIP

Library
University of Texas
at San Antonio

PRINTED IN THE UNITED STATES OF AMERICA

Y el pesar de no ser lo que yo hubiese sido,
la pérdida del reino que estaba para mí,
el pensar que un instante pude no haber nacido,
¡y el sueño que es mi vida desde que yo nací!

—Rubén Darío

And the pain not to be what it was I have been,
the loss of the kingdom that was mine on this earth,
the thought that for naught I could never have dreamed,
and the dream is my life since my moment of birth!

Contents

Acknowledgments 9

Introduction
    Diana Glad 11

The Mirror

Chapter 1. 27
Chapter 2. 43
Chapter 3. 57
Chapter 4. 71

The Hunting Lodge

Chapter 1. 87
Chapter 2. 101
Chapter 3. 117
Chapter 4. 131

The Sun Window

Chapter 1. 145
Chapter 2. 159
Chapter 3. 171
Chapter 4. 184

Heads and Tails

Chapter 1. 201
Chapter 2. 213

Acknowledgments

I WOULD LIKE TO ACKNOWLEDGE CARLOS ROJAS'S VALUABLE SUGGES-tions and words of encouragement throughout this project, and to thank him and Eunice for their generous hospitality to me and my husband at their home in Maçanet de Cabrenys, Spain, during the initial translation phase. I am especially delighted with the collage on the cover illustration, which is the author's design and creation. A true debt of gratitude is owed to Emory University for funding the translation project and to President William M. Chace for championing the cause. Susan Ashe's stylistic advice is also gratefully acknowledged, as is Frederick Langhorst's generosity in sharing his precious time and computer skills. The assistance in the preparation of the manuscript on the part of my colleague Laurent Ditmann, Chair of Foreign Languages at Spelman College, proved to be an invaluable favor and one for which I shall always be appreciative.

Very special words of acknowledgment and gratitude go to my husband, Hans van den Reek, for his unflagging encouragement, boundless patience, and never-failing faith in the project.

Introduction

Diana Glad

THE GARDEN OF THE HESPERIDES IS A CONTEMPORARY MYTH ON THE theme of the heroic quest. As the title suggests, Carlos Rojas has drawn his inspiration from the classical legend of the labors of Heracles in pursuit of the golden apples of immortality hidden in the shadowy land of Hespera. Rojas recreates for the reader this twilight realm where the sun returns each evening to die and to wander somnambulant until dawn in the netherworld. This is also the place and time for dreaming: the irrational domain of psychic creativity. Fittingly, in Rojas's novel the characters are surreal creatures wandering, as if in limbo, through the pages of the text. All are either dead or at death's threshold; yet they dream that they exist and spar for autonomy with their author. Their struggles for authenticity ultimately reveal as much about the writer's quest, and dreams, as about those of his characters.

The novel has two principal protagonists from the Spanish art world: the renowned seventeenth-century portraitist of the court of Philip IV, Diego de Silva Velázquez, and an unnamed twentieth-century surrealist artist whose life story closely matches that of Salvador Dalí. The text, likewise, has two principal narrators. They, along with the anonymous author who plays a cameo role, intrude into the text to explain how these artistic kinsmen converge across three centuries of time.

The surrealist painter's life is narrated by the ghost of his brother and namesake, who was born at the dawn of the twentieth century and died a child. It is the specter of this precocious two-year-old that serves as the begrudging storyteller. His first words, directed to the reader, introduce a portrait apparently done of himself. Yet the face in the portrait is that of an adolescent; it is not his *vera effigies*. As if in defense of the function of art as that of a mirror, the ghost protests that his portrait does not reflect his reality or his time: "I am not the boy in the glossy print. I did not live long enough to be that serious sepia-faced youth. . . . I was a child of flesh and blood, and if I was born a

11

buffoon, it was by the grace of God or Satan himself" (17). The portrait is entitled *Portrait of My Dead Only Brother*, the modified title of an actual painting by Salvador Dalí, of a brother who died before he was born and who was also named Salvador.[1]

Other family ghosts haunt the house and hint that the novel is more than a surreal roman à clef of the life of the historical Dalí, who was—at the time of writing—an old man on his deathbed in his native Catalonia. As he lies dying, the phantoms of the contemporary protagonist's mother, father, and erstwhile lover, Federico (García Lorca), repeatedly beckon the artist to join them. Unless the reader believes in ghosts, he or she quickly suspects that this text, like the fictitious portraits it describes, is no *vera effigies*. The spectral narrator may pose as a child born of flesh and blood, but he suspects that it is ink that runs through his veins.

The artist is also portrayed as a mere character in a manuscript, but his character is fleshed out and given serious psychological attention that resonates with Freudian overtones. The arrival of the family ghosts unlocks memories that he thought he had banished to the darkest recesses of his psyche but now return to haunt his sleep. Drifting in and out of dreams and madness, trying to unravel his memories from hallucinations, the artist is particularly tortured by a dream of having been seduced as a youth by his mother. His dream can be read as either a figment of a collective oedipal fantasy or a repressed childhood memory that informs the artist's surrealist imagery. It will prove to be the venom that gnaws at his psyche, yet the germ of his artistic expression.[2] Like Salvador Dalí's most renowned painting, *The Persistence of Memory*, the novel reflects the persistence over time of the subconscious memory in the creative process. The telling of the painter's story is an exploration into the irrational, a search that is guided by Dalí's aesthetics of critical paranoia.

The storytelling likewise reflects serious literary questions regarding the role of myth in relationship to literature, biography, and the arts. Interspersed within the surrealist painter's story is the supposed autobiography of Diego de Silva Velázquez. It recounts the historic Velázquez's youth in Seville, his meteoric rise to fame as the court portraitist of Philip IV, the untimely death of both daughters and his first granddaughter, survived by a second who (like the Dalían sibling) is the namesake. The story of Velázquez is being transcribed by one of his models, the dwarf and court scribe, nicknamed "El Primo" (which can mean either cousin or fool), as he poses for a portrait with a large volume in folio on his tiny legs. Like the ghost brother's in the contemporary narrative, the portrait of the scribe is also meticulously visualized for the reader—not as a fanciful image, but as the verbal mirror of the real portrait done by the historical Velázquez that now hangs in the Prado Museum. Through the portrait, the reader sees what appears to be a faithful transcription, or reflection, of a *vera effigies.*

At first glance, this manuscript serves as the mirror of art, which reflects reality. Yet soon the author's hand intrudes into the in folio on the scribe's lap to remind both scribe and artist that they are no more than characters in a script despite their semblance of reality. They are line figures drawn in ink—a series of scratch marks, indistinguishable from the squiggles in the various manuscripts that comprise their text or from the brushstrokes on the canvases that frame their context. Their fictional existence serves as the metaphor for the themes of autonomy and authenticity recurrent in the novel. As a metafictional device, it establishes a tension between literature and the visual arts and between history and fiction.

These artists and their subjects exist only as the mental constructs of their author. The visions are the stuff dreams are made of but, blurring the line between object and subject, they also dream and beckon to the reader to join in. Much like the viewer of a surrealist canvas, the reader follows these somnambulant creatures through the labyrinthine folds of their collective revelries. In one dream, Velázquez sees a future artist whom he heralds or prefigures—the surrealist painter of the contemporary narrative who, much like the historical Dalí, reverentially imitates the master painter in search of authenticity.[3]

The novel is complex—more aptly called an enigma. Indeed, a clue for deciphering the code lies in the depiction of the dream portrait, *Incredible Enigma in Velázquez's Studio.* The title may call to mind Salvador Dalí's *Twist in the Studio of Velázquez,* where spectral cardboard cutouts dance the twist to the images of the royal family depicted in canvases, or mirrors, on the wall (*Dalí,* illustration 133*). Incredible Enigma in Velázquez's Studio* is a painting by the surrealist protagonist of a dream he had as a young man, immediately following his first homosexual encounter. Even in his sleep, the protagonist realized "that he would paint the portrait *'d'après* Velázquez,' and he felt certain that he had been transformed into an authentic artist" (61). The portrait is a sort of montage of three of Velázquez's most famous paintings: the portrait *El Primo* of the dwarf, the self-portrait of Velázquez looking into an imaginary mirror included in *Las Meninas,* and the back view of Venus gazing into a looking glass in *Venus of the Mirror*. The canvas is unveiled to the reader by the hand of an unnamed art critic who, like the unnamed author, intrudes into the text to describe the surrealist portrait in minute detail. The critic/author does not decipher the enigmatic reflection of Venus as dark streaks in the mirror; and the reader is left to conjecture her, or his, identity. While failing to grasp the elusive mythical Venus, what *Incredible Enigma* does capture is the baroque artist in the act of painting, the dwarf model in the act of writing, and the surreal protagonist in the act of dreaming. Their activities are identical since each—artist/writer/dreamer—ultimately seeks to authenticate himself through his art. Self-confrontation (facing oneself in the mirror) becomes the protagonists' labor. Writing their stories will prove also to be an heroic labor for the anonymous author, a bit character in self-conscious search of a hero in the mirage of his text.

The enigmatic artist-as-hero can be explained psychologically for the reader who looks for a privileged meaning impressed by the artist, intentionally or unwittingly, into a work of art. To read *The Garden of the Hesperides* as a psychological roman à clef of the identity of the unnamed artist, one could attempt to use Dalí's own paranoiac-critical method to trace the surrealist images that hide in the folds of consciousness of the contemporary artist/ hero. But perhaps that would be tantamount to studying the language of surrealism with the tools of irrationality and deceit, since the method conceals as much as it reveals.[4] In *The Myth of the Birth of the Hero*, the psychologist Otto Rank (1894–1939), a contemporary of Freud and prominent for applying psychoanalysis to creative activity, applied a more detached eye. Rank elaborated on the creative urge of the artistic personality by tracing what he believed to be fundamental links between the creative artist and the hero. Never doubting the power of the hero myth, the question that Rank raised is why one would choose the aesthetic form to satisfy the heroic quest and answered by arguing that both artist and hero seek to transcend the limitations of their birth in search of a higher, self-created destiny.[5]

In *Salvador Dalí or The Art of Spitting on Your Mother's Portrait*, Carlos Rojas mentions that Rank's *The Trauma of Birth* was one of Dalí's favorite books in that it celebrates the creative impulse in art and literature for providing the experience of rebirth (40). Rojas also reports Dalí's claim that the famous eggs in *Oeufs sur le plat sans le plat* (*Eggs on the Plate Without the Plate*, 1932) and in *The*

Sublime Moment (1938) are embryonic images—from memory—of an idyllic, albeit unfeeling, life in the womb:

> In Dalí's paradise lost there is no human love; instead, the living and the dead are reduced to spectral, metaphoric appearances: the two fried eggs as the identical images of the painter's and the dead brother's embryos. . . . Birth means being expelled from this eden into the earthly world, as in the universal myth of the first sin and the fall of humankind. Dalí seemed to be absolutely convinced of this idea, which he backed up with Otto Rank's *Trauma of Birth* at the time he wrote his autobiography, around 1942. . . . *Oeufs sur le plat sans le plat* and *The Sublime Moment* are intuitions of life in the womb, that Dalí could only remember and explain after years had gone by. (38–39)

If the reader elects to read *The Garden of the Hesperides* as a roman à clef of the life of Salvador Dalí, the traumatic memory of a uterine paradise lost would appear to fall like a yoke over the frail (pencil-thin) shoulders of the Dalían hero-protagonist. Nevertheless, interspersed throughout the novel are reminders to the reader that the surrealist artist is a projection of the author's willful fantasy, rather than a mirror into Salvador Dalí's psyche. The surreal character's evanescent existence is bound in the flimsy pages of a manuscript of an unnamed author: "reduced to [a] mere shade in the imagination of a pervert" and "condemned to his twisted fantasies" (59). The reader may perceive in this condemnation a veiled allusion to accounts of another paradise, created with the absolute foreknowledge that it was to be lost and would become the object of the death-defying quest of the hero myth.

Despite the oblique correspondence between *The Garden of the Hesperides* and the Eden of the Judeo-Christian tradition and the garden of the setting sun of classical mythology, the reader is left free to interpret whether the contemporary text reconstructs or deconstructs the myths of paradise lost and regained. The anonymous hero-artist of the contemporary text dreams that he reclaims himself and his kin from the shadows of oblivion by capturing, from the elusive mirror of memory, their specters in a family portrait. In doing so—and again in answer to Rank's question as to the choice of the aesthetic form to satisfy the heroic quest—the creative impulse provides, like a dream, the experience of spiritual rebirth.

Times change, and perhaps a question more germane to our age would be why one would choose the aesthetic form to authenticate the myth of the hero or, for that matter, any transcendental myth. In the more than half a century since Rank offered his theories of trauma and sublimation, the power of the myth of artist-as-hero and the viability of psychoanalysis to explain it have been rendered all but impotent by the skepticism of late-twentieth-century literary and cultural criticism. Inquiry into grounding truths or myths has been replaced by the deconstruction of any metanarrative that makes claims of being an all-explaining authority. The sign of the postmodern times this surrealist artist lives (dies) in is that our age no longer believes in signs, including myths and metaphors, except as signifiers that, like reflecting mirrors, point only to themselves. These are but some of the dilemmas that the metafictional hero-protagonists and un-named author of *The Garden of the Hesperides* confront.

Does a postmodern hero exist or is he perishing along with the modernist privileged status of authority? In their introductory chapter to *Literary Theory Today*, Peter Collier and Helga Geyer-Ryan suggest that the variety of responses to the tenets of post-modernism precludes any over-arching conclusions as to the current literary debate. They argue that the modernist stance, while tottering or placed on its head, is not played out: "The destabilization of the critical metalanguage of modernism has, clearly, not been fatal. . . . Certainly, no one critical language can now claim hegemony" (8).

My reading of *The Garden of the Hesperides* is in support of their claim. The choice of a dying artist for the author's perishable contemporary hero reveals, I think, not so much the main character's puniness in comparison to yesteryear's immortals but rather the author's admiration that his hero has the will to survive at all. Here the author shows remarkable talent in creating a visual icon that captures the tension among the surrealist, modernist, and postmodernist literary theories at play in his contemporary myth. A deadly serious parody of twentieth-century literary theory, his central character is precisely this—a character on paper—who nonetheless seeks authenticity in defiance of the times that wore him so thin. Whether a surrealist reflection, a modern mental construct, or a postmodern deconstruction, this hero persists in believing in the redemptive power of art to elevate humanity beyond its mortal limits. His aesthetics is his faith, and tapping the source of his aesthetic inspiration becomes his heroic quest.

The myth from which Rojas's novel takes its name proceeds from the classical legend of the hero who must find The Garden of the Hesperides that holds the immortal apple tree given by

Gaea to Hera as a wedding present. The tree is attended by the three beautiful daughters of Hespera and guarded by a demon dragon. The hero is Heracles, son of Zeus and the mortal Alcmene.[6] Mortal by birth, Heracles must claim his legitimate place in the pantheon of gods by plundering the garden and making off with its immortal fruit. Before he can present the bounty, he must win a wrestling match with Antaeus by tearing his adversary from the grips of Mother Earth.[7]

In the contemporary myth, the author uses Dalían imagery to displace Heracles, the legendary virile hero, with Oedipus, *le fils de sa mère*. The protagonist's struggle is not only with Antaeus but also with Gaea, the Earth Mother: the masculine and feminine oppositions of the artist's psyche. The Venus of his dreams, whose face he could not confront in the mirror of his art, on one level, is the daemon mother to whom he is bound by dread and desire. Recalling Salvador Dalí's *Enigma of Desire: My Mother, My Mother, My Mother* (1929) and *Specter of Sex Appeal* (1934), she is at once Eros and Thanatos (Descharnes, colorplate 15 and figure 30). The labor of this hero is to confront the seductive specter who banished him from his garden of innocence. His ambivalence towards Venus, the icon of erotic femininity, mirrors a fascination with and abhorrence of his own androgynous nature. On a more latent level, the object of his desire is inverted in *l'amour obscur*, symbolically reflected as the dark streaks in the looking glass of his Venus. The protagonist's is a divided self, and his struggle is his wrestling match with the demon of his fragmented psyche.

In the end, it is the medium of art that proves the transcendent agent for the apparently irreconcilable opposing psychic forces at battle with one another. The surrealist painter dreams up a press conference during which he announces his final masterpiece, entitled *The Garden of the Hesperides*, and—in his ultimate delusion—declares himself the resurrected, self-created, mythic dragon slayer: "According to the myth, Hercules destroyed the demon dragon and stole the apples. Myth lies! Only art can reduce the demon to its own image and likeness, and that's what I plan to do as soon as I steal the golden apples. I'll rob them from my own *Garden of the Hesperides* where I will depict the final setting sun at the threshold of eternity" (194–95).

As predicted, the dream canvas is illuminated by the golden apples of the mythic garden; but the subject matter is an all-too-mortal ensemble portrait in chiaroscuro. *D'après* Velázquez, the artist depicts his extended family (including himself, his mother, his homosexual lover Federico, and Freud) in the exact pose of the master painter, the ladies-in-waiting, and the royal family in *Las Meninas* reflected in an imaginary mirror. A homage to the baroque genius for catching a moment in a mirror, the surreal portrait is a perfect meeting of the illusion and the arrested moment that captures the fiction, the art, and the pathos of the contemporary fable. It permits the reader to visualize *The Garden of the Hesperides* as if he or she were viewing a painting with an inward eye or from the mirror of memory.

In "Ekphrasis in the Contemporary Spanish Novel," Jeffrey Bruner sees the eponymous portrait as the visual metaphor of *The Garden of the Hesperides*. Drawing parallels between Velázquez's baroque painting and Rojas's dream canvas, Bruner argues that the most important correlation is "the self-portrait stance of the artist who gazes eternally into an invisible mirror. The anonymous Painter's reflection in *El jardín de las Hespérides* is identical to that of Velázquez in *Las Meninas*. In this way, Rojas has stretched the very nature of literary representation to its limits, for in this novel he achieves the (metaphorical) transformation of a verbal text into a visual work of art" (85).[8]

Also *d'après* Velázquez—who originally entitled the canvas of the Infanta and her ladies-in-waiting *La Familia*, seemingly to assert his right of place in the royal family—the spacial mirror into which the artist gazes includes yet another self-portrait. Painted as if in a mirage and half-hidden in darkness, the author's nondescript face peers out from the surreal protagonist's masterpiece. His reflection, as if in the shadows of his artist-heroes, appears to reflect the author's yearning for his own right of place. Using words and lines of text to depict the visual imagery of his painter-protagonists, the writer fantasizes for himself a place in the family lineage of visual artists and portrays the act of creation—whether with brushstrokes that paint the faces or, as here, in a literary ensemble portrait that gives voice to them—as a heroic labor inasmuch as the creative act is the battle of the psyche in confrontation with one's personal ghosts and demons. The artist's quest for rightful place in an idyllic garden of his own creation is, through the process of identification, the author's own. Just as the identity of the unnamed surreal protagonist has fused with that of Velázquez, so also does the writer's with that of his spectral characters.

Unwavering in the persuasion of the redemptive power of art, *The Garden of the Hesperides* celebrates the artists' life-work as a struggle for identity and self-determination. And, just as all labors have deliverance as their goal, the ghost narrator wishes his creator an equal part of the release he senses for having come to the end of the line: "Perhaps this unknown author will come to share the peace I feel as I let myself go without fear or protest. It is as if I have returned to Calador Bay, where in my brief life my father taught me to swim. I let myself sink into waters that become more golden as they deepen and reach toward oblivion, at the secret point of infinity that can only be the end period of a novel entitled *The Garden of the Hesperides*" (214). The novel closes with a luminous glimpse of deliverance, thus carrying to fruition the language of metafiction as the (trans)parent act of labor in the creative process.

Rojas's myth is not a tragedy, although the lone survivors at the end of the novel are the unnamed author and the green-eyed demon—at once personal and yet as old as time. The demon— the self-professed *auteur* of the world's stage—appears in myriad roles (envious voyeur, lizard in the garden, pox–infected whore) as the specter of sex appeal, but whose ultimate guise is the mask of death that looms like a shadow over the cast of characters and yet serves as the deus ex machina to resolve their drama. The protagonists wage a heroic, self-determining battle of the psyche torn between its instinctual urge to accept death and return to earth's womb in hope of a spiritual rebirth and its intentional impetus to confront the contingencies of mortal existence before vanishing into the light of oblivion. It is precisely this struggle of the psyche that elevates the artists beyond their dependence upon the alienating happenstance of existence.

Myths do not answer riddles; they posit them, as does Rojas in his contemporary fable. Nevertheless, understanding *The Garden of the Hesperides* as a visualized Freudian family romance is crucial to unveiling one of the myriad layers of symbolism in the dying hero's dream canvas and that of its namesake, the author's dream novel. Their manifest content visually depicts the dream of reclaiming the idyllic garden via the surrealist technique of superimposition: in this instance, superimposing the uterine images of water onto those of earth and hidden treasure inherent in the myth of the Garden of the Hesperides. It is the dream world of oedipal-centered dread and longing to return to the golden waters, the womb of Mother Earth, the paradise lost at birth. The latent content of the novel is of an existential and metaphysical nature verbally presented in the jealous, sibling squabbles over who is the legitimate son that find their parallel in the battle for autonomy waged between the narrator and his author who, like Cronus—the Titan of Time—creates and destroys his offspring.

In the epilogue, the author's voice fuses with that of his narrator—the "other" author with whom he had earlier been feuding over control of the text—to admit that their story, regardless of authorship, is but a mad attempt to stave off the inexorable effects of Time on their history: "To die is to dream, definitively so for us ghosts, and to go stark mad. In my dream, a demented unending delirium, I was a wandering soul in a book; and I had a brother conceived in carnal rage after I passed away. Now my eyes open, I see that neither brother nor book ever existed. . . . Death is not a novel but a fistful of remembrances scattered by the winds into oblivion" (201).

The novelistic equation of limbo to a memoir (a book of remembrances that scatter like pages into the void) is as much a metaphysical theme as a novelistic frame. Once they cross over the fictional threshold, the the wandering souls vanish into the blank pages of the epilogue, despite their fleeting persistence in a manuscript as evanescent as memory or a reflection in a mirror. As one more spectral persona in the script, the author's inclusion of his self-portrait is no haughty claim to immortality for either himself or his artistic protagonists. Like them, he too has striven to capture a moment in an imaginary mirror before he too vanishes into the void. For the novelist, it is a moment for which he can merely search by means of the distorting lenses of history (time) and art (space) yet wherein he intuits the perennial reenactment of the infinitely evasive heroic quest. Ephemeral constructs and fleeting reflections of his creative mind, his literary portraits (his own *vera effigies* included) disappear at the precise moment their creator puts the end period to his novel and, looking up from the page, searches for his own shadow in the timeless mirror of art.

Carlos Rojas is eminently qualified to write this homage to two national Spanish heroes from the art world. As professor and researcher, he has dedicated his career to the field of Spanish letters. As scholar, he has lectured and written extensively on the literature, history, and art of his native Spain. Among his books on art criticism are *El mundo mítico y mágico de Picasso* (The mythical and magical world of Picasso, 1984) as well as the aforementioned *El mundo mítico y mágico de Salvador Dalí* (1985). He is the author of twenty-one novels, which he chooses to call fables, and has won the most prestigious awards in Spain: National Prize for Literature, 1968; Planeta, 1973; Ateneo, 1977; and Nadal, 1980.

His art of fabulation is to translate into fiction the myths that translate reality and to recreate myths that explain his country's genius and its fractious past. His protagonists resonate with the historical events and biographies of Spain's greatest artists, men of letters, despots, and demons.

Rojas frequently juxtaposes national histories and sacred texts. Among his other fictional biographies worthy of special mention are *Auto de fe* (*Act of faith*, 1965) on the Spanish Hapsburg Charles II, known as "The Bewitched;" the bedeviled play he wrote on the last temptation of Christ; *El valle de los caídos* (The valley of the fallen, 1978); *Yo* (I) *Goya* (1990), on the life and monsters of Francisco de Goya; *El ingenioso hidalgo y poeta Federico García Lorca asciende a los infiernos* (The ingenious gentleman and poet Federico García Lorca ascends to the inferno, 1979), where the poetry of the assassinated poet takes on a Dantesque prescience in the context of the Spanish Civil War; *El jardín de Atocha* (1990, translated in 1996 by Cecilia Lee as *The Garden of Janus*), a search for the real and the apocryphal Cervantes in another mythical garden not unlike that of the Hesperides; and *Alfonso de Borbón habla con los demonios* (The Bourbon King Alfonso XII speaks with his demons, 1995). His *Sueño de Sarajevo* (The dream of Sarajevo, 1982) has in its cast of characters two renowned figures in European letters—Descartes and Ulysses Personne—who enter a mental sanatorium located on a magic mountain in the Pyrenees on June 28, 1914, the start of *La Grande Guerre*. Inextricably bound in these narratives is a signature theme of Carlos Rojas: rational man's failure to prevent the monstrous carnage of war due to his failure to reconcile with the other in himself.

Notes

1. See Carlos Rojas, *El mundo mítico y mágico de Salvador Dalí* (1985); or, in English translation, *Salvador Dalí or The Art of Spitting on Your Mother's Portrait* (1993). Rojas contends that Salvador Dalí was tortured by the suspicion that he was conceived to replace his brother, Salvador Dalí Domènech, who died at the age of two (6–7).

2. There is no doubt as to Rojas's knowledge of the historical Dalí's dream. In his biography of the artist, *The Art of Spitting* (121), Rojas quotes it verbatim. It is the novelist's contention that this alleged nightmare formed Dalí's sexual paranoiac complex.

3. In *Dalí* (1968, see illustration 135) Max Gerard quotes Dalí's proclamation of indebtedness to Velázquez: "Velázquez has taught me more about mirrors, light, and reflections than tons of scientific treatises. He is an inexhaustible treasure."

4. For example, Dalí chooses to conceal as much as reveal his "Venus de Milo with Drawers" with the cryptic explanation: "Freud discovered the world of the subconscious on the tumid surfaces of ancient bodies, and Dalí cut drawers into it" (see *Dalí*, illustration 148).

5. See Robert A. Seal, *In Quest of the Hero* (1990), 59–60.

6. See Thomas Bullfinch, *Myths and Legends: The Golden Age* (1932), 179–180.

7. See Robert Graves, *The Greek Myths: Vol. II* (1979), 85–86 and 145–47.

8. In this article, Bruner provides an excellent description of ekphrasis by likening it to a mirage.

Works Cited

Bruner, Jeffrey. "A Picture is Worth a Thousand Words: Ekphrasis in the Contemporary Spanish Novel." *Journal of Interdisciplinary Studies, Cuadernos Interdisciplinarios de Estudios Literarios* 3 (1991): 71–89.

Bullfinch, Thomas. *Myths and Legends: The Golden Age.* Reprint of *The Age of Fable.* London: Ballantyne Press, 1932.

Collier, Peter, and Geyer-Ryan, Helga. *Literary Theory Today.* Ithaca: Cornell University Press, 1990.

Morse, E., *Dalí.* Translated by Robert Descharnes. New York: Henry Abrams, 1993.

———. *Dalí.* Translated by Max Gerard. New York: Henry Abrams, 1968.

Graves, Robert. *The Greek Myths: Volume II.* Harmondsworth, Middlesex: Penguin Books, 1979.

Rojas, Carlos. *El jardín de las Hespérides.* Madrid: Editorial Debate, 1988.

———. *El mundo mítico y mágico de Salvador Dalí.* Barcelona: Plaza y Janés, 1985.

———. *Salvador Dalí or The Art of Spitting on Your Mother's Portrait.* Translated by Alma Amell. University Park: Pennsylvania State University Press, 1993.

Seal, Robert A. *In Quest of the Hero.* Princeton: Princeton University Press, 1990.

The Garden
of the Hesperides

The Mirror

1

No, I AM NOT THE ADOLESCENT *MON SEMBLABLE, MON FRÈRE* IS gazing at on the dust jacket of yet another art book interspersed with illustrations of his sketches and paintings. I did not live long enough to be that serious, sepia youth on the folio splayed across his bony knees. I see the shiny-haired boy on the glossy cover and wonder how my brother dared call the painting *Portrait of My Dead Only Brother.*

Directly behind my so-called *vera effigies,* and barely more than shaded in, is a studio with a vaulted ceiling where an artist in black satin paints the portrait of a dwarf reading a book. In the background, a naked woman reclines on a blue-draped divan, admiring herself in a mirror held by a winged cupid. All four—the model, the painter, the cherub, and the woman in flesh tones whose face shows misted in the looking glass—belong to my brother, inasmuch as he spent a half century repeating them in a palimpsest of variations.

None of them, not even the boy with the great shock of hair who is supposed to be myself, has anything to do with me. I am not, and I was never, the disgusting long-faced adolescent in the illustration who looks as if he could be masturbating in the depths of a closet while dressed in drag as a bride. I was a child of flesh and blood, and if I was born a buffoon, it was by the grace of God or Satan himself.

With tears in his eyes, my father used to reminisce almost daily about my funny little ways during my short stay on earth. How he would smile, his bald pate shining like quartz, as he talked of how I cheered him up with my antics. At the time my brother was no more than a lad himself, long before he set out to make the world his stage. In a sailor-suit with white stockings and buckled patent leather shoes, he would sit on Father's lap, enthralled and consumed with envy. Cinnabar skies lowered on the endless afternoons of that Indian summer while my father still talked about the myriad charms of his ill-fated prodigy.

As if on cue, yet always by surprise, the office door that led to the terrace overlooking Calador Bay would then open and close.

27

The recurring marvel would seem to both of them to be over in a flash: the exact time no more, no less needed for the latch to lift and the handle to turn before some spirit or equally invisible gust would coax the door shut with exasperating slowness. Accustomed to the mystery, they watched in silence, knowing that my ghost had just tiptoed across the threshold.

At such times, my brother hated me so intensely that he wished he could kill me, strike me dead all over again, and then crush me with his tiny buckled shoe as easily as one might tread on a tear drop or quench a sigh. Unaware of his son's malice, my father would merely shake his head and softly announce every year on the same day and at almost the exact time: "Summer is over and tomorrow we head back to Fondora."

The following afternoon they would drive home by carriage with the wind at their back pushing them inland across the plains. The first autumnal hurricanes always arrived with their departure, looming over the olive groves and stripping the trees—as Federico would later say—"to their gray souls." The bells on the mare's harness jingled and the sky, that yesterday glowed like the mouth of an oven, was now a limpid transparent blue.

When yet a child, my brother thought of colors as people, believing that he could fathom their souls, and that these were as different and even opposite to their appearance as are humans. At the base of the shimmering firmament, he intuited long cobwebs and the milky light of a pale January. Later, seated on a little stool at our mother's feet in a hackney cab upholstered like a passenger train in patterned plush of purple and mauve grape vines, he would stare at her as if trying to print her indelibly on his mind. It was, as I see now, an ironic habit, since my brother's memory can keep pace with my own, that of a specter for whom nothing slips between the cracks. As late as yesterday, ancient, sickly, shakily awaiting a death that never comes, *mon semblable, mon frère* described to his nurse the buckled patent-leather shoes that he outgrew eighty years ago, which were either thrown away or handed down to another child.

Gazing down on him with a doting smile, my mother would ask: "Darling, what is it that you want, my darling?" My brother would respond with a vague, distrustful glance, as if afraid that she could read his mind. Perhaps he was thinking that he was so much the spitting image of me that my baby photograph hanging in our parents' room and the one of him in his bedroom were identical, even though I had been dead for years when a photographer from Pomerania—complete with monocle, goatee, yellow duster, and silver-stained hands—captured his image in a studio on the Rambla de los Pájaros in Barcelona. However, since nothing stays the same in this masquerade, in time my brother started to look more and more like my mother.

Staring at her in that carriage next to her husband, who slept with a cold pipe still clenched between his teeth, my brother said to himself that there never had been a more beautiful creature than she on the face of the earth. "Darling, what is it that you want, my darling?" In spite of his raging self-centeredness, there was absolutely nothing that he wanted. He was as enraptured with the idea of sharing that woman's beauty as his Venus would be on seeing her image in the hand glass held by the cherub. The more he looked at her the more he admired the contrast between her fair skin, a pale pink tending toward snow white, and her dark eyes framed by jet-black hair parted down the middle and pulled back over the ears. Hers was, as she was well aware, a face of singular beauty. Chiseled from marble and balanced upon a swan neck, her face turned into an animate but illusory mirage as her complexion took on the iridescence of mother-of-pearl.

My brother must have noticed that his features not only matched our mother's but that time would make them indistinguishable from hers. Indeed, a few years after her death, he turned into a flowing-haired cravat-sporting ephebe. If his huge eyes seemed smaller in comparison, his somber gaze matched hers. As time passed and my brother's fame spread across the globe, he persisted in staring wide-eyed, as if in a trance, whenever he posed for the press. He thought he was aping other eyes even bigger than his own—Dalí's—unaware of how closely he resembled the woman who gave birth to the two of us in Fondora. Yet perhaps he noticed nothing that stormy morning since he was but a child and, moreover, overcome by an unforeseen fit of terror. While our father slept, rocked by the motion of the racing coach and the howling wind, his curved pipe fallen into his cupped hands that met across his portly belly, pearl-gray vest and gold watch fob, my brother suffered his first bout of pure fear. He was terrified that he would be caught in the open stare of those jet pupils and would vanish as surely as the winter light was eclipsed by the autumn skies. When our mother reached over to pat his knee, he shuddered as if he had been touched by a spider. "Darling . . ."

Dead and invisible, although eyewitness to them all, I remembered the journey back to Fondora that I had made in the very same hackney carriage before my brother was born. It was late

October and I just had my first birthday. The warm, golden summer had lasted unseasonably long, the sea was still, flat as polished slate, and the listless leaves hung green on the branches. Although our father, the Garden-Variety-Legal-Beaver as my brother would later mock him, had to return to his law practice, it was decided that my mother and I would stay at the beach until we were swept home by the high winds.

They chased us away as all fall broke loose on my first birthday. My father traveled back with us, his monogrammed Roskoff watch tucked into his dust coat and the few wisps of hair that he still had left slicked back at his temples. He had come to give his wife a hand with packing her hat boxes and the canary cage they dared not trust to the servants. I am inclined to believe that he must have also returned, as he did almost every Sunday, to Calador Bay because of me—the beloved first-born son and namesake—on whose birth certificate was stamped, at his expressed will, not only his name but both surnames. Whenever we were apart, he felt lonely, homeless as a stray dog, as if stripped of a pound of flesh and another of soul which had been tossed into the gutter.

That day he held me on his lap and told me stories about sales contracts whereby covered vineyards and well-watered orchards changed hands as though by elfin magic as in fairy tales. It was as if I were not his legitimate child but a bastard son who had just come of age and for whom he would create a position as his legal assistant and call "nephew"-the way lecherous priests refer to their sacrilegious offspring.

As opposed to what happened on my brother's trip, the only one who, unmindful of me, dozed off that morning was my mother. I saw her rest her head against the seat back, and I followed the outline of her purplish eyelids, parted lips, and pulsing veins in her long slender throat: she looked just like a lily as she leaned on one hand that had aimlessly settled on the lid of her hatbox. I was as engrossed in her as later my brother would be while sitting in the very same carriage; watching her, I spontaneously uttered as if in a trance my first words: "In this circus, Father, the only reality is death."

Like Farinata in Dante's inferno, whose fate made such an impression on my brother when he reread La Commedia while illustrating the Joseph Foret edition, we the dead all have a clear memory of the past, uncanny insights into the future, and a rather murky sense of the present. I can remember the ruins of a mill and a cluster of poplars twisted by the gale over the banks of a creek, which I saw through the coach window at the precise moment that I burst into speech, to my father's shock and delight. Resplendent with wonder like a Rembrandt saint—whose light, according to my brother, emanates from the virginal core of its inner being—my father took my head gently between the rough palms of his hands more suited to a blacksmith than to a practicing lawyer.

"What did you say, my son? Repeat what you just said!"

"I said, Father, that in this farce the only reality is death."

Dispensing with vulgar babbling, I enunciated crisply and articulately. Honestly, I must confess that I am still quite proud of my witticism even though at the time I had no inkling that my impending death would doom me to the confines of this limbo, in other words, to the front and back covers of this book. Really, it was not bad at all for a spontaneous aphorism out of the mouth of a babe who had spent the summer of that year crawling on all fours. I have no idea, however, from whence the statement sprang, and I will never know whether it came from an atavistic collective memory tucked away in my ancestral genes or if it was an inexplicable burst of my brief and absurd genius.

Years later, on the afternoon when a French monoplane either lost its course or suffered engine trouble and landed in a potato field in Fondora and the entire town council came out to present the keys of the city to the pilot—the most unexpected of our visitors—our father told my brother of my miraculous prophecy. For some reason, he whispered the words as if they were a jealousy guarded family secret, while the mayor in frock coat and silk top hat welcomed the bewildered aviator: "*Bienvenu, monsieur le voleur! Bienvenu, monsieur le voleur!*" Head bowed in silence, my brother listened to his father until the confession whipped him into a sudden rage.

"If Adam was the last man on the earth to know for certain who his father was," he shouted at ours, "you cannot swear that today I am not my dead only brother!"

Nevertheless, the entire scene—the aeroplane, the council in black tails and tie, my brother's bellows, and the horrified expression under my father's soot-black eyelashes—belonged to a still unforeseeable future. For the time being, my world was restricted to me and my parents riding in a carriage scented with chamomile that some peasant girl must have carried in armfuls on an earlier trip. We left behind the mill and the poplars doubled over by the gale as if they were drinking from the banks of the creek. Unvarying and endless fields spread out around us: plowed and sown fields that now exist only in my memory. In that closed universe, not so different from the wombs with skylights that my brother was to paint at a later date, my father hugged me tightly and I could smell the pungent scent of cigar from his kisses on my forehead, eyes and cheeks.

"Wake up, wake up at once," he shouted, trying to rouse my mother from sleep. "Our boy is talking and saying incredible things!" My mother awoke so fresh and with such ease that she might have been pretending to sleep. She gazed at me with eyes black as raven wings and, while as ever adoring her, for an instant I thought I hated her. Looking right through me, she seemed to perceive my invisible double crouching behind me, as she asked: "What's happened? What did the boy say?"

"I said that I've got a secret tucked between my name, my shadow, and my reflection in the mirror." My response was confused, timid because my voice now sounded alien, but I soon came to grips with myself and my fear. "Listen to me carefully for perhaps one day my shadow will no longer be among you." Since death was still an unknown to me, I am not sure I believed my own words. But did I talk! I talked non-stop for the ten brief months left to my stint on this earth still wrapped as I was in, what my brother was to call, the golden guise of a half-baked seraph.

My mother never shed her polite reserve when hearing me speak but continued to stare as if through a glass darkly, perhaps intuiting another child inside me for whom my mask and disguise were a mere rehearsal. I grew accustomed to detesting her while she came to ignore me in her pursuit of my inner phantom. In hatred and jealous rage, I endeavored to be like her in order to win her back: so that she would be completely mine, from her eyes to her most secret self, so that we would fuse together as one. If my brother later feared lest he end up a prisoner in her jet-black pupils, like the devoured sons of Cronus who stare with fear and trembling from the monster's orbs, I would have gladly plunged into the depths of my mother's eyes. It was my fervent wish to immerse myself in them just as a child dreams of jumping through a looking glass or diving into a pond of yellow lilies painted in watercolor. Maliciously, I tried to identify completely with the woman who brought me into the world and began to feel like a little girl next to her. Had I lived, I am sure that Federico would have fallen in love with me and not my brother, and we would have loved one another with all the possessive and passionate affection that I longed for but never found in my mother.

Such reasoning was absurd because, had I survived, my brother would never have been born. Nor do I suppose I ever would have met Federico or that he would have uncovered the "gray souls" of the olive trees that surrounded my house. It is more likely that I would have ended up a clerk in my father's law firm and he, a powerful virile man, would have grown old discussing law briefs with me, hiding his broken heart for having sired a homosexual.

Just as the living are snared in the brambles of life, we the dead get tangled up in our digressions. Threading through my ball of yarn for memories, I return to the image of my father gaping in sheer joy and total incomprehension at my outbursts of wisdom. He felt like the venerable patriarchal scribe witnessing the debate in the Temple between the Holy Fathers and the Christ Child, even though Jesus must have been twelve at the time and I would not live to see my second birthday. I was no more than two feet high when my father first took me to the casino to amuse his friends and clients. I would say things like: *Speech was invented to teach man the value of silence.* Or *Two things separate us from orang-utans; we bury our dead and they don't nag.* Or *The devil's most treacherous ploy is not to pretend that he doesn't exist but to trick us into believing that there truly is life after birth.* Or *Earth is the hell of some destroyed planet, and on the day of Armageddon we will resurrect into the black hole.* Or *We live in a dream world, in the nightmare of a lunatic who lavished upon us a universe hostile to life.* Or *If a rich man enters into the kingdom of heaven as easily as a camel passes through the eye of a needle, then paradise is just like Spain, a land of paupers.* These whimsical notions were celebrated in my father's tight-knit circle of freethinkers, republicans, anarchists, and Esperantists.

It was about this same time that a local Fondoran photographer had me sit for what was to be the last, and long since lost, photograph taken of me—the one that would turn out to be my brother's spitting image. Shortly thereafter I fell sick and died, although I do not like to think about that. It does not grieve me to recall my feverish coughing spells, my dying gasps, because physical pain and pleasure seem somewhat elusive to memory. Yet, my sense of being abandoned and uprooted remains as vivid today as on the afternoon I saw my little body shrouded under the spray of white lilies, knowing myself reduced for eternity to a shade invisible to the eyes of the living.

The only person to whom I could confide how forlorn I felt as they lifted my tiny remains onto the shelf in the cemetery vault was my brother, even though he never paid his respects and we may never resolve our dispute as to which of us is the other's shadow. Occasionally, when the fancy struck, he sent flowers, calling from New York or Paris to his home at Calador Bay and having his chauffeur or staff decorate the tomb with a wreath of roses. They were always roses, arranged and delivered according to his instructions and whims: fresh cut that very morning, dripping with dew, and the thornier the better.

He liked to boast to his following of worshipers, sycophants, and downright delinquents who paid him homage at his suites in the Saint Denis or Hôtel Robert, "I am the serial murderer of my only dead brother. Sometimes I strangle him, sometimes I kick him to death. But I always execute him with utmost discretion and respect. Only this morning, I had flowers delivered to his tomb. We are inseparable namesakes. One could not exist without the other, we are one another's reflection. At times I have even believed that we exist on alternate days but that neither one is aware of the switch. Obviously this is a lie, since each time he tries to come back to life, I destroy him. Since the dawn of my youth, I can remember his useless yet cunning attempts to return to the world of the living. He has never taken me by surprise, and whenever he tries to crawl out from the ranks of the dead, I tread on him. Gentlemen, it's an open-and-shut case." Ironically or hypocritically, all would nod in assent. It was the unwritten rule that, in his mock court, his word was law.

Only on surprising and rare occasions would he talk to me about these parasites. Then he would retreat into his shell, cross with himself for having allowed me a glimpse of his soul. In the evenings, after most of his young minions had crawled back into their cells, his listless gloom would shift into fevered sexual arousal. An obsessive voyeur, he would improvise obscene, baroque orgies, striking the floor with his cane to work his models into a frenzy, while the youngest—a little blond creature, wide-eyed and naive as a china doll—was sodomized by a butcher from Les Halles. The brute would roar and pant while she twisted and screamed in a spasm of desire.

"*Pour vous, mon sublime Maître,*" she shouted to my brother. "I sacrifice myself for you, my Master!"

"*Non, non, pas pour moi! Pour mon frère mort dans les limbes!* May his soul wandering in limbo find eternal rest and disappear into the void! Period, the end!"

"*Pour le frère mort de mon Maître! Point et à la ligne! Pour son silence! Pour le néant!* For the final silence of my Master's dead brother! For the void, void, vooiid!"

On another attempt to obliterate me from his memory, he had a long rug brought in and placed diagonally, still rolled, in the middle of the parquet floor. Brandishing a cane that the Kaiser had used during *La Grande Guerre,* he called for another attendant of his royal bed chamber—a tall svelte Tuscan with black hair flowing over her shoulders. My brother ordered her to strip naked, crawl head first into the hirsute tunnel, and burrow her way through on hands and knees. I imagined her sobbing piteously, her voice and spirit broken, too weak to advance or retreat yet driven by fear to push forward while my brother boasted of having reversed the process of childbirth. He trumpeted that instead of copying the birth of a male infant through a woman's vagina, he could bring into the world a full-grown woman via his metaphoric male member. The finale to her rite-of-passage intoxicated him. The rug seemed to narrow at the far end and the girl had to squirm inch by inch through the half-clenched fangs of her serpentine birth canal. Covered with sweat and tears, she pleaded with my brother to cut it open to rescue her. Peering through the opening and into his victim's eyes, he would shudder with unspoken glee. No pagan flaying the skin off a martyr ever derived such sadistic, silent pleasure as my brother's on seeing her straining to expose a shoulder or a breast, elbowing her way out of the vise. When the girl would finally free herself and collapse in hysterics on the parquet floor, the excitement of her sublime master changed to a demure mask of cruel reserve that vaguely reminded me of someone else.

Only now can I place the expression. It was the same as our mother's on the day of my funeral. Veiled in black silk and in heavy mourning, she remained seated in a mahogany chair beside the half-open door to the balcony. As the women left, they would kiss or embrace her. Their husbands, either neighbors or clients whose property rights—a grain mill, an oak grove, a herd of sheep—my father had defended in the past, whispered their condolences as they tiptoed out, hat in hand. Motionless, her bowed head resting on her hand, neither blinking nor responding, my mother stared blankly through the glass doors. Just as the same likeness of Her Majesty the Queen appears on each new mintage of coins, in that pose, her veil half shading her face, my mother would have been identical to my brother in his youth. Even through her mourning veil and black shawls, hastily dyed for the occasion, the men could not help undressing her with their furtive leers.

She did not go to the cemetery because it was not the custom at the time. She was confined to her home, as if instead of burying her son she had just borne him. Prostrated by sorrow, neither could my father escort me to my grave. The man whom my brother would later call Cronus had collapsed into a leather arm-chair in a paroxysm of grief. I will never forget his torrent of anguish, which Federico would have called a river and which the townsfolk found unmentionable and unthinkable, worth only a few brief huddled comments in the casino before being relegated to oblivion. A physician with a shaggy salt-and-pepper beard, his thinning hair parted low and combed over his temples (the same doctor who, forty years later, would appear in one of the most reproduced of my brother's oil paintings, the one seeking the echo of silence that preceded the creation of the firmament) came to the house twice to make my father drink the murky concoction that he prepared from saffron-colored powder and chamomile tea. After a few sips, my father sank into his winged-back chair and shook the house with thunderous snores, making my mother wince and silencing the buzz of family and friends that filed through the house offering their condolences. Three or four hours later, my father awoke from God knows what dreams to wail even more scandalously, and the doctor was again summoned to prepare a sleeping powder.

In such circumstances, and in spite of the obstinate nature of the Garden-Variety-Legal-Beaver, it was no surprise to see my mother's will prevail to prevent him from attending the burial services. More surprising was the fact that the family members respected her wish to be left alone that evening to care for her husband by herself. After the mourners had taken their leave, my mother and father were left with my ghost as dusk fell and a full August moon appeared. Outdoors, the neighbors lit gas lamps and set out wicker chairs and earthenware pitchers for an after-dinner gathering in the sultry night air. The hours dragged by until their voices fell silent and the neighborhood retired for the evening. It was so quiet that one almost could hear the grass grow in the parterres in the plaza and the water slither through the shadows under the twinkling constellation of The Bear. Gazing at my mother, who still sat by the glass doors, her ankles crossed under her, her chin resting in her hand, I felt more hers than ever, even though I was a mere shade among the shadows: her chiseled features in the half-light and the majestic curves under her mourning weeds were mine and mine alone. At the same time, in a sudden pang of irrational jealousy heavily laced with self-pity for the recently deceased, I hated her for not having shed a single tear the entire day.

A stroke of bitter chance make my father echo my resentment. "Cry!" he screamed at her as he twisted around in his chair.

"Why should I cry?" My mother answered softly, as if she were speaking to herself.

"Because our only son is dead, you bitch. Cry!"

"I know he is dead, but he will not be our only son, I can assure you."

"And I can assure you that we will never have another child, because I shall never touch you again. You disgust me."

"I disgust you because I don't cry?" My mother crossed her hands on her lap and leaned back as if she were posing for a portrait. "Who should I cry for? For the boy, for you, or for myself?"

"Not for me, I don't need your pity. I don't even want it," he roared.

"Perhaps not, but you deserve compassion as much as I. We've both made mistakes."

Now he seemed to be the one who did not understand. Writhing in his chair as if shackled, he beat on the armrest with the flat of his palm. The blow sounded like the crack of a whip in a night that had gone quiet but for their voices. From time to time, I suspected that, lying in bed beside their open windows, the neighbors were eagerly eavesdropping. Later, I felt certain that the three of us were alone in a dormant or indifferent universe.

"You're out of your mind," said my father, but fatigue had softened his voice. At first I thought that, aware of my presence, he was talking to me, reproaching me for the madness of my untimely death. Then I realized that he was talking to my mother.

"I was out of my mind once," she said, "one night early in my pregnancy, when I dreamt about the son that I would have. He was admiring himself in a mirror. Seeing his reflection, as beautiful as a summer morning, I knew that he would never die."

"You're demented, you monster! We've just lost our child, and you indulge in foolishness rather than mourn him."

"We have lost our first-born son, and you were the fool for conceiving him simply to carry on your bloodline and your name. I should have known that the poor child would never be the chosen, predestined, immortal son of my dreams."

"I don't give a damn about your dreams! Why should I listen to such nonsense? Shut up or leave this house. I never should have brought you here in the first place."

"Leave? You can't throw me out yet. Not until we conceive the son who will never die. As for the boy we buried today, fate made a rough draft of him and then threw him away."

"I hear you and I can no more admit that you exist than I can accept that God of yours," my father hissed at her. "I only know that I despise you—more than as a woman, as one abhors an idea or a religion. Leave me alone and get out of my life."

"I'll leave but only after I prove to you that I exist," answered my mother with a smile. "Hate me for what I stand for if you want, but see me for who I am." She rose slowly to her feet and began to remove her black mantilla and shawls, dropping her hairpins, one by one, onto the floor. Her mourning veil slid from her shoulders as her long tresses cascaded down her back. She slipped off her dress and petticoats and held them up in front of the half-closed doors to the balcony as one displays a costume for a carnival that is never to be. Head high but her defiant eyes now submissively half closed, she unhooked her whalebone corset in a gesture of silent sacrifice to invisible and inexplicably demanding gods. She tossed her camisole on the stack of clothes and, looking at her husband out of a mask of indifference, sat down on the edge of her chair to unfasten her shoes and stockings. Although later my brother was to see him as Cronus, the God of Time, who has sired and will devour us all, my father was no awesome deity to whom my mother offered body and soul. Slouching, sunk into his winged-back chair, his rage and hatred spent, he looked exactly like the portrait that my brother would later paint of him—not that my father could ever make heads or tails of it—and with age he would become his own image captured and immortalized in the still life of an oil painting.

Completely naked, my mother again stood, raising her outstretched arms. The moon blanched her breasts, hips, and open palms and seemed to transform her into a statue newly emerged from the shadows. Her outline blurred, she took on a shimmering, shy milkiness as if in defiance of the very powers that tried to subjugate her to their laws and whims. Although dead, I envied her as intensely as I had defied her as a child, whenever she looked through me as if I were the vicarious shade of an unborn infant. After my first bout of confusion—the perplexity of one who realizes that he is lost in his own nightmare and incapable of cutting short the dream—in death I felt the same jealous pangs for those feminine curves that in life I had wanted for myself. Enraged, I lamented that I had not been born that woman or at least shared her beauty. I fantasized that, if I could retrieve the life so abruptly snatched from me, I would grow to look so much like my mother that one day, as hers began to fade, she would envy me my perfect features.

"What do you think you're doing, exposing yourself in front of the balcony on the day of your son's funeral? Do you want the neighbors to wake up and stone you to death?"

"I only wanted to prove to you that I exist, before you kick me out of my house."

"You aren't the woman I married or the mother of the son I've lost. I don't know you."

"Not even now?" My mother smiled once again. She stood, resting against the back of the mahogany chair adorned with the carving of a pineapple or lemon pear. "Are you sure that you still don't know who I am?"

"Go to hell. You've lost your mind and now you're acting like a slut."

I thought that, carried away by yet another sudden, violent rage, he would storm out of the house slamming the door behind him and leaving my mother to collect her clothes and walk away into a scandalized night: censored and damned but ever obedient to the will of her lawful husband. Hands clenched against the arms of his chair, elbows pressed down, my father shook his head like a raging bull ready to charge. Then he fell back gasping and muttering obscenities, reduced to cursing himself in irrational, impotent fury. The church bells had just tolled; if I were my yet-to-be-born brother and namesake, I could tell you the precise number of times. Although he now confuses the day and month of his appointments, there was a time in the past when he was such a fanatic for precision that he would have wanted to know the exact instant, hour, and year in which the kitchen maid in Vermeer's painting—the one that hangs in an Amsterdam museum—poured milk from a pitcher. He used to say that it was at such sacred moments that the entire universe was recreated in a cosmic hush.

"It is you who're behaving strangely," said my mother between the bells' strokes. "You want to toss me into the gutter, but you can't summon the strength to get out of that chair. What kind of man are you, blubbering like an old woman? You claim that our son was a genius because he spoke on his first birthday. How ashamed he would be to see you grovel."

"Our son can't see because he is dust and ashes," my father roared in pain. "My grief is mine and you have no right to mention his name."

"No, of course not! I wouldn't dare defile your sorrow with my words." Flashing anger in the distant heavenly light, my mother pointed her forefinger at his face. "I will walk out of this house stark naked and on my own two feet, because I despise you."

"Not anywhere near as much as I detest you!"

"More, much more! At least now you know the unveiled truth, the truth just as naked as I am now. I don't hate you. I loathe you. Our son had to die before I found the courage to tell you to your face. Never forget it. What the hell! I don't give a damn if you do or not. When you get lonely once I'm gone, you can stick your nose in your dictionaries or play with that medal Zamenhof gave you at the Esperantist conference—the one you display behind glass in your office. Can't you see how ridiculous you are, what vulgar, pretentious taste you boast as self-appointed expert in law and would-be revolutionary!" Throwing back her head, her disheveled hair falling wildly on her shoulders, she burst out laughing. I thought she was mocking her husband, partly out of scorn for the undignified grief he flaunted and partly out of a cruel, almost brutal, delight in seeing that virile model of manly integrity reduced to its own parody.

Her laughter pealed, crested, and spewed in the night, like fireworks that soar in the darkness to erupt into a panoply of stars. Then it plummeted, ricocheting raucous as the clatter of a hailstorm off the rooftops. Leaping suddenly to his feet, my father let out a low curse and struck her across the mouth with the back of his hand. My mother did not utter a single cry but the blow so staggered her that she knocked over the chair beside her mourning clothes, which lay in a heap on the floor. Snorting like a bull, my father grabbed her by the shoulders to keep her from falling. A trickle of blood stained my mother's lips, slicing across her smile of scorn. I was terrified that my father would strike her again but, to my surprise, he clasped her face in his hands and smothered her eyes, temples, and bleeding lips with kisses of unbridled passion as if he wanted to devour her. Just as surprisingly, my mother freed one hand and, with her long fingernails, slashed open his face from forehead to jaw. I saw him pull back and blink, stunned, his wife's head still clutched between the palms of his hands. Mucous clouded the pupil of his eye and his astonished face took on the helpless look of, let's say, a man standing before the Sphinx, who beholds a falling meteorite smash a child mutely gazing up at the sky. Before he could gather himself together, my mother pointed at his shirt front and, poking her index finger into the stitching of his embroidered vest, recited with a smile:

> To stay healthy and nonpareil
> throughout the month of September
> don't touch the destructive snail
> or poke your wife with your member.

Fleeing from her shocked husband, she ran onto the balcony and, bearing her nakedness to the moon, screamed: "Mark my words—don't touch the destructive snail or poke your wife with your member." With her back to the plaza beneath the balcony window, she repeated the refrain, raising an arm in salute like a crazed vestal virgin on the threshold of her temple, admonishing her emperor as he set off to inspect the Tyrrhenian vineyards and the turbot fishmongers. It remains a mystery to me why the whole city did not bolt from sleep and whatever dreams lurked behind its windows at her frenzied screams that had only the stars as witness. Had the city awakened, it would have been aghast at the month-long ban on lawful carnal knowledge—an all-but-forgotten injunction from a quaint old proverb—just as a rumor, centuries earlier, of bubonic plague or yellow cholera springing up on Tuesday in the Barcelona market and spreading by Thursday to Fondora and by Friday to Bisbal had a hair-raising effect throughout the neighborhood.

Meanwhile, with the furor of a man who is about to avenge a monstrous offense or to throw himself into the morass of Lerma to strangle the hydra, my father overcame his stupor and charged onto the balcony. The sight of his wife raving and gesticulating stark naked on a stone ledge above the street exhausted his patience and stoked his wrath. Eager as he always was to curse the gods, passionately defend free love, or fervently adhere to the anarchistic principles urging the dispossessed to burn the landed gentry's fields and poison their wells, in a stream of invective that conservative cronies endured with stoic boredom or mock patience, like Caesar himself, he would not tolerate his wife's being the object of public scandal. With one kick of his high-buttoned boot, he broke two panels in the balcony door. Then he attacked my mother. When she tried to protect her face with her arms, he knocked her down, spat on her breasts, and brutally dragged her across the stone floor. I was afraid that he would kick her to death and stomp her soul into the stone, just as years later my brother would stamp ink silhouettes in his lithographs.

Once again in my innocence I was wrong. With an agility that belied his corpulent frame, he threw himself on top of my mother, unbuttoning his trousers to rape her as she panted and moaned. With her blood-stained smile, she seemed more amused than defiled, as if this were the ironic fulfillment of her sexual fantasies. For a few immortal moments when, as *mon semblable, mon frère* would say, the clock stops and human identity dissolves into nothingness, my mother closed her huge jet-black eyes, shuddered from head to toe, and shrieked with pleasure—a shriek that somehow disappeared in the barbaric grunts of my gorged father. Lying close to one another, prone on the balcony floor, they smiled silently at a black-mouthed snail in its tiger-striped shell that clung to the railing. Delicately, my father picked the snail up in his fingers and placed it on my mother's upper thigh, barely visible in the early morning light. *"Cargol I dona encornada,"* our father said as if reading the title of some future *objet trouvé* by my brother. Absentmindedly caressing my mother's enlarged nipples, he explained: "Snail and Cuckoo Wife. You see, this is not September but August, the sixth of August." Ignoring him, she followed the path the snail traced across the fine mist that dotted her groin and pubic hair. Rising from the sea, the sun painted her abdomen and thighs first in bronze and then in hyacinth. Our mother greeted the new day with open arms, her hands raised to the sky. "Look at the golden rain," I heard her say in a hushed voice. "I have finally reached a state of grace, and we have conceived an immortal child."

Lost in their earthly delights, our mother and father failed to notice a man with a pointed silvery goatee watching them from a balcony across the street. His face seemed calm but somber due to the furrow between his graying eyebrows. His eyes, focused in attention, were a perfect malachite green.

2

I REMEMBER THAT IT WAS TWO OR THREE WEEKS AGO, IN MIDWINTER, when you mentioned that you had seen a snail beside the front door of Freud's London home. You said: "It had probably been on that brick wall for quite some time. It was so still it might have been dead, but it was either sleeping or dreaming." Aware that at times I could not understand you, even if you were my brother, I did not answer. At dawn and dusk you were almost incomprehensible because, if fatigue or anger did not overwhelm you, the sadness that comes with overcast sunsets would defeat your spirit.

"What was the snail's dream?" I finally asked on one of those whims by which the deceased seek to escape the tedium of our death. "Perhaps it was dreaming about you and me at this very moment, as I tell you how I found it on that brick wall just above the handlebars of a bicycle painted a brighter red than a London double-decker bus." The unexpectedly youthful tone in your voice, so at odds with your appearance, startled me. From your looks, anyone would have thought you even more ancient than you were—a faded, decrepit self-portrait in an antiquated frame on its last hinge.

"A bicycle?"

"Perhaps it was a child's tricycle, a brand-new shining red tricycle." You nodded and proceeded to ramble in a fit of excitement. "Freud too was a snail. He was dying of cancer and one could already see his skull through his skin. It looked just like the shell of a mollusk."

"I believe you. That's how you've painted him."

"Yes, several times."

We fell silent—I, the specter of a child whom only you could see, and you, close to death's immortality, your reflection cast as if in a mirror in my limbo, which is this book—and I thought of our mother lying naked beside her husband on a now demolished balcony in an otherwise deserted dawn. Idly, I wondered whether the snail on the London wall was tiger-striped and black-mouthed

43

like the one she absentmindedly watched as it crept over her groin and across the fine web of vaginal mist on her pubic hair.

"Edward James took me to see Freud," you said in a whisper. "It was one of the epiphanies in my life, yet I've forgotten the name of the street and the number of the house."

"You've forgotten them?"

"Completely. It was so long ago."

"They'll come back to you."

Your ancient hands trembled on the blanket over your knees. Bundled up in flannel pajamas and a woolen robe, you looked like a skeleton that had plopped down in the chair. You shrugged your shoulders and smiled. "Why should I bother to remember his address? Just so I could give it to you, my dear dead brother? What difference does it make now anyway? Of course, I should mention that he moved shortly thereafter and I never went to his new home. I was never to see him again." In the pause that followed, we both stared through the window at the winter morning. It had snowed briefly during the night and the last traces were already melting in the square where the sidewalks were crisscrossed as if by the footprints of a mad hare that had lost its way home. A quartz-pale ray of light cut across the scene, etching a cityscape of facades and motionless trees. You stared in dazzled rapture, seemingly at a polar mirage.

"Go on," I urged impatiently.

"I showed Freud one of my paintings. To be exact, it was the *Portrait of My Dead Only Brother* that I had just completed. After studying it closely and attentively through his thick glasses, he said, 'Young man, do you know that, in another era, you could have been a Grand Inquisitor?' 'I am now. I interrogate my finished canvases with fanatic stubbornness, but they never reveal their true meaning to me,' I answered back."

"Is it true that, in another time, you were a Grand Inquisitor?"

"Just me? Aren't you and I fused into one and the same manifest monster, the horrid head of the Holy Office?"

I was frightened by the impatience and dead seriousness in my voice as I questioned you. I suppose that each man is an incarnate myth in some occult hierarchy that includes all humankind. Nevertheless, and only because of your appointment with Freud, I agreed then and there that you and I must have been the first judge and executioner to preside over an Inquisitorial tribunal. You paid me no heed and we each continued our own train of thought.

"How odd that I should forget Freud's address. I mean his London address because I remember that, in Vienna, he lived at 19 Gergasse. Yet I never was able to see him while I was in Austria. Every afternoon I called on him, just to be told that *Doktor Faustus* was either out or otherwise engaged."

"They say that you forgot to die or else that death grew weary of knocking on your door. Is that so?"

"Dying requires a difficult apprenticeship, brother dear," you immediately replied. "Few master it correctly. We simply grow used to its hardships. You can't possibly understand because, being of tender years, you passed away as easily as Mozart played the clavichord in the innocence of his youth. The fact is that I hadn't given death much thought until I met Federico. It was in the Students' Residence at the University of Madrid. He was so obsessed by the inevitability of death that he thought up a game to pre-empt the ineluctable moment of truth."

The mere mention of the art of dying had perked you up. In your mood swings, you were host to a multitude of inseparable strangers that never failed to take me by surprise. In a flash, all traces of old age in your speech and appearance had melted more quickly than the snow in the flower beds.

"A game of luck or magic?" I ventured to ask.

"Perhaps both. Federico was a talented comedian. Since every actor requires an audience, he would take us to his room, by strict invitation, to view the dress rehearsal of his death scene. Stretched out on the bed with his arms crossed over his chest and his face twisted into a hideous grimace, he portrayed each stage of his decomposition. It took five days for his flesh to rot away. Then, in a husky grunt that seemed to come from the depths of his soul, he would mimic the thud of his coffin lid as it fell closed. He described in detail his corpse oozing inside the casket. Last of all, with the fading rays of dusk, he would describe the funeral procession through the city streets to the family mausoleum. We would all shudder as the hearse creaked over a ditch or hit a pothole. By that point, we agonized as if caught in an nightmare of being eaten alive. We had never taken part in a game that so held our fascination. Sensing that he had us on the edge of our chairs, he would leap from his bed in a wild fit of laughter and shove us out the door. Then he dropped into a deep sleep from which he would awake a day later without recalling a single dream."

Half closing your eyes, you fell silent. Seated cross-legged on the red upholstered divan in my sailor's suit, I was baffled. Had you expired as abruptly as you had revived but a moment before, or had you retreated into your memories of Federico's histrionics? Were you spying on me through your white eyelashes to catch me off guard? I knew you were not dead since both of us are mere characters in a book—one, the specter of a little boy who died before you were conceived; the other, the shade of a fictitious old man whose death the real world vainly awaited year after year. You seem to have inadvertently discovered the limbo where my soul wanders and your mirror image goes in search. You once had the screeching blue-eyed young girl dedicate her sacrifice to me: *"Pour le frère mort de mon Maître! Pour son frère dans les limbes! Point et à la ligne."* But there is no "period, new paragraph" separating us in this space of ours, populated as it is with words. Anything as complicated as our destiny must be inseparable. So this room with its view over the plaza, the scarlet couch and your carved oak chair—said to be a Renaissance replica of the throne of the *Can Grande della Scalla*, lord of Verona—and the entire house for that matter, are a mirage of the home that, a quarter of a century ago, you had built on the same site. The earlier one— the home where both of us were born, the one with the snail on the balcony railing—had been destroyed years before. Our parents had moved at about the time when the Pomeranian photographer took your picture in his studio on the *Rambla de los Pájaros*. The house was razed shortly thereafter in the long winter months of the hurricane season. Unseen and heartsore, I peered at the truncated staircase climbing to nowhere, the scarred outer shell, the last vestiges of the demolished floors.

In its place a warehouse was built that as time went by would keep changing hands. Before the war, it belonged to a greengrocer, a sculptor, a cabinetmaker, and then served as headquarters for a coalition of the anarchist/labor movement. During the Civil War, it was the headquarters of the United Socialist Party of Catalonia and, immediately afterwards, it became a discreet brothel where the rosary was said every night. Later it belonged to an importer of spices—cloves, black mustard, nutmeg, caraway, and pure Tacari pepper. During the era of the Consumer Society and the Moral Majority of *Opus Dei*, it was bought by a mechanic, who turned it into a used car lot. Every owner either filed bankruptcy or was driven mad and fled because, although I had no part in the haunting which I am only beginning to understand myself, they would hear my childish voice coming out of nowhere and pronouncing those aphorisms and homilies that so delighted my father in my tender youth. "Listen to me carefully," I would say, "for perhaps one day my shadow will not be among you" or "Know that I've got a secret tucked between my shadow and my reflection in the mirror" or "Don't forget that the devil's most wicked ploy is not to pretend that he doesn't exist but to trick us into believing that there is true life after birth" or "If I deign to speak to you wretches, it is to distinguish you from chimpanzees, apes, and orangutans—you bury your dead and they don't nag."

Finally, one afternoon when you had just awakened from a nap, you made a telephone call from New York, giving orders to acquire the warehouse, to tear it down and build in its place a copy of the family home just as it was when we came into this world.

"*Mais, pourquoi?*" your wife asked, fearing or perhaps hoping that you had gone completely mad.

"*Qu'importe pourquoi? Pour mon frère mort!*" you snapped back, as if your dead brother were reason enough. The original plans of the building had disappeared in a fire, a move, or a bombing during the war. For that matter, blueprints would have proved useless because you dictated the design from memory or whim halfway around the world. Architects, contractors, and masons went out of their minds trying to carry out your contradictory and impractical instructions. The house became a winding labyrinth of rotundas, passages, atriums, halls, tunnels, parlors, bedrooms, baths, pools, antechambers, matching chambers, studies, waterclosets, archways, vaults, miradors, oriels, and bay windows of heavily-draped beveled glass, where any rational being would have gone stark raving mad. Even today your doctors, bodyguards, secretaries, valets, and nurses would lose their way if most of the rooms had not been closed off.

You found the house quite to your satisfaction when, years later, you came to inspect. You meandered through your chaos as confidently as another man could follow the lines traced in the palm of his hand. You ordered the walls of that confused maze of craftsmanship to be decorated with paintings, sketches, engravings, ink drawings, and sculptures which you had done in your youth—before meeting Federico in Madrid—when you were considered the least talented of all the young hopefuls, with the possible exception of Federico himself before he met you. You first had tried to model your monstrosities on Matisse and ended up with a hodgepodge that looked more like the tapestry cartoons of a Goya. You then attempted to copy Picasso and instead painted distorted El Greco caricatures. No matter, once you had seen your jealously guarded squiggles and doodles flaunted on the walls, you locked the doors with six turns of the key, tucked the roll of blueprints under your arm, and took off for Paris whistling a Catalan dance tune, a *sardana*. It was only after your wife's death that you returned, ready to bury yourself in the patchwork of your paintings and in a labyrinth as contradictory and unruly as your own life.

It is widely believed that you had built that intricate monument not as your dwelling but as your tomb. I have no doubt this may be true. But you and I must be forgetting that the house is the fiction as well as the limbo we share, in our respective dying and spectral forms. In a bout of insomnia, the first night that you spent in this bedroom, you called out to death and I appeared once again before you. You gave me a weary look of displeasure and said: "Will I never be rid of you, even when I'm dead?"

"I have no idea, and I doubt if whoever is writing all this has either. We're in his book, but the book controls him as much as it does us."

You seemed to nod in agreement, but a second later I noticed that you had dozed off again, smiling. And that is where it all stopped, with you either dreaming or pretending to sleep. Your bony profile, against the headrest of Can Grande's throne, reminded me of a greyhound. At times I could have sworn that, although death ignored you, the relentless light would rub you out before my very eyes.

"I'll never understand," you whispered with eyes closed, "why we were born as identical and inseparable as Siamese twins, even though I'm alive and you're not. Or why our father insisted that we both be named after him, or why you had to pick this moment to show your face again."

"Maybe it all adds up. As brothers we have the same name; our photographs as children were as alike as two drops of water. But the fact is I can't answer any of your questions. Isn't it said that at the brink of death we meet up with our deceased family or friends?"

"It is redundant for us to meet," you barked back, "because I always knew you to be so close beside that my shadow and my memories might well have been yours."

A sudden whim made me turn away, peek down on the plaza through the frost on the pane in the crisp morning air, and ask: "Are you sure that I'm the only one of your dearly departed to appear to you?" You sat up and rested your forehead against the glass. A pale, hesitant sunbeam was falling from the slate blue of the January sky. Below we saw our parents and Federico strolling through the snow-covered flower beds in front of the house. The three of them were wandering in circles like Picasso's blue waifs— man, woman, and pale youth—who walked aimlessly along the seashore on a turn-of-the-century winter morning. Our mother was wearing the black satin strapless gown in which she had scandalized an entire city while, with one arm resting on her husband's, she had applauded Gherardo de Sagra in *Filottete.*

In my memory, the past was a winter scene of gas lamps and leafless trees through which our parents strolled. For the first time since my death, they were performing their social obligations by attending the opera on a January evening as mild and clear as if it already anticipated springtime. Our mother was wrapped in a feather boa that tumbled over her hips and breasts, partially hiding her low decolletage. My father, who had recently put on weight, was dressed in a tight-fitting tailcoat and a shabby gabar- dine. Their acquaintances and clients greeted them along the way: *"Bona nit, señor. Bona nit, señora."* He responded by silently touch- ing his cane to his top hat. If the speaker turned out to be one of the few luminaries with whom he associated, my father would doff his hat when passing. Dressed in tails, he seemed short and stout with his bulging jowls and potbelly. In contrast, our mother's long-limbed beauty was more delicately set off by her festive finery. They made such a mismatched pair that they could be mistaken for victims of a spell that turned him into his own caricature and blinded her to the change.

From some dark recess of my mind—one that calls forth brief flashes of memory—I recalled that de Sagra would die that very year and that the theater where he sang his last opera would be turned into a museum dedicated to my brother's work. Ironically, it would remain empty forever, stripped of every canvas, sculp- ture, or sketch. As soon as they had finished the preparations to house the greater part of his private collection, he had second thoughts about donating a treasure created by his own hands. So time passed while, to the dismay and alarm of the authorities, he could not bring himself to part with what had already been placed in storage. Suddenly, toward the end of what had been an overcast Advent, the tide was heard rushing through the deserted halls as if the building had been transformed into a gigantic snail. At midmorning came the sound of wavelets calmly lapping the foot of the winding staircase. The engulfing water mounted to the balcony, over whose old railings the scandalized public had leaned one evening when, after taking her seat in the theater box borrowed in the absence of its privileged owners, our mother had sown the seeds of desire and scandal by letting her boa slip from her shoulders. With not a single jewel at her throat, she must have seemed even more undressed. There could be no nakedness so stark as that of a statue. Perhaps her sphinx-like air combined with her well-known reserve to fuel the indignation and resentment behind the impertinent glances. The disconcerting aloofness of her manner made her immodesty seem all the more an affront. Our father pretended to sleep through the performance; but under his furrowed brow he was reveling in the hate and envy directed at him because of the lust and outrage of others. A moment later, the lights were dimmed, and *Filottete* opened to the now long-forgotten applause for de Sagra before the audience settled down to enjoy the opera.

Years later, the rush of the sea could be heard from the upper gallery as it spilled over the empty spaces that had once been the front rows and orchestra pit of the former theater now converted into a deserted museum. The gallery came crashing down with a thunderous roar, a splash of shadows, an invisible spray, and again silence reigned. Afterwards, of their own accord, a multitude of visitors from around the world would fill the vacant halls that were to have exhibited your canvases. Soldiers, school children, and tourists came, as did the local bourgeoisie with a few hours to kill between High Mass and the Sunday bullfight. Nuns from various religious orders, pupils from a boarding school that bears your name, political refugees from the southern cone of South America appeared along with Asian ambassadors with orchids in their lapels. What more can I say? They pushed and jostled, eager to hear the mysterious high tide and the rumored schools of fishes, invisible as the waves, that struggled to escape to the surf through the huge chambers of that most singular chambered nautilus. The never-before-seen Grand Guignol spectacle fascinated and delighted you. They were perfectly matched to your own flair for the extravagant, as if the mysterious events were a reproduction of your own clownish pranks. You knew nothing, however, of that evening—the night of the last performance of Gherardo de Sagra in the Fondora opera house months after my death—because, although you had already been conceived by the woman whose wandering soul years later would stroll through the plaza with her husband and Federico, you had not yet been born.

From his seat, our father must have reminisced back to the Sunday afternoons when he used to demand silence at home so that, with his ear to the tulip-shaped speaker of his gramophone, he could listen to Gherardo de Sagra sing *Fedora* or *La Forza del Destino*. Then my mother would take me out for a grenadine soda or maraschino sherbet. From his memories, flavored with Romeo y Julieta cigar smoke and steaming espresso coffee, our father would return to undeniable fact that it was de Sagra himself, in the flesh, singing beneath his theater box. So close was de Sagra that, with a single leap to the stage, Father could have embraced him as proof of his very existence. He did not throw himself onto the podium but leaned head and chest over the velvet-cushioned balustrade, as if to push through the shadows with his bald pate in search of the hidden source of the *romanzas* and arias.

Father was so absorbed in the music that he completely forgot about his wife, immersed as always in her haughty disdain; but I saw Mother slowly extend her naked arm to stroke her husband between his legs. Enthralled in *Filottete*, he paid no heed to the hand fondling his groin, but Father snapped out of his trance when she unbuttoned his trousers and took his penis between her fingers. Staring him full in the face, Mother endured his shocked look without altering her aloof demeanor. Her indifference crushed him and silenced his protests before he could utter a sound. Meanwhile she kept on stroking him with her fingertips and palm, arousing his pleasure, slowing or deferring its pace, as she listened to the suppressed panting of a man progressively losing all control. From time to time, Father's passion for the music conquered the temptation of the flesh and, with half-closed eyes, he would shake his head like a dying bull, slipping into a state of sated pleasure that more modern folk soon would call the annihilation of ego and the self.

At other times, I thought I could read his forehead, scrawled as if by veins of resinous feldspar, like the mouthing of a frogman through the glass mask of his diving gear. I imagined him tormented by a hatred equal to his desire as he recalled in shame and rage the sight of our naked mother, screaming from another balcony: "Don't touch the destructive snail or . . . !" At last, following a singularly inspired aria, he collapsed against the balustrade biting his knuckles as the enraptured audience fell into a respectful silence and then an interminable applause. I can still see Gherardo de Sagra bowing to the public with the tired courtesy of a dying man who, unaware of his destiny, detaches himself from his dreams and subconsciously renounces the world.

Years after the tenor's voice fell silent and the memories of our parents were swept away, you sat up tremulous, ravaged and gaunt, on the throne of the Can Grande. Reduced to a blubbering skeletal bone, you turned to the balcony and pointed an index finger at our mother. "Look at her! She walks barefoot in her long skirt, but she glides over the snow as if on air!" It is true that she moved with the lightness of a feather held up by the wind. Nevertheless, and even in the fictitious light that we phantoms share with mirages, the cold had blushed her cheeks and blanched the cleft between her breasts. In the distance, she stared at the horizon as if in an hallucinatory trance; but her gaze was so penetrating that, as it glanced over the window, we both felt a shiver pierce us.

Walking slowly in circles, her husband and Federico could have been mistaken for father and son—their features may have been different but they undoubtedly shared the same bloodline—both as roughly hewn and dark as farm hands or hardware salesmen. The Garden-Variety-Legal-Beaver kept the fiftyish face and build that you had drawn of him when, well into your prime and after many false starts, you finally found the firm hand and the originality of a true artist. Father's mouth and jowls bulged, but his eyes shone as innocently as those of a lost fawn. With his hands clasped behind his back, Federico kept his head at a tilt, as you said he used to do when alive. In profile, the light cast a blue shadow across his thick stubble of beard and the rugged black eyebrow that almost joined his bushy sideburn. I wondered how Federico could ever have loved you—his opposite—and, at least for the time being, could find no explanation. Meanwhile, you were hailing the specters, waving to them wildly, and trying to force open the window sash.

"Cease and desist," I said, feeling pity for you in your frustration. "They won't answer, because the dead only commune with one other. I am the sole exception, in that I speak to you and you perceive and hear me, perhaps because we are condemned to live and die inseparably. Life and death are merely quirks of our fate." You looked as if you had not understood a single word. However, through the closed window I heard the voices of the shades as clearly and as crisply as if they were carrying on their conversation in the next room. Word for word, like a medium, I began to repeat their words to you.

"It was a mistake for us to be summoned here. We're not even sure who called the meeting. Either my son is stranded somewhere, since I for one don't see him, or else he is still among the ranks of the living," fretted Father. "Perhaps he'll turn up soon. He never was overly punctual," Mother replied. "You can never count on him," muttered Federico to himself. "He is a fraud to the core. I should know, even if in death I've never stopped loving him!" With the hint of a smile on her pursed lips, Mother shot Federico a disapproving glance as she paused to eavesdrop on his conversation with her husband.

"In all those summers you spent with us, I never once suspected that you were homosexual. I suppose I never dared let the thought cross my mind because, had I found out, I would have thrown you out by the seat of your pants. But now, in this spiral of eternity, whoever you were when my son brought you into our home seems a trivial matter. I think about who I once was, and I don't recognize myself. We were shadows then and now death is our only reality. There's no doubt about it even if it doesn't make sense."

"That's why I'm surprised that I still love him," Federico said smiling. "It's like clinging to a dream."

"I had no idea you were a queer," Father, ignoring him, stubbornly persisted in repeating himself. Then, studying Federico carefully, Father confided to him: "On the other hand, you see, I would have believed any of my son's aberrations, or denied them for that matter, because I never understood him either."

"You didn't know him because you never learned to love him," Mother cut in, her voice lacking all hint of reproach. She might as well have said that the sun rises in the east and sets in the west. As if confirming a fact of life—for you the living, that is— her voice was matter of fact. "It was I who forced you to conceive him, even though you despised me even as you planted your seed in my body."

Sputtering in frustration, you squirmed and writhed on the Can Grande's throne. "Tell them I must speak with them!" you begged, reaching your hands out to the apparitions. "Tell them I'm here and I want them to see and hear me before they leave."

"I can't, because they can't see me any more than they can you."

"Beseech them anyway, if you're truly my brother!"

"Perhaps it is precisely because I am that they don't see me. You can ask them whatever questions you want once you're dead. That is unless, as Father says, by then everything will seem superfluous to you."

With a wave of your hand you told me not to be a snippet and to simply relay the apparitions' words. Meanwhile, his head held high and his hands clasped behind his back, Federico occasionally poked at a branch with his foot or sank into silence. Father absent-mindedly pulled from his right pocket a cigar and a box of matches with a sketch of some transatlantic liner presumably sunk or torpedoed during the signing of the Peace of Versailles or the Treaty of Locarno. Having lit the cigar, he tossed the burning matchstick into the air, and watched it vanish into the light like water into water. Mother stood shivering nearby, and I still don't know whether it was from the cold or because she sensed our presence, so close yet so inscrutable. She then gave a sigh and, as if walking on air, resumed her barefoot stroll. Unexpectedly, Father paused and remarked to Federico: "You remind me so much of my son!" Turning toward his wife with a wave of his had, he summoned her from her feigned introspection. "Look at the resemblance. I never noticed it when Federico used to come to Calador, but he and our son are identical. Don't you see it?" Before our mother could answer, Federico interrupted: "Sir, it never occurred to me that your son and I were alike." "No, not that son—I was thinking of our first-born! He died in infancy— an archangel. The years passed and I grew old surviving him, but I never got over my grief at the loss. It's as if his body were still warm under his little blue shroud. . . . Dear, don't be shy. Speak up. Tell us if he's not the spit and image of our eldest son." "Perhaps," our mother answered doubtfully, "but I really don't think so."

You looked up and gave me a sidelong, dubious glance. "He means you, but Father is spouting nonsense. You don't look at all like Federico. Even now, with both of you dead, you're as different as night and day. I was the only one you ever resembled. You were the rough draft and I was the finished portrait. At this very moment, you could pass for a caricature of me as a toddler."

"If you say so. . . . But just look how Father's expression has softened speaking to Federico."

The Garden-Variety-Legal-Beaver was spilling out his heart: "Never in all eternity could I tell this to another soul. It is as secret as the memory of that life, even when it passed on, which I couldn't share with any one. If I confess it to you now, it is because you loved my other son; and he was as cruel to you as he was to me. At times I was so beside myself that I felt like taking off in a boat on the high seas and never returning. Or I would decide to throw myself head first from a balcony like the one where we conceived them both."

You and I noticed, or at least imagined, Federico's smile during the pause in my father's harebrained story. His eyebrows knotted in a frown, Federico said softly, weighing every word: "I too considered suicide, when he deserted me. In one of my poems, I am watching a little boy eat oranges in a brook. Perhaps he was your first-born son, the one that you say looks so much like me." "It's quite possible." "Is it true that they were both conceived on a balcony?" Federico asked, both amused and amazed. "Yes, indeed, and in the presence of a snail," Mother added her detail with studied indifference. Ignoring her but working himself into a lather, her husband continued: "In our bedroom, I kept a photograph of my dead son. Although at the time I believed in Satan but not in God, I would lock myself in my room to pray: Forgive me, my son, for having conceived your brother on the day you were buried and for having given him your name, since it is mine also. It was all a tragic mistake, and we never should have conceived him to try to resurrect you from the dead. If there were any justice in this world, you would still be alive and he never would have existed."

Forcing myself to feel the compassion that I merely pretended, I reached over the back of your armchair and rested my hand on your shoulder. "If you'd like, I'll stop repeating their conversation." Leaning forward to hear them better, you answered: "They're only saying what I already know. I used to spy on Father by peeping through the keyhole. Almost every night I heard him say those very same words to your photograph. Step back a little. You're blocking the light and my view of the apparitions." I obeyed as Mother paused beneath the leafless trees in front of the window to whisper: "It's too late and far too cold here. My son is alive and we're waiting for him in vain. Someone has the time and date confused. Let's go to the sea where it never snows."

Neither talking nor looking at one another, the specters reversed the direction of their circles. Federico and our father nodded their heads in silent agreement as if dropping off to sleep. Erased by the morning mist, they disappeared into the gray dawn. They formed a trio of forgotten figures, as if in a family portrait corroded by time. They then were transformed into isolated images, submerged in a stream and frozen in glacial ice. When they finally melted away, leaving no trace except for our memory of their visit, I leaned toward you and said: "I had no idea that death does not stop us from aging. Did you notice the silver sideburns on Federico and the white streaks in Mother's hair?" "No, I couldn't make them out," you lied, hiding your shivering hands beneath your shawl and averting my eyes. "Mother was right," you continued, "it must be very cold outside, but I wonder why they would return to the sea, even if it never snows there. I'd never go back to Calador Bay. There are too many people and too many boats. Besides, it frightens me to think of

Velázquez painting in his sleep beneath the waves." I let you ramble uninterrupted, but at your first pause and in order to calm your nerves, I asked if you preferred me to remain silent.

"I'll fall asleep soon; and if death takes pity on me, perhaps one day I'll find eternal rest. The only two things I fear are insomnia and immortality. But first I want to confess that I am very happy."

"Happy? Why? Because you saw Federico and our parents, despite the fact they failed to notice us behind the windows panes?"

"Oh no! That's of no importance and I've almost completely forgotten about them," you smiled maliciously. "I'm happy because all of a sudden I remember Freud's address in London and the house with the red bicycle and the snail beside the door. He lived at 39 Elsworth Road, near a very well-kept park. What do you think about that?"

3

"It frightens me, too, to think of Velázquez painting in his sleep beneath the waves."

Granted, sir: you control—or think you control—us all. So all right, you are the author of this limbo and this book, where—presumedly at your beck and call—my parents and brother, Federico and I, along with a whole cast of named and nameless characters, appear and disappear according to the roles you have assigned us. I want to confess to you, whoever you may be, my sincere belief that we, your characters, influence and define you no less than you conceive, breathe life into, and mold us. You are not the same man today that you were before starting on this book, which belongs just as much to us as to you. For that matter, and this may be hard for you to accept, you will not be the same man when you finish it—that is, if one day you do complete it and believe that you have relegated us to total oblivion in your mind. Shredded from memory, as you would put it.

So it is, my good sir, that while you construct your text word by word, like a mason who builds a stone lodge and covers it with a pitched red-tiled roof, you run the risk of losing balance, slipping, and disappearing into the pages of your own text. Should that happen, you could be mistaken for any one of us. I could appreciate the irony of walking into a bedroom in this absurd labyrinth of a house, mistaking you for my dying brother and not discovering until the funeral that the corpse is not his but yours. You, I repeat, you—whatever name you go by—could be killed off between the lines of your own prose in the character role of one of your own creations. The ultimate irony would be your metamorphosis into a minor character insignificant to the plot line. Let's take by way of example my parents and Federico returning as a trio of shades, similar to Picasso's early figures. I can picture you as one of those lugubrious long-legged dogs that absentmindedly walk with Picasso's blue beggars along beaches tucked away in some museum. I dare say that your metamorphosis into one of Picasso's scrawny strays would be a clever touch, and even obliquely relevant since my brother—as you depict him, awaiting the most drawn out of death scenes—also reminds me of a scrawny greyhound.

"It frightens me, too, to think of Velázquez painting in his sleep beneath the waves."

It might not be too far-fetched to think of Velázquez—not me, or my brother—as the inspiration, the raison d'être, of this manuscript. No matter how voluminous a text may be—a million words or such vast reams of paper as to accommodate every tome recorded down through the ages—behind the printed page there exists a world for which the script is a paper mirror. Half a century ago, my brother did an oil painting and entitled it, *Incredible Enigma in Velázquez's Studio*. Although he would not actually admit that he considered it his finest work and would merely shrug his shoulders each time I asked if it was his favorite, he never parted with it. He refused to sell it even in his most dire economic straights, such as when he and his wife were starving artists in Almería, holed up in a country inn with a barred window overlooking a desolate garden of centaury and prickly pear plants and awaiting in destitution the interminable arrival of a money draft from Baron Drameille. Even in that predicament, he would not part with his *Enigma*—in spite of the fact that the copperskinned gypsy woman who owned the inn offered to pardon the entire tab in exchange for the painting. "I feel like I'm looking at hell through a keyhole, . . . at hell through a twat," she confided. He did not sell it the following autumn either, when *madame la baronne* posed naked but for her monocle in his atelier at Chateau de Carry-Le-Rouet and insisted on purchasing the picture. That russet-flecked fall afternoon was straight out of Mallarmé—*jonché de taches de rousseur*—and my brother had just put the finishing touches to the nude portrait of the Baroness de Drameille. The delight of *la baronne* was so heartfelt that, without bothering to remove her monocle, she offered herself to him on the divan— with the prior approval of her husband, who had granted it at once the night before when she first confessed her desire or caprice. My brother shook his sculpted head—that of a Corinthian hero stamped in relief on a medallion, or perhaps that of Cellini's beloved model. In his stumbling French, my brother replied: "*Excusez-moi, madame, mais je suis presque impuissant même avec ma femme*. Forgive me, but I am all but impotent even with my wife. I would hate to make a fool of myself or disappoint you, especially after the kindness that you and *monsieur le baron* have shown me, but I believe that evil spirits have consumed my manhood with the same craven appetite with which Rubens's *Cronus* devours his son in the Prado Museum."

"It frightens me, too, to think of Velázquez painting in his sleep beneath the waves."

Although my brother had traveled the world over with his painting tucked under his arm or in the safe of an ocean liner or hotel while he attended the *vernissage* of some art exhibit or a royal ball, it was only on rare occasions that he showed the painting in public. He would then call another raucous press conference that quickly turned into a jostling free-for-all of cameras, microphones, and outlandish questions: "*Maître, maître,* is it true that, as Altizer claims, God is dead? Or, by chance, are you His reincarnation?" Answer: "I am only my brother's brother. He had to die so that I could exist. A unique individual such as myself spans more than one lifetime. Just as *The View of Delft, Ladies-in-Waiting,* or the *Mona Lisa* each grew out of an earlier study, I too needed to be twice conceived and born again." Such dithyrambic flaunting was pronounced with his hand on his heart; but rather than striking a mythic stance, it seemed more like he was rubbing salt into an open wound. When the *Incredible Enigma in Velázquez's Studio* was unveiled, he appeared actually to shrink. Due perhaps to his change of demeanor—now almost stutteringly shy—or to the near-frenzied anticipation of the press, the painting was to be received as a total disappointment meriting no more than bewildered silence and servile respect. In a high pique, my brother would then snatch up the frame and begin to stalk up and down glowering and spouting nonsensical Iberian rhymes and tongue twisters to an amazed audience from genteel Gallic France: "Seven judges sat on a wall, seven judges had a good fall, seven judges broke gavel and ball." Or "The sky's a swath of silt and sand, whoever sifts the shifty strand, a good silt-shifter is the man. Go out and sin no more. Amen."

"It frightens me, too, to think of Velázquez painting in his sleep beneath the waves."

Incredible Enigma in Velázquez's Studio. A few days after the specters' appearance, my brother asked that the painting be removed from its mother-of-pearl inlaid chest and propped against the wall so that he could see it as he reclined on the feather pillows of his bed. Studying the painting, he became lost in thought as if asking the figures on plasterboard for answers to questions that he had never before dared pose. Only then did I make any claim to understand his outlandish statement that once his masterpieces were finished he could no longer fathom their meaning. Although his eyes were a shade darker than those of the man he called the Garden-Variety-Legal-Beaver, they had the same expression. It was the look my father gave me in the casino when I played the Christ Child declaiming words of wisdom to the Elders. My brother would imitate the agonized disbelief in my father's eyes— the burning spark in the iris of his pupils—when peering into the crib where I lay dead, he collapsed in despair, only later, enraged with fury, to conceive my sibling.

"It frightens me, too, to think of Velázquez painting in his sleep beneath the waves."

You, my dear author, must be taken as unaware as my brother, by the *Incredible Enigma in Velázquez's Studio*. On this very page, I look up from *mes limbes* and, by chance, see your detailed critique of that painting. It is as if you had a sudden, irresistible urge to put an end to our story or to weave us into the plot of another quite different book. I read your prose with open eyes, or with closed lids, the way a seer reads destiny on the soul's slate. I tell my brother that our mirror may be about to break and our text reduced to a blank page—ripped to shreds by the author or abandoned for a new theme. Perhaps my brother's *Incredible Enigma in Velázquez's Studio* will be the starting point for a chronicle of the life of the painter of *Ladies-in-Waiting* and *The Spinners*. Perhaps its our time to bask in the eternal oblivion known as the void. My brother shakes his head pensively on his pillows and replies that, on the contrary, he feels alive again. He refuses to believe that the author can weave a tale around Velázquez and fail to include any mention of our part in the story. The two worlds must be joined, our dear author, in your critique of his *Incredible Enigma*. Unfortunately, my brother's eyes and memory are not what they once were; your gloss of his painting is forgotten, muddled as his memories. He asks me to read it aloud and, without further ado, I obey.

The work, Incredible Enigma in Velázquez's Studio, *is a mere thirty-three by thirty centimeters. Due to its small size and its devotion to detail, it could be called a miniature. Painted with camel-hair brush-strokes in oil on gesso, it is undated, although the artist must have painted it in the summer or fall of 1935, during his second visit to the United States. The work is stamped and signed in cursive on the back, under a stanza from "Nocturne" by Rubén Darío: "And the pain not to be what it was I have been, / the loss of the kingdom that was mine on this earth, / the thought that for naught I could never have dreamed, / and the dream is my life since my moment of birth!" Painted on plasterboard with the glossy sheen as if of enamel, this minute pièce forte*

*depicts, to the viewer's left, don Diego de Silva Velázquez facing front
in a pose reminiscent of his self-portrait in* Ladies-in-Waiting, *although
the Red Cross of the Order of Saint James does not appear on his chest.
Likewise, the canvas that he is painting is on its side, as opposed to
upright like the tall easel that we see in the foreground of Velázquez's
canvas. On the right in the painting is don Luis de Acedo, Haedo o
Aedo— whichever of the three versions of his last name is the correct
one— Court Jester to Felipe IV and Secretary to the Royal Chamber and
Bearer of His Majesty's Seal, officially charged with the authority to sign
and seal in the King's name. He is seated on the floor, leafing through
the same huge in folio as in the Velázquez that hangs in the Prado
Museum. Beside him are several other manuscripts, an inkwell, and a
quill pen. That courtier and jester's true likeness, resurrected a half
century ago in America, is the exact copy in miniature of the portrait
painted in 1642, or perhaps 1643, by don Diego de Silva Velázquez. The
single discrepancy consists in the background style of the two works—
one being baroque and the other surrealist. To the back of the original
jester, and stretching into the horizon, is one of the blue translucent
landscapes for which Velázquez is renowned. These do not copy nature
but rather resemble a palimpsest of tapestries contrasting with the true-
to-life figures in the foreground. In the painting done three centuries
later,* Venus of the Mirror, *Venus poses with her back turned between
Velázquez and don Luis de Acedo. She is depicted with the same attention
to detail as the learned clown who is decked out in black vet. This is the
nude that once belonged to the Duchess of Alba, the very one that was
to be removed at her death by that flimflam of a Prime Minister, Manuel
Godoy, who hung it over his bed until his eventual fall, and that is now
in the National Gallery. Although the modern painting is a replica in
miniature of the goddess's flesh tones and hair arrangement, not to mention the mirror and cupid, the coverlet and bed curtains— there is one
more discrepancy between* Venus of the Mirror *and* Incredible
Enigma in Velázquez's Studio. *In the canvas that now hangs in London, the mirror, hand-held by a winged putto, captures in halftones the
shadowy face of a woman whose identity is debated. (Those who believe
it to be the reflection of the goddess differ sharply from those who believe
that, thanks to a miracle, a peasant girl's face peers from the glass.) The
mirror on painted wood, now faded into purple streaks, has absolutely
nothing reflected in its shaded glass. It goes without saying that all the
figures— Acedo, Velázquez, Venus, and Cupid— are repeated obses-
sively in many of the artist's other oils and sketches, such as* Portrait of
My Dead Only Brother *(1960) presently hanging in the Tate Gallery.*

Although my brother gave the air of having more important
things on his mind, he listened to your critique most attentively,

his hands crossed over his lap shawl. As soon as I finished my reading, he corroborated all the details except for the date of *Incredible Enigma in Velázquez's Studio*. He responded to my silent and quizzical look of surprise by admitting that he was to blame for the mistake. The correct date was 1925, instead of 1935, as he had told you. I listened in astonishment; it was as if the true-to-life reproduction in this book of yours had suddenly muddled each and every perspective into a sort of a cubist still life, or as if some angel had announced the Resurrection of the Flesh in that demolished theater once inhabited by whispering snails and howling winds.

As soon as I recovered my power of speech, I asked him where he could possibly have met you, our author, if you had conceived and given shape to a world where we existed as mere shadows of our former selves—him, still in life, and me in death. He answered that, as a matter of fact, it was at the Saint Denis Hotel, the day of Kennedy's assassination, where you and he first crossed paths. It was the year that would go down in history bordered in black—the day the whole American populace grieved, within the four corners of their homes, in the streets, on the beaches, or hanging from tree branches, or clinging for dear life to window ledges, or clutching old-fashioned barbers' shears in their hands. Instead of the assassination of a too-soon-forgotten President, it was as if the family's beloved pet dog had been poisoned or a prized tropical fish found dead in its aquarium in the foyer. He added that he had forgotten your name and face, that his memory was not what it used to be, either in real life or in this mere reflection, where it was muddled and blurred by outside hands that tapped or plugged the source from a spigot within their palms.

I ought to excuse such lapses, since my brother was soon to be turned into a memory as fleeting as that of any other mere mortal who must accept that his life's work will outlive his bodily remains. I asked him how I could have missed that meeting at the Saint Denis Hotel—I who have tagged along like his shadow since the evening of his conception in my presence and that of a striped black-mouthed snail. Eager as I was to point out the tiniest discrepancy and to correct each error in the events that I must have also witnessed, I doubted the truth of his trip to London to visit Freud, simply because I could neither recall nor substantiate it. But he silenced me with a wan, superior smile and a weak raise of his pale hand. Wandering spirits can also doze off and sleep for years as did the legendary Rip Van Winkle; and there were times, he went on, when he did not cross paths with my errant and snoozing soul after I disappeared among the summer cicadas and the Queen Anne's lace at the iron grating beneath our porch at Calador. But eventually I awoke at his bedside, aboard the *Mary Tudor* in the middle of the Atlantic Ocean, unaware of having been asleep and incapable of recalling a single dream.

I let him ramble on, and he assured me, sir, that it was during your meeting at the Saint Denis that you were inspired to write this book and to make of it a limbo—the truth through a glass darkly, as in his oil painting of Venus. He said that perhaps some subconscious urge impelled you, our author, to capture us poised between life and death while he was expounding on his *Incredible Enigma in Velázquez's Studio*. The inevitable day had arrived when you could not free yourself from either of your two works in progress, not from the pages of this, our space—where my brother patiently awaits his death and I my yet-to-be-unfolded redemption—nor from the tale lifted straight from Velázquez's canvas of the painter and his picnic companions. Your chronicle of a painting will unfold, therefore, with the story of me and my brother, just as the golden vines climbed Solomon's column in search of the dawn breaking through an oriel window. In the end, the two narratives will merge and, together, will provide the clue to the other's mystery—that is, of course, unless art and eternity are merely two more preposterous follies invented by man. "I have spoken," he said and crossed his arms on his chest, frail as a reed. He then lost himself in the contemplation of his *Incredible Enigma in Velázquez's Studio*. Looking at us then—the way you, our dear author, regard us now—anyone would have thought that my brother had dismissed me from his mind, or that I had sprouted wings and disappeared just as my sleeping specter, according to my brother, had vanished through the iron porch grating at Calador Bay.

I asked him why he had lied in postdating the painting by ten years. His only response was to say you, sir, had not been fooled even though, out of respect for authenticity, you had included the alleged date verbatim in your notes. I insisted on being told the reason behind his deception, and he replied that the truth would take us back to July or August 1925, when he was still in his early twenties. Months before, during the Christmas holidays, I had once again slipped absentmindedly away by dozing off on a park bench in Fondora while my brother fed bread crumbs to some frightened doves. The summer afternoons were so sweltering that the iron gratings and balustrades seemed to melt beneath the

lacquered overcast skies, and the nights quivered with an excitement that silenced the dogs and the crickets. It was as if the stars
were twinkling above a wasteland. Although it does not figure in
any of the biographies yet written about the poet, Federico made
a surprise visit to that hellish cauldron of Calador Bay. He was
much changed from the young man that my brother had brought
home before—*No, in all the summers you spent with us, I never
suspected that you were queer. I suppose I never dared let the thought
cross my mind, or else I would have thrown you out by the seat of
your pants.* He was jumpy as a fish swimming upstream, or else,
hangdog and gloomy, withdrawn from the world and from those
around him.

Fearful that our father would guess the reason behind such
abrupt changes in Federico's behavior, my brother took him to
the family's mountain refuge, a restored shepherd's hut on the
highest part of the ridge. From the crest of a cliff that projected
over the water like the prow of a ship, they inched their way across
steep slopes overhanging a diaphanous blue sea that allowed the
sun's golden rays to penetrate the sandy depths of the chasms
where corbina darted in and out of the submerged crags. They
were taken to the refuge by a guide yanking at the halter of a
dapple-gray mule irked by its burden of tools and supplies. Brown
as a nut and silent as a stone, the mule driver left my brother
and Federico on the mountain peak with the promise to return
in a week to collect them. Although the purpose of their escape
was to paint and write—Federico had started another book of
poetry and my brother a work in three panels—they did not daub
a single brushstroke or jot down one stanza during their lonely
retreat. Their days passed with long lapses of silence when neither one could look the other in the eye nor face up to what they
were mutually avoiding. At dawn, with the first pale rays of the
sun rising from the sea, my brother would leave Federico sleeping
with his head tucked to one side and stumble outside to greet
the new day. My brother told me later, as he stood in front of his
Incredible Enigma in Velázquez's Studio, that at the time he thought
that he went out to find me, hoping to wake me from my dream
on the park bench. However, instead of seeing me materialize, he
was to witness the rebirth of the world.

Testing the overhanging cliff with the toe of his sandal so as
not to fall into the star-studded darkness, he leaned out and saw
all creation reduced to the sea and the granite crest that loomed
over the water like a ship's prow: a sort of headless *Victory of
Samothrace* with huge breasts and a single arm, crowned by my

brother turned into a jay. While the sun burnished the water in
its fiery rays, my brother contemplated the ever-repeated resurrection of the world. At dawn the landscape slowly came alive,
and the cliffs were transformed into a mob of naked Titans, gigantic fauns, profiles stamped on coins, women sleeping prone on
the jagged crests with their faces to the sky, humpbacked penitents, Michelangelic hermaphrodite slaves and catamites, all
struggling in vain to break free from some cruel catatonic spell.
It was as if a doddering old man were slowly and methodically
changing the slides in a magic lantern. Perhaps it was the one I
had before my brother inherited it, the one with color transparen-
cies of Antarctica and of the Velázquez galley of fools—don Pablo
de Valladolid, Barbarossa, el Niño de Vallecas, Calabacillas, don
Juan de Austria, and don Sebastián de Morra—that miniature
squirearchy of buffoons awaiting the arrival of His Majesty's little
"cousin," the absent Primo.

Light changed the contours of the rough crags that surged from
the sea before a universe surprised by its own rejuvenation: a
firmament that each and every morning must thrill at the outrageous spectacle of rocks tortured in expiation of the sins of a still-
to-be-created mankind. As you, sir, must have already anticipated, I am thinking of those who would later defy Father Time
to erase some ironically imperishable instant—the moment that
Justino de Nassau hands over the keys of the city of Breda to a
most respectful Ambrosio de Spinola, the precise and no less
sacred hour when an unknown Flemish girl begins to read a letter
in the dim afternoon light of Delft or Rijswijk, the second eternalized by a prisoner standing with arms spread before a firing
squad, or the fleeting profile of the octogenarian Titian contemplating his image and likeness in the background of his self-
portrait.

"It frightens me, too, to think of Velázquez painting in his
sleep beneath the waves."

Frightened. My brother was frightened of Federico. He knew
that Federico was in love with him ever since they met at the
Students' Residence, just after Dalí had been expelled from the
School of Art. The poet followed after my brother, harassing him
with the melancholy look of a black-haired gypsy virgin nurtured
among prickly pears and olive trees in the pale moonlight, and
now unhappily betrothed to an assassin with the face of Apollo
who had stepped straight out of a cypress grove littered with
Roman amphoras of olive oil from the First Empire. When he
could not find him, or did not try, they would meet by chance in

the Retiro Park, the Royal Hunting Lodge, the Patio of Kings, or the Prado's Patiner room—the one that adjoins and leads to hell on the other side of the wall by way of the River Styx painted on a canvas. One morning in January, in a corridor of the student dorm, Federico embraced my brother and kissed him full on the lips. He had not imagined that he would ever again be caressed in such a way—not since those early childhood days he tried to forget, when he had been fondled like a little lamb: *y yo queriéndote tanto, tanto, cordero mío.* In his adolescence, he was equally terrified at the thought of going to bed with a man or with a woman. Only much later would fornication with either sex be a matter of total indifference to him, just as one recalls but does not fear an outbreak of the plague or the madness of a stranger. Although unmoved, he was flattered that Federico desired him because my brother sensed that this would breathe creative originality into his fledgling stabs at art. He also believed himself more intelligent, in that the power of observation begins with the recognition of one's own limitations. Although he never admitted to it, my brother lived in a constant state of crisis, a contagious affliction that Federico could not help catching. If what the one wrote was, indeed, as clumsy and devoid of originality as what the other painted, even more painful was the mute proof of their still embryonic talent, their consistent failure to realize their potential. In other words, without daring to admit it—concluded my brother, absorbed in his *Incredible Enigma in Velázquez's Studio*—they were tortured by the premonition that they would never develop into the artists they truly were.

It was on one of those nights that the aurora borealis had awakened my brother. Overwhelmed by a splendor that lit up the skies as if all the blood shed by the sons of Cronus had been set ablaze in the firmament, he raced barefoot and naked to the cliff above the surf. The air smelled of ozone, and the scent of scorched rockrose and Scotch broom wafted in from the burning inland fields. Barely awake as he searched for me along the crags, he saw herds of animals leaping two-by-two, for his eyes alone, out of the midnight sun, ages before man first walked the earth. Horses, goats, and wild dogs took shape in that red glow. Gentle mares and heavy-maned coursers lay on the flinty rocks and, as they stood up, their neighing mingled with the roar of the waves. He saw the dogs greeting the sudden dawn with smoldering eyes and endless yowls. He saw the translucent shapes of rams with horns sharpened to points by centuries of tempestuous winds. My brother thought he was in the presence of fantastic creatures resurrected from the mythical world of medieval bestiaries. The apparitions, however, suddenly vanished; it was as if a shepherd's inaudibly high whistle had scared them, forcing a retreat to their shadowy kingdom while the pungent scent of scorched steppes vanished into the blazing night. It was then that he noticed Federico, naked and visibly shaken, staring from the doorway of their hut. My brother was so startled that he barely contained a scream of terror. His friend advanced toward him, caked in blood and with horns on his forehead and a gaping hole in his chest. Years later, my brother said one would have thought that Federico had just been shot and miraculously had gotten to his feet in order to walk up to him and to point him out as the assassin. No matter; the terrifying vision—a parody of Banquo accusing the innocent Macbeth—lasted merely a few moments. As he approached, Federico's wounds healed and the poet changed back into his tanned body the color of burnished bronze. Without looking one another in the eye or exchanging a single word, as the aurora borealis began to vanish into the sea, they stood naked and motionless on the deserted cliff top.

Still silent, but moved by an identical impulse, they took off in a run toward the cabin that served as their shelter. Federico was in the lead because the poet's bare soles were as tough as a wayfaring gypsy's. Bursting into the tiny hut, they snatched up Federico's quatrains and my brother's preliminary sketches like armloads of dried straw and kindling and, as if making away with battle spoils, ran back, breathless, to the cliff. There they made a pyre of paper and canvas while the very wind paused to watch. As soon as they had stacked up their poems and sketches, they stepped back to await a miracle, as imminent as it was inevitable. One would be hard pressed to find an explanation—whether farfetched or plausible—of what happened next. This my brother accentuated from his bed, shrugging his shoulders in bafflement. Let us just say that the scorching summer winds, so hot they can set an entire mountain ablaze, shattered the proverbial glass. In any case, and by all his gods, my brother swore to me that with the last streamers of light from the aurora borealis, and in less than no time at all, the poems and canvases went up like matchsticks as the night closed in around them. Watching the bonfire above a frieze of terrified gulls nesting among the rocks, the two young men burst into shrieks of laughter. Hands to their mouths, their naked bodies doubled over as they sniggered and guffawed, they bowed to the first stars appearing in the sky. Tears that tasted of the salty night air ran down their cheeks into the beards that had sprung up on that sleepless midsummer night, as Federico would later recall and my brother would repeat in his atrocious English, "that summer night without dream." The beard was heavy and dark on the rough jaw of the poet, but sparse and straggly on my brother's cheeks. Gasping with laughter, they watched until the last sparks of their bonfire had gone out, and then they returned to their hut, still shaking from head to shoulder.

My brother had just lain down when he overheard Federico quietly laughing to himself, perhaps in his sleep. Later, as my brother began to doze off, he felt Federico slide into the cot, moaning and crushing him with his muscular arms as if he were trying to break him in two. Unnerved and realizing that he was in a helpless and irrevocable situation, he closed his eyes believing that he had a vision of our dead mother looking at all the buffoons in the magic lantern. For a fiery eternity, he was violated that dawn in a manner that was to remain indescribable right up to his final years when trying to reconstruct the scene with all the sharp detail he had used to capture his nightmares on canvas. He told me that he had been struck by the notion that he and Federico were make-believe players in that outrageous scene. Their true selves had remained on the cliff, laughing at the midnight sun while they destroyed poems and sketches that should never have seen paper in the first place. Or perhaps, naked and dreamless, they were sleeping in separate cots awaiting a new dawn: the true dawn of a day like all the rest, with stars twinkling in the semi-darkness. Both parties to the rape were reduced to mere shades in the imagination of a pervert who, in his hatred, had condemned them to his twisted fantasies.

My brother at first suspected, while Federico held him in his arms and turned him into one more pederast, that they had been changed into their own ghosts by a lewd whim of mine. He thought I, even in death, hated him and had chosen those means to avenge myself for his having outlived me. Then all of a sudden it occurred to him that perhaps it was not I but our father who had dreamed up his defilement. After all, our father also hated him for being conceived on the day of my funeral. My brother had no inkling at the time that, one afternoon in the distant future, he would overhear our father's specter confide to Federico's apparition that it had never occurred to him, watching the two young men stroll arm-in-arm, that the poet was a sodomite. My brother then concluded that if he and Federico were players in someone else's nightmare or madness, neither my father nor I could have conjured up his brutal attack. This left only Velázquez himself as the suspect. The two young men were, my brother decided, the sketch that don Diego left unfinished so that the world would never condemn him for his salacious spirit, which he kept hidden behind a mask of dashed hopes and disabused illusions. Or perhaps they were the canvas that Velázquez worked on at night in his studio in the Palace Treasure House, under the cover of darkness and behind the king's back.

Ripped apart by searing pain, with Federico stretched over his body and biting vampire-like into his flesh, my brother had to admit that what was happening was real. Even in his anguish, it struck him that if he was providing pleasure to a man, it was more than he would ever give to a woman, afflicted young as he was by impotence. At the same time, he was certain that his paintings also would excite a pleasure akin to the sexual, even if he would have to outlive those who professed to love him or to have been sensually aroused by him. All at once, he fell fast asleep, as Federico rolled over howling like a beaten dog, perhaps one of those greyhounds into which you, sir, can metamorphose if you lose your footing and fall into your book. My brother then had a dream about a light which only years later would make any sense to him. He tried to describe it to me as being like the beam from a skylight in an abandoned house where a crime has occurred, or from a November morning when the mist outside is still at odds with a topaz dawn. In his old age, and in front of his *Incredible Enigma in Velázquez's Studio,* he understood that the light was the faint glow from the ocean depths: the muted splendor of two opposing colors, that of the aurora borealis on the breaking surf and of the magic lantern that beamed its light over the snail slithering across my mother's *mons veneris* after my brother's conception.

As I listened to my brother, I noted a certain contradiction in his story. It was on the basis of my own testimony that he knew the factual circumstances leading up to his conception on that particular dawn. It could not be possible that, years before I had revealed it to him, he had also dreamed of that early morning light in Fondora and had fused it with the brilliance of the midnight sun. I could only deduce that you, sir—the jailor of this our limbo—had shuffled the pages of your story at random and left the result to chance. If all of us—the living, the specters, and those characters relegated to memory or a passing mention— have been our own mere reflection in the mirrors of your written pages, perhaps you yourself have gone mad and been converted into your own parody—just as my brother assured me that I was merely his premature rough draft, his caricature by anticipation.

"It frightens me, too, to think of Velázquez painting in his sleep beneath the waves."

My brother snapped me out of my wayward digressions by pointing to his *Incredible Enigma in Velázquez's Studio*. He told me that while he slept, and in the warm glow that he later would transpose onto canvas, the four protagonists of the work—don Diego, the buffoon or "little lizard" as dwarfs were called at Court, the nude with her back turned, and the cherub holding the mirror—all appeared to him in a dream. He knew that the following morning he would begin to paint them *d'après* Velázquez, and he felt certain, albeit with total indifference, that he had been transformed into an authentic artist. Never before nor since the midnight sun had he painted nor would he ever paint again his own dreams, even though his finest works would one day be recognized as universal reflections of mankind's nightmares.

As soon as he awoke, he set up his easel and worked ceaselessly, almost breathlessly, until late into the night. Only then did he notice that he had not seen Federico once that day. Believing that he felt no shame or resentment whatsoever for having been sexually assaulted, he decided to take a rest and go look for his friend. He found Federico seated on the rocks, with one foot in a cavity where the waves paused after breaking against the reef. The two young men looked at one another in silence, and my brother was not surprised to notice that Federico also had changed. His look was guarded and stern, as if he had just confronted himself in the secret core of his destiny. My brother talked about his recently begun work, and Federico asked the meaning of the scene in Velázquez's studio. My brother told me that he had merely shrugged by way of reply. Or perhaps he responded that he would never understand it himself until someone did a copy or a rendition that would unravel the mystery. He told me that he decided not to add: "Even better, perhaps if one day, either in our lifetime or later, someone enlivens my painting by writing a story about it and giving voice to its characters, so that they themselves can clarify its meaning, without bringing our lives into it."

4

W_HILE HE SITS FOR ME, LUIS DE ACEDO STARES AT ME OUT OF THE_
corner of his eye. Don Luis de Acedo, Hacedo, or even Aedo— just a
few of the surnames he delights in using— is called "Primo" by His
Majesty, as if they were truly cousins. Buffoon, gentleman of pleasure,
and court jester, Primo addresses Their Sovereigns familiarly and could
make the now defunct Queen burst into laughter at his pranks. One look
at him during Mass at the Alcazar was enough for Her Majesty to
command her retinue: "Nom d'un chien! Get that man out of here
before I wet myself!" Queen Isabel was French and had a consummate
ability to scandalize our then fastidious and circumspect court with her
salacious outbursts. If she lived today, her allusions to the monthly curse,
to her almost endlessly difficult pregnancies, or the labyrinthine female
libido, would not raise an eyebrow. Rumor has it that the Queen's shade
now visits Sister María de Agreda, imploring her prayers for release
from purgatory where Her Majesty is expiating the sins of vanity of
dress and levity of tongue. Her tribulations in the nether world, and the
changes in this, have just entered my mind when Primo startles me by
reading my thoughts.

"Don Diego, today's mores and the lewd games in the Retiro would
have embarrassed whores when we were young. This kingdom always
sways between paralytic and epileptic spells."

"I was thinking about the same thing. Now hush and hold still. Your
head moved and it looks as if the light is painting a cloud in your
right eye."

"Leave that cloud out of my portrait. It doesn't exist. As Your Honor
so often says, painting only understands truths; for farce and mockery,
life will suffice."

"Truths . . . yes; but only up to a certain point. Truth is always a
question of limits, don Luis. If you exceed them, you run the risk of
turning into another Michelangelo and painting the Sistine Chapel. May
God save us from falling into such perverse temptation."

Primo smiles and I continue painting. Damiana, reclining nude upon
the coverlet of the Barbary divan, also smiles into her mirror. Naked as
on the day he was born, Francisquito de Asís y de la Santísima Trini-

71

dad— the tiny son of Luis de Acedo and his unfortunate young wife—
kneels as he holds the mirror. His father wanted me to attach two wings
and a quiver to the boy— as if he were Eros, and Damiana, Aphrodite.
"Don Luis, don't dress the child up. Art doesn't understand masquerades.
Theatricals are too close to life's own mockeries. Farce and history pass
away; but art endures." "It is true, don Diego," Acedo finally conceded.
"Do you remember in this our Court of Miracles, as Your Honor calls
it, a royal decree forbidding ladies to wear decolletage for any occasion
or to wear the short veil in church? Only whores could expose any part
of their breasts, but they had to throw on a shawl before entering the
sanctum. The law only incited the ladies to flaunt their breasts in public
and to attend Mass donned in mantillas." "Our laws, Primo, are forgotten even quicker than our dead." Acedo shoots me a look from those eyes
of his that sometimes have the look of two scarab buttons. "Did Your
Honor already forget yours?" "I don't remember them if I don't see them.
In the recesses of my soul they appear to me, frozen as if in a pose for
one of my paintings." "You're lucky to see them. I can only remember
their names. I lost my wife less than a year ago, but her face is already
disappearing into the mist of past time. I don't think you understand
me, because you have the memory of an artist."

Although Acedo's wife made a tempting model, out of sheer indolence
I never painted her portrait. Tall, wheat-haired, and rosy-cheeked, she
was a lady-in-waiting at our now defunct Queen's table. She married
the court jester not out of admiration for his sharp wit, but on account
of his phallic endowment that was the talk of the palace. His Majesty
himself sponsored the wedding and laughed benevolently at his favorite
clown's infidelities. Acedo's bride never recovered from her first labor
pains and passed away in sleep, on Christmas Eve, during the recitation
of the rosary. I told Primo that I understood him very well, because I
found it as hard to remember the living as he did the dead. If I didn't
glance into a mirror from time to time, I would not know who I was or
what I looked liked. As a matter of fact, I am not so sure that I do
recognize myself. At times I thought, if the true artist exists through his
paintings, I could only perceive my innermost being by contemplating
all of my work together. Unfortunately my canvases are few and far
between. My enormous talents have been surpassed by my lethargy—
Rubens assured me as much— and my few paintings are scattered halfway around the globe. Some were lost the year we moved from Calle de
la Concepción Jerónima to the Palace Treasure House, or perhaps they
were carted off prior to my first trip to Italy by some unfaithful servant—
whose name I have also forgotten. At Pacheco's home in Seville, there
still hangs the portrait I did of him before he became my father-in-law.
Absentmindedly studying it while I applied the finishing touches after

months of work, Pacheco let out a deep sigh: "I have nothing more to teach you. In centuries to come, my name will be remembered only because you were my student."

His Holiness Innocent X, may he rest in glory, was less impressed when I finished his vera effigies in Rome. "Troppo vero! Troppo vero, figliuol! Too true to be true, my son! I am not like that at all! I am merely an irascible old man born to be a soldier of fortune but resigned to the role of Pope in this world of make-believe!" Since I always considered servility avoidable and anger futile, I replied that I could erase his portrait in a trice if it had offended him. "Let it be. If he lived to see it, Titian would envy you; but I, personally, prefer that bust of your mulatto servant, the one you exhibited in the Pantheon on Saint Joseph's Day. I asked myself why I couldn't have been your servant, and why he couldn't have risen to my throne. If the Creator were black, a mulatto Vicar of Christ would be more fitting than a redheaded pontiff." His Holiness then gave me his blessing, and two gold chains that, had my daughters lived, would have been theirs.

Given the impossibility of assembling my canvases so that they could serve as my full-length mirror, I decided to paint a pair of oils, both at the same time. I am not shuttling from one easel to another like a spool; I am painting Primo's portrait while he and Damiana pose nude for another canvas that I have already conceived and will execute later. I intend not only to illuminate the hidden similarities between two quite distinct works but also to shed light on the raison d'être of an artist named Diego de Silva Velázquez, whom I have never understood even though he and I are one and the same man. When I showed Luis de Acedo my charcoal sketches, he was so delighted with the project that he offered to give written proof of his satisfaction and even to allow his son to sit for me. "Don Diego, you will enter a labyrinth of your own genius and making, one where you would be irremediably lost if I were not there to guide you by the hand. In this adventure, I will be your Lazarillo— your Seeing Eye and your scribe." The Marquis del Carpio y de Heliche, don Gaspar Méndez de Haro, was similarly agreeable to my plan of doing a mythological nude of his mistress Damiana and offered to purchase the painting as soon as it was completed. But, once again, he refused to allow me to paint his portrait or, for that matter, that of his wife, the most renowned beauty in the court. "My dear friend, the marquise and I are devout Christians; we aspire to no more on earth than dust, ashes, and nothingness— el polvo, la ceniza y la nada. If you immortalize us in an oil, you will condemn us. There is no greater sin than the sin of pride or more satanic an arrogance than the desire to be eternal. Besides, why should I agree to your painting this mug of mine? To frighten and scandalize generations to come?" He then rubbed his pocked

*horse-face, in which two sparkling eyes belied the ugliness of his other-
wise hideous features. I asked why he would agree to Damiana's damnation, if posing for me meant our condemning her to immortality. The
marquis shrugged his shoulders and seemed to weigh his reasons before
exposing them. "Damiana is a pagan child. She lives only for sensual
delight and her longing to play the part of someone else. Paint her as
Aphrodite, but she'll discover a woman quite different from either Damiana or the goddess when she looks into the mirror. Paint her from behind.
She has a wantonly exquisite bottom that would bring Phidias back to
life if he could spot it through the flames of hell."*

*The cloud has vanished from Primo's eye, and with Venetian red I
outline his eyebrow on the canvas.* "Draw a piece of paper with your
signature in my hand," *Innocent X said when he posed for me,* "so
tomorrow no one will mistake me for Julius II, and you for Michelangelo
Buonaroti." *I have already sketched Damiana and will depict her from
behind as the Marquis del Carpio y de Heliche suggested. I'm not doing
this to obey his wishes but because her buttocks are most worthy of a
nude, as I found out when I saw her naked for the first time in my
studio. Besides, if Rubens lived, he too would paint her from the rear,
because don Gaspar Méndez de Haro's mistress has the breasts of a child,
with tiny nipples the color of strawberries.* "Caro ragazzo, l'impor-
tante e avere il senso della storia universale." *When he visited Madrid the year Breda fell, addressing me in the familiar as if I were his
lackey, Peter Paul Rubens said,* "My dear boy, we must have a sense of
the universal. Par malheur, *we live in an age when everything is diminished. Anger is reduced to resentment, love to lust, hope to greed, and
faith to beatitudes.* Nello stesso modo, *and to my greater distress,
women's tits have shriveled to such a degree that it's not worth catching
a peek at them in the midst of this* épouvantable décadence *that be-
sieges us. When I see how near we are to the end of the world, I can
truly say that I wish I had never been born."*

"Don Diego," *Damiana says to me without turning her head while
Francisquito de Asís y de la Santísima Trinidad giggles and guffaws for
no apparent reason,* "is it true that you claim a coat of arms bearing
thirteen sheaves on a field of silver, and eight gold crosses on crimson?
I've heard say that you are descended from the old line of the kings of
Alba Longa."

"Perhaps it's pure poppycock. What little bird told you?"

"Don Gaspar Méndez de Haro mentioned it when he told me you were
going to paint my portrait. But the rumor is spreading like wildfire from
the court to the Caños de Peral."

"I heard the same from my grandparents and even my great-grand-
mother, whom I still remember telling me in Portuguese. The legend*

originated in Viana do Castelo or Vila do Conde and came down through my ancestors, the Rodríguez de Silva. I don't know if it's true."

Primo listens, scowling so intensely that even his son stops giggling. I could engrave, sketch, or paint Primo from memory as easily as I could write the "Our Father" blindfolded in legal script, if I were inclined toward such nonsense. Primo stares through me as if I were invisible and he were speaking to his portrait, rather than to me or Damiana, as he replies: "Don Diego may or may not be descended from the House of Alba Longa, but I've have always sensed that his blood will course spectacularly through the watersheds of time. It will form the blood bond of future generations of august descendants. Three centuries from now, kings, princes, grand dukes, scattered across a Europe quite different from our own. . . ." He pauses, waiting for me to shrug my shoulders or to comment on his startling prophecy; but in the end it is Primo who is disconcerted by my silence.

"Your Honor, if you don't believe me, the least you can do is laugh."

"Laugh, Primo? Never! To me it's a matter of total indifference whether I'm to be the ancestor of future royalty; but the idea is no more incredible than the rest of my life. Like Polycrates, I learned at a young age to fear my own good fortune. All that has happened to me thus far might sound fine in some unfinished fable; but in an existence we assume to be real, it just doesn't ring true."

"For farce and mockery, life will suffice." Admiring herself in the mirror and lightly caressing her inner thighs, Damiana quotes the buffoon quoting me. She then turns her head slightly and looks at me from half-profile. "But if only painting understands truth, as for existence— for what we call existence— I say that only the theater exists."

"Then all the world's a stage, if you say so."

I then tell Damiana the most incredible story, the story of my life, one that don Luis de Acedo knows all too well. Once again I am the young initiate in Pacheco's studio, who left the atelier of the elder Herrera when he slapped me for painting a pitcher as it looks and not as it is. "A painter who uses only his eyes should pluck them out!" Although I am a mere boy of twelve, my father insists that I enter into an apprenticeship with my new teacher. Pacheco will instruct me in drawing and painting as well as bas-relief and engraving; he will furnish me room and board, clothing, shoes, and medical attention for all illnesses of less than two-weeks duration. At the end of six years when my apprenticeship is completed, he will provide me with breeches, underwear, shoes and stockings, two shirts and ruffs, a broadcloth cloak, doublet and waistcoat, plumed hat, and silver-buckled girdle: all new and as stipulated in the contract.

After less than a month in Pacheco's home, he asks me why I am content to paint cluttered still lives: cellars filled with smoked hams, rounds of cheeses and stalks of celery illuminated by the light of a cooking range. "I learned it from Herrera El Viejo," I reply. "He taught us to give witness to things as they are and not as we want to see them. To learn this, he said, there is no better university than a handful of carrots or a head of garlic." Quite different from the hot-tempered but prodigious Herrera, my level-headed and courteous new master teaches what he does not know. His paintings are a useless collection of rubbish. He was commissioned to do a Christ on the Cross, and when it was hung, the young girls of Triana began to chant: "Who pasted you up there, my Lord / tasteless and dry as stale cake dough? / You'll claim that it was Love, sweet Lord / but I say it was Pacheco." In spite of his courtesy, the man is irritated by my laziness. Whenever he sees me stretched out on my back, my arms folded and my eyes wide open, he asks: "Why don't you at least sleep in these siestas of yours?" "It's not worth the trouble; we dream enough awake." "Doesn't it worry you that your sloth will waste your talent?" I shrug my shoulders. "If I have any, I'm too lazy to kill it off." He smiles and leaves; but he comes back the next day and distractedly contemplates the portrait of a street urchin that I am taking an eternity to complete. "I'm going to make you court painter," he whispers. "If I then marry Juana off, I can die in peace with no business left undone."

Pacheco is a widower and his daughter manages the household affairs. I have watched her grow from a ten-year-old into a girl of fifteen. And I now pass my final test of apprenticeship by turning eighteen. On a silver locket, I do an enamel profile of Juana with her thick curls spilling over her shoulders. "One day soon I'll do an oil painting of you," I promise, "a full-length on canvas." To my surprise, she bursts into tears and says that I'm a liar. That I will be leaving the studio because I now have more commissions than her father. That I will never see her again, neither at her home nor at the Mass that she and Pacheco and the apprentices attend in the Chapel of la Gorgoja on Sundays and other holy days. Emotional outbursts have always taken me by surprise and, to silence her, I take Juana in my arms and kiss her. I then undress her and— although my only sexual experience has been at the flea market with the Baratillo whores, where the older apprentices have taken me— I surprise myself by making love to her on the crimson-splattered drop cloths while a finch warbles in the window. As soon as Pacheco returns, I tell him everything and ask for his daughter's hand in marriage. He gives me an emotional hug, crushing his starched ruff and shirtfront against my shoulders. I think I am doing him a favor and feel as happy as if I had paid off an outstanding debt. Then I ask myself if I will ever feel for Juana the love they talk about on stage: a world where everything real exists, according to Damiana. It will take me years to realize I am inca-

pable of loving anyone, except for my daughters and my first grand-
daughter. All three have died— as all Madrid knows— one, a grown
woman, and the other two, while still little girls. And I don't understand
my destiny.

"When I turned twenty-three, my father-in-law took me to the court
so I could paint a portrait of Their Majesties. The King and Queen never
granted me an audience, but I did paint the poet, don Luis de Góngora
y Argote. He told me: "There are only two truths: art and death. This
is their correct order, because art outlasts men and, thus, transcends
death." Francisquito de Asís remains silent, and Damiana listens half-
turning aside, but seated on the floor, Primo writes furiously in an open
in folio almost bigger than himself.

"The following year, Pacheco and I returned to Madrid where he per-
suaded the Count Duke of Olivares to obtain permission for me to paint
Felipe IV on horseback: all completely lifelike, with the snow-capped
Guadarrama in the background. The sovereign was so pleased with the
equestrian portrait that he had it exhibited on Calle Mayor in front of
San Felipe. That autumn, by order of three royal decrees, I was paid three
hundred ducats for the painting and I was taken on as court portraitist at
a salary of another three hundred. I remember that the contract had to
be authorized by His Holiness, Pope Urban VIII himself, but that it went
smooth as silk."

"It's like the life of a saint, a chosen one, a Christian Midas who
converts all he touches into art," Damiana sighs. *I can't tell if she's being*
honest, mocking me, or putting into prose some verses from a play by
Valdivieso that she has just performed in the Buen Retiro.

"Saint I am not, and if the death of my daughters was the price I had
to pay for everything that's been handed me, I would have rather been
born blind, so I could never have painted."

An artist who only uses his eyes should pluck them out! *I*
learned more from Herrera than from nature, not to mention Pacheco or
myself, although I have not set eyes on Herrera since the day he slapped
me. I think of El Viejo while Damiana pinches her nipples to keep them
rosy. He used to seat his apprentices on benches or stools while he paced
up and down the workshop grasping a dog whip. Blind is the artist
who only sees! *he would roar, as if we could understand his aphorisms.*
To reduce the world to the sphere of what we can see is to dimin-
ish it to the range of our limitations! *He made each of us recite what*
he had just taught us, and anyone who could not do so verbatim received
a rap on the head. Herrera would never paint Damiana in the mirror as
we see her but, rather, as she truly is: an actress dying to be someone
else on the stage, or finding herself through the myriad Rosauras, Belisas,
Filis, and Lucindas whom she plays. If I had Herrera's energy, I would

treat this as my masterpiece: one that, due to lethargy, I may never finish even though I almost picture it in my mind's eye. I would paint myself doing a studio painting of some everyday scene of courtly life— let's say, Primo or another midget carrying bonbons to a princess, or perhaps a lady-in-waiting offering her a flower. In the background I would include Their Majesties, watching everything through a window like a mirror, or like a portrait where the King and Queen can be seen through the window.

"If your story appeared in a book of the lives of the saints," comments don Luis de Acedo, "you would be the most noteworthy of all. Not because you're an artist— Saint Luke was too— but because you're a sloth. Did you ever stop to think that you have never taken one step without someone pushing you from behind? Your father forced you into Herrera's studio and then into Pacheco's, when you were ready to give up on art and loaf your life away. In spite of what Your Honor may have thought then, you did not seduce your future wife. She and her father seduced you into joining their family. Pacheco brought you to Madrid, and His Majesty named you court painter. If you hadn't met your father-in-law, you'd still be in Seville, staring up at the clouds. On the other hand, I dare not imagine to what heights you could have risen if you had the right patrons. And with no more contribution on your part than your indolence and the singular talent that you've managed to hang on to without the slightest effort. I presume that the proper sponsors could have made you chancellor, sovereign, or perhaps Pope or Holy Roman Emperor."

"I never stopped to think about it, Primo, because it was all there before my eyes. I'm the man that others wanted me to be. While my life is hardly a saint's, it does seem about as probable as the inventions of our chivalric romance writers. And by the way, speaking of storybooks, what are you so furiously scribbling in that huge in folio?"

"Everything, don Diego. We're all in my book— you, Francisquito de Asís, my portrait that you're painting, the nude that you're going to paint, and of course Damiana and I sitting for you, not to mention this cozy studio or your confession of being the man that others wanted you to be. I must get down all the facts, to the minutest detail, so that some day tomorrow no one will think that my portrait is the work of your son-in-law, señor Martínez del Mazo, instead of your own."

"You'll run out of ink in your ink pot, don Luis. So we have a book within a painting: yours inside mine."

"Or perhaps a painting within a book," Primo answers deep in thought and with his delicate eyebrows furrowed. "I'm talking about the portrait of us all, here and now, in the work by another writer, Don Diego. This is very strange, but at times I have a deep feeling that we're not who we think we are."

"It may be that we're turning into our portraits. That's why the Marquis de Heliche won't allow me to paint his, . . . so he won't commit the sin of pride and be damned along with immortality."

"The marquis is already damned for the sins of the flesh— even if I worship him and call him my godfather." Damiana smiles and shrugs. "I won't say any more because we have a child in our midst."

"I wasn't thinking about portraits or mirrors," Primo replies, ignoring Damiana. "Although I can't prove it or even explain it to myself, I'd say that, on occasion, someone spies on us from the other side of time."

"It's true and I've also sensed it!" Damiana shivers, startling me by the fervor of her conviction. Her skin, the color of virgin nectar in overflowing honeycombs, turns to gooseflesh from her throat to her buttocks. "Someone is watching us— someone we can't see— as if we were little fishes in a pond. Someone who's coming closer and closer, to poke us with his finger to prove that we're alive! Don Diego, I'm so afraid, I'm so cold!"

"Pull yourself together, woman. There's nothing to be afraid of; only His Majesty and I have keys to this studio. Even the charwomen straightens up only when I am here, and no one but the King touches a brush or a chalk without my permission."

Shortly before my first trip to Italy, my father came from Seville to visit us. I was too young to realize that he knew he was dying and wanted to bid me a silent farewell. With the help of the apprentices, my servant Pareja prepared him a room in the loft, directly above the corner of the studio where I do most of my work. If an agreeable insomnia got me out of bed in the middle of the night to finish a chiaroscuro of faces framed in candlelight, I could hear him pee into the chamber pot and then get down on his knees to pray. There were few other occasions for me to overhear him, because he was so reticent that only my little girls were deemed worthy of his trust. On the saint's day of John the Baptist, or thereabouts, my father was in my studio watching me paint a nocturnal landscape in the broad daylight, when the King unlocked the door and appeared, as was his habit, without warning or escort. My father attempted to kneel before him to kiss his ring; but the King put a stop to it by embracing him as I made the introductions. Likewise, out of affection for me or deference to my father's age, His Majesty always addressed him as don Juan, or Your Honor, or señor Rodríguez de Silva, rather than in the familiar. My father would doze off in boredom as soon as the monarch began gossiping about art with me: "It's a well-known fact that El Greco, for whom my grandfather had little respect, used to say that Michelangelo was a good man but an execrable painter." The *sovereign then laughed so uproariously that his blue eyes filled with tears and his pronounced jaw became all but dislodged.*

The following Sunday at the conclusion of Mass, the King again appeared in my studio to ask about my father. I told him that he had returned to Seville, taking the Saturday coach from the Calle de Toledo. The King shot me a long look, inadvertently showing his left profile that he almost always shielded due to a deformity on the temple. "You should never have allowed him to go. I should have warned you, but my courage failed me. I'm afraid you'll never see your father again, because he had the glow or aura of one who is close to eternity. You must believe me. It has been my plight to see many in my family pass away: my parents, my brother, and six of my infant children." A few days later, I received a letter from my sister and brother-in-law, saying that my father had died in his sleep at his home on the Square of Sweet Success.

"I fear that there is no past, present, or future," continues don Luis de Acedo, seated on the floor. "Whoever is spying on us must be lurking from a century still to come. He has tucked our space and time, like an embroidered page marker, into his book. There he describes us as I write in my in folio, Your Honor paints me, my son holds the mirror, and Damiana shivers naked."

"Primo, you're afraid we may not be who we think we are," I cut him short with a wave of my brush, caked in auburn from painting his mustache in the portrait. "If our here and now were not the Treasure House, this day of the year of Our Lord, but the pages of a story, we would be mere characters in an unpublished novel."

"And I tell you gentlemen, while you tie yourself up in your tongue twisters, our spy does not live in future time but is lurking behind that door!" Damiana screeches hysterically. "In no time flat, he'll push it open and show up in the mirror!"

To be or not to be is all the same to me. Even in our dreams we change according to our shadows and chimeras. I have decided to paint myself painting the portrait of the Infanta and her servants. Their Majesties will be peering at us from a window, a mirror, or a painting— in the final analysis, each one is the human eye. If he lived, Herrera would see that I did not squander my apprenticeship— although, as he must have expected in the core of his being, I have reversed his precepts. If for El Viejo, reality exists and our only duty is to uncover it, for me reality is my point of view. Herrera could respond, that in my future masterpiece, the sovereigns' view from the canvas was necessarily circumscribed in another, and yet another ad infinitum. He would add as his final argument that the moment a painting is placed on public view, it ceases to reflect the artist's perspective.

The door to the studio now opens and His Majesty the King appears on the threshold wearing a nightshirt and dressing gown loosely fastened at the waist. From his sleeve he pulls a eucalyptus-scented handkerchief and delicately lifts it to his nostrils, simultaneously raising his palm to stop us from kneeling to kiss his hand. The stark nakedness of the boy and Damiana behind the scribe's in folio forces a bemused smile across His Sovereign's delicate lips.

"Continue, my friends; I don't mean to interrupt," says don Felipe IV. "I missed Mass because my cold has kept me bedridden. I got up and thought I would shake off my headache by seeing what don Diego was dabbling with in the Treasure House."

"More than one headache is in store for you, King of Spades and Spaniards, if you step into this studio." Primo uses the familiar, in the custom of jesters addressing the King. "You and that closet Republic of yours don't add up to much; but we, here in this chamber, don't count at all except in the vivid imagination of a novelist and a book reserved for the future. The instant you step into our void, you will be turned into one more chimera. And I can't promise, in this tale that entraps us, that you'll be allowed to pursue your wanton pastimes of hunting to the hounds, attending the theater, and falling in love."

"Primo, I love it when you thunder like a prophet," replies the monarch in a reverential tone, "and I'm much obliged for the advice you give me from your shadowy kingdom. But I must admit that the portrait don Diego is painting of you— not to mention that body on Damiana— seems more real than my court of powdered dandies. I'll take my chances and step inside."

"Sir, don't come any closer unless it's to get me out of here!" Damiana is all but groveling. "I'm so frightened and so cold!"

"What's the matter, my little lamb? Only old men at the gates of eternity tremble from fear and cold," the sovereign reassures her softly, arching his blond eyebrows. "The beauty and passion of youth should be enough to stoke your courage and fire your soul, even if you posed naked in the mountain wind."

"When Your Majesty was about to enter, I feared you were the one Primo said would change us into shadows. The moment he appears in the mirror, he'll lock us up in this studio and throw the key into the sea."

"The sea is far from here, Damiana. Many in this court will die never having seen it."

"Then the Manzanares river or the Buen Retiro pond! My Lord, help me escape even if I must leave as I came into the world! Perhaps your will alone can challenge the man who transformed us into our reflections, in a book more huge and terrible than Primo's."

"*Don Diego, don Luis, is this the way to treat a lady? How can you let her shiver with cold fear in your presence?*" *Drying a tear from his eye brought on by a sudden coughing spell, the King continues to chide:* "*I must say it seems to me an unpardonable slight.*" *He then lies down on the divan with Damiana in his arms and comforts her like a child.* "*Hush, hush, my little dove, nothing bad can happen if your monarch is here to watch over you.*" *The actress sniffles, sighs, and finally calms down. Like a lullaby, The King sings her a medieval love song by Villasandino:*

> *Prithee, fairest beloved, pity my plight*
> *For I languish consumed by love at first sight.*
> *Your beauty ensnares me in my prison hell.*
> *My crime's of the heart, I'm a caged Philomel.*
> *Release me, release my sad song in your praise.*
> *The past shan't be lost, I'll remember always.*
> *Though your comeliness be the source of my pain,*
> *I pray thee, fair lady, be fair once again*
> *To your humble servant and your loyal swain.*

Visso enamorosso, / duélete de mí, / pues vivo penosso / desseando a ti. / La tu fermosura / me puso en prisión; / por la cual ventura / del mi corazón / nos parte tristura / en toda sazón: / por en tu figura / me entristece assí. / Todo mi cuidado / es en te loar, / que el tiempo passado / non posso olvidar: / farás aguissado / de mi te membrar, / pues siempre de grado / leal te serví.

His Majesty has a lovely baritone voice and adds a Portuguese lilt to the old Castilian, which reminds me of the speech of my grandfather in Seville. "*Diego, my friend,*" *he addressed me, even though I was just a boy, seeing through me in his cobwebbed mirror of old age,* "*You're headed into perdition if you trust a woman who dances the* saltarel a la francesa *in the meadow.*" *Irked by a sudden swelling itch, His Majesty rubs his pudendum against Damiana's buttocks. She briefly considers his advances and, feigning sleep, refuses the entreaties of her royal swain. But she succumbs. The woman lives only for sexual pleasure and, according to the Marquis de Haro, her drive to become someone else. Arching and thrusting her hips, she seems determined to polish them to a Florentine finish. With one hand, don Felipe IV unfastens his dressing gown and, lifting his nightshirt, enters Damiana in a single thrust.*
Primo is scribbling furiously in his book, and the scratch of the goose quill is the only sound in the tedious moment of silence. Francisquito de Asís y de la Santísima Trinidad holds the mirror to the improvised lovers and stares, neither shocked nor amused, with the rapt attention of one

studying a species distinct from our own, or counting grains of sand in search of the last number before infinity. Damiana bursts into peals of laughter, and the King joins in hearty chorus that, by degrees, turns into intermittent fits of the giggles, and then a brief moment of silence, as the lovers try to salvage the last shred of pleasure before it fades into fleeting memory. The boy also laughs wholeheartedly, as if mocking them. He stops, however, when the actress begins to moan, pitching her head and rolling her eyes like a martyr on the rack, ready to burst like a pomegranate. Raising a Titian-red eyebrow, Primo surveys them with professional detachment before returning at once to his in folio. From time to time, he glances the lovers' way, but appears to be doing a sketch of the coupling rather than a written testimony. Inspired by don Luis, I place a sketch pad on my easel and rapidly begin drawing the royal fornication. The girl is panting for air, breathless as a fish washed onto the shore, and trying to rediscover her human voice. The monarch mounts her from behind and presses her breasts in his pale hands until his knuckles turn pink. To my horror, and without realizing it as I sketched the couple, I see that it is not Damiana and His Highness that I captured in carnal company. It is the unnatural act of two minuscule men on an unfamiliar mountain crest. I am so taken aback that I throw the crumpled page on the floor so no one will see it. Primo continues writing, and his tiny son moves the mirror from side to side so as not to miss the reflection of unbridled passion.

"Diego," the King once asked me in this very room, "did you ever make love spontaneously, almost without realizing what you were doing?"

"I don't think so, Majesty. If I did, I don't remember."

"Then you're lucky. In matters of lust, the worst punishment is recall."

Like a wounded doe, Damiana sends a scream to high heaven and, spent, slumps across the faded quilt as don Felipe, growling like a wolf, sets his teeth into her shoulders. Exhausted, now both collapse on the divan while silence hovers over their last intermittent panting. The King's right hand rests on her left hip. Distractedly, with her back still turned, the actress takes his scrotum in her palm. Close in body, they seem more estranged in soul than Aldebarán from his land. Primo sets his quill in the inkwell and, crossing his arms, glances impassively toward me.

"Don Diego, whoever is setting us down in his book has put the end period to it— at least for the time being."

The Hunting Lodge

1

THE ARCHITECT OF MY LIMBO, THE AUTHOR OF MY PRISON, SHOULD either stop or else break off writing long enough to set me free. It is exhausting, demoralizing to be a child who died near the turn of the century, to wander through these paper passages as counterpoint to a brother who usurped my existence in order to be made flesh. I am worn out from bickering with him, from watching over his interminable old age, from being his constant companion since he was no more than a twinkle in our mother's eye. If that weren't devastating enough, I now find out that I slept through months, entire years, while he was surrendering to Federico or having other experiences, still unbeknown to me, that changed him into a stranger before my very eyes. Maybe it is best this way because his mere presence is debilitating, oppressive as the visit of our family ghosts—my mother, barefoot, her half-naked breasts tinged blue in the quartzlike winter light, my father, strolling through the plaza on his way to a sea where it never snows, Federico, thinking about a child munching on oranges in one of his poems. They too are wandering souls, pitiful apparitions who show up in advance for an appointment my brother refuses to keep.

To top it all, I must now grope through the tedious, baffling passages of someone else's text, set in a time and place that no longer exist. If it is true that my brother, as he has said so many times, was frightened by the thought of Velázquez painting in his sleep beneath the waves, what is the meaning of Velázquez's studio in a royal palace? I also wonder why the buffoon's journal reflects my own author's point of view. Where's the missing link? I think I understand the analogy between Federico's seducing my brother on the cliff top and Felipe IV's trysting with Damiana, just as Velázquez inadvertently sketched both couples intertwined in the act of intercourse. It is possible for past events to recur in the present, or to repeat themselves in the future, so that anyone presumptuous enough to pass judgment on time can bear witness. Yet I cannot help but think that these couplings also are linked to some event I don't comprehend, just as the snail on our mother's *mons veneris* would be confused with the snail on the doorjamb of Freud's home in London somewhere else in these pages.

It is frankly a matter of total indifference to me whether or not the various strands of this plot ever come together, as long as I break free from the frame. I want to be the one to put the definitive end period to the story, to conclude it once and for all and not merely for the time being. (My thoughts echo Primo's words to Velázquez while, sated with pleasure, Damiana and the King collapse in exhaustion.) I dream of losing myself on a blank page, of slipping into the void, as if my prison and I had never been invented. I grope through the labyrinthine inner ear of a deaf-mute in the hope of falling through a gap of his memory and being able to sleep at last, free of nightmarish souvenirs, in an eternal vacuum. If only the author would respond to my pleas, my desperate cries for help, I might resign myself to wander through the maze of this text. I can't wait to tell him my heartfelt conviction that his characters shape him as much as he molds us, to warn him of the danger of falling into his own pages and turning into one of his own inventions. He could end up Francisquillo de Asís in the Velázquez studio or Pope Innocent X, shouting "*Troppo vero! Troppo vero, figliuol!*" from the Vatican. But I keep running up against the stony silence of our jailer and creator who refuses me his voice and his presence.

To tell the truth, although he may pretend to be invisible, I have my doubts as to whether our author is omniscient. While I was asleep, I missed out on what was happening to my brother. Therefore it is quite likely that, in the world outside his book, he has also missed essential facts of my brother's life and has even confused him with another artist—Salvador Dalí. Our author would not be the first to mistake one for the other or to mix them up while shuffling through their lives and their art. In the Chicago Art Institute, and the Statens Konstsamligar Moderna Museet, canvases by the two of them—painted more than half a century ago and years before they ever met—seem the work of one and the same man. My brother would remember those exhibitions with, depending on his frame of mind, a sarcastic sneer or a noncommittal shrug whenever he mentioned Dalí and the myriad coincidences that zigzagged through their destinies like a pair of swords crossing in an interminable duel.

"Although I am just a few years older than Dalí and had made my mark as an artist barely before he did, we crossed paths only

once—in London at the outbreak of the Spanish Civil War. Up to
that time, we seemed fated to search one another out to no avail.
In New York, Dalí would check into the Saint Denis because that
was where I always stayed; in Paris, I made a point of staying at
the Hôtel Robert, where he kept a suite reserved. By pure chance,
we met in the lobby of the Queen Alexandra. Independently, we
both had gone to London to pay a visit to Freud. As you may
recall, I stopped by 39 Elsworth Road four or five days before
Dalí. He told me that when his day came to render homage to
Doctor Faustus, the red bicycle and the snail were still by the
doorjamb." (The truth be told, Dalí and my brother spoke in such
hushed voices that I could not make out a single word.)

"When I told Dalí that I had pictured Freud's skull in the shape
of a snail, he nodded, replying that he saw it in the same way. It
was not that we were subconsciously plagiarizing one another.
The fate of all mankind, as decided on Judgment Day in the Valley
of Jehosaphat, is to be resurrected as snails praying for immortality of the soul to a God who is deaf, dumb, and blind." (I dare
add just as deaf and dumb, as invisible and unseeing as you, sir.)
"Like birds on a wire, we hover at razor's edge, counting sheep
combing the seashore for wild mushrooms among the pine
cones." Among the prickly dwarf palms in the cozy vestibule of
the Queen Alexandra, seated in a armchair embroidered with
vine tendrils and satyrs, my brother was reading a newspaper
article about the civil war in Spain. The *Times* reported that
churches were ablaze and blood poured through the streets, that
teachers and farmers were shot at the crack of dawn, that cities
were rocked by bombs while raped nuns cried out in chorus, and
soldiers were herded into bullrings and machine-gunned by firing squads. On the same columns a few lines up, he had been
caught off guard by the brief report of Federico's assassination.
My brother folded the newspaper and stared at me stupefied, as
if I, the specter of his only brother, were an unwelcome stranger.
His face impassive, as if unaware of my apparition, he remained
silent for a long time. Then, without once mentioning Federico
or his death, my brother invited me for a stroll through Marble
Arch. A few days later in the same lobby, Dalí waited an eternity
on end for us to notice his presence. When my brother finally
looked up and saw him, the two regarded one another in silence
and then embraced closely. Afterwards they drew up a pair of
armchairs and talked for hours in a low voice and intimate tone
that made their voices unintelligible to anyone but themselves.

"We agreed that we had a lot in common but could not determine who was who's double. Dalí was born in Figueras; and I in Fondora, which is in a way its alliteration and metaphor. We were both sons of provincial lawyers and preceded by an ill-fated elder brother, after whom each of us was named."

It was still winter. That morning his servants had seated my brother on the carved chair that had been sold, in Pistoia or Pisa, to his late wife as a Renaissance copy of the throne of Can Grande, the protector of Dante in exile, to whom the poet had sent an epistle on the meaning of his *Commedia*. This my brother would sometimes recite in Latin: *Sciendum est quod istius operis non est simplex sensus, immo dici potest polisemus, hoc est plurium sensum.* . . . It had started snowing again and, from the bedroom window, dawn was breaking through gray overcast skies onto a plaza vacated by strolling phantoms. Watching the clouds' shadow fall across the snow, I knew that if I could not overhear the conversation between Dalí and my brother, you, sir, would have no idea either of what they confided, nor could you have always told them apart.

"I mentioned to Dalí that you had died nine months before my birth while his own brother died at the age of seven, three years before he was born. Dalí just shook his head and admitted with a smirk that he had spread that story himself; his namesake actually died at about the age of two; precisely nine months before he came into the world. He had lied about the dates for two reasons: he had no desire to be taken for a reincarnation, a stand-in for his parents' first-born son; nor did he want that part of his life-history to be confused with mine, because we were too alike as it was. 'You're wasting your time lying to the world because you and I suffer from a dual, lifelong form of alienation. We were both conceived to bring back a dead child, whose name and bloodline are repeated in us. As long as the other lives, neither you nor I can be certain of our identity. Before this meeting today, you cannot know how many times I called out to you in my sleep, only to awake in terror because I was screaming not your name but my own,' I told him."

Listening to my brother, I felt a sudden shiver and the urgent desire to be rid of him once and for all. It was, sir, your folly alone that kept me bound to someone who refused to die, who detested me since he was able to figure out my existence. To abandon him would have meant my escape from this hem of words, to the sea where it never snows and where January's curved horizon may be the image and likeness of the eternal void.

"I asked Dalí if his brother ever haunted him, and he denied it with a shocked look. Although he was used to other specters, such as that of his adorable cousin who emerged from Cadaqués Harbor every summer on the anniversary of her death, he never ran across his ghostly counterpart, his double. If he ever had, he would have been driven mad with fear." My brother told me that he replied, "But I see my brother. Right now he's sitting on the floor, leaning against that Doric column in the middle of the lobby." Dalí shuddered and asked, frowning, "Are you sure it's your brother and not mine?" "I'm sure. He's two years old, but because of his height he looks more like three, and at that age he could only be mistaken for me." Wide-eyed, craning toward me as if suddenly beginning to perceive my features, Dalí asked, "Did you ever bump into Federico's specter?" "Once, when he was still alive, in the early dawn of the day he first had me. For an instant, and in the light of a sudden aurora borealis, he turned into his own bullet-riddled, blood-stained ghost. He advanced grimly toward me, remorsefully exposing the gaping hole in his chest. At the time, I wanted to believe that I dreamed the premonition, along with everything else that had happened that morning. Still, after he was actually assassinated, he never appeared to me again."

It would take many years, more like centuries to my mind, for Federico's shade to link up with those of my parents in their house vigil in the plaza. Beside Can Grande's throne, listening to my brother, I looked distractedly at the snow-covered plaza. A woman holding a child by the hand had just appeared below the window and was walking toward the flower beds. She wore a wide-brimmed hat with a veil, buttoned boots, and a full-length overcoat. Her right hand, with which she held the child, was gloved, her left was tucked into a fur muff. I remembered her from a remote winter as pale as that morning in Fondora. She was my mother. She was strolling with me through the snow during the last Christmas season that I was to spend on earth. Her silhouette paused below the windowpanes, as if listening to the priory bell toll the hours, hours that could have belonged to the past, to the present, or to an illusory juxtaposition of both.

"Federico first seduced us with his make-believe death in the student dormitory." My brother was quoting Dalí in the Queen Alexandra. "It was such a believable farce that he was, at the same time, our brothers. Ironically, he resurrected each of them by playing dead. He made us his lovers because, in his arms, we thought we too could assume the role of our respective dead brother and thus prevent his haunting. In fact, all we did was to surrender to Federico's love, hunger, or caprice. He turned us into what we never wanted to be: a pair of queers." My brother said he told Dalí that for inexplicable but self-evident reasons, it was only at the moment of yielding to their lover that each had been converted into a true artist, just as Federico did not become a true poet until he had forced himself upon them. "If we had not given in to him, we never would have become who we are in the eyes of the world." "In the eyes of *this* world," Dalí could not help but amend his comment. Once my brother stood corrected, however, neither he nor Dalí could dodge the shadows that bore their names and cheated them out of half their existence. Dalí had thought he was long rid of his tormentor when he received news of Federico's assassination. That day he crushed the newspaper with savage fury, shouting: *"Olé! Olé!"* Naturally he felt obliged to add wearily that he was not celebrating the crime but the hoped-for disappearance of his personal Cain, the brother though dead before Dalí was born who pursued him relentlessly. He now admitted his error and that he could have spared himself those shouts that, once quoted in the press, rang out half way around the world, because the child who died so that he could be conceived was indestructible.

"Didn't it ever occur to you that, in a way, you and I murdered Federico?" The question apparently caught Dalí by surprise, overwhelming him. My brother recalled him writhing and digging his knuckles into the armchair to protest: "You and I? Where'd you get that idea?"

"If Federico had not molested us, he would have never become a great poet and, perhaps, would never have been killed. Being himself was his crime." While Dalí silently agreed, a premonition assaulted my brother. "I don't know whether it will be to you, me, or both of us, but one day Federico will beckon. I, for one, will not heed his call."

While he was speaking to me from the Can Grande throne, a cabriolet pulled up in front of the door, and my father stepped down into the plaza. The reins grasped in his bared knuckles, the driver was wrapped in a fur-collared overcoat and wore a Russian cap of curled astrakhan. When he doffed his hat and leaned down to give my mother a kiss through her veil, to pat me on the head, and to shake my father's hand, I recognized him by his receding hairline, his temples pale as the snow itself. It was Uncle Santiago, my mother's older brother, whom the family always mentioned with reverential respect during his prolonged absences. My father extolled his devotion by pounding the table-cloth with the flat of his hand after a Christmas Eve supper or the mid-day dinner on New Year's Day, as he toasted to the health and happiness of his brother-in-law living in London, not far from Marble Arch or from the Queen Alexandra, as my brother was to remind me after our uncle's death. More reserved in her emotions, my mother would share in her husband's eulogies with a brief comment or a simple gesture, the expression of her well-pondered agreement. A bachelor surrounded by an singularly enigmatic aura, Uncle Santiago was the well-to-do traveler of our caste. As a customs official, he had made his fortune in contraband, but had lived for years in London where he owned a firm that imported oranges. "Mandarins, tangerines, plump navels from Nules, Mallorca, Bedmar, Malta, Nice, and Java. Bitter oranges or juicy sweet, of every shape, size, and taste . . . ," my father would marvel, as if he were taking inventory of precious stones yet to be mounted.

In the meantime, sir, you were introducing my uncle into your book, making him chat briefly with my parents before my mother climbed aboard the cabriolet and settled me on her lap while my father waved them good-by. Perhaps it is worth explaining that my uncle is neither a figment of your imagination nor the shadow of a shade—in other words, a ghost of my fancy. According to my brother, my uncle's existence is verified in several texts on the Spanish Civil War. At the very outset of the conflict, he donated part of his fortune to Franco's cause via the Duke of Alba, the insurgents' representative in England. Without further comment, such historians as Thomas, Jackson, and Vila-San-Juan dedicate half a footnote to him. At the age of ninety when almost at death's doorstep, he tottered at my brother's side to attend the *vernissage* at the Tate Gallery. It was the first retrospective of my brother's work, so it must have been sometime in the spring of 1950 or 1951. I once asked him why he was so determined to haul to the museum an incontinent old man half choking on phlegm, dragging him almost by force from his convalescent center where he was squandering his last lucid years with his memory still intact. Before he answered, my brother's expression grew somber. Then, with a shrug of his shoulders he replied that he had never been afraid of any of his ghosts, dead or alive, the one exception being yours truly.

Seated on the imitation throne of the *Can* of Verona—called *Grande* due to the lord's titanic height and broad shoulders—my brother, ironically gaunt and diminished by old age, continued his story of his encounter with Dalí. After affirming their shared complicity in Federico's death, my brother asked Dalí how old he was when his mother passed away. Somewhat perturbed and suspicious of a hidden motive behind the question, Dalí replied that it was just after his seventeenth birthday. To this, my brother responded that he was at the same adolescent stage when he lost our own mother, who died with her gloves on, toppled by a heart attack into the rosebushes she had been pruning. Sprawled among the flowers, she lay lifeless on a balcony similar to the one where she had conceived her son, with no other witness to her passing than my poor soul who forgot that it was dead. Her seizure caught me by chance at her side; I had just stepped out to join her while she sunbathed one warm Sunday afternoon in April. Forgetting that only my brother could see me, I shouted for help to no avail—just as I now plead with you, sir, to rescue me from this limbo—although, by a stroke of luck, the plaza was filled with people. A French aeronaut, Monsieur Archiprêtre or Archimandrite, was lifting off in a balloon and all Fondora had thronged to watch in amazement. The Fondorans had seen silvery single-engined aeroplanes and remembered magazine shots from before the Great War of biplanes with canvas wings lashed together by cords. But a balloon would take them back to more remote times, when the first aerostats went up over the fountains of Versailles and, in the gardens, an orchestra performed, *Music for the Fireworks of His Majesty the King.*

Perhaps our ancestral fascination with the past is even greater than our hope in the future—including our eagerness for immortality—for the crowd waxed ecstatic over the amazing feat of Monsieur Archiprêtre, or Monsieur Archimandrite, dangling overhead in his straw basket. The throng had its back turned to the scene of my mother's death because the balloon had veered southward over the highway to Barcelona. In the course of the balloon's descent, the aeronaut was the first to catch a glimpse of our mother and to signal at her with his telescope, flapping his arms like a windmill and shouting words that were carried away by the breeze. Those gathered below must have wondered if the dizzying heights hadn't affected his mind: what devil of a message was he trying to tap out with his Saint Vitus dance? Only when he was able to make himself heard— *Une femme! Une femme est morte ou au moins évanouie, là-dedans, sur la balustrade!*—did the public spin around to find my mother, either dead or unconscious, sprawled over the balustrade. Up went an earth-shaking scream similar to that which rocked the Middle Ages during an appearance of Halley's Comet. Fondora's roar roused my father, who was listening to the gramophone records of Gherardo de Sagra's *Othello*, having refused to watch a spectacle so beneath the dignity of a freethinking barrister as that of a balloon being raised to high heaven. Running out onto the balcony to see what was going on, he stumbled against my mother, who was doubled over the railing like a glove, and also tripped over my specter, numb with fear, of which it goes without saying he took no notice.

Alerted by telegraph, my brother returned home from the student residence in Madrid. He arrived with a yellow pallor, puffy eyes, and in a light-weight suit freshly dyed in mourning black; but throughout the candlelight vigil in the chapel as well as during the funeral, he kept his lips pursed and his eyes dry. Many years later, my brother told me that Dalí had confided in the lobby of the Queen Alexandra that he sobbed when they buried his mother. He then swore to become immortal in the eyes of mankind, in order to restore her to a vicarious life, a life that he was to give to her. My brother had accepted this confession with some skepticism. Dalí was offended and said that he was sure that I— "the sprite who, you say, spies on you and who is right here with us"—would believe him without batting an eyelid. "It could be, but we'll never know; we're talking in such low voices that he can't hear a single word. At this very moment, he is leaning against that column bored out of his mind."

Thereupon assuming the role of a Grand Inquisitor, as he later described to me in his bedroom in Fondora, my brother asked Dalí why he steadfastly refrained in the whole course of his work from painting his mother, alive or dead, when she had been a proud beauty, judging from the few remaining originals or copies of photographs of her. This fact seemed even more incomprehensible set against the many portraits in oils, pencil, and watercolor he had done of his father, sister, grandmother, stepmother, even of his dead cousin complete with straw hat and ribbons: in sum, of all his other relatives. Determined to keep the matter to himself for obscure if not inexplicable reasons, Dalí muttered that it must have been an oversight on his part. My brother shook his head. "Your attitude is inexplicable and your answer implausible. The motives behind such an omission can hardly have escaped you. When you first exhibited your works in Paris, you scribbled across one drawing, *'Parfois je crache par plaisir sur le portrait de ma mère'*— Sometimes, for pure pleasure, I spit on the portrait of my mother. Spitting on an image is the same as trying to erase it."

As my brother speaks to me from his throne, you, sir, are erasing the view below the window—the plaza with parterres and palm trees where the apparitions of Federico and our parents held vigil, or where the throng gathered to admire a balloon suspended in the air. Under the winter sky, fields of snow now appear along with Uncle Santiago's carriage, the horse galloping at full speed. As always with me on her lap, my mother and her brother carry on a conversation in English so that I cannot understand them. She had learned English in Barcelona, at a private school run by Irish nuns dedicated to Saint Teresa. My mother frequently described the city of her girlhood and her mosaic-walled school beside the Tibidabo Sanctuary as if they were an Eden irretrievably lost once she moved to Fondora to marry my father. She used to tell me that at noon every day, the gentlemen's carriages would line up along the Paseo de Gracia. As they filed by, the occupants would greet one another from their coupés, their buggies, their victorias, and their open four-wheelers. At two o'clock on the dot, when the receiving hours of the Marquise of Mindanao were over, the discreet bourgeoisie, preceded by the aristocracy, returned to their homes.

Asleep in my mother's arms I would dream, or think I was dreaming in my half-slumber, of a parade of carriages—berlins, phaetons, landaus, chaises—cantering across the gray horizon until they vanished into the mist of a far-off Advent. When Uncle Santiago stopped the cabriolet in front of a lodge bordered by a frozen creek and a windbreak of black poplars, I peeked through my eyelashes. I saw the country house that he had acquired the previous spring to idle away his leisure vacation hours and that now, carried away with his purchases, he wanted to show off all decked out and furnished to his sister and brother-in-law. My father, busy with clients at his law office, regretfully had to postpone his visit. My uncle's Bengalese valet was waiting for us on the steps of the front entrance. He was attired in a tunic and leggings that came to mid-calf and had a turban wrapped around his head. My uncle curtly introduced him to my mother as Sanianayake, and the valet then offered to carry me in his arms into the house, believing as did everyone else that I was dozing. My mother consented to his holding me while my uncle helped her down, but she immediately clutched me to her bosom once she alighted from the driver's seat. We were shown in to a library, lined wall to wall with blue-bound French books, where they laid me on the cushions of a leather couch while the ever-respectful Sanianayake withdrew.

Mute and still, my mother and uncle paused for an instant to check on me. I have never been sure whether my childish slumber aroused their tender admiration or whether they wanted to make certain that I was asleep. Almost on tiptoe, they then stepped back to the library window which the cold had almost covered with hoarfrost. Outside a storm was raging anew and the row of poplars seemed to tremble. Beside the bay window and in front of a table inlaid with mother-of-pearl, I saw a winged-back chair. It was exactly like the one which my father was to collapse into when they buried me at midsummer of the following year, before conceiving my brother in a furious fit of desire—the very brother who is now as ancient as Uncle Santiago the day his nephew took him to the Tate Gallery to view his exhibition, the very brother who commented how in the Queen Alexandra, unbeknown to me, he had told Dalí, "Do you know why you never included your mother, alive or dead, in your paintings? You blotted her out of your work because you are merely my reflection, just as I am my brother's, and some day someone will write a book to prove it." Then, without waiting for him to reply, my brother asked Dalí to accompany him to his suite in the hotel to view his *Incredible Enigma in Velázquez's Studio.*

My brother paused in silence as he recalled the meeting with Dalí, and I saw myself once again stretched out pretending to be asleep on the leather couch in front of the library fireplace where pine cones and kindling blazed beneath two logs of live oak. Suddenly, my mother and my Uncle Santiago embraced and began kissing with calm and unending relish. Theirs was not so much the kiss of lovers as the lingering, complacent caress of man and wife, who greet one another after a long absence endured with impatience. Slowly they drew apart and, with the snow-covered trees as witness, Uncle Santiago began to undress my mother. Without a single word, he gazed upon her, naked and barefoot, and then he placed the palms of his hands on her shoulders, urging her to step back so he could get a better look. He scrutinized her as carefully as would a sculptor his newly completed statue, or perhaps with the desire to confirm beyond any doubt her identity in living flesh, as opposed to the specter she would be in this book. Expressionless, with neither a blink nor a smile, he recognized the impassive, placid eyes that stared into his own. His wandering gaze—so like that of my mother's— passed over the throat and breasts, the groin and pubic hair, the hips and knees of a woman who might well have been mistaken for a caryatid caught in eternal stone but for the sudden erectness of her thick nipples and the swelling of her ample aureoles. Having identified the nude, Uncle Santiago raised my mother's hand to his lips and kissed her fingers. If later in Fondora, on the night of my brother's conception, our parents' coupling was to have the air of a sacrifice to stern and invisible deities, the love tryst of my mother and my uncle seemed more appropriate to a stage than to a mating ritual. They might have been performing a pantomime of love, played out since the dawn of creation by the same couple under different names.

Seeing the mirage of that winter day through the window pane, I grasped that Uncle Santiago and my mother had made love before, behind the back of the Garden-Variety-Legal-Beaver. But they had never been so completely hidden from the world before giving themselves to one another with only the snow-laden fields as silent observers of their passion. After kissing her fingers and gazing deeply into my mother's eyes, Uncle Santiago led his sister to the wing chair. With the grace of a *maître de ballet* directing the leap and adjusting the lace of his prima ballerina, he spun her around and positioned her elbows against the back of the chair. As my mother parted her thighs, he let out a sigh, loosened his trousers, and entered her in two thrusts, pinning her shoulders with his hands. In silence—he very erect and she bent forward—they gave rhythm to their pleasure, and aroused each other's frenzy, the brother drawing back to thrust again, the sister quickening the arch and sway of her buttocks. From the oak-lined road, I could hear the rattling of a buggy and recognized the bell jingling on the horse's collar. It was the bay of Fondora's postman. The canvas top of the cart scraped against the window casement, but the frost on the panes screened the room from casual glances. Deaf and indifferent, the enrapt lovers paid no heed to the three distinct raps of the knocker against the front door. Someone—it could only have been Sanianayake—answered and I heard the creak of the door opening onto the grove. The door closed and, from the sound of the post-horse trotting across the snow and an occasional ice patch, I guessed that it was nearing the end of its route and heading back toward town. Meanwhile, raking the winged-back chair with all ten fingernails, my mother began to moan. Although her cry of pain and joy had not yet come, any moment she might erupt into a wail of delight and torment. Into and from her my uncle came and went with the unrelenting and unhurried persistence of cascading water that bores into the rock below.

Seeing them spirited up from distant memory and through the window overlooking what had been the plaza, I impatiently beckoned to my brother. My manner must have been imperious because he rose tremulously from his throne and, groping for his walking stick, obeyed. Standing at my side before the window, he seemed to catch his breath as, without warning, he found himself confronting that mirror of the past. Only the fixed stare beneath his matted eyebrows betrayed any qualm at our mother's surrender to Uncle Santiago. He must also have been disconcerted to see me, alive and feigning sleep in the library, to hear the church bells toll the hours of some lost time as, unexpectedly, Sanianayake entered the room. Having lightly rapped with his knuckles, he opened the door without waiting for a reply. His blank expression did not alter in the least at the sight of the coupled figure of brother and sister; but he did pause in the doorway, waiting for Uncle Santiago to signal him to come closer. As the servant slowly approached, my uncle did not withdraw from my mother who continued to moan through clenched teeth, either disdainful or unaware of Sanianayake's presence. The servant held out a silver platter bearing a sealed envelope addressed to my uncle. Uncle Santiago released his hold on my mother's buttocks and, ripping the envelope open, coolly read out loud the single sentence scrawled across a card: WORDS FLY FASTER THAN TIME AND IT IS TIME TO PUT AN END TO THIS CHAPTER. He placed the note back on the tray and motioned to Sanianayake to leave the room. The Bengalese bowed ceremoniously and left, closing the door behind him. Thereupon, consumed more by fury than desire, my uncle redoubled his assault. With a scream of agony and excitement, his beloved sister collapsed in a swoon across the back of the chair.

Years later—so many, many years later—my brother was to stand at my side watching them from his bedroom. I thought I could read his face, motionless as a hieroglyph whose meaning could be deciphered only through cryptic paragraphs in an unknown tongue. He bore the same rapt expression that came over him whenever he contemplated one of his masterpieces, such as, *Incredible Enigma in Velázquez's Studio.*

Uncle Santiago continued thrusting into his sister until he realized that he would not satisfy himself that morning. As he pulled abruptly away to button his trousers, my mother fell from the chair onto the carpet and, still breathless, her eyes closed, clutched hold of his knees. Mentally dismissing her, Uncle Santiago crossed his arms and stood erect in front of the window. "I love you so much that I feel truly alive only when I see you," my mother said in a whisper. "Why hasn't my husband noticed? One look at me should be enough for him to tell. I know he would kill me because he has the temper of a wild beast. I'm afraid of him. I want to leave everything and run away to London with you and my son. When will you take us?" My uncle studied the gray windowpane without answering. "One day they'll catch us together and inform on us," my mother continued. "Sanianayake has already seen us," replied Uncle Santiago. "He came in and brought an anonymous note which said that words fly faster than time." "I wasn't talking about your servant," insisted my mother. "Sooner or later, others will find out about us, if they haven't already." Slowly she gathered up her golden hairpins that my uncle had strewn across the floor when he let down her long locks of hair before undressing her. Even more slowly she smoothed her thick disheveled mane and fixed it into place with her pins. "Didn't you hear footsteps?" she asked in a hushed voice. Scowling and preoccupied, her brother shook his head. "No. There's no one here," he said.

"I thought I heard footsteps in the snow, outside the window." Uncle Santiago unfolded his arms and placed his palm on her forehead. His gesture seemed not so much a caress than the act of exorcism of an invisible demon who lurked stark-naked within her body. Trying to force her lover to meet her gaze, she raised her head. "Perhaps you're right," my uncle agreed. "I too have the feeling that strangers are watching us from the depths of some book, or from some other place that can only be limbo. The eerie thing about it is that, in their eyes, I think we're dead."

2

"Look!" you said to me, "it all disappeared in a trice—the snow-covered fields and the library with its roaring fire, where you pretended to be asleep while Mother gave herself to Uncle Santiago. Look out at that deserted plaza in the winter sunlight. It's the one you walked through hand-in-hand with the woman who brought us, like identical twins, into the world. If you first strolled there alive holding hands, you do so again, now dead and changed into your own shadows." I was on the point of interrupting you to say that we did not walk hand-in-hand through that plaza twice but three times—the last time, in this book, where memories turn into words and, having tried in vain to flee from irrevocable time, are impressed on bound pages. But I held my tongue, because I was tired of arguing, although I could not help think that you, of all living beings, would have understood.

"We are nothing but decalcomania—like that stuff of yours," you told Oscar Domínguez about twenty years ago. "Your decalcomanias mirror our destiny. You heat your canvases with a red-hot flatiron, then you hurl your paints across them and press them in with a sheet of glass to achieve a chance transparency or some other random effect. Well, time treats us in exactly the same way. While our past is still warm, time daubs it with huge brushstrokes of memory, smears them in passing, and leaves us uncertain of the true parameters of our identity. When we try to compare ourselves with the person we once were, we run up against superimposed phantom smears. And these are our personae, I can assure you." His eyelids half closed, Oscar Domínguez nodded without glancing your way. Meanwhile, seated on Madame of Drameille's *pelouse,* you eyed me as I, invisible to everyone else, listened to your words. I had the premonition that Domínguez had already started counting his hours on the fingers of one hand and that soon, having finally confronted the decalcomania of his identity, he would kill himself. In the last few years, his skull had been swelling relentlessly into the shape of a zeppelin and pressing on his brain. Between attacks of searing migraines, he would slip away into an introspective silence or else break out in scandalous shrieks of hilarity.

The now widowed baroness of Drameille had invited you and the Rambouillet Ballet Company to a cold buffet at her home in Argenteuil to celebrate your birthday, after the ballet had agreed to stage in Paris your *Incredible Enigma in Velázquez's Studio.* Your wife did not wish to accompany you as she was staying in New York at the St. Denis with one of her young lovers before joining you and me in Calador for the summer. You left her in the arms of a hairy Armenian who played shadow tricks with his hands, projecting the silhouette of a horse-drawn carriage at full gallop similar to the one where I pronounced my first words: "In this circus, Father, the only reality is death."

In the parterres of *madame la baronne,* and under a red May moon, waiters in white tie and tails served at brocade-covered garden tables because the guest list was too long to seat everyone formally in the dining room. Like an emperor and his aging empress, you and your hostess sat at the edge of the swimming pool on the mosaic-inlaid curved stone bench which you personally designed for the baron and baroness. Madame de Drameille ordered dinner to be served: aperitifs, wild boar and salmon from the Vosgues, prosciutto, champagne, coffee, and *gâteau feuilleté à la crème,* all served on little Japanese trivets that seemed more suited to hold flower vases than dinner plates. You had barely sampled that *nature morte* when you asked for a sketch pad and immediately started drawing. While you sketched a landscape of blazing cypresses, Rachel de Drameille enjoyed her meal and chatted away without interruption. On the subject of her deceased husband, she seemed to be inadvertently quoting verses from Aragon: *"A-t'il aimé vraiment? A-t'il vraiment revé? Je ne saurais te dire."* Oscar Domínguez was standing there staring at her, his mouth agape. After a while, she fell asleep slumped over the marble mosaics, her monocle dangling over her chest. The servants retired for the evening, the water glistened green along the pool ledge, and the stars gazed down in bewilderment.

On a sudden whim, under the half moon, the Rambouillet dance troupe began to disrobe in a whirl of costumes and laughter. They leaped naked into the pool: some diving with the arched leap of dolphins, others clasping hands to jump in with a flurry of teasing squeals. The remaining guests avoided being splashed in peals of laughter. Only the baroness remained asleep while you— *mon petit chou surréaliste*—sketched on without pausing to catch your breath. Having finished your perspective of the flaming cypresses, you reduced and transformed it into the netted slaughter of a school of tuna. The head and chest of a very young ballerina surfaced from beneath the water, supporting herself on the edge of the pool, her tiny nipples the size of a child's—"*nello stesso modo* to cause me even greater sorrow, women's nipples are so shriveled it's not even worth the trouble to look at them, in the midst of *l'épouvantable décadence* that is wearing us down." Teary-eyed and blinking, she called to you: "*Maître, maître,* isn't it true that long ago we were all fishes and that our ancestors came from the sea? Wouldn't you like to do us the honor of joining in?" You seemed tempted to oblige by plunging into the green abyss with your shoes on, to fulfil your recurrent dreams of returning to a greenhouse where swirling images from the womb and the subconscious, protected by translucent panes of glass, encircled madness or the origin of life.

In the end you simply shook your head and continued your butchery of tuna stuck like pigs by fishermen, while the ballet troupe finished their swim and stretched out on the lawn beneath the moon, red as the half-open mouth of a furnace. The naked dancers soon became entwined in languorous kisses and unending caresses. Then, in slightly less than the flick of an eyelash, they all joined without a word or a sigh in frenetic copulation. It was as if a multitude of slender statues had come to passionate life but was denied the voice to call one another by name. The other guests, equally silent, watched without altering either gesture or stance. The men propped their chins on their hands, and the women sat erect in their chairs with their palms open on their thighs. Suddenly, as Oscar Domínguez pierced the night with laughter, the younger couples slowly began to undress, without so much as a glance between partners, in seeming obedience to an irrevocable destiny written in the water. They quickly joined the orgy on the lawn where everything was a chaos of arms and legs tangled like proverbial straws in a haystack. Watching you watching the satyrs and bacchantes, I concluded that you assumed the free-for-all to be in your honor, as if divine voyeurs, concealed in the night but conceived in your image and likeness, were coaching those passion players to render you homage.

Almost inadvertently, you transformed the slaughter of netted tuna into a snarl of worms like a snake pit. Or perhaps one rough sketch changed into another on its own volition, just as we determine events in this book that the author did not foresee when he began it. Once the linear perspective was completed, it pleased you to see how the pattern changed as the worms became a single couple joined in a carnal embrace. Turning to the drawing pad, you smoothed it across your knees with the flat of your palms. You then noticed that it was not a pair of lovers that you had traced but rather two faces. Blurred and partially superimposed, one in the light and the other shaded, they were the coupled likenesses of you and Federico. Or perhaps they were your face and that of Oscar Domínguez, fused on the same shield like regal Siamese twins, one gleaming in the sunlight and the other, already dead, in the shadows.

At this point in the evening with the Rambouillet dance troupe, you interrupted me to give an impromptu monologue: "The way our father worshipped your memory was something to see. In the niche in the bedroom where anyone else would place a Virgin with a draped backdrop, he enshrined your last portrait—the one where you so resembled me—all dressed up in the sailor suit that your specter is now wearing. And if that weren't enough, each and every night, to show his veneration, he had to light a votive candle in your memory, as if you were some holy innocent watching over an atheist. He lit the candle as soon as our mother fell asleep at his side, put it out before she awakened, and hid it like a thief, furtively tiptoeing in stockinged feet. When the German photographer, the one with the silvered hands and the yellow duster, snapped my picture on the Rambla de los Pájaros, my mother placed the photograph on the white chest of drawers in my bedroom. Perhaps she wanted me to get used to seeing my image on paper—as if that were the finest mirror—so that little by little I would come to see myself as her immortal son: the one conceived under the golden rain. She was mistaken, because when I caught the similarity between my photograph and yours, the picture so worshipped by our father, I was consumed with jealousy. It wasn't my image in that portrait, although I hadn't forgotten the Pomeranian photographer adjusting my pose with his silver-stained hands and shouting, to our mother's delight, 'Wünderhubsch! Wünderhubsch!' It was your ghost.

"I remember another May evening—it was on one of my earlier birthdays—and, of course, with moonlight just as red as that shining over Rachel de Drameille's pool. You were seated on top of the chest of drawers, as usual spying on me. You never took your eyes off me as I crouched under the sheets not listening to a single word you were whispering while beckoning me to play with you from the shadowy threshold of sleep. Frightened as I was by the incredible similarity between your specter and my snapshot in its frame by your side, I was no less afraid to slip into a nightmare, where you would pursue me with your staring eyes so as to leave no doubt that you were the boy in the sepia print. At that age—I must have been six or seven—it would have been most unfortunate, because only asleep do we free ourselves from one another. If you can disappear into your dreams—as invisible then to my eyes as to any one else's, alive or dead— my nightmares hide such intimate secrets that not even you can penetrate them.

"Overwrought from your lurking in the shadows of my insomnia, my head against the pillow, I burst into tears. I was mortified when you, pretending to comfort me, began to caress my hand that was clenched on the quilt. Anyone who claims that a ghost's touch is cold as ice is either lying or deceiving himself. Yours was as warm as that of a frightened little animal, a lost bird or a stray cat whose fur sparks if you pet it on a slate-gray rainy afternoon. I awoke our father with my sobs, as I suppose I half intended to do all along. Lighting his way with a candlestick, he came into my room in his stockinged feet and paused at the foot of my bed. His eyes were lidded from drowsiness, his head heavy and crest-fallen, while the moon and the candlelight sparkled on his bald crown as if it were feldspar. Quietly, with the candle in one hand, he picked me up with his free arm to take me to his room. I shot you a look of triumphant malice but started cursing under my breath when I saw that you were following us like a shadow that I could not rub out. Our mother was asleep on the conjugal bed, her back turned and her arms stretched out at her side over the comforter needed that spring when the rose bushes were drenched in an early morning hoarfrost. In the afternoons, dressed as in summer, she would sunbathe in a wicker chaise longue on the same balcony where she died, when one April Sunday her hour had come, to the shock of monsieur Archimandrite or Archiprêtre dangling in a straw basket from his balloon. My father tucked me in beside her, under the quilt with its lingering scent of the cedar chest, and I immediately pretended to doze off, just as you confessed to feigning sleep in Uncle Santiago's library while he and his sister made love.

"You settled down comfortably on a rattan chair, cross-legged as a Turk, with your hands on your knees and a knowing grin on your face as if you had guessed that my sleep was a pretense. In its niche behind the votive candle, your picture attracted our attention and once again began to arouse my jealous intuition that I was not only your homonym but also your resurrected stand-in. Gazing at your portrait, our father was taken by a sudden impulse and, dragging his flannel nightshirt across the waxed floor, he rushed out of the room tiptoeing hurriedly back with my picture in hand. He placed it in the wall niche beside your own and, now completely awake, he stood stock-still contemplating the side-by-side photographs. While he absentmindedly nodded his head, I read his thoughts as clearly as if he were writing them down in that angular lawyer's script of his. Although to another's eyes the likenesses were identical, our father could clearly tell them apart. From the irrevocable perspective of the man who had sired us both, I was nothing more than your counterfeit copy. From that night on, it was his conviction that I came into the world on the heels of your death only to usurp your existence."

I replied that I was tired of the whining pity you lavished on yourself. If you could not forgive your sin of having been born, neither could I absolve myself from another guilt: that of dying with the sunset the night before your conception. For the rest, the only living witness to my death, the author of this chronicle, must take the blame for our transgressions. By masterminding my limbo, he took responsibility for our fate. It therefore falls to him, and to him alone for his own salvation, to redeem us all: our mother, for wanting to conceive you as soon as I was laid to rest; our father, for giving you his name and mine; and our own anonymous jailor, the scribe of this fable, for making me your posthumous custodian.

With a toss of your long white hair, you brusquely answered: "Why do you talk about my father as if he were yours? What makes you so sure that he was?" I was left speechless. Not really certain that I had understood you correctly, I managed to ask: "Why wouldn't he be?" With a vague incredulous look, you went off on another tangent and started talking about your exhibition in the Tate Gallery. And all the time you kept looking at me as if, from the far recesses of memory, you were groping for the long-forgotten answer to my question.

As you led him by the arm through the halls of the museum, Uncle Santiago had stopped in front of the *Incredible Enigma in Velázquez's Studio*. He wanted to know who the nude in the painting was. You answered that the painting was a copy of *Venus of the Mirror* and that Damiana, an actress and mistress of the Marquis of Heliche, probably posed for the artist on the insistence of the grandee. Sputtering in impatience, the old man raised his voice and pounded the floor with the tip of his Indian walking stick. He had seen *Venus of the Mirror* many times in London and he had not the slightest interest in the identity of the seventeenth-century model. He only wanted to know the identity of the woman with her back turned in your painting, since it was obvious that you were Velázquez in *Incredible Enigma*, even though you had taken the Velázquez of *The Ladies-in-Waiting* for your model.

As if his question were purely academic, he did not bother to wait for a response but immediately asked what the jester could be writing in his in folio. This time, you replied that the subject was unknown to you and highly debatable to boot. It was even possible that you and Uncle Santiago meandered through its pages in the same way as you strolled through the Tate Gallery. The old man half agreed with a shrug and then stopped in front of *Portrait of My Dead Only Brother*. Coming straight to the point, he said that you had botched the portrait, that the only model you really needed for it was any randomly chosen photograph of yourself as a child. It was common knowledge that you and your brother were so alike that either one could have been born twice.

"As luck would have it, you dozed off that day, just as you vanished into sleep the morning that Federico molested me. Don't believe me if you don't want to, but what I'm going to tell you is the truth and nothing but the truth. We had just left the gallery when Uncle Santiago asked me to take him to Hyde Park. He was feeling better than he had in years and wanted to make the most of the exceptionally sunny afternoon to see the gardens around the Serpentine. In the park, we sat under a weeping willow where, leaning on my arm, without preamble he blurted out in a whisper: *I shall die wondering whether your brother was or was not my son.* He caught my look of shock from the corner of his beady eye and figured that he needed to say it again: *I shall die of old age pure and simple, in my sleep any day now, without ever knowing whether your brother was my son.* He went on to say how, in adolescence, our mother and he became lovers without anyone ever discovering their secret. *Perhaps because for us it was as inevitable as life after birth. We couldn't live without one another, just as you'd think you didn't exist if you looked in the mirror without seeing your reflection.* They never felt a qualm of guilt about their incestuous love nor did they ever quarrel or blame one another, although they kept in infrequent contact after Uncle Santiago became a customshouse inspector in Port-Bou and later moved to London. Struggling to express himself, the old man confessed that, if they were to be neither betrayers nor betrayed, their love was irreducible to the written word and demanded their total submission. Nevertheless, he continued, as soon as he received the wedding invitation, he understood our mother's marriage to an undistinguished lawyer much older than she. He was certain that his sister, married or single, would give herself to him as joyously and as meekly as in their first embrace the minute they set eyes on one another. *I must say that I could never take a woman without the memory of your mother diminishing her before my very eyes as soon as I tried to make love to her. I repeat "to make love" because love, heartfelt and true, was something I could never cherish for anyone else. As time passed, I found that I had stopped desiring other women altogether and that their very company was odious. I suppose that I never married because I was trapped in my love for my sister, although there were other reasons that could and did determine my bachelorhood. But whatever they were, I don't believe that after the death of your mother I ever bedded with anyone else. And if I did, it was like leafing half-asleep through a book where, couched in ambiguities and lies, someone claimed to be telling the unquestionably true story of your life.*

"I listened in silence to his confidences which he broke off at mid-point to repeat the question he had posed in the Tate Gallery: Who was the nude model in the *Incredible Enigma in Velázquez's Studio?* It was when I had just decided on the composition in the preliminary sketches for the painting that I remembered finding one of the few postcards that Uncle Santiago sent from London while my mother was still alive. It was a print of *Venus of the Mirror,* and I used it to retouch the nude and the cherub in my painting. On the back I read a brief note to my parents in English which would take me several years to decipher, before the post-card was finally misplaced. "Cardinal on vacation hung from Blackfriars Bridge," Uncle Santiago had written. "Scotland Yard rules out foul play but Seagulls suspect murder."

In icy rage—a restrained ire that impedes us specters from either shrieking or sobbing—I protested that only our father could have conceived me, judging from the deference and devotion that I inspired in him while alive and, above all, dead. A man may be wrong up to a point when going on sheer instinct; but he can never so patently deceive himself. The afternoon of my funeral, before Mother incited him to seed you in her, I saw Father overwhelmed by grief that could only be provoked by the death of an only son—and one so alike that there could be no doubt that he was flesh of his flesh. You interrupted to remind me that neither of us looked in the least bit like our father, that it was Mother we favored—and Uncle Santiago, if only for being her brother. Staunchly refusing that he had sired me, I did admit to sharing his somber look and patrician features. According to the old man surrounded by Hyde Park's pigeons, not even our mother knew whose child I was. You feigned indifference as you relayed our uncle's words; yet I knew you were eager to pick a fight with me. *Before your mother became pregnant with your brother,* Uncle Santiago told you, *your father would go for months when he only desired her from time to time, though they had not even been married for two years. Many a Sunday, the day set aside for the delights of the flesh if he so deigned, he became distracted or simply neglected his wife. On those afternoons, he would be so absorbed in his records, caught in the throes of the prelude to "Tristan and Isolde" or the graveyard scene in "Don Giovanni"— the one that, if I remember correctly, begins: "Ah! Ah!, questa è buona / Or lasciarla cercar. Che bella notte! / E più chiara del giorno, sembra fatta / per gir a zonzo a cacciar di ragazze."* On other occasions, again according to Uncle Santiago, our father worked on his Esperanto exercises, as he basked in the allegro or the adagio of the *Concerto in D Minor* of Johann Sebastian Bach. With rapt concentration, he translated in hushed tones the texts that afforded him almost as much pleasure as the baroque background music for violin and clavichord. They were well-known fragments from primers that Uncle Santiago could recite from memory or improvise correctly, since he too had been a fervent Esperantist. *Sukerplantejo, "The Sugar Plantation." La infanoj supreniris en tramon kaj venturis tra la Mefa strato, kiu havis grandajn palmojn ambauflanke, preter bitukoj kaj grandaj, bankaj domoj. miuj Vardenoj similas las internon de flordomo hejme. Sed estas longa tempo de kiam mi vidis tulipojn, diris Vilhelmino. Beldau ili sin trovis apud longa, blanka marbordo, brilanta en la sunlumo. óa sabloj estis plenaj de homoj, kelkaj surhavis bankostumoyn, kaj aliaj nur tolon Kirkau la korpo, kiu brilis kiel nova, kupra cendo en la sunlumo.*

"During the autumn of the year you were conceived, Uncle Santiago was convalescing at our parents' home," you proceeded, following the thread of Uncle Santiago's confessions beside the Serpentine. "In London, he never fully recovered from a bronchial pneumonia that he had contracted in August, when a bad wind caught up with him on the golf course of Torquay or Plymouth. As soon as he described to them the Catalonian sun-drenched Indian summer, before the winter high winds swept the cattle from their pastures, his English doctors recommended the climate of Fondora. Nevertheless, he had to show them the spot on an atlas, pointing it out with his forefinger and reading the name with the aid of a magnifying glass, while all the while they shook their heads in ruddy amazement that such improbable cities could indeed exist. That was years before our uncle's purchase of the lodge in the oak grove and, it goes without mention, before the note that Sanianayake would bring on a silver platter—while Uncle Santiago cavorted with Mother, and with you as witness: WORDS FLY FASTER THAN TIME."

I interrupted you to point out that the full message was WORDS FLY FASTER THAN TIME AND IT'S TIME TO CONCLUDE THIS CHAPTER. "No, not yet," you replied. "Whoever's writing this won't find it the opportune moment. If he wanted to end it, he would have sent another *valet de chambre* to alert us." You closed your eyelids, and I presumed that your memory had gone back to the confessions in Hyde Park. But you suddenly leaned over to ask me, "Have you ever noticed how the future determines the past? Will our image and likeness be captured in a book because we predate its writing or do we merely live for someone to compose the chronicle of our life? If the latter were the case, then our fate would be backward. Our life would be nothing but a marginal note on a mirror and its written account would be the whole truth."

Realizing that it was futile to say anything, I remained silent. Indeed, you were listening to yourself and I was no more than your sounding board. Abruptly, in yet another of your mood swings, you returned to the Hyde Park gardens. You then told me how our parents had taken Uncle Santiago into their home— before you converted it into a chaos of passageways, arched vaults, shuttered windows, skylights, nooks and crannies; before we even existed. Our uncle began to regain his health the moment he stepped down from the hackney coach and his brother-in-law welcomed him with a bear hug on the front threshold. That autumn, the incessant love trysts between brother and sister resumed with an indiscreet and obstinate ardor that even in old age kept Uncle Santiago in fear and trembling. In the morning, as soon as our father left for his law office, they would roll on the waxed floors or romp on the still unmade beds, they would cavort standing against the oak dining room table, or our mother would straddle Uncle Santiago's lap with her legs circling his hips. They would steal away to the rooftop on sunny November days; they would sneak inside the great white armoires with the half-moon mirrors or lounge behind the chinoiserie screen, while the clock on the Court of Justice tolled the hours. They were never caught snuggling behind the staircase or wedged between the fish in the aquarium and the bird in the cage. They frisked before the iridescent daguerreotype taken on our grandparents' wedding day—in the yesteryear of the First Republic when President Estanislao Figueras resigned and went into voluntary exile in Paris, leaving a note to his friend, our grandfather: *I m'en vaig perquè del pais n'estic fins els collons.* "I'm leaving because I'm up to my balls with this country." It was a phrase that would send our father into gales of laughter whenever he quoted his deceased father-in-law.

Their love was high pitched: they screamed out one another's names as if being so alike they had lost themselves in one another's arms. Or, in matching throes of frenzy, they would swap insults with the unleashed tongues of common barmaids or drunken sailors. So as to postpone indefinitely the annihilating explosion of pleasure, they would make love in silence as if silently enduring the torture of the rack. They loved tenderly, sighing and whispering their bliss. They assaulted one another savagely as if in a back-alley mugging—my mother throwing herself at her brother's feet, while he savored his last morsel of toast and honey or distractedly read his newspapers, to sink her head in his lap and to spit on him, to tear and bite him. Sometimes Uncle Santiago pounced on her in the front hall, pinning her down with his palms and taking her while an unsuspecting mailman slipped a blue telegram beneath the door. They made love dressed in the other's clothes, since they were the same height and almost the same weight. Uncle Santiago would put on my mother's wedding gown, still a crisp white as if it had just been returned by one of Picasso's stoop-shouldered ironing women from his blue period, even though the blue period was still far off and the lace sleeves had started to yellow. Naked, our mother would slip into one of her brother's nightshirts—the ones from Regent Street, embroidered with his monogram—and they would make love with their eyes open so that he could recognize himself in her, and she in him, as they fused in the scream of a shared orgasm.

"They so sated themselves that, in our father's presence, they never spoke and rarely looked at one another." With calm deliberation, you proceeded to paraphrase Uncle Santiago's confession, carefully choosing your words to comb out the tangles of the past, the knots of futile memories, and the conjuring of pallid ghosts. "They were not pretending. They were simply saturated. Our father was unable to interpret such estrangement and asked his wife if she had tired of her brother's visit. Would she like him to invite his brother-in-law, discreetly but firmly, to leave at once? She only gave a shadowy smile as, in the mirror, she adjusted the veil of her hat. Uncle Santiago was still asleep when our parents buttoned up their between-season overcoats. It was Sunday morning and fall was approaching. As was his habit on holy days ever since they married, our father accompanied his wife to the church where she heard Mass while he set off for the lowland oak grove to sing to himself in the heart of the forest. You may recall that he had a beautiful tenor voice and could do an accomplished imitation of de Sagra's arias; but he was reticent and miserly with his gifts. Like a personage in a Wagnerian cast of characters, in the Mad King of Bavaria's court or in the Nuremberg of *Die Meistersänger,* he would share his talents only with the clouds, the rocky cliffs, and the thickly wooded gullies. If we ever caught him singing, it was due to carelessness on his part. And he would blush hotly as if caught pilfering. As the city slowly roused itself on its day of rest, he returned on foot to Fondora and stopped by the casino for a mid-morning snack of squid and marinated anchovies. He and his cronies discussed the latest news—Canalejas's entry into the cabinet or the escalating prices of bread and veal. In the early afternoon with his gabardine slung over an arm, he made his way home, occasionally stopping to chat with a friend or nod to an acquaintance with a preoccupied glance, a stoop to his shoulders. He must have completely forgotten his vow to send Uncle Santiago packing off to London. In the most intimate and tucked-away corner of his being, I figure Father never wanted to be free of his presence, because Uncle Santiago was almost as indispensable to him as to our mother."

At that period, your father was suffering from a premature and prolonged sexual lethargy. You were still quoting from Uncle Santiago's astonishing confidences: those inspired by your *Incredible Enigma in Velázquez's Studio* and his demand to know the identity of the woman looking into the mirror in the oil-on-wood painting in the Tate Gallery. *Whatever the motives for his impotence— a weary foreboding of his yet far-off old age or perhaps the disillusionment of being buried in law briefs when as a youth he must have dreamed that he was a born revolutionary tenor, a sort of self-styled Chaliapin singing his elegy to Bakunin in the snow— your mother told me that, before my return to Fondora, he had spent weeks without touching her or explaining the reasons for such neglect. But, once she and I resumed making love behind his back, we inadvertently put a spark under him. I should add that an act of commission is the same as an act of omission, since it's a natural law that what we do or leave undone affects the lives of others, in accordance with the all-encompassing laws of the absurd. Our furious love-making must have left your mother with a sort of hidden aura, a secret murmuring like that of an underground spring, because my brother-in-law unexpectedly began to take her in their matrimonial bed with a previously unrevealed craving. Below the crucifix with its Romanesque Christ, in the niche where your mother placed it and her husband replaced it with the portrait of your brother, he would mount her two and even three times each morning. A subconsciously envious grudge seemed to make him possess her with blind and persistent rage. Inadvertently, he was jealous of a nameless lover whom he would not have dared to imagine. He had never before been able to excite her, but at those times she would swoon— crazed by his kisses, his bites, and his goring thrusts— or wake me in the middle of the night with screams from clear across the house. In those moments of frenzy, your mother said that she once shredded the pillow with her teeth and, on another occasion, she fainted at the agony of her own pleasure. Some mornings, when she was making love to me, she seemed to go stark raving mad. Between fits of orgasm, she would call out your father's name or confess to me as if I were her husband. She would tell me that, beyond the borders of her very self and even beyond the floodgates of her bliss, she had loved her brother since the moment she reached the age of reason and could distinguish between right and wrong. I would never know whether in her delirium she really thought I was her husband or whether she was mocking me by calling me by his name, challenging me to give her an all-consuming pleasure in her incestuous adultery.*

Engrossed in thought among the pigeons, Uncle Santiago recalled the day our mother held him at arm's length when he went to kiss her. She later confided her absolute certainty that she was pregnant, although she would never know if her child was the son of her brother or her husband. *Quoi qu'il en soit,* until the baby was born, she refrained from sex entirely in order to meditate and regain her center. It was useless for our uncle to put forward the idea that no one encounters his true self in the center of his being. As in the eye of the hurricane, there is nothing there but unbridled silence. Refuting his theory and refusing him, our mother once again raised her hand in open rejection. He knew her too well to believe her capable of concession, and that very day decided that his convalescence was over. The next morning, he invented a telegram calling him back to London, said his good-byes to our father, and took the afternoon express to France en route to Great Britain.

"A coughing spell cut his story short, but I couldn't let him off the hook," you said, gazing at your trembling hands. "He was dying, and I wanted the whole truth before he went. So that he wouldn't give up the ghost on the park bench, I drove him back to the convalescent center; but on the way I resumed my interrogation. Was or wasn't my dead brother his son? Irritated and exhausted, he replied that neither he nor she ever knew. The Garden-Variety-Legal-Beaver never so much as suspected and idolized you from the moment of your birth to the day of your death—or perhaps, to put it better, to the day of his death, because he dedicated his life to loving your shadow. Around the time of your first birthday, Uncle Santiago returned to Fondora. He was not to know until much later that his absence was due to a double-edged uncertainty—the fear that you were or were not his flesh and blood. Either possibility was equally frightening, just as other horrors—such as being or not being alone in the universe—inspire in us an identical dread. It was only when he saw in you only our mother's features that, even though by inheriting them you ironically resembled him, Uncle Santiago resigned himself to the fact that he would never be able to know whose child you were.

"At the time, he felt that, after such a long separation, the incest with his sister had come to an end. He still loved her but sensed that, for both, their passion had been spent. At times, he imagined their past relationship occurring in a different dimension: on the ocean floor or in a madman's fable. For all that, he was surprised by the vehemence of their embraces when they were once back in bed. With somber fatalism, he accepted the eternal return of his destiny; but he was intimidated by Mother's insistence that he take her and you away from Fondora and to his home in London. But it was you who wordlessly forced Uncle Santiago to refuse her pleas. If he had been certain that you were his brother-in-law's son, he would have happily obliged. But because he thought he might be your father, he lent a deaf ear to her entreaties. To take you and Mother into his home would be tantamount to broadcasting their incest and inviting the world to damn you as their bad seed. Torn with the certainty that he was losing his beloved sister by ignoring her demands, he left her in Fondora and returned to London with Sanianayake."

They were never to make love again, and, you hastened to add—still quoting from the old man—that, after my death, when you were a mere tyke, he felt the vague though unprovable suspicion that she had taken another lover. His confidences ended at the gates of the nursing home, where you said good-by knowing that it would be for the last time. As a charming nurse came to take Uncle Santiago by the arm, he recited a verse from Apollinaire, long lost in the benighted folds of his memory. *Nous ne nous verrons plus sur la terre.* Then he raised his shaky right hand to your face and cupped your cheek in his palm. With a trembling smile, he said: *You should have been his father. It's you your brother truly takes after. Even more than your mother.* As he held you in his gaze, a cloud came into his eye and he began to forget you. *You . . . who are you?,* he asked puzzled. Waiting on the sidewalk, your arms crossed, while he was escorted through the hydrangea-filled garden, you did not reply.

"You know the end as well as I," you whispered. "Three days later, they called to tell me that Uncle Santiago had died and would be buried in his gardens in Croydon the following morning. My wife, due to sloth or perhaps fear, did not wish to pay her last respects. Although she knew little or nothing about our family, she tried to safeguard herself against all of you—the living and the dead. She figured the whole lot of us to be either gone in the head or possessed by the devil. Maybe for the first time I missed you, wishing you'd wake up and come with me to Croydon. It was raining when they laid him in the ground, at the edge of the meadow beside a willow copse. Beneath a pewter sky, a soft and silent rain seemed to spread over the universe to where it reached the void. It was our uncle's wish that the ceremony be simple, with only his servants and me in attendance. Beneath their umbrellas, I saw his chauffeur, his cook, and his gardener. Ever since Uncle Santiago became a recluse in that nursing home, they had wandered in that house like lost souls, absentminded ghosts with no owner. Their homelessness was even more pathetic remembering his legacy to them of a country lodge where they would be forever lost, even to themselves.

"I could see, sheltered in the gazebo, the grayish outline of an old man hunched over in a wheelchair spying on me through his specs. Suddenly, as if heeding my silent summons, you appeared at my side, rubbing the spiderwebs of sleep from your eyes with your left hand. You took hold of my hand with the right. Shivering and only half awake, you glanced at the invalid in the wheelchair. *It's Sanianayake,* you said in a whisper, *his Bengalese valet and secretary. Beware.* Meanwhile, with neither cross nor name on his tombstone, in accordance with his wishes, they lowered Uncle Santiago's varnished coffin into the grave. In the mute fragrance of the damp upturned soil, we heard the rain ricochet off the wooden casket. Sanianayake beckoned to me, and slowly—with you still holding my hand—I entered the gazebo. As you must recall, trying to stand up he grabbed hold of my sleeve and gasped: *Are you by any chance his child?* I told him that I was not

Uncle Santiago's son, but he insisted, bobbing his head up and down while you and I looked at one another dumbfounded: *Oh, yes, you are. I can still see you asleep on the couch at his country lodge, when he was making love to his sister in front of the window. From the outside, they looked perhaps like two figures in a painting.* Rather than seeing me, he must have perceived you through me as clearly as I make out your specter. Then he began to speak in his guttural English that had faded with time. Your hand trembling in mine, you begged me not to listen to him. The man, you insisted, was either lying or deranged. *Before he died he asked for me,* he whispered. The chauffeur drove Sanianayake to London. Two of the gardeners at the nursing home rushed him in through the hydrangea garden. His head silhouetted against the pillow and the sun glistening off his temple, our uncle immediately recognized his valet. *Sanianayake, watch over my son when I'm gone,* he said neglecting formalities. Sanianayake tried to reason with him, reminding him that his son had died as a child and that the news of his death had been cabled from Fondora. *Old age is tricking you,* Uncle Santiago interrupted. *I assure you that my son is alive and is exhibiting his paintings at this very moment in the Tate Gallery. Just day before yesterday, he himself took me to the exhibition. You must promise me that you will always protect him.* So as not to contradict him, Sanianayake gave his promise, and our uncle smiled from his death bed. *Good, that's good, but now I must sleep.* He had barely closed his eyes when he opened them again, either in acceptance or shock. He looked at me in a way I will never forget and smiled. *Sanianayake,* he said, *my only regret is passing on without ever knowing who sent that message you brought me. I mean the misplaced telegram, the one that said that words fly faster than time and sooner or later irrevocably each and every chapter must end."*

You fell silent and I too remembered the morning in Croydon. Thick slabs of sod were being hastily shoveled back into the grave. Sanianayake was nodding away, and you were as immobile as if you had been planted upright in the gazebo. That was when, among the servants' umbrellas, I once again saw the man with the malachite eyes whom I had surprised leaning out of a window the morning you were conceived. He smiled, seemingly pleased that only I could make him out. As I watched him, I noticed that he was not in the least bit wet from the dampness. But I stood chilled to the bone watching the wretched rain.

3

AND THERE COMES THE TIME WHEN, IRREVOCABLY, EACH AND EVERY chapter must end.

Did we ever really live through what you now write about, or had you decided beforehand on the broad outlines of our existence and we resigned ourselves to interpreting your notes? If this were so, our lives would merely flesh out the rough sketches that you, sir, then fashioned into our definitive literary portraits. Such was the theory that I advanced to my brother who, as usual, shrugged his shoulders. "You may be right. All this may be nothing but a hasty blueprint that the author has yet to polish. In that case, we would exist somewhere between the scribbled notes and the printed page—as you're my rough draft, I'm your finished copy." He paused and then continued: "I recall reading that in some spiritualistic seance, a towering visitation hovered over Victor Hugo. The poet demanded her name, and she equably replied that she was Death. Before it occurred to him to ask if his hour had come, the shadow told him that every soul materializes twice: once, as a human being and, the second time, as a specter. That, as you saw with your own eyes, is just what happened to our parents and Federico. Our fate—yours and mine, however—is precisely the reverse. You first appeared as the phantom, and then I showed up in person." I asked him the reason for this turnabout, and he attributed it to a possible error in the original text. "Though for all I know, Death herself could have slipped up. She too must be getting senile in her old age."

It was once again autumn, approaching the ninetieth anniversary of my conception and Uncle Santiago's convalescence from pleurisy at my parents' home. My feeble brother, to the amazement of his doctors, felt a sudden surge of vitality. They could not hide their astonishment at seeing him eat with moderate appetite, at hearing him sing his favorite *sardanas* or read aloud from *La Divina Commedia*—his favorite bedside book and, so he said, Modigliani's—while he recited in excellent Italian: *Gridò: Ricordara ti anche del Mosca. / Chi dissi, lasso! Capo ha cosa fatta. / Che f'ul*

mal seme per la gente tosca. Closing the book and readjusting his
eyeglasses, he then explained that Buondelmonte dei Buondel-
monti was engaged to an Amidei, from Florence; but he left her,
almost at the altar, to marry a Donati, with a more handsome
dowry. All the Amidei blood relatives foregathered, but they
could not agree on the most appropriate punishment for Buondelmonte's failure to keep his word. It was then that the sardonic
Mosca dei Lamberti broke his silence and presented his view:
"*Cosa fatta capo ha.* The guilt and the culprit share the same head.
Let's chop it off and be done with it!" This is indeed what they
did, at the foot of the statue of Mars, sparking off the civil war
between the Guelfs and the Ghibellines. Such were my brother's
favorite verses—faithfully rendered here, to the point of exaspera-
tion, like endless echoes of an echo.

At times, my brother intentionally contradicted himself. "I may
have been wrong," he admitted one morning, "to believe that we
were nothing but a scratch on a mirror and that reality was confined to the pages of this chronicle. Have I ever mentioned
Hugues de Saint-Victor, a twelfth-century theologian and canon-
ist at the abbey of Saint-Victor? His works were recommended to
me by that monocled seductress, *madame la baronne.* According to
the prelate, the world too was a book, the work of God, where
each individual was a word filled with meaning." He lowered his
voice, fearful that you, sir, could overhear him—even though he
was about to deny your existence. "At times, I'm inclined to think
this book is anonymous."

The light around us was golden and resplendent as if it had
been glazed by autumn. That morning, my brother woke up demanding to be taken to the oak grove where Father spent his
Sundays singing on the sly. A mob of clamoring doctors, wardens,
nurses—their nerves set on edge by the unpredictable patient—
argued noisily about the dire consequences that could befall such
an outing. They were apprehensive because for months, perhaps
even years, he had refused even to set foot in the plaza—right
below his bedroom window—where the shades of our parents
and Federico gathered. The protestors finally gave in while my
brother enjoyed his breakfast, gloating as if he had known all
along that they would agree to his whim. After bathing, shaving,
and dressing him, they bundled him up in his fur coat and, as
he insisted, his astrakhan cap. He also asked for his Bally calf-
skin boots, the high-tops that made his ankles look trimmer by
pinching his heels until they were ready to pop. With his hat and
overcoat on, he demanded one of his canes: not the chrome-

plated crutch with the padded armrest but the silver-handled cane with the greyhound's head. Seeing it in his hand reminded me that, if our parents' ghosts could wander like Picasso's blue beggars on a turn-of-the-century beach, you could stumble into the pages of your own book and turn into one of Picasso's scrawny sniffing dogs—just like my brother who looked so much like a greyhound himself.

As if half reading my thoughts, my brother raised the head of his cane and said: "Federico, you may remember, thought that my profile had been poured from a mold similar to this handle. Or perhaps he noticed the similarity after you slipped away in sleep, on the night of the aurora borealis. In any case, I am taking on the silhouette of a dog, just as he predicted." His cortege of befuddled jailors had no idea who he was talking to and were baffled by his wicked laugh. They could not tell if he was mocking the whole world or had completely lost his mind. His rapid-fire orders had them at his beck and call and, after several back room consultations turned into shouting matches, they escorted him to his car and settled him into the richly upholstered seat cushions between the tassels and fringes of the rear window shades. I sat down on my brother's lap and, perhaps simultaneously, we were reminded of Uncle Santiago's parting words in London: *You should have been his father. It's you your brother truly takes after, even more so than your mother.*

The chauffeur stopped at the edge of the woods, and his wardens had barely helped my shaky and trembling brother out of the car when he recovered instantaneously to improvise yet another farce from his vast repertoire. A pair of nurses wanted to support him by the elbows for his woodland stroll, but he refused, shouting and flailing his walking stick so wildly that it was by a sheer miracle that he did not decapitate them. Stooped over his cane, he then started alone up the rosemary-bordered path, shadowed by my invisible presence. The instant we turned our backs on his escorts, he grinned maliciously, his lower jaw hidden by the collar of his overcoat. A mucous veil clouded his bleary pupils, which he rubbed with a gloved forefinger, highly pleased with himself. "I faked that temper tantrum. All my life I've had to play the artful dodger so as to keep you from swallowing me whole, and it hasn't been for nothing. I was cool as a cucumber back there; I staged that scene to get rid of those women. You don't know how they hate me when I act like that. If looks could kill! I can read in their eyes how disappointed they are that I haven't keeled over from a well-deserved thrombosis. To coin an old phrase—What gall!" Looking at me from the corner of his eye, he burst out laughing. "This is just a little game for me but, believe me, it's so much fun."

This nonsensical chain of events—my brother's recovery, his hasty outing and staged tantrum, and even that ridiculous get-up of Persian lamb cap, fur overcoat, and high boots on a sunny October Saturday, not to mention his care in the hands of nurses who hoped with every breath that he would die—shows not only a cross-section of life but also, sir, an insight into your imagination as you worked out our characters and wrote the final revisions to this book. Again, as if he were reading my thoughts in order to refute them, my brother contradicted me: "In all sincerity, I assure you that a book, like the one Saint-Victor wrote, serves us as guide and groundwork, and our every word contributes to its nonsense and attests to its folly. Strangest of all, I'm convinced that this book is anonymous." "Anonymous? How can that be? Didn't you tell me how you met the author on the day of Kennedy's assassination? Didn't you lie to him about the date of *Incredible Enigma in Velázquez's Studio*? Didn't we agree that, whoever he is, he breathes life into your painting by transcribing it? And didn't we read together a fragment written on a mirror, the scene where Felipe IV appears in the text—or steps into the live painting, whichever you prefer—possesses Damiana and makes her moan like a wounded doe, at which point the author ended the scene, 'at least for the time-being'?"

"That's all partially true," my brother admitted, pausing absentmindedly to poke a carline thistle with the tip of his cane, "but I'm also convinced that the man who visited me in the Saint-Denis was an imposter, or else, when I mistook him for our chronicler, he entered into my make-believe. It's chance and chance alone that arranges these words, and the spaces between, as if it they had been tossed into the air to fall into random patterns that would tell our story and quote our conversations. All this seems far more plausible and marvelous than the invention of some would-be characters according to the whim of their author. Our chronicle obeys the wise rules of fortuity, the one and only sense of the absurd."

I remained silent as I pondered your possible nonexistence. I tried first to imagine you, sir, as merely invisible, as invisible to the world as I myself am—except to you and to my brother. Something in me refused to believe it, and I would have hazarded an opinion but was distracted by my brother's abrupt withdrawal into himself. He was being led through the underbrush like an entranced seer following a zigzagging divining rod into the purple heather, across a patch of toadstools, over a dry brook, and through the thorny brambles of a lavender field. The silver-headed cane seemed to take on a life of its own and to lure him deeper and deeper into the oak woods. Amazed at its obstinate speed, I wondered where the chase would lead us. To my bewilderment, it stopped in a clearing over which loomed sharp granite crags. Thumping the ground with his cane, my brother pointed out a yellowed piece of paper at the edge of a wild strawberry patch. I realized that this was the end, or the quest, of his pilgrimage. I bent over to retrieve the paper while he all but collapsed onto a rock, the driving force of his energy abruptly spent. His gloved hands trembled so much as he fumbled in his coat pocket for his eyeglasses that I had to salvage them from their case and position the lenses in front of his dazed eyes. Hampered by his fits and spasms as he fought to regain his breath, I unfolded the paper across his knees. It was fine linen stationery on which was typed a half column of doubled-spaced text, bordered in black ink; across the entire page was scrawled in red a huge 'Z'. It was as if, on rereading it, the author—no question but that it was you, sir—had slashed it with his ball-point pen. "I don't see any other pages," my brother said, squinting round the clearing. "This must be the next part of don Diego de Silva Velázquez's story; but fate can barely have begun this section when it misplaced the page." I tried to express my qualms about the likelihood of chance being not only the author but also his own censor, but my brother cut short all debate and again urged: "Read, read it out loud. The type's too small and, with my cataracts, I can't even make out the lines." I read slowly, dutifully pausing at the commas and periods in the text and trying to render what I assumed, judging from my brother's account of Velázquez's cool disenchantment and professional apathy, an appropriately reflective and slightly aloof tone.

Morning has broken with clement and clear skies in the ever uncertain Madrid springtime. At the crack of dawn, I dress, go down to my studio, and then stroll through the cloistered gardens. This is my favorite time of day, and I declare it out loud even though I do not know to whom my soliloquy is addressed. A topaz sky is fanning out in the east, while the moon still shines over the Casa de Campo, the Royal Hunting Lodge. In the half-light of dawn, the world looks like one of the unfinished landscapes that I like to use for a background to my portraits. I had just finished the equestrian painting of the Count Duke of Olivares when His Majesty the King came into the studio to see it. Pointing to the canvas with his forefinger, he smiled and said, "It is supposed to look like the sky over Fuenterrabía in flames, but it seems to me that there's a half-woven brocade at the back of your painting. A make-believe truth lurks behind your make-believe lie." I replied, "Your Majesty, every daybreak paints the world into a half-woven tapestry, as you so aptly describe my landscape." Absorbed in my painting, he distractedly nodded in agreement and, once again, pointed to the painting. "The portrait is not finished either. In your frustration, you've smudged out part of the horse's hooves." I replied that, to be precise, it was due to uncertainty rather than frustration and promised myself to do the final touches without delay. But the Count Duke soon fell from power and I never did complete it.

As soon as I had finished reading the passage, my brother snatched it out of my hand and, after checking both sides of the page, slipped it into his coat pocket. I asked him if he had a premonition that he would find that piece of paper in the clearing. He shook his head, and studied the cane in his hands. "It never crossed my mind and, anyway, it must be out of sequence. If some day our lives do turn into a book, this paragraph belongs in the notes for the next chapter. I was looking for a man, not a scrap of paper." "A man?" "Let's just say 'Father.' Weren't you the one who told me that, when I was a child, he used to hide in the woods to sing?" When I asked what a ghost had to sing about, my brother lost his patience. "If he shows up, it won't be to imitate de Sagra but to fetch me. He's not sure if I'm alive, even though I didn't make the rendezvous in the plaza when they came at my supposedly appointed hour. Maybe he's hoping to find me in this wilderness. For every word we left unspoken, between the two of us there's twice as much that needs to be said." "Why would your paths cross here?" Scowling, my brother raised his forefinger to his lips. "Shush! Didn't you hear footsteps in the leaves?" Someone had been creeping up behind us in the undergrowth, and I could picture him searching the heavens and the bushes with his gaze. I asked myself if it could be you, sir, coming to say that it was time to take leave of one another, that my brother died a very old man whereas I would return to life at the appointed Resurrection of the Holy Innocents.

I was so delighted that I wanted to yell out a few of my aphorisms, the ones that echoed in our bewitched home in Fondora: *I hold a secret between my shadow and my reflection in the mirror . . .* or *. . . You wretched humans bury your dead, while chimpanzees, macaques, and orangutans dispense with such nonsense.* I held my tongue, because the man who appeared in that rocky neck of the woods was none other than the specter of Uncle Santiago. At his death, capricious eternity had discarded his decrepit image and restored to him the mark of a dandy in the autumn of his life: blue suit, beige overcoat, gray-tipped hair receding at the temples, salt-and-pepper British moustache. He stopped and spun around and, as if that spin were a conjuring trick, our father appeared through the foliage, pulling a spiderweb off his forehead. They stared at one another in shock before Uncle Santiago said: "I saw you in the plaza with my sister and Federico. I thought I might find you here later on, but I didn't expect you so soon." "How did you know that I might show up?" Standing very tall and erect with his hands in the pockets of his trench coat, Uncle Santiago smiled. "All Fondora used to whisper behind your back how you would hide out here to sing your arias." Our father shook his head in amazement. "It's true, even though I forgot all about it. I haven't a clue how they found out, because I didn't tell a living soul. In fact, today I have other reasons for returning." Without spotting us, he looked around to make certain that no other specters were spying on him. He then took Uncle Santiago by the arm and said: "As a youngster, I used to come here to have secret talks with my father. You never met him because he died before I was married. He was a pharmacist. He left my mother for another woman. Leaning against that rock over there, with his hands on the crook of his walking stick, he confided that he had never stopped loving me but that the narrow-minded Carlist ideas of my mother's family became intolerable. Try to imagine him as a pompous federalist and atheist during the Restoration: the provincial Jacobin who would become in old age a staunch supporter of Lerroux and follow an identical path of conservatism. No matter, it was he who made me a rebel." Uncle Santiago again smiled, probably thinking that this self-professed rebel was but an eccentric parlor incendiary and a conspicuous member of the establishment. His brother-in-law did not catch the irony. Transported to the past by his memories, he added a few more details to his portrait of our grandfather. "He introduced me to the books on which I modeled my spirit. It was at his insistence that I got my hands on a copy of *Du Contrat Social* and brought it to these woods. That day, he had misplaced his reading glasses and, without them, he couldn't make out the print. *Open it at any passage at all*, he told me, *I know entire chapters by heart.* I opened at random to page 43 and began to read, while he nodded following the words: *Comme un pâtre est d'une nature supérieure a celle de son troupeau, les pasteurs d'hommes, qui sont leur chefs, sont aussi d'une nature supérieure a celle de leur peuples. Ainsi raisonnait, au rapport de Philon, l'empereur Caligula; concluant assez bien de cette analogie que les rois étaint des dieux, ou que les peuples étaint des bêtes."*

Father broke off his recitation and glanced at our uncle in amazement. "Haven't we seen that passage quoted in another text?" Uncle Santiago shrugged his shoulders. "I don't think so, but we will. The book that you're referring to is still unpublished. Did you come here in search of the old man?" "My father? I should say not! All I remember about him are his tortoise-shell eyeglasses. I was waiting for my son." "Which one?" There was an anxious interest in our uncle's voice, which up to then had sounded cynically indifferent. "Which one do you think? The one who stood me up in the plaza. I think he's dead, but I'm not sure. It's more like a sixth sense, something you couldn't understand since you never had sons of your own flesh and blood. I mean, of course, as far as I know."

Suddenly taciturn, Uncle Santiago did not respond. Taking his hands from his pockets, he rubbed them together in the sunlight. They were an almost transparent white. "You had another son, your first-born, who died in his childhood. Maybe you've forgotten his face along with your father's?" "I loved that child as I loved no one else in the world," Father answered in a tone so emphatic that it rang false. "Yet, whenever I try to remember him, I confuse him with his brother." He paused and then forced himself to add wearily: "It's the other one I'm looking for, just as I waited for him once before on the beach. He may still be alive." Malice sparked in my brother's eyes. He looked into mine with a grin as he faced me. "You will note that our father has tossed you into oblivion but cannot admit it. He's the same ego-maniac he was in life when he used to accuse me of turning him into a King Lear. Yet in my mind he was nothing but the Garden-Variety-Legal-Beaver. It wasn't out of love for you that he constantly compared me to your shadow, and poisoned my childhood with jealousy into the bargain, but out of hatred for me." "Why should he hate you? You were his son, too." "Because, unlike you, I didn't die and was growing to manhood at his side. *Bref, mon frère,* because he sensed that I would outlive him. He could never forgive me such a sin, and now he feels cheated that I can still draw breath, even though old age has turned me into an empty shell."

"You may be right," I admitted grudgingly. What I was about to add I do not know, because I was silenced by his furtive look and his simultaneous gesture for silence: raising a forefinger to his lips and holding up his other hand, palm outstretched. Beyond the gigantic rocks and the oak woods we heard loud voices, the strumming of a guitar, and laughter clear as a bell, a little girl's laughter. Surprised, my father raised his translucent frame and, shooting his brother-in-law a dubious look, stretched out his arm in the direction of the sound. "Not one single Sunday in my life did I ever cross paths with anyone in this corner of the world. Who can be roaming around here now? It can't be my son, because I would recognize him instinctively." Feigning indifference, his face half-turned, Uncle Santiago listened. He was deliberately parsimonious in his response and refused to look his brother-in-law in the eye. "These woods don't belong to you, nor are they fenced in. There's room theoretically for everyone—for us and all those who still draw breath. But the strange thing about those chords is that they seem more remote in time than in space." "What do you mean, in time? What are you getting at?" Uncle Santiago shrugged. "Forget it. Let's find out who else is with us in this dark forest. Let's settle, once and for all, if they're spooks or witches." They ducked into the woods Indian file, my father in rear guard.

I thought of you, sir, and felt a shiver. I feared they were nearing the end of their story, their text cut short by your decision to toss it into a fireplace or a waste bin. My fear was short-lived since my brother reappeared, leaning on the handle of his stick and shouting for my help. "I don't even have the strength to stand up because of this goddamn old age! You can at least give me a hand, since you who robbed me of half my reason to live." I came running and asked where the commotion was coming from. "It's in the direction we should be headed!" My brother pounded the ground furiously with his cane. "You're my nemesis, and you act more innocent now than when you were a child spouting about how the devil tricks us into believing that he doesn't exist and worse, that real life begins at birth. But our luck is with us, something marvelous and unforeseen is about to happen, and I refuse to allow only our father and uncle to witness it. It's the Peeping Tom in me, and your constant harassment, that made me the artist I am. Even though I no can longer paint, I never lost my curiosity, just as you never stopped haunting me."

If he was telling the truth, it struck me as rather odd, sir, that, denying your existence, he could assure me that chance was the sole author of my limbo. But I had no time no reply because my brother was beating his way through the brambles toward the sounds of voices and hiking canes. I do not remember how long we tracked the ghosts before we came upon a picnic in a clearing beneath skies a deeper shade of blue than Fondora's. Everyone was dressed as if in the seventeenth century—the age of worldly disillusion. In the meadow, a group of men and women were having a party, along with two little girls and a midget. The strumming came from a *vihuela* expertly played by a young man, and a *guitarrón* almost as big as the tiny musician who accompanied him. The laughter came from the two girls—one, a toddler and, the other, approaching adolescence—playing tag and trying to keep in time with the rhythm. A tall nobleman—dressed in a velvet jacket, hunting boots, breeches fastened tightly at the knee, and a heavy silver buckle at his waist—lay stretched on the grassy heath, propped up by an elbow. He was flanked by a couple lounging on the grass, their heads turned his way. The woman's profile was pale, and her wheat-colored hair was tucked into a little snood. The man was more advanced in age, with wasted features yet jet-black temples, and a starched lace collar. A young lady with a broad forehead and large protruding eyes was setting out on a picnic cloth an assortment of bread loaves, preserves, fish fritters, smoked sausages, cheeses, fruits, and wineskins that she took from reed baskets. From time to time, she shot a mother's protective glance toward the slope where the little girls romped. Kneeling among the ringed napkins, she unloaded her arsenal of pastries, brioches, marzipan cakes, and cream puffs. It was then that I noticed that the younger girl was her daughter and that concern for her was keeping the watchful mother tense.

"Is this Carnival season or are they ghosts like us?" Our father seemed stupefied as he queried Uncle Santiago. "Use your powers of observation and imagination, my friend. Why would masqueraders abandon the merrymaking just to come to these woods all decked out for Mardi Gras, which if I'm not mistaken never occurs in November? Besides, they're not self-conscious enough to be in costume. Here bread is bread and wine is wine, and what we're witnessing is a family picnic." In a hesitant tone and despite himself, our father ventured to guess: "The Velázquez family, right?" "My hunch was not far off," said Uncle Santiago, nodding in confirmation. "He's younger than in *Ladies-in-Waiting*, but there can be no doubt that it is Velázquez himself. The look in a person's eye never ages." I watched my brother, daring not to expose my thoughts: how, for instance, don Diego de Silva's epoch now shows up in a living family portrait after its first appearance as scribbles on a mirror. I should like to know if a twist of fate has not scrambled those times with our own. Or was it you, sir, who made our paths cross so that you could weave them into your book?

"Younger, yes, than in *Ladies-in-Waiting*," my brother repeated, leaning heavily on the handle of his cane, "but older than in the alleged self-portrait that hangs in the Prado. He couldn't have been much more than twenty at the time, judging from the smooth, starched collar that he was wearing—it wasn't introduced at Court until 1623. Perhaps that paragraph on linen stationery wasn't so misplaced as we thought. It could be the lead-in for this vision. But now let's be quiet and listen to what Uncle Santiago has to say." There was a new fragrance in the meadow that I recognized at once as the scent of wild rosemary. Purple thistledown was in flower, and bees were buzzing among its prickly spines. My brother unbuttoned his fur coat and removed his cap, stuffing the crushed astrakhan into one of the pockets. His long hair hung limply from the sides of an otherwise bald head, giving him the distracted look of a lunatic. He was mistaken when he told me to listen to Uncle Santiago, since it was Father who was talking in gloomy, pensive tones. "I thought, when I was alive, that I knew these woods like I knew my own land; but I don't recall the sloped clearing that Velázquez now shares with the other shadows. It's all very strange, and I admit that I'm afraid. I've tricked myself once again, because my son will never find us. Let's go to the sea, where it never snows." He took our uncle by the arm, but his brother-in-law held back. "It won't snow here either," Uncle Santiago said smiling. "Look at the skies and those birds flying. By noon, we'll be suffocating from the heat. The woman next to Velázquez is already fanning herself with her hand. I don't know who she is, but I recognize that dwarf with the guitar. He's a court jester by the name of Aedo o Acedo. His portrait hangs in the Prado, and your son copied it in one of his paintings. He himself showed it to me at one of his exhibitions in the Tate Gallery."

My brother took off his coat and draped it round his shoulders. "You surely must have recognized Luis de Acedo, the buffoon," he challenged me, not without a hint of disdain. I had no time to take offense, because he went on with a flourish of his impressive gift for recall. "The woman at Velázquez's side is his wife. Her portrait, which her husband also painted in profile, now hangs in the Prado, its original site being Their Majesties' Art Gallery at La Granja. Until quite recently, the museum questioned the model's identity, believing her to have been a prophetess. The gray-haired man in mourning, the one with the pleated lace collar who looks

like a cross between a goatherd and a horse doctor, is the artist's
father-in-law: Francisco Pacheco. The Prado acknowledges a similar portrait as the work of Velázquez but is reluctant to name
Pacheco as the model. Having seen two other portraits of the
young woman, both painted by her father, I immediately recognized the young woman setting out the picnic. One of those
paintings is in the Wallace Collection in London; the other, in the
Duke of Devonshire's private collection at his home in Chatsw-
orth. She is Francisca, Velázquez's daughter, the famous *Lady with
Fan*. I'll guess the older of the merry little girls to be her sister
Ignacia, and the younger, her daughter Inés Manuela. But the
most striking of them all, to my mind, is the young man so spirit-
edly playing the *vihuela*. You have no idea how thrilled I am to
come across him in this hallucination. There is an anonymous
portrait in the Kunsthistorische Museum in Vienna of an uniden-
tified model whom I have always maintained was this youth—
the artist, Juan Martínez de Mazo, the son-by-marriage of Velázquez—immortalized there in vain by his father-in-law. If I weren't
running out of time and sense, I'd write a book to prove it."

Our father must have changed his mind about returning to the
sea where it never snows, for he suddenly embarked on a lengthy
monologue that held my uncle enrapt: "Our son must have been
about eight or nine when we took him to the Prado. He had
already decided to make a career of art, although he had no more
talent with a brush than an ape with a pencil. We arrived at the
Atocha Station and went directly to the room with *Ladies-in Waiting* so that he could fully appreciate the painting's reflection in
the suspended mirror facing it. It seemed even more real in the
mirror image than on canvas." As I eavesdropped, I wondered
at my forgetfulness. Perhaps I had been asleep when they paid
that special visit to the Velázquez masterpiece—a canvas, according to my brother, where time and space converge to tie the
universal knot. However, he must have vividly recalled the trip
to the museum because, still gripping his cane, he bobbed his
head in silent confirmation. "So fervently had my boy wanted to
see the painting that I thought, as I led him by the hand through
the museum, he would be overjoyed. Although I hadn't the faint-
est inkling of the scandal that was to ensue, I suppose my wife
must have been expecting it. She lagged behind us morosely as
if we were about to witness a dear friend's beheading. The very
instant we reached *Ladies-in-Waiting*, my son shook off my hand
and, screeching like a banshee, attacked me. He kicked me in the
shins and tried to scratch out my eyes. It all happened so quickly

that I barely had time to react while a crowd gathered round and a museum attendant gawked cross-eyed in astonishment. We couldn't make heads or tails of the child's screaming fit. Although we were used to his temper tantrums, it was the first time we had seen him so hysterical, so enraged. I don't know how I managed to yank him up and whisk him out, kicking and screaming, in the crook of my arm. And that was our exit from the Prado. My wife trailed behind with down-cast eyes, followed by an entourage that, to my mortification, was quite a mob by the time we gained the street. We had a hotel room reserved on Carrera de San Jerónimo, and it was a relief to slam the door in the faces of the bemused guests who paused to witness the spectacle. Once inside, I threw my son onto the bed and slapped him with the back of my hand. That didn't stop him from picking up a pitcher and smashing it against the wall, almost hitting his mother in the face. Then, my son abruptly stood up and calmly asked: "Why did you take me to see *Ladies-in-Waiting* if you knew I couldn't step into that mirror hanging in front of the painting and kiss Velázquez's hand?" Smiling and staring away into the distance, Uncle Santiago continued to listen. As if the apparitions were also drinking in our father's every word, even the guitar duet in the clearing had stopped.

"Haven't you heard all this before?" My father sounded perplexed. "No. I had no idea," replied Uncle Santiago, and I believe he was telling the truth. It must have been out of adoration for my brother that our mother kept the incident quiet. "I thought he was stark raving mad. From that day on, I began to hate him and took to reciting in Esperanto: *There is no worse evil than madness— the abuse of the strong by the weak in a shroud of innocence.* It was then that I came to realize the boy was the macabre parody of his brother. When my first-born son died at the tender age of two, I sobbed in lonely silence, for with him died the only genius I would ever sire. My poor angel! I profaned his name and mine by giving it to his caricature." As was his habit when a card game started warming up, he loosened his tie and unbuttoned his collar. "Don't you think it's getting hot?" Without waiting for a reply, he went on. "Now I realize my mistake and, if he were to show up, would gladly admit it. He tried to reverse time in order to kneel in the presence of Velázquez! He tried to jump into that mirror facing *Ladies-in-Waiting*, right next to the balcony window! I guess every artist must feel the same temptation, but only my son could have put it into action or words! I'm going to beg Velázquez not to fold away the picnic cloths because in no time at all, and dead like us, my son is coming to kiss his hands!"

He was running toward the thistle-covered edge of the clearing when his brother-in-law grabbed him by the arm. "I'm afraid that you'll be wasting your breath," he said slowly. "The whole vision and everyone with it will vanish if you take one more step. You saw how hot it suddenly became, and you must have noticed the eery scent in the forest. Our sunlight is colliding with that of a late springtime. You were certain that you knew every corner of these woods, but you never before came across this out-of-time picnic spot. It never existed, nor does it now. Either I'm mistaken or that outing took place in a meadow belonging to the Royal Hunting Lodge, from three centuries ago."

I was shocked to find myself repeating his words: "The Royal Hunting Lodge, from three centuries ago?" Nodding in agreement, my brother raised two fingers to his lips and pointed toward our uncle so that I would pay attention. "Everything is as simple as it is inexplicable," he proceeded, measuring his words. "For reasons unknown to me, we are eyewitnesses to an actual scene from the life and time of Velázquez. The artist, his family, and the jester are not specters like us. They are removed from this tedious eternity where you and I bore one another to tears. Don't ask me how an hour of the seventeenth-century can appear to some bystanders from the twentieth. If a single instant captured in *Ladies-in-Waiting* can repeat itself in the Prado mirror, the boy who wanted to step through the looking glass will have to explain how. I'm not up to the task. If you give no credence to my words, put them to the test. A *guitarrón* and a *vihuela* sound close enough to the *bandurria* you were once so fond of playing. And if I remember correctly, you were a man with a healthy appetite, as opposed to your wife and my sister who barely touched her food. Well, let's see whether the buffoon and his companion will let you lend a hand in the strumming, or whether the girl with the big round eyes will offer you some bread and wine. Try to join the outing. If they all don't vanish on the spot, taking their picnic cloths and thistles with them, I'll apologize and beg your forgiveness for having led you astray. Is it a deal, my friend?" Our father did not answer.

And there comes the time, irrevocably, when each and every chapter must end.

4

*I MUST SQUARE ACCOUNTS WITH THE ROYAL HUNTING LODGE. AFTER
disguising it, time and time again, as tapestry for my regal backdrops,
I must bring it out of the closet— like a taboo portrait of a nude painted
square in the face. But I know I'll never repay my debt to these vast
woodlands bordered by granite walls overgrown with wild thistle. One
of these days when I'm up to my ears in boredom, I may ask my son-in-
law to prepare a cartoon of this pastoral setting here at the base of the
thistled slopes: one with him and Acedo playing their guitar duet, my
daughter setting out the platters, while the little girls frolic in the
meadow and I chat world-weary with my wife and father-in-law.*

*"Say no more, don Diego," Juan Bautista will reply. "I can picture
that afternoon as if I were reliving it. It'll be a snap to prepare not one
but several cartoons."*

*We'll continue our contemptible charade and I'll remind him to call
me simply Diego since we're fellow artists and, after all, he is the father
of my granddaughter. If he persists calling me don Diego, I'll have to
call him señor Martínez. It is his family name, Martínez del Mazo, that's
prized at court.*

*"No need to bring it up," the scoundrel will gloat shamelessly. "I'll
start at once." And he will, knowing all along that I'll never complete
the painting and that my resolve, like so often before, will vanish into
the abyss. Slacking it off may be inevitable in this case, even though
capturing the ephemeral tic-toc of time in the air has become my lasting
obsession. Or at least it's one of the few projects I haven't relegated to
oblivion in my self-betrayal. To tell the truth, my son-in-law has proven
a disappointment to me, and he's too observant not to notice. When he
married Francisca, I thought I saw in him what Pacheco must have seen
in me as a youth: an authentic artist worthy of carving a name for
himself. I soon realized I was deluding myself. Juan Bautista is an affable
mediocrity in whom I wanted to relive my youth. No need to bring it
up, don Diego.*

*"Don Diego," he addressed me after the birth of my granddaughter,
you think that I married Francisca and fathered your grandchild in order
to weasel my way into the family of the royal portraitist. But I did so*

131

to join my bloodline with the Portuguese pedigree of Alba Longa, to let it flow with the tide for centuries on end, and to mix my red blood with your blue."

"Stop this nonsense. I only know for sure I'm half Portuguese, because my paternal grandparents came from either Villa do Conde or Viana do Castelo. They spoke Castilian almost as execrably as don Peter Paul Rubens," I'll jokingly add. "It's as embarrassing as being a new convert to the faith."

Juan Bautista is quick with a laugh, but this time too quick to be convincing. A nagging voice in the dark recesses of his soul keeps reminding him he's a nobody and would never be a court painter if I weren't his father-in-law. He is also well aware that I am who I am despite my efforts to the contrary. My apathy gnaws at him more than his own insignificance. I may lose patience with his bombastic affectations, his constant forced laughter and his pretense at being a musician and dancer; but he has enough honor to balance out the defects, his and mine. It's best to entrust him with the memory of this afternoon, to have him etch into acid our little picnic. Once set to print, it could end up as the illustration for a book dedicated to another artist, perhaps still unknown, perhaps yet to be born. Juan Bautista would gladly comply, but I see no reason why I should. It's best to keep still and send the afternoon to oblivion.

"Don Luis, keep still and send this afternoon to oblivion," I tell the buffoon sitting cross-legged on the slope sucking on a stalk of mint.

"Don Diego, where will the blue of today have gone tomorrow? If everything gets tossed into the illusive files of memory, I wonder whether the void itself isn't an illusion." He shrugs his shoulders and shoots a sideways glance at Pacheco stretched out asleep on the ground. "What do old men have to dream about? Their dreams of childhood?"

"I doubt it, don Luis. Symmetry doesn't exist in life. That's why man invented the mirror."

"But not art," cuts in Juan Bautista, propped up on his elbows in the field. "You can't hang a mirror over a portrait."

"Or a window," I add. "But one day, I should like to incorporate a mirror image into a portrait, creating the sensation of an open window on canvas."

"I don't mean to offend, but knowing your indolence, I doubt very much that these eyes will see that painting before they're swallowed up by the grave," replies Primo as a smile spreads over Juan Bautista's face. "And don't promise to do my portrait after I'm dead, because I don't intend to go to the devil denouncing you as a liar."

"Don Diego will capture your living image," my son-in-law breaks in, "but he better get a move on if he's to finish your portrait while your head's still on."

The buffoon laughed, but action was rolling offstage. On Pentecost Sunday, he saved his neck by a hair's breadth. All Madrid was abuzz with gossip. He was en route with the Count Duke of Olivares to the inauguration of the aviary at the Buen Retiro Park when they were attacked by masked sharpshooters hiding in ambush behind the acacias of the surrounding hills. They sent the head of the coachman flying, along with the faint-hearted soul of the Count Duke, as the carriage keeled over breaking the axle and three spokes of a wheel. The highwaymen made a clean escape across the slopes of San Jerónimo el Real, leaving the quivering Acedo and Olivares to crawl their way out of a carriage window.

"Help! Help! I'm being murdered by heartless thugs," screeched the overlord of Spain, as Acedo sniveled: "Heaven above, hear my confession! These sonsofbitches have cut me down without time to repent for my sins." Shortly thereafter, Acedo burst into my studio in the Palace Treasure House, coming from the Archives of the Royal Mint where he moonlighted when not amusing Their Majesties. "Don Diego, rumor has it that the masked men were after Olivares, but his incompetent government had nothing to do with the ambuscade. Doña Isabel just confided a most terrifying bit of gossip. Word is going around that some husband or jealous father hired those tigers to avenge the dishonor of a daughter or wife. But, miserable wretch that I am, I don't even remember! Going after the Count Duke was icing on the cake—a hundred years of indulgence for killing a thief. Oh forgive me, Your Honor, I forgot Olivares was your protector at Court."

The rumors will prove true, and the skies soon come crashing down. The latest rage is for the maids-of-honor to take as lovers the palace midgets, ironically renowned for the steel and stretch of their sabers. Among those gay blades, and at the hour of lusty valor, it is invariably Acedo who cries "touché", even though scandal nips at his heels like hound after hare. His protector, and mine, had barely been disgraced when Marcos de Encinillas, His Majesty's Intendant, stabbed his wife on her return from a secret meeting with Primo. They say the smiling adulteress was sniffing a rose from Picardy and singing a ditty that went something like: "So sad am I, so out of luck! / Cruel death from out my heart did pluck / sweet love that like a dart had struck" when her husband slashed her throat, slit her tongue, and then plucked out her eyes with the tip of his dagger. The case was quickly put to rest as the judges made their standard decision— an unfortunate and gratuitous homicide; no verifiable guilty party. Primo has his connections and was not summoned for interrogation. The palace intrigue continued, unbeknownst to me, until His Majesty called me to his chambers to say: "I'm thinking about dumping Encinillas and appointing you my Intendant.

In spite of your obvious sloth, you've got a better mind than most, including mine. Tell your friend, the buffoon, not to seduce any more wives of jealous assassins. Things get so bloody messy."

Yesterday don Luis showed up at my studio and Juan Bautista immediately let him in, knowing full well the amusement I derive from his jokes and the respect I have for the windbag's judgment. "Don Diego, we should make the most of this spring weather and organize a picnic, before the summer storms roll in. Your father-in-law will have a nice memory to take back with him to Seville, and the little girls have been cooped up too long in the Royal Palace. They need to hear the songbirds and to smell the scent of wild marjoram. If you decide to come, I'll put celery in the picnic basket and dye your horse's tail pink." Laughing, I asked him why he would pack celery or paint my horse's behind. He immediately rationalized such foolishness with his unfailing logic. It so happened that a Cypriot delegation had been granted an audience with Their Highnesses. To the Queen they presented ceramic jars of pickled celery, a delicacy on their island; to the King, a large earthen jug filled with Famagusta ink: the juice of a grenadine-like tree in which they dipped their horses' tails in order to ward off flies. Since doña Isabel does not care for celery and don Felipe finds painting an ass pink a custom more suitable for gypsy queers, the earthen jug and the ceramic jars went to their favorite buffoon.

"Don Diego, forget about capturing my portrait and your window in a mirror. Immortalize our picnic instead. As court portraitist, you may be more renowned than Rubens himself, but I think your calling is for group portraits. Paint our ensemble in this meadow and future generations will marvel how Velázquez made his contemporaries so lifelike that their figures seem more like ghosts than painted images."

I hold my tongue and again marvel at how he can guess my thoughts. Yet I know I will never capture this afternoon on canvas, either out of lethargy or for reasons unbeknownst to me. There is another ensemble being conjured up in some dark recess of my soul. I see the buffoon on canvas scribbling in a huge book and a nude woman lying, her back turned, looking into a mirror held by a winged putto. I recognize the setting to be my studio and watch as the door opens and His Majesty tiptoes in. With a pair of sure strokes a hand scratches a zigzag across that vision, shredding and erasing it. This is no idle daydream but a glimpse into the future for reasons beyond my ken; but my hunch is— when Primo poses for me, book in lap, along with the nude model and cherub— I will have completely forgotten that today I imagined them together.

"Yes indeed, don Diego, more like ghosts than painted images. Why should specters seem more real than paintings?" I pay him no heed, lost

as I am in my inner mirrors. I must paint the hunting lodge square in the face, like a taboo portrait of a nude, after disguising it time and time again as tapestry for my royal backdrops. Behind the vera effigies *of Acedo, I'll paint a panoramic view of the snow-capped peaks of the Guad-arrama wreathed in pale clouds. "Don Diego, why should specters seem more real than paintings?" My destiny veers between my incapacity to accomplish my goals and my urgent need to recapture what's lost in the folds of memory. I have a premonition that someone will commission me to paint a nude— the exact living copy of the woman I see with my inner eye— lying naked with her back turned and admiring herself in a mirror. I'll sketch the model and the buffoon together and then transpose them onto separate canvases. The complication, the enigma, comes from my presentiment that the entire scene— the woman in living flesh, the cherub, the mirror, don Luis and his in folio, me and my canvas— will end up on someone else's easel in a century yet to come.*

Meanwhile in the here and now, Juana and Francisca begin to gather up the picnic cloths. Juan Bautista gets up to give them a hand and starts tying the napkins into rabbit ears, while the little girls howl in delight and Pacheco continues his siesta in the glade. The spot has seemed different since the moment we arrived, and it's unsettling to note the change. "My parents used to bring me here as a child, to hear the songs of the skylark and the golden oriole, or to gather truffles for salad. We used to call them wolf farts," don Luis was recalling. We were ready to leave when the skies suddenly clouded and we were caught in an afternoon shower. The downpour stopped as quickly as it had begun, and Saint Martin's rainbow dipped into the clearing. It was impossible to restrain my daughter Ignacia and my granddaughter Inés Manuela who gleefully raced, equally childlike in their delight, to paint themselves in the colors of the arco iris. When the sun came out, the meadow felt oddly dry beneath our feet, as if it had never rained. Even Pacheco, a man short on words and imagination, had to admit the chimeric quality to the scene: "My word! If I hadn't seen it with my own eyes, I would say it was a chapter from a pastoral novel. No, from life itself."

"Don Luis, what are you brooding about now?" I ask while he crouches pensive and circumspect at my side, his arms clasped around his little legs.

"You don't want to know, Your Honor."

"Tell me anyway."

"My parents died together in their sleep, from a matched pair of cardiac arrests. That was years ago, before you arrived from Seville. The leeching physician said their simultaneous death was unprecedented in the annals of medicine. My father, renowned for his penmanship, had engraved the royal initials on the Court Seal. From the time of the other Felipe, he *had worked in the Palace Mint, and His Majesty called me there to offer me an apprenticeship in the archives. Although still a boy, I had nice handwriting and the reputation of being a discreet fool at court."*

"You're not telling me anything I don't already know." I say shrugging my shoulders.

"But what you don't know only Their Majesties know, if they haven't forgotten my secret. I'm referring to my premonition of my parents' death the very night they died. I can only assume that, as they passed away, they must have appeared to me in my dreams, waving to me and calling my name. They scared me. They weren't little people like me but full grown, and in my nightmare they seemed like giants, like flames in a fire out of control. Come with us, Luisito, *they beckoned.* Let's play 'cup in ball' and 'all fall down' in the lovely gardens of this city."

"Did you find out what city they were talking about?"

"I had the hunch it was Hell; but when I asked them where they were, they said in the capital of a kingdom just like our own, ruled by another Felipe IV."

"By Whose grace?"

"Satan's, I suppose. But that's just my best guess, my gifts are not so far-reaching. But then I saw, years later while I was napping like your father-in-law this afternoon, my hapless Marta de Encinillas moments before that bastard stabbed her. She was bare-foot, offering to go wading with me in the Retiro pond. Through her camisole, I could see her nipples, luscious and plump as muscadine pears.

"Was I in your dream? Smothered in the aura of that dead woman?"

"Many years still await Your Honor, painting or pretending to in your studio," he answers immediately. "But I'm afraid, once your father-in-law returns to Seville, you won't see him again. Although he's sleeping peacefully now, he has no idea he's hanging onto his soul by the skin of his teeth."

"If he dies in his sleep, at least he will have realized one dream. Of that I'm sure, Primo, because I was that dream. I'll never forget the first time Pacheco brought me to Madrid, determined to make me court portraitist, while I lagged behind grumbling under my breath that I was only doing this for him, and for Juana. I wanted everything to end up as disastrous as it portended to be, so I could remain in Seville where a less demanding future awaited me. We stopped at the home of the King's confessor. Father Fonseca was Andalusian, a countryman and friend of Pacheco. When I showed him the charcoals in my portfolio and my rolls of canvas, he called a colleague of his— a clergyman no other than don Luis de Góngora— and asked him to pose for me. The poet surprised me by being even more tongue-tied than I, limiting his response to a mere wave of the hand as I recited his poem to the Marquis of Ayamonte,

as if viewing the portrait of the defunct marquise and addressing her as she strolled through the luminous night: en noche camináis, noche luciente. *In my innocence— I was not even twenty-three years of age— I marveled that such a hermetic man could imagine a green aquatic satyr with flowing white mane, the face of a lecher and the tail of a dolphin; or streams with as many ears as pebbles in its river bed, better to hear the song of the mountain sirens. I think the only words of his I understood were: Of the two truths, it is art that has survived death."*

Their Majesties never saw my portrait of Góngora, despite Fonseca's scheming, because they had rescheduled the deer hunt in Riofrío. When we returned, at Pacheco's insistence, a few months later, they had a different portrait to admire, none other than that of Fonseca himself who would go to wit's end to keep pace with Góngora. The Count-Duke of Olivares presented the portrait to Their Sovereignties, assuring them that if there was ever a Spanish Titian or Rubens, it was I. The painting so highly pleased Their Majesties that King Felipe asked me not to leave Madrid until I had completed an equestrian portrait of his royal personage. The monarch waxed enthusiastic over his effigy: "Young man, I see the real me here, I get an inner glimpse into myself and shudder to think how alike we are." He immediately decreed that no one else would ever paint his royal portrait. Before taking the stagecoach to Seville to share the news with Juana and to make preparations for our move to the court, Pacheco and I celebrated with a bottle of red Valdemorillo in a tavern in the Plaza Mayor.

"Son, the instant I laid eyes on your sketches, I knew you would be court portraitist." My usually reticent father-in-law was shouting, pounding his fist against the table. I replied softly: "Sir, to be precise, if it weren't for you, I could have never been His Majesty's portraitist. It just wasn't in me to do it on my own." Since then many years have unfolded, and today the jester is convincing me that Pacheco is dying. My indifference frightens me; I foresee his death as coldly as that of a stranger. I wonder if I've ever truly loved a living soul, apart from my daughters and granddaughter. Has art taken all my affection? I ask, knowing full well it's not true. I don't love art either. It comes easily to me and breaks the monotony. If it began to bore me, or I began to repeat myself, I'd put down my brushes. But Pacheco interrupts my reveries by sitting up and rubbing the sleep out of his eyes.

"I truly had a most amazing dream. You, don Luis, were playing a duet with Juan Bautista, while Francisca set out picnic cloths and Juana kept a watchful eye on the girls scampering in the glade. Suddenly I heard the voices of invisible beings. One said quite clearly: For reasons unknown to me, we are eyewitnesses to an actual scene from the life and time of Velázquez. The artist, his family, and the jester

are not specters like us but are removed from this tedious eternity where you and I bore one another out of our minds."

"*What else did he say?*" *Acedo had a worried and pensive air not at all in keeping with his usual cynicism.*

"*I couldn't catch the rest or else I've already forgotten. Then the same voice exclaimed in a distinct and matter-of-fact tone:* Let's see whether the buffoon and his companion will let you lend a hand in the strumming, or whether the girl with the big round eyes will offer you some bread and wine. If they don't all vanish the instant you intrude in their picnic, taking their cloths, their meadow, and thistled slopes along with them, I'll apologize and beg your forgiveness for having led you astray. *Now if you don't mind, I'm going over to those thistles to take a pee.*"

Pacheco gets to his feet with a lightness belying a man his years, unaware that he has one foot in the grave. His age shows as he stumbles up the slope, his arms hang heavily from his stooped shoulders. The still taciturn Luis de Acedo follows him with his eyes and, for the first time, predicts the one aspect of my destiny that he will repeat frequently on future occasions: "Don Diego, the death of Pacheco will not be your only misfortune; but in centuries to come, from your bloodline will issue dukes, princes, and even kings of distant lands."

"Primo, stop preparing my way; you sound like John the Baptist. And that's the name of my son-in-law, not yours." *I laugh at my own joke.*

"Those royal heirs shall be his also. But don't ask me how I know. I suppose I was born with this talent, just as you were born a gifted painter . . . with neither inkling nor say in the matter."

"That could be. Tell me what other misfortunes await me once Pacheco's gone."

Primo stands up and, turning his back to me, stares off into the horizon. With the pursed lips of an acolyte and the wounded pride of a charwoman, he pretends to ignore me. As it is not by nature his wont, I am disconcerted by his strange turn of mood.

"Answer me at once, don Luis, or I swear to Christ I'll give you a lashing as soon as we get back to the Palace."

"Thou shalt not take the name of the Lord Thy God in vain." *He half turns, and his tiny silhouette is etched against the sky.* "Let me remind you, so you won't get too worked up, that Your Honor is incapable of raising a hand to anyone."

"Speak!"

"Leave it be."

"I command you to speak your mind."

"Don't press me."

"I want to know."

"It's better if you don't. I'll talk, but only because you force me. I never asked to be accosted by premonitions, and I hope to God they're but a fool's fears. I cannot help but dread that you and doña Juana will bury your daughters."

"Who spreads such lies?"

"No one. It's not even my voice I hear whispering the future. Let's drop it once and for all. Take me for the fool I am."

I hold my tongue but am convinced that he is not spouting nonsense. I've seen too many of his predictions come true not to pay heed to his words. For my part, I never imagined that Francisca and Ignacia would go to their graves before me. The very thought is an outrage. To lose them would run counter to every law of life. I cannot comprehend how or why we, their parents, should outlive them. I'm too much the coward to even imagine it. Yet the coldness in my voice frightens me as I tell the midget: "Proceed."

"I would sooner cut out my tongue or burn it with a hot coal."

"Nor do I want to hear, but I'm listening."

"The blood of those future kings will not be that of your granddaughter, Inés Manuela. It is in God's plan that she departs even before your daughters, so that you will be given another granddaughter. She will be identical to the first and also will bear the name Inés Manuela. Some are fated to repeat themselves; in contrast, there are others— like you and me— who break the mold. We were born exceptions— you, the exceptional artist, and me, the exceptional runt— and could pass for a pair of monsters."

"What's monstrous is that I must outlive that child!"

"It's not for me to judge," replies Acedo, turning his face to wipe his nose. "I can only predict the facts; I can't interpret them."

"We must be the most perishable of ghosts if our portraits have more life than we." You're fortunate, don Diego, whispered that disbelieving cleric, don Pedro Calderón, as I decorated the curtain for his mystery play, The Resurrected Man, performed in Retiro Park last Easter Sunday. Lucky indeed, because the creatures you paint are long-lasting. The ones I dream up—all-powerful Emperors and theological virtues like Christian Faith—don't outlive the effeminate actors and whorish actresses that play their roles on the stage. Pacheco returns from the thistle patch and, his back turned to don Luis, stands in the high grass listening to the songbirds in the near pines. From his vantage point, one could say that another forest was looming in the light of a distant winter, as if the world were reduced to a double stage drop— one of which was transparent and shedding life and light onto the other. Indeed, that is how I painted the back flats for The Resurrected Man, with a make-believe Valley of Jehosaphat hanging *behind a translucent curtain depicting the Retiro within the Retiro.* My most honored friend, *Calderón told me when he saw the stage effects,* you will never live in peace unless you take at least one step beyond this world of appearances that deforms its every reflection like a turbulent river. *He then walked away to read his missal at the edge of Retiro Pond. He had sired the sacrilegious son of his unmarried cousin and lived in mortal dread that the boy would be stricken by a foul wind.*

"Don Francisco," I call to my father-in-law, "can you hear the voices clamoring that they can read an untimely page from my history?"

"Or the voices of those wanting to borrow our vihuela and guitarrón, but fear that we'd vanish like a scratch on water?" Pacheco turns to ask the dwarf and then shakes his head. "It was a dream. All I hear now is the song of the skylark."

"Only its song?"

"Nothing more."

"And the only voices you hear are ours?"

"Just ours. The others . . . are already fading from my memory."

Nor can I hear other voices because the children's laughter drowns out those of Juana, Francisca, and Juan Bautista huddled together by the roadside. I can swear the pines are disappearing and the outlines of a darker forest— a rocky oakgrove thick with underbrush— is appearing in their place. One could say that someone is erasing a landscape with a sponge to sketch another over it. My dear Diego, you may not believe it, *I again recall don Pedro Calderón's words as I was working out my stage effects,* but I conceive a work where one character knowingly lives the dream of another. Let's take as a case in point, that you were certain that you were you, but also the hallucination of Titian, so to speak. *Perhaps one day I'll confide in that alchemist of a priest the slow-motion transformation of this pine forest, so he can finish scribbling his farce or drama— one where I live the dream of my father-in-law, even though Pacheco is a far cry from Titian.*

I can also make out in that rugged oakgrove four figures separated into two groups. The first is comprised of a pair of old men, pallid and translucent as ghosts. One is short and stocky, with a bald crown and bulldog cheeks; the other must feel he cuts a better figure, being tall and thin with a moustache the same shade of silver as the hair on his receding temples. They are talking, but I doubt I could understand them even if I could hear what they are saying. Behind them I see, though they do not, the vitreous specter of a child and an old windbag so pale and shaky that, although alive, he looks more decrepit than the spirits. They are wearing outrageously tight-fitting boots and clothing, but the most eccentric of the two is the old man on his last gasp. With his curly cap of

Persian lamb and his fur overcoat, he looks like a Turkish general on a winter campaign. I have no idea what they are disguised as, perhaps as men of that far-off century when, according to Acedo, my descendants will rule the palaces of Europe. The apparitions turn to smoke and, as they vanish into air, the oaks melt back into pines. I recall the morning the King showed up at my studio to view the besieged and burning Fuenterrabía in the background of my portrait of Olivares. His Majesty assured me then that it was no war scene but a painting on tapestry.

The oakgrove has barely disappeared and the piney woods reappeared in its place, like the dawn returns its image to reality, when I bite my lips and force back a scream. The horror of losing my daughters and my granddaughter assaults me, along with the irrevocable conviction that the predictions of don Luis will come true at their foreordained time. If I must outlive the three, it would have been better never to have conceived Francisca and Ignacia. I married Juana to please Pacheco, and I fathered the girls to please Juana each time she wanted a child. Francisca, Ignacia, and Inés Manuela did not ask to be born either; when they were, it never occurred to me I would lose them. I would trade everything— my other granddaughter yet to be born, my descendants the Kings of Europe, my reputation, my art, my life— if Francisca and the girls could remain in this clearing, as if eternalized in a painting that was at the same time the Garden of Eden. I suddenly notice that my father-in-law is studying me as if he were reading into my eyes. Then I tell the jester and Pacheco: "I'll never paint this picnic because I could never know what limit to impose as I frame it. It's best to let someone capture us and the Royal Hunting Lodge into words, into straightforward words, without failing to describe our ghosts." The buffoon agrees while Pacheco yawns and smiles. One could say he shares our presentiment of his death and accepts it as meekly as he admitted his mediocrity as an artist. "Abandon this project, just like so many others you've refused to complete," he whispers. "This has been a most agreeable outing, but it's time to return home. I've led a full life but I'm tired."

The Sun Window

1

Everything vanished: our father, the slopes, the Velázquez outing at the Royal Hunting Lodge, the picnic cloths, the thistles, the low walls, the piney woods, and the wild grapevines. Seated on the trunk of a felled oak—his brother-in-law apparently dismissed from his mind, perhaps determined to await the arrival of other specters—Uncle Santiago was left alone with his thoughts.

"I didn't know Velázquez had two granddaughters named Inés Manuela and that the second was named after her dead sister."

"I found it out through Dalí, in London," my brother immediately replied. "All humanity must be filing in succession through these distorted mirrors of time. How else could we explain Velázquez watching us watching him? Or Pacheco overhearing in his dream the voices of Uncle Santiago and Father?"

"I was wondering how we could read the thoughts of Velázquez if they weren't yet published. Velázquez must have suspected something himself when he left it up to his author to paint the picnic in words."

Stroking his cane and studying Uncle Santiago, my brother remained silent. Finally he whispered, "Father has disappeared into the painting Velázquez abandoned. He stepped into the picture frame, and that's why we can't see him."

"Do you think he plans to come out?"

"I don't know and I could care less about the fate of the Garden-Variety-Legal-Beaver. Alive or dead. He caused me too much grief in his lifetime to track his footsteps into eternity. I only know that Uncle Santiago didn't come to these woods in search of our father, or else he wouldn't still be here."

"Who's he waiting for?"

Frowning evasively, my brother shrugged his shoulders. "I'm not positive but I think I know who it is. If my hunch is as keen as the court jester's, I'll let you know in due time." His face turned peevish as, through the trees and thick underbrush, he noticed his chauffeur and nurses stalking him. Squinting over his eyeglasses to get a better glimpse, he began to shriek like a man possessed. "Death and damnation! Can't you give an old man one last chance to enjoy these woods in peace before he goes to his hell hoping to never again cross paths with the likes of you?" Not content to shout, he began to snarl like a rabid dog and to stamp the ground with his walking cane. His tantrum subsided as soon as the intruders discreetly slipped from sight. It was simply another of his scandalous charades.

Meanwhile Uncle Santiago, totally oblivious, had stood up and was heading down a craggy path to the hollow. "Let's follow him!" shouted my brother excitedly. "I think I remember where that path leads. With the rain we've had lately, it's probably covered with underbrush and washed away in places. You may have to give me a hand, although I'd rather not touch you unless I have to. I've told you before, you dead have that panicky feel of trapped birds." I made no reply and he made no attempt to use me for support. The juniper-lined path, although narrow, was as clear as if the shrubs had been pruned before leading us down those haunts. About halfway down, we heard the sound of flowing water and could make out a stream winding its way through the hollow. "I used to come here when I was a boy to bathe my dog," my brother said smiling. "It seems like yesterday, but it's been so many years that even you won't remember. There's a source in that rocky cliff where a spring breaks and cascades over the creek. I used to try to catch trout with my hands, but they always slipped away in that ice-cold water." I could vaguely recall the spring but could no more recall the scene he described than if it had been a dream, one of those shadowy childhood dreams that I had long forgotten.

In the pond below, we saw our mother swimming naked. She was floating on her back, her hair flowing round her face, her thighs pressed tightly together, and her arms extended wide for balance. If it were not for an occasional flick of the finger, just enough to keep her afloat, she could have been asleep in the brook. She had laid out her clothes and shoes to dry at the water's edge, and once again I was reminded of the morning my brother was conceived. I saw her naked body on the stone balcony where later she was to die. If that remote dawn had painted her first in bronze and then in hyacinth, the rays of this Indian summer sun seemed to bleach her skin white. Only her pubis reflected the colors of the rainbow, as water and light converged on the downy hair that curled between her legs and up her belly.

His arms crossed at the water's edge, Uncle Santiago watched her in silence. "Hey, Sleeping Gorgona, you're going to freeze your soul in that creek," he finally called out. "Don't forget, we dead are nothing but spirit. The rest is all mirage, a fleeting mirage we shed as we slip into the void and disappear, as if we had never been born."

My brother was eavesdropping on the couple's chance encounter. He kept his voice to a whisper. "Look at Mother. She's as startled as a water nymph caught unaware in Arcadia by a scowling faun. What's this about ghosts disappearing when their souls freeze over? Don't tell me the dead die twice!" I did not respond, as I had no reply to give. The sound of the current dropped to a low murmur as my mother stepped from the pond to embrace her brother.

"How you've aged! Death has turned your hair gray." Shaking his head, Uncle Santiago placed his hands on her naked shoulders to keep her at arms length. "No, it hasn't. I started turning gray in my lifetime, about the time you left us. But I was to age far more than this before dying. I must have retained the looks I had when you passed away, so that you would recognize me." Trying to pry into my uncle's eyes, our mother stared at him, perplexed. "I barely recognize you. Why do you pull away and reject me? Are you no longer my brother? Weren't you once my lover? Didn't you come here looking for me?"

"To tell you the truth, we've met up by chance. I just ran into your husband in the oak grove. He was waiting for your second son. The lad must be quite old by now but he never showed up."

"He never made his appointment in the plaza either." Shivering and hugging her naked body, she crossed her hands round her elbows as she had done when strolling with the shades of Federico and our father. "It's freezing out of the water." She suddenly lowered herself up to her neck into the pond and sat on the sandy floor of the riverbed to lean back against a sun-bleached boulder on the shore. His back turned to the rushes, Uncle Santiago draped his overcoat like a cape over his shoulder before asking in a hushed voice: "Are you positive your son is still alive?" Our mother eyelids drooped as she replied. "Positive. When did you see him last?"

"It was in London. He took me to the Tate Gallery where they were exhibiting a retrospective of his life's work, but I only remember two paintings."

"Which two? What did they represent?" Although her eyes were closed as if lulled by the sound of the stream, her voice sounded like that of a judge interrogating a witness.

"One was entitled *Incredible Enigma in Velázquez's Studio*. It portrays Velázquez, standing at his easel like in *Ladies-in-Waiting* but painting the portrait of the jester scribe that hangs in the Prado. In the background is *Venus of the Mirror*, her back turned as she gazes into a cherub-held looking-glass. I mentioned to your son that he painted himself disguised as Velázquez. He didn't deny it; but when I asked who Aphrodite was, he refused to answer."

"He must have had his reasons."

With a mere shrug, Mother changed the subject and reminded her brother of the September afternoon when he had first taken her to that bend in the river. They must have been very young because it was before I was conceived. Uncle Santiago was to return to London the next day and Father had taken the morning train to Barcelona to settle some legal disputes, leaving them alone until nightfall. They went to the pond, which had been deeper before the riverbed shifted, and raced to throw their clothes off and to dive in. With only the fish as their witnesses, they swam splashing and fondling one another in delight. They made love standing in the water, Mother's back braced against the smooth boulders warmed by the interminable summer sun, and together reached climax with violent screams and moans. Limp as two rag dolls, they let their bodies drift until the cool water slowed their beating pulse and restored their lost breath. The current carried them to the shore of the pebble beach where the specter of our uncle stood with his overcoat draped over his shoulders. Naked, they lay down at the edge of the marshy reeds and fell into a dreamless sleep until sunset, when they were awakened by the sounds of padding hoofs and lapping water.

Clutching onto her brother as she stifled a scream, my mother saw a stray boar shoat drink from the water's edge. Sensing that the wild boar would not harm them if they made no abrupt move, Uncle Santiago restrained our mother from fleeing or frightening it away. It was later that our uncle admitted that he was afraid her heart would burst in her chest from beating so violently. Its thirst quenched, the beast looked up at them with a flash to its beady eyes that they would take to their graves. But the look was less fierce than bewildered, somewhat allaying Mother's panic as her brother smiled and beckoned it with an open hand. The young shoat gingerly approached, head lowered and eyes aglow but less startled, as if it were resigned to the strange, immobile bodies of its doubtless first human encounter. It came within reach of Uncle Santiago and began to lick his hand like a playful puppy. Only then, and to Mother's obvious distress, did her brother dare to address it. In a low voice, he asked what angels or devils had sent it. If it had come to punish him and his sister for incest, Uncle Santiago demanded that the avenger hear him out before expelling them from Eden with a fiery sword. It was no crime of theirs that they were conceived by unsuspecting parents incapable of foreseeing the future they were to give to their children. Nor was it the brother and sister's fault if they were fated by the stars to fall everlastingly in love. Since they had neither created themselves nor chosen their destiny, they could not repent for who they were. If they must appear before the Supreme, All-Seeing and All-Knowing Boar, they would stand naked again on Judgment Day and confess that they had acted in accord with their conscience in loving one another as they did. The shoat must have understood Uncle Santiago because it turned on its haunches and, kicking up a trail of dust, took off through the rushes and into the woods on a full trot.

"I suppose the cub must have pardoned us in the name of the Supreme Boar because it left us this paradise. But I never imagined I would meet up with your naked shade in this river," admitted Uncle Santiago.

"You never answered my question," Mother persisted. "Did you come here in search of me, or did you have another motive?"

"I saw you in the Fondora plaza with your husband and Federico. I don't recall when it was. In eternity, there are times when everything seems to be happening in the present, then swept away by oblivion or turned into a carbon copy of some remote past time. I suppose I was looking for you, to find out if your first son was mine or my brother's-in-law."

"When I was pregnant, I swore on oath to you I would never know because your embrace was identical to my husband's. Don't you remember the times we made love and I began to rave, calling out my husband's name to confess my adultery and our incest?" Her shoulders exposed in the river, Mother shrugged before deliberately adding: "But today you didn't come for me. You were looking for the child whose face I've forgotten."

"Look in the water and you'll see him. His face was identical to yours. We always thought that, since he favored you, he also took after me. I'm convinced that since he was my son he had my features too."

"There's nothing more to say. I don't know if he was yours or my husband's child."

"But I know. Even though I can't prove it, I know now he was mine!" Uncle Santiago screamed at her. "I fathered him. I feel it in my bones just as I remember making love to you in life on this very spot."

"You can make love to me right now," my mother answered softly. "Love is inseparable from desire, and I still want you."

"No. This is no time for lovemaking. We mortals die too soon and arrive too late for any brief moment of eternity."

"Are you so sure?"

"Positive. Just as you're certain that your other son is still alive."

"And you think that because we're dead we can't feel desire?"

"Our time to love has passed like clouds into the void."

"That's not so. I feel your attraction and I desire you." Like a languorous statue supported by its stone cushion, our mother slipped into the water and splayed wide her legs. In the rays of the afternoon light through the current, they looked brown as toast. A school of tiny fish darted knifelike between her thighs. Her eyelashes shone copper beneath her dark brows and the hair on her pubis reflected the colors of the spectrum, like Velázquez's rainbow after the storm. Her eyes closed to the indifferent skies, she raised a hand to her rainbow hair and began to fondle herself. She caressed softly at first, her entire body immobile in the current except for her right hand, so white around the knuckles that it seemed to take on a life of its own. She methodically made love to herself by thrusting her fingers once and again into the crook of her thighs. Uncle Santiago impassively watched. It seemed as if his face had changed into a lifeless mask that robbed him of speech and shielded his thoughts. The rushing current accompanied his sister's high-pitched moans as she thrashed her head against the rock, as if trying to stamp her profile into the stone. There was a rustle among the reeds like that of a stealthy lizard, and green great-winged butterflies lighted on the pink soapwart leaves. In the abruptly quiet afternoon woods, a worm-eaten oak fell with a crash while a lone eagle soared high above the tree line.

"It's the Final Judgment, straight from Bosch's triptych," whispered my brother. "Everything ends as it began: with the temptation of man in the Garden of Earthly Delights."

Our mother's moans rose to a lament, almost a dirge. She plunged her fingers deep inside her body in a furor akin to rage or despair. In my mind I saw a procession of penitents—men and women of all ages, and all yet to be born—filing down the lane to appear before the Supreme Boar. Their voices joined in lament with the buzz of swarming bees to give chorus to my mother's doleful wail. Spent, she slipped full-length into the water, her

voice breaking into a silent scream. The current softly brought
her to water's edge where Uncle Santiago helped her to the shore.

"I have never been in such pain. I thought I was dying for the
second time."

"Late again," said Uncle Santiago, wrapping his overcoat
around her. "Didn't I tell you we're never on time for eternity?"
Seated there beside the stream, he took her in his arms and comforted her by brushing the hair from her eyes and drying her
tears with his perfectly starched handkerchief. No sooner had
she regained her composure, it was his turn to cry out: "Look over
there! Do you see what I see?" He was pointing in the direction of
the dunes at the base of the heath and the rushes. "There we
are! That's us just as we were in our youth when we came here
for the first time!"

At the foot of the moor, two naked lovers lay sleeping in one
another's arms. I recognized them at once as the couple to whom
Sanianayake handed the note warning that words fly faster than
time. My brother agreed. "That's them all right. They're witnessing a scene from the afternoon they made love and fell asleep
not realizing that they would be awakened by the boar cub. The
mirage can't last any longer than their dream." No sooner had
he spoken, the illusion disappeared as quickly as the Velázquez
picnic had vanished. The specters, each caught up in his or her
memories, maintained a moment of silence.

"We wash away as if our destiny had been written in the sands
of a river," whispered our mother. "Let's go. I'm feeling cold
again." Absorbed in his thoughts, her brother remained seated
on the shore as he watched her put on her clothes. Fully dressed
and standing by his side, she beseechingly placed a hand on his
shoulder. "Let's go now. This place gives me the shivers." "Not
yet. First I have to make sure the boy won't show up. Even though
I can't see him, I feel his presence and know he was my son."
Our mother did not answer. Standing erect at his side, she was
following the flight of an eagle above the trees.

I heard my brother's sudden, stifled laugh. His was the laughter
of a free man upon realizing that all is for naught and all knowledge is in vain. Our mother would have agreed. Had she not just
said that we are washed away as if our destiny were written in
sand? And wasn't my brother fond of saying that our destiny was
traced, without rhyme or reason, in pure air?

"At last, the truth!" shouted my brother. "You're Uncle Santiago's son. He didn't figure it out until he died. Mother may not
be lying when she insists she doesn't know whose child you were.

But the fact remains, the Garden-Variety-Legal-Beaver was not your father. He was mine, even if he hated me for conceiving me so soon after losing you. Fate wasn't content merely to cuckold him. It made him worship your image on his altar and to never suspect you were not his son but the offspring of incest and adultery."

Even though it repulsed my brother to touch me, so intense was his joy that he grabbed me by the arm and tried to convince me by the sheer force of his words—words that neither my mother nor Uncle Santiago, poised like a pair of statues carved from the same stone, could overhear. I pulled away to protest that none of it was true, that we were full brothers who shared a double bloodline. "No one makes the mistake you accuse him of! He couldn't have loved me the way he did if his instincts told him that I was a bastard and not his first-born son!" I shouted in vain because he did not even hear me. Nor was I listening to what he had to say.

When at last I began to follow his line of thought, my brother was talking about another autumn, in Paris some twenty years before, when he and his wife were awaiting the departure of the ship that would take them from Le Havre to New York. I had not appeared to him since the previous spring—a season that I remembered as struck by violent storms—and he seemed almost to miss me. He wondered whether, on awaking from my sleep, I wouldn't be lost in a world that had changed each day and night of my absence. He was staying in his suite at the Hôtel Robert, killing time in the final days before the ship's departure watching his wife heat her cocaine or his minions make love on the carpet for his amusement. One afternoon he was driven by boredom to take a solitary stroll through the Allée de la Reine Margarite that ran along the lake at the Bois de Boulogne, while his chauffeur waited on the Avenue des Acaces. He was thinking of all the lost souls that filed past that spot since Proust was a child and Madame Swann crossed those woods with a bouquet of violets in her hand.

My brother was abruptly awakened from his daydream by a sudden flash of inspiration. Imitating Dalí as so many times Dalí had imitated him, he decided to do an exposition of oil paintings entitled *Visions of Federico,* where the outlines of his self-portrait would merge with those of the assassinated poet. In the background he would paint places that they had shared, the Madrid of Alfonso XIII or the shepherd's refuge on the cliffs. Perhaps he would even write inscriptions taken from *Les Chants de Maldoror* that had so excited them when first discovered: *I am yours, you own me, I no longer live for myself!* or *Young man, you who have borne such cruel pain! Who could have forced such an atrocity on you?* or simply *Here lies an adolescent. Please refrain from praying.* Once back at the Robert, he proceeded to sketch his first drafts with the frenzy of a man possessed. He continued work throughout the evening and into the night; but at the break of dawn he threw his pencils and charcoals into the hotel's fireplace, a plaster imitation of a marble chimney from the Second Empire. Without realizing it, in the attempt to join his self-effigy to the portrait of the poet, he had succeeded only in tracing my profile.

"Even though you were lost in sleep, you showed up in my sketches. Without my even realizing, you made me transform my portrait and my memory of Federico into your own image and likeness. I cursed both your death and the day my parents conceived me to give you another life. You terrorized me yet once again, so I called Fondora to placate you with fresh flowers for your tomb. My staff told me they were about to call me, to tell me my father—you heard me, my father and not yours—was dying."

My brother's face grew somber as he shot a glance toward the mirage of Uncle Santiago and our mother in the lake. They were silent and appeared to be eavesdropping. It had been years since my brother and father had spoken, but he knew that he would be on the next plane to Barcelona, no matter how he feared flying, to pay his last respects while the man was still alive. He woke his wife to tell her the news, but she merely lifted her eyeshade to grumble: "Don't ask me to shed tears. Dead or alive, your father's the same bastard. A real *cochon!*" She turned her back and fell asleep.

While his secretary was on the telephone to Air France, my brother recalled the scandal Picasso raised when his own father died. Don José Ruiz Blasco, the monkish, melancholy artist who gave up painting because he had nothing more to teach his son, had died in Barcelona the summer of 1913. Picasso was vacationing at the time in Ceret in the foothills of the French Pyrenees with Fernande Olivier and the Braques. To the shock of those French rationalists, he not only refused to attend the funeral but invited them to a bullfight in Figueras the following Sunday. Don José already was in the Barcelona Southeast Cemetery awaiting his final judgment when Picasso, dressed in mourning, boarded the express train to offer condolences to his mother.

"A few years ago in Paris, and in this same hotel, Dalí told me of Picasso's conduct, adding: 'Picasso's behavior was consistent, considering that he spent a lifetime evoking and conjuring his father back to life in his work. He sometimes depicted him as he was, at times he disguised him as a sculptor or as a blind minotaur. Picasso even offered his own body, his very eyes, so that his father could share in fame with him. Why should such a submissive son bother to attend his father's funeral? Since the age of fourteen, when he painted his first important work—the one entitled *Science and Charity*—Picasso's destiny, his father's, and death have been inseparable. You remember the painting where don José is the physician consulting his pocket watch at a woman's deathbed. From that moment on, his son's existence was to be no more than a race against time in the presence of death.' As if distracted by other thoughts, Dalí paused for a moment before telling me that he did attend his own father's funeral: 'While he lay in state, even though we despised one another, I kissed his purple lips. They tasted like saltpeter. It suddenly occurred to me that I had never kissed a man on the mouth, not even Federico when we were lovers,' Dalí reminisced."

My brother arrived at Fondora at the close of the evening vigil to find the house a confusion of strange people rushing about in tears and hysterics. Inexplicably, he fervently wished that I would awaken to be by his side. He felt like a clown required to put on successive faces. He needed me to assure him that his only act in that circus was to be himself, living my life with my name. The man who just died conceived him, inadvertently, for that very role. "Brother, brother," he repeatedly called out, "why have you forsaken me? Where have you gone in your sleep?" He was told that his father, the Esperantist, the atheist who denied God with anarchistic zeal, had just passed away in the comfort of all the sacraments. No one knew whether or not he was blaspheming when, at the height of his deathbed conversion, the old man shouted: "How can I doubt in Divine Providence that gave us Franco? How can I deny the existence of God when I see the sublimeness of His dandelions of the field?"

When Father asked his house staff if they had notified my brother, they lied mercifully: No, it was not necessary that his son be notified since his illness was nothing serious. His head peeking over the edge of the blankets, our father broke into laughter: "Ill? I'm not ill. I am just sick of life. I want to say good-bye to my son. I want to remind him I still curse him. I'm giving up, but I won't let this moment of weakness change my convictions. I have spoken."

Those were Father's last words. He died the moment my brother walked into the house. A neighbor ventured to say perhaps it was for the best, and my brother roughly shoved him away. Then, brushing out the wrinkles of his coat sleeves, he apologized for his behavior. They had already closed the dead man's eyes, but my brother asked for a few moments alone with his father prior to the customary preparations of washing and dressing the body for viewing. Once inside the bedroom, my brother was surprised to see the long-forgotten portrait he had done of his father hanging on the wall above the bed, badly in need of cleaning and restoration. The painting was an adolescent work, done several years before my brother was to become a true artist, an artist he never would have been if it weren't for Federico. It was more a multicolor smudge of heavily applied impasto in imitation of a fauve Matisse, but my brother was surprised to see it over the bed of the man who refused even to speak to him. He was more shocked to see my photograph in the wall niche. It was yellow with age but still framed as my brother remembered it from his childhood. His own photograph, the one taken by the goateed Pomeranian, was nowhere in sight, and my brother felt certain that his father must have thrown it into the trash when he disinherited him.

He placed his hand on the dead man's bushy brows and, like Michelangelo after finishing his Moses, shouted: "Now speak to me, you dog!" A shiver ran through him and his palm turned cold as ice as if he had just touched a jellyfish on the beach. Forcing himself to control his revulsion, he leaned over the body and kissed it on the mouth. He let out a hair-raising scream when Father bit him on the lip and stared at him through wide-opened eyes. The bedroom once more was filled with strangers. They saw the old man stare, heard him sigh, watched his hands tug on the quilt, and began to speak of a miracle. The doctor, summoned posthaste to examine Father, proclaimed him unquestionably alive and perhaps even aware of what they were saying. Turning to my brother, he added, "If he's regaining his will to live, it may save him." The doctor called the revived man by name but only received a fixed stare in response. He administered an injection to stimulate his patient's weak pulse and left shaking his head. When the doctor returned late that night, Father was unable to move or speak, but he seemed lucid.

"I kept watch from an armchair at the foot of the bed, in view of his impassive stare. I asked if he would like me to turn down the light and noted a slight movement of his eyelids. Taking that for a reply, I turned off all the lamps except for the one on the night table. For hours on end, between the visits of a starched-capped nurse, we listened to 'The Kreutzer Sonata' by Beethoven. My father followed the cadenza-arpeggio of the piano with his eyelids and an occasional twitch to his mouth. I recalled that he had once mentioned how Kreutzer—a violinist for *La Chappelle du Roi* and later the director of the Paris Opera—had refused to perform the sonata that was to immortalize him. *Pay attention to the music. Pay attention to how Beethoven describes May skies. Now hear the sorrow that rises from the earth. Don't you hear it? Have you no ear for music? Your brother, even though he died so young, could hum all the way to the first presto.* Then he turned his back to me and was lost to the record on the gramophone with its tulip-shaped horn. I answered that I could understand Beethoven because Ruisdael attempted the very same with his landscapes with windmills in the background. Since my father had never heard of Ruisdael, my impertinence infuriated him and he slapped me. *Damn your insolence! When you talk like this, you can't know how much I much I miss the other child!*

"Father lived through the night and, in the morning, began to talk. *Why did you come back?*, he asked. My brother replied that he had no special reason to return nor did he know how long he would stay. *Don't go away. Not until I tell you my nightmare.* My brother promised to listen but only if our father did not overexert himself. The story would not overtax him in the least bit, Father replied, because he was in total control of his strength. He then asked that our mother be called to share in his confidences. Running my tongue over my lip where he had bit me, I told him that Mother had passed away years before on the balcony of our old house. He seemed startled for a moment but then nodded his head in agreement. *I came to believe her death was part of my nightmare, but now I remember. She died while a trapeze artist soared overhead in a balloon. It's not always easy to tell the difference between what we've lived and what we've dreamed.*

"I inadvertently replied, 'Or for that matter, between what we've lived and what we've painted.' But he ignored me as he continued in a confessional tone: *I dreamed a life I never lived. In my dream, as in real life, you died young, leaving me amazed by your good looks and your precocious talent. But, and it horrifies me even to recall it, your grave was still warm when we conceived another child, your exact look-alike as well as your living parody.* I made my father repeat what he had just said, because it crossed my mind that it was I who was dreaming all this: our home in Fondora, my father on his deathbed, and, naturally, myself listening to him. I also asked him to describe the other child in his nightmare. I wanted to know how he saw me in his dreams, even if he pretended not to recognize me when awake. *In spite of hating him as I did, I was so weak that I gave my name to the impostor. It was yours too and I hated him for what I did. While still a child, perhaps even before he began to reason, I detested him for inheriting your name and your looks, even though I gave them to him. And he must have known that I could never love another son the way I loved you. Mad with jealousy, he despised me in turn.*

"My father paused at that point, and I asked him what happened to the intruder in the nightmare. He answered that the dream spanned the entire life of the imposter who went quite mad in his obsession to be, if not the favorite, at least one of a kind. He forced himself to become an artist even though he was born without any talent. He even amassed a fortune equal to that of Rubens in his day. Clutching at the sheets, my father hissed: *The nightmare ended in this very room, with me in this bed and him in your armchair. I realized that it was he and not you the moment I felt my dream slip away. When I woke up—it couldn't have been more than a few seconds ago—I saw you here at my side, and I realized that my life was no more than an old man's dream. You never died as a child, nor did your brother ever exist. At that moment I asked why you came back to Fondora.* My father said no more, and once again I told myself that none of this was real. If anyone was dreaming, it was I. It was then I realized why you were absent. Only when one of us is asleep can the other be free of his presence."

Still standing motionless in front of us, Mother and Uncle Santiago watched themselves in the stream. "It's all so odd," our uncle was saying, "I am convinced that your oldest boy was mine and that, in spirit, he gets closer and closer to us even though we cannot see him. Can you also feel his presence?" Our mother answered: "All I see is our reflection in the water. We are alone among the shadows of the trees."

Then my brother told me how our father burst out laughing when it occurred to him that his dream in that bedroom was truly his life. No dream, in all his fantasies, could be so incredible as that reality. "He died laughing. I wondered if he was delirious. He had been mocking me pretending to confuse me with you. No matter, he died convinced that you were his son and he persists in that delusion. He has no idea that you were not his first-born but the bastard fruit of incest." My brother burst into hilarious chuckles that seemed to make his birdlike head and long curls bob in joy. Neither Mother nor Uncle Santiago could hear his shrill laughter. Enraged, I tried my best to deny it: "I was just as legitimate as you were! Which son our father chose to love or to hate was no fault of mine!" "Finally, everything makes sense," my brother cut in. "You died so young because you came from bad seed. Like rotten fruit, you were destined to fall with the first storms. When brother and sister cross, there can only come a monster. Even your precocious speech and nonsensical aphorisms that so amazed the Esperantists of the Casino were nothing more than the hallucinations of a freak." I was too weak to reply and, seeing the outline of my hands start to blur, realized I was dozing off. Just before disappearing in sleep, I saw my brother's chauffeur and nurses come rushing pell mell down the slope. Oblivious to us all, Mother and Uncle Santiago stood motionless on the pebble beach. I became painfully aware of how removed we were from one another and that, although forced to coexist, my brother and I lived the most isolated loneliness—one among the living, the other among the dead.

Scorched dry by the autumn sun, a tree branch overhanging the stream split and fell with a crash into the stream. I began to count the waves it made. They rose in ever larger concentric circles only to disappear, leaving no more trace in their wake than I leave in my sleep. At the very last moment, immediately before falling into my blindman's dream, I saw the man with malachite eyes and the Vandyke beard—the man who had casually leaned over his windowsill to witness my brother's conception. He stood watching us all from atop a high boulder, pointy as a French baguette, and seemed to grin.

2

THE EARLIEST DREAM I VIVIDLY REMEMBER IS THE ONE WHEN I vanished before your eyes at the edge of the creek. I cannot say for certain whether it was a repeat of a nightmare or the recall of memories that I had tried to block but that had returned, implacable and diaphanous. At any rate, to thread through these tangled thoughts, everything must have begun with another *cauchemar, mon cher frère,* that repeatedly hounded you as a child and that, years later, you were to call a painfully disturbing premonition of being sexually molested by Federico.

We are back to the time our parents are restoring the old fisherman's hut on the cliffs. You still delight in those few—never more than three or four—days of solitude that you enjoy there each summer. Steadfast, you will insist they were not only the happiest days of your childhood but perhaps of your entire existence. You would give your life and your worldly reputation to relive them. Your joy is such that you tolerate my presence and almost forgive me for having been born with your name. You and our parents climb on foot to your retreat while a fisherman tugs at the mule loaded down with the family's barest necessities—white linens and embroidered sheets scented with lavender, tableware and silver packed in a wooden box crafted from a champagne crate with handsome brass reinforcements, mimosa firewood for flavoring sea bream grilled on a low flame, a set of cooking ranges, a pair of plaid hatboxes for our mother's sunbonnet and our father's straw boater, not to mention the fishing poles and reels, and the canary cage.

The only bed is a feather mattress spread out on the open patio. You sleep peacefully between our parents and, at times, can hear them talking to one another in the unrecognizable language of sleep. As you will confess much later, you think of me and remember how our father tried to catch a glimpse of my shadow as I lifted the door latch to half-open his office door. Then you imagine me the night on the rocky cliff, sitting all alone in death beneath the stars, facing the sea and watching the distant lights of the fishing boats. During siesta time, the tide recedes along the golden strip of beach at the foot of the rocky slope. Then you and I escape to race like rabbits across the peaks or frisk about the rocks like lizards darting in and out of cracks. Sometimes we have contests throwing pebbles into the sea. You envy the long trajectory of my toss when the stone slaps flat against the surface and skips across the waves.

Later you will tell me that, once back in Fondora, you were to pay a high price for such happiness. Night after night you are accosted by a recurring nightmare. You are once again on the rocky cliffs but the cabin is empty and my parents and I have disappeared. You sense that someone is lurking behind you but you are afraid to turn around and face him. Petrified, you imagine the pursuer to be a Titan with your own arms—it is yourself you see, aggrandized by the concave mirror of the skies, or perhaps a huge monster with my pallid features that so much resemble yours. You run panting, but you will be overtaken if you pause for breath. You feel the space and time separating you from your pursuer become smaller with each stride you make. You want to scream but your voice gets caught in your throat. You will lose your footing and fall into the sea if your hangman does not catch you first. The golden beach is far behind and you race across the high bluff where the path narrows and the rocks are knife-sharp. You know that deep beneath the sea lurks yet another chimera that you can see clearly in your dream. It must be one of the Sirens that your father describes as he translates into Esperanto the Catalán version of *The Odyssey: Come hither, Odysseus, great glory of the Achaeans! Bring in your ship and listen to our song. For none has ever passed us in a black-hulled ship till from our lips he heard ecstatic song, then went his way rejoicing with greater knowledge. For we know all that on the plain of Troy Greeks and Trojans suffered at the gods' behest. We know whatever happens on this bounteous earth.* You awake sobbing as your mother comes running into your bedroom. She is wearing a long dressing gown, very open and trimmed with flounces. In her hurry to console you, the lace slips off one shoulder and exposes her nipple. It is bleached the color of marble by the moon beaming into the window. She sits on the bed and presses your cheek to her breast. You fear that your face will burn her while your cries settle into sobs and sniffles. The way your heart is racing, you are afraid that it will burst and rise to your throat and strangle you. All the time, you feel once again like an infant, and you would like to take her pale nipples into your mouth and swallow them.

The scene then changes as quickly as lightning flashes across the darkest night. I do not know whether I truly am recalling the dream I had on the sea cliff or whether I was remembering some secret you confided in me—one that we both long forgot since neither could bear to recall it. I only know that another night you also dream you returned to the rocky bluff, where once again at cliff's edge you flee in breathless terror. A soft rain falling from a zinc-colored sky has turned the sea gray and the horizon dark. Barefoot, you are afraid you will lose your step and slip over the rock. Meanwhile, your pursuer cannot tell your gasps for air from the roar of the waves. He is now so close that, if the sun were to break through the misty-green morning fog, his shadow could swallow you whole. You are drenched, blinded by the rain that turns into a flood of tears. You awake screaming.

Alarmed by your cries, Mother stumbles against the furniture in her path as she rushes into your room. The moon that had bleached her to a marble white now bathes her in silver. Naked and barefoot, her hair falling wildly down her back, she does not think to slip into the dressing gown that each night she drapes over the modest chair at the foot of the bed. Although distraught, you rationalize that she, in her husband's absence, must prefer sleeping naked on hot summer nights. The aroma of jasmine and gardenia fills the night air as a prick of your conscience warns you that the Garden-Variety-Legal-Beaver is in Barcelona on business, closing the sale on some terraced orchards behind your Calador home. They were the property of a client who was financially ruined from trying to import fricasseed hare and vinaigrette brains from Paris.

Without rhyme or reason, one flash of memory triggers another, and you tell yourself that our father must be in the hotel with the oval mirrors next to the Pomeranian's photography studio. On your visits to Barcelona, the family liked to stay there as it was a popular haunt of famous bullfighters. Our parents say that on their honeymoon they saw Guerrita himself, then at the height of his success, long before he was to forsake the ring in disgust. He was sitting in the lobby on a sofa of amethyst brocade, presiding over an impromptu gathering of admirers and snapping a reedlike cane against his boots of cordovan leather. *Don't cry, my son. It was just a nightmare, like everything else in this world of shadows,* your mother tells you as she once again presses you against her. Your heart beats at your temples and your panic threatens to split you open like a pig on a spit. Suddenly you feel a hand slip between your thighs and icy fingers start to caress you. In vain you tell yourself that you are dreaming and that your screams will snap you out of your delirium. It is indeed in vain, because the only dream that day was mine as I witnessed your seduction as clearly as I recall it now from memory. *I sense that I will soon be leaving this deceitful world,* says your mother as her fingertips arouse you. *There is nothing wrong in physical pleasure, since the body is condemned to die anyway,* she continues before breaking into peals of laughter in the moonlight. *But why should I be speaking of death now? In moments like this, aren't we eternal?* She takes off your nightshirt while you submit like a rag doll whose only life burns in the fire of its taut loins. Her legs outstretched, Mother straddles you and uses her hands to help you penetrate her open body. No sooner does she feel you inside her, she grasps hold of the sheets and sways her hips in resolute crescendo until she writhes in an agony whose very existence seems to you unknown and unimaginable. I dream that you reach climax together. Your cries are indistinguishable before she collapses on your chest, panting: *I love you, I love you so much, my little lamb.*

In the same nightmare, I foresee your teen-age shyness with girls, who make wicked jokes about your dainty mannerisms. It is a Saturday night after a violent rainstorm. Gas lamps light our way past the rose bushes and acacia shrubs along the boulevard. Together you and I stop beneath the marquee of a watch shop to stare at the couples strolling arm in arm or kissing in the doorways. Your neighbors pretend not to notice the pained, envious look on your face and pass by without speaking, as if you were a stranger lost and alone in his own city. By degrees, the pavement turns iridescent as the lamps in the windows are lit and the stars take on a reddish glow. "Let's go," you say in a low voice so that no one will think you crazy for talking to yourself. The years pass and, in my dream, are shuffled with ever increasing speed, as if time rushed their course before they were spent. Smiling gypsy models now sit for you. They seem to undress you with their dark, longing glances. As one girl poses for you with a spray of hortensias across her lap, she says that, as dark and handsome as you are, you could be taken for a full-blooded gypsy. In panic you invent an excuse to get rid of her.

One Sunday afternoon, while your father sings to the oak trees or enjoys an aperitif of vermouth and olives, Mother shows up at your studio. Silently, she glances at your canvases and absent-mindedly leafs through your sketches in a half-open folio. She says that you should paint a portrait of her looking over the balcony at an imaginary city. Blushing, knowing that you will never paint her, you avert your eyes. What is more, you seem to have lost your touch with the brushes or charcoal. You wonder whether you should give up painting for good, like an addict hooked to a destructive habit. Another afternoon, still in the far-distant future, Picasso, crestfallen, will tell you that his father did just that: *Although I owe everything to him, the poor man was a mediocre painter. Renouncing his art was perhaps his greatest accomplishment.* You decide not to renounce yours once you realize that you have nothing else to do with yourself. Left with only free time and no goals, you would turn into the same wandering soul alive that I am dead.

In Madrid you receive the telegram from Father saying that our mother had suddenly died on the same balcony where she hoped to view the columns of her legendary city. You will have to come to grips with your adolescence and admit that the reason for never drawing your mother prior to her death on that jasmine-scented night was that you silently half-believed that she would seduce you. Alarmed, you ask yourself whether your subconscious could have desired her so instinctively as to have magically charmed her into your bed.

You return to Madrid in the fall to find out that Federico is convalescing in Granada. He is stricken by a relapse of muscular paralysis that, as a child, kept him invalid for an entire year. It will be mid-January before you see him, lame and sallow, in sharp contrast to his natural olive-colored complexion. You can hear his footsteps as he approaches tentatively from behind. He calls you by name and lays a hand on your shoulder for support. You realize that the monster of the sea cliffs, whose face you dared not turn to see, was a premonition of Federico. Once the message has been decoded, you turn to confront your destiny. Federico expresses his condolences for your mother's death while you wonder what quirk of fate could have brought you together that winter morning. Suddenly, but not altogether unexpectedly, he hugs and kisses you on your cheeks, eyelids, and lips. His tongue tastes like salt and tobacco. You know that you will succumb to him, even though his love leaves you as indifferent as does that of any woman. You will never allow Federico to completely possess you because, by his macabre pantomime of his own death, burial, and decay, you have identified him with my ghost—the irretrievable core of your being. You also give yourself to him in order to exorcise the specter of sexual abuse by our mother. Only by sacrificing yourself to the metamorphosed chimera of your nightmares can you expiate your guilt for having been doubly victimized—by Mother and by me.

While Federico kisses you, I once again sense that, just as you were born from my ashes, we exist in two separate versions of a script by an unknown writer—not the one you refuse to admit who visited you in New York, but another author whose existence I do not doubt even if you deny it. I feel he included us all in his book. In the first draft, Federico makes an obvious pass, leering at you while offering his condolences; but you reject him. In the second version—the lived script—Federico wrestles with you as if you were Antaeus and he Heracles, suffocating you with his hugs and kisses and tearing you away from Mother Earth—your dead mother.

Then my memory blocks out entire years of your life while I sleep. You meet the woman who will be your one and only wife during the first Paris exhibition of your etchings. You were introduced to her by Rachel de Drameille, who whispers behind her back that she is a two-time divorcée and the talk of all Paris for her ménage-a-trois with Peggy Guggenheim and Yves Tanguy in a picture-book cottage, complete with stork's nest on the rooftop, tucked away in Mantes-La-Jolie among the linden trees and strawberry fields. Like a prayer book, the divorcée carries a translation *des poèmes choisis* of Federico, with a prologue by Cassou tracing the theme of loneliness in Spanish poetry since the time of Góngora. She opens the anthology to read to you: *I want to cry aloud in anguish / so you will love me and sob with me / the evensong of the nightingale / pierced by a dagger with your kisses.* She remembers that you had been his friend and asks if he dedicated the poem to you. "*Mais non, madame,*" you reply coolly. "He must have written it for another lover. I turned him into a poet but didn't inspire his verses. When I left him, he tried to kill himself out of despair." Surprised by your cruelty, she looks up with a steadfast gaze. You force yourself to meet it and to peer into her eyes, from whose depths there seems to shine a summer moon. "*Que voyez-vous?* Tell me what you read in me," she asks. "When I try to read your present life, I can't fathom it," you reply at once. "But in some remote past and in another reincarnation, you were an abbess with the same green eyes you have now. You headed a convent on the trek to Santiago. No pilgrims passed by without being bewitched by your glance. You first served them a dinner of trout in hot pepper sauce and chilled claret wine. Then you sported with them under a flurry of fine linen sheets. When they fell asleep, you slit their throats with your teeth. It has all been recorded in a long-lost poem by a forgotten poet, Villaespesa. Like Federico, he was Andalusian, but more gifted in imagination."

Duly impressed, she exclaims: "Of course, it is simply too true! I have always dreamed that in another life I was his green-eyed abbess." You quickly slip away, unsure as to the cause of your fear—the woman or your sudden sexual urge despite your dreadful impotence. That summer, she and Peggy Guggenheim make an unannounced visit to your home in Calador. They are on their way back from Morocco and Guggenheim wants to purchase two of your paintings for her collection. She buys the best she sees and leaves by herself because your future and only wife asks that you paint her portrait as the abbess with the green eyes. Aware that she will seduce you, you agree. Your dread is such that you no longer desire her. While she poses for you one Sunday morning, you blurt out that you will take her to the ends of the earth. You close the sketchbook where you have been working. She follows, obedient as a lamb, as you slowly make the climb to your fisherman's hut. You barely reach the crest when you hold hands and, unflinchingly, stand at the edge of the precipice. At your feet, a bed of immobile clouds extends from the reefs to the horizon. A single ray of sun breaks through it across the bay, lighting the churning gray surf at low tide. *Voilà la mer moutonnée et nouveau-née*, you say to her in a hushed voice. There beneath lies the sea, foaming and newly born, yet older than the beach, the fish, or the shadows.

She turns disconcertingly defenseless and fragile, leans her head on your chest, and breaks into silent tears. When you console her, she trembles in fear. Suddenly you realize that you could possess her, on that dawn of creation as the sea emerges in search of the shallows at the foot of the cliff. At this moment she would yield to your every whim. Without complaint and only to please you, she would throw herself from the cliff. You and I exchange a long glance, and I read in your eyes a glint of sarcasm and lechery. Slowly, at a pace so different from that mad, nightmarish race to the edge of the abyss, you lead her to the fisherman's hut. With one foot, you open the door that your father adamantly refuses to lock, and thus defies the wind to blow the whole thing away if it so chooses. Everything is the same inside as on that early morning when you began the *Incredible Enigma in Velázquez' Studio*, although the aurora borealis no longer lights up the walls. Standing, you undress her with prudent efficiency and toss her clothes onto the floor. She gives herself to you with her eyes closed and head back, as if offering her throat to be slit. Supporting her by an elbow on her hip, you lay her on her side on the cot. Your glance once again meets mine and we both think how much she resembles the *Venus of the Mirror* in your reproduction. It is as if she walked out of the painting to lie down in the same hut where, years ago, you unknowingly painted her portrait in premonition. Quite different from your usual shyness, you strip off your clothes and, with violent thrusts of your body, you take her from behind as if you were ravishing one of your own works of art. Yet through some quirk of fortune, by possessing her you transfer the outrage done to you by Federico, with an act of violation in atonement for other wrongs.

Your future wife submits and arches her hips to meet your thrusts. Panting and groaning, you try to force orgasm while she remains silent, her eyes closed and her teeth clenched. She later admits that she postpones her climax for a more intense pleasure. When at last she comes, with a scream that matches your own, a pelting rain begins to pry at the windowpanes. From then on, you will always take her from behind, sometimes with ardor and at times with amused detachment as if you were never inhibited by women from fear of impotency. You will make love not only at home or between bed sheets in hotels but also in unimaginable places worthy of the lechery of eccentric Uncle Santiago. For example, in the box seats at La Tour de Nesle during a performance of Maeterlinck's *Marie-Magdeleine,* for which you did the stage decoration and costume design. She straddles your lap and writhes in contortions while the chorus cries out on the stage to stone the sinner to death: *Honte! Honte! Chassez-lui! Chassez-lui! Lapidez! A mort! Les pierres! Les pierres!* The curtain descends and the Voice responds from the sets for the one among them without sin to throw the first stone: *Que celui d'entre vous qui est sans péché lui jette la première pierre!* You cast an arrogant look over my shadow as if daring me to partake in the sports of the flesh or accusing me of having died too young to know what they were. *I am condemned to put up with you because you came before me on this earth and with my name. Your punishment is to witness my delight in pleasures that have always been denied you. You're like a jester that shares the bloodline of a King but is deprived of royal privileges.* I ask you whether that does not make us metaphors of Velázquez and Luis de Acedo in your painting. You give a pensive shrug to your shoulders. *It could be. All my paintings are mirrors, although not even I understand the hidden meaning of the images they reflect.* Those years will be your most creative, as you so many times will sadly repeat to me. You refer to a period long ago that begins with the *Incredible Enigma in Velázquez's Studio* and ends with the *Portrait of My Dead Only Brother,* in whose backdrop you include the enigmatic studio transformed into a blurred miniature. You become irate when critics say that what preceded or came after is of negligible worth.

One summer afternoon, between *Incredible Enigma in Velázquez's Studio* and *Portrait of My Dead Only Brother* —while I once again temporarily disappear in sleep—you do a pencil drawing of Aldous Huxley that, upon his death, his widow will donate to the museum in San Diego, California. *There are artists who know how to grow old and artists who don't.* You mention to me later that Huxley said these words while posing for you. *Goya knew, and so did Titian. We will never be sure if his extraordinary* Burial of Christ, *which hangs in the Prado Museum, was painted when he was ninety-eight or ninety-nine. I suppose to grow old with your talent intact must be adequate preparation for immortality. Let me wish you a very happy immortality.*

That autumn, you and your wife will be invited to Argenteuil by the Drameilles so that you can design their pool and mosaic garden benches. It is then that, invisible to other eyes than yours, I awake and once again witness another scene from your life. Madame la Baronne puts you up in one of the guest rooms on the ground floor whose windows open onto a rose garden beneath an iridescent moon. You have no sooner settled in than you and your wife begin a screaming argument. In your rage, you forget that I am present. You shout obscenities and beat on the bed with your cane, while the pallor of your only wife belies her feigned composure in demanding that you keep your voice down so as not to disturb your hosts or the servants. You are beside yourself with anger because you have found out that, while you were in California doing the portrait of Aldous Huxley, in Paris she had resumed her affair with Yves Tanguy. Although you are left cold or even amused by her casual flings—with the androgynous, languid young men that your models bring to the studio, or the minions who bask in your fame and fortune—you go into fits of jealousy if she goes back to her lovers from before you met. *Bref, espèce de putain, tu es une sale garce et je te déteste!* She locks herself in the bathroom so you can gain control of yourself. She comes out naked, brushing her hair. You kiss her passionately, force her onto the bed and, bracing your hands against her breasts and hips, try to take her from behind.

Suddenly she turns and says: *I want you to talk to me and look me in the eye when we make love.* Threatened, your manhood fails you and shrinks to the size of a child's, as a long-forgotten terror returns to haunt you. You turn your back to her to hide your panicked face in the pillow. She sits on the edge of the mattress and lights up a Gitane, looks up at the iridescent moon and, omitting any mention of Tanguy as if he had never crossed your paths, puffs on her cigarette, and describes in detail one of her bisexual young lovers, his virile skills, his adolescent penis—as rosy and erect as the red lily emblazoned on her family shield. The boy is so strong he can mount her for hours on end, bring her to multiple orgasms, and read at the same time the verses from hell of Francesca da Rímini in the *Divine Comedy,* the edition that you illustrated. *E quella a me: Nessun maggior dolore / Che ricordarsi del tempo felice / Ne la miseria: e ciò sa 'l tuo dottore.* She does it to inflame you, but you are devastated. As you yourself will attest, you will never be able to make love to her, not to mention any other woman, again.

And now, my brother, I am not so sure if I am dreaming or remembering another of your quarrels. You and your wife are returning to the United States about the third winter of World War II. In New York, you refuse to exhibit your works with the surrealist exiles from Europe. *Why relive old feuds when we ourselves have changed?* You do a one-man show of your last twenty works which is, according to your wife, the scandalous success *le plus fan . . . tastique* she has dreamt about for months on end.. You believe the public identifies your chimeras with the monsters of the universal subconscious that began that war. *Dalí painted his premonition of the bloodshed of the Spanish Civil War or at least that's what he called one work, which of course has nothing to do with our tragedy. In mine, the Civil War is reduced to a dress rehearsal for the final farce. It's all scenery and costumes, but in the midst of the make-believe, they kill one another for real.* Then you smile wickedly. *From this war, my brother, will come the end of the world. Our private war will be settled in the Valley of Jehoshaphat, because the day is coming when all humankind will devour itself and we will all disappear into the same shadows.* I will never know whether you are sincere or whether you are mocking the war and mankind.

Heaped with praises since the opening of your art exhibit—a smash success with the critics and in terms of sales—you are ready for anything. You hum tunes while your wife drives your Cadillac up the Hudson to a spot between Cold Spring and Nelsonville. It is a summer house loaned to you so that you can enjoy a restful weekend. For hours you drive through a grayish countryside, between cattle pastures and past huge road signs recruiting for the armed services. Suddenly she brakes at the bend of a blind curve. Two young men in grubby sneakers, heavy sweaters, and khaki pants signal for you to stop and pick them up. Without bothering to ask, as if you were as invisible as I myself, she offers them a ride. Unabashed, she asks with obviously wicked intent: *And you, young men, what have you done to help the war effort and free the world?*

They are Catholic seminarians, returning from their Christmas vacation to their diocese in Beacon, in Dutchess County, where you are headed. They tell you how the seminary's old Ford they were driving had given up the ghost that very morning, before you were sent by Providence to rescue them from despairing that no one would take pity on them. You ask your wife in French if she is planning on parodying the old Duchess of Alba, Goya's mistress, who waylaid a seminarian reading his prayers in the Retiro Park and took him to her palace where she seduced him. His innocence lost, the nearly-ordained priest madly asked her to marry him; but her pleasure was sated and her curiosity satisfied. "So she tossed him into the gutter, *tu sais.*" She won't answer you, caught up as she is in telling the seminarians that you are a Swiss couple on a diplomatic mission to the United States. Your task completed, you will be spending a few days at the summer home of some friends just above Cold Spring. Perplexed, they look you over wondering what sort of embassy would send a creature decked out in gold bracelets and amber necklaces.

In Cold Spring, they insist on taking the side road with you. They grew up in the area and know it like the palm of their hand. You have no difficulty finding the place, and your wife insists that they stay for lunch since they are not expected back at the seminary before nightfall. There is a wet chill to the air, and so you turn on the heat and, at your insistence, they light the firewood stacked in the chimney. In the living room there is a bar, as well-equipped as the fireplace, where she prepares some mint juleps with Kentucky bourbon for the three of them while you watch them inscrutably over the rim of your Perrier, hardly taking a sip. As I watch you slouch down in the armchair next to the fire, I am reminded of our father the day of my funeral. Without realizing it, you have stolen the look of abject sorrow he wore the afternoon before conceiving you on the vanished balcony. Out of the corner of their eye, disconcerted from seeing you remain so passive, the seminarians glance your way as your wife begins to kiss them. Their laughter becomes louder and soon they pay no more attention to you than to a long lost memory as their day opens to unexpected horizons. In record time, she has gotten them to undress and to take turns making love to her. They possess her with the virgin clumsiness of untamed colts, with one panting to catch his breath while the other mounts her. *I want you to speak to me. I want to look you in the eye when you make love to me.* Your wife does not glance your way as she straddles her partners, but neither does she close her eyes while she screams and writhes as if in epileptic spasms. You also avoid my glance as she falls asleep with her erstwhile lovers lying across her like two statues knocked over by magic charm.

Your eyebrows furled, your attention seemingly fixed on some remote past, you impress me as one whose center of being can open and close like a book to any random gust of wind. It dawns on me that you have no idea how different we would have been, despite your wasting your life trying to be unique, if I—the ghost of a precocious misfit—had lived to old age like you. In the first place, I have no doubt that I am far more rational. I cannot understand how you so perversely insist that I am the son of Uncle Santiago, and my death the sinful consequence of incest. You truly cannot believe such nonsense. You lie to compensate for your own guilty secret, your subconscious desire for Mother to seduce you. Since that distant moonlit night, she destroyed your will so completely that, even in death, she could force you to give yourself to Federico. What is more, it was she who made you impotent with other women, if—like at Medusa—you dared look them in the eye. She castrated you forever, although you justify sodomy with your wife as vengeance for your rape by Federico. Finally, she almost ruined you as an artist before you had the chance to become one. Your canvases reflect nothing but the monsters that possess you, although you disguise your truth with the occult language of imagery so obscure that at times not even you can decipher it. In times of war, the collective conscience of guilt may be recognizable in your work; yet your confessions and chimeras are inalienably your own. It falls in place now why you could never accept me as first-born, the name my father gave me, or the love he professed for me long after my death. I suppose that for these same reasons you never learned how to grow old, despite Aldous Huxley's best wishes. There is no one behind your tragic mask. You have outlived yourself and turned into your own mockery, as you wander lost in a book that may never see print.

3

My brother fell asleep shortly before dawn. I wonder if he is dreaming about his interview with his author in New York, the day Kennedy was assassinated and Americans climbed to the tops of the trees and to the very clouds to grieve and then forget. If he has returned to that afternoon, in sleep he must remember the interviewer's name and face that his conscious mind forgot. Even though at times my brother contrarily denies the man's existence, I believe their meeting was the starting point for the convergence of our lives with that of Velázquez. It is also possible that my brother is now confiding to Oscar Domínguez his personal view that our lives are parodies of his decalcomanias: *Time splashes memories like brushstrokes over the past, smearing them a little more with each new day until we are left uncertain of the true parameters of our identity.*

No matter which is my brother's dream, I leave him in a knot of blankets and blue sheets. Like a game devil, I clamber up to the rooftop to dangle my legs over the eaves and to spy on the plaza below. Dawn is breaking over an all but abandoned Fondora, as if during the night its denizens and ghosts had filed out in one long procession and lost their way in the shadows. Everyone left, I repeat, except me and my brother, so that we could settle our differences without the restraints of judge or jury. They no sooner had marched out when spring came tiptoeing in. The morning is crisp and breezy, and a hint of rosemary fills the air. Over the pastures lies a fine mist that will evaporate as soon as the wind grows calm and the day turns warm.

I somehow sense that our author is nearby. I feel him at my side even though he is as invisible to me as I am to the eyes of all except my brother. What is more, I could swear that he, overwhelmed by the tedium of writing his book, would like to set fire to these pages and throw me off the rooftop into the smoke. But perhaps I am hallucinating. In fact, what I see below are Mother and Uncle Santiago. They hesitantly enter the plaza from opposite directions, from the right and the left of the par-

171

terres as if afraid to cross in front of our house. Our mother is barefoot as usual and holds the long train of her evening gown by her fingertips. Uncle Santiago is about the age he was when Mother collapsed like a hankie over the balustrade. He seems to have slipped back across the span of time to somewhere in his forties. Judging from his clothes—a snug-fitting jacket with short lapels, the spray of violets in his buttonhole, square-toed patent leather shoes—he is dressed in a style fashionable during the teens. Exchanging glances, my mother and uncle sit on a curved-back stone bench. It is covered with black and white mosaics and stands next to a flower bed of frothy hortensias. "So you're still waiting for your son," asks Uncle Santiago, thinking of my brother. "If he hasn't died yet, he must be ancient." Our mother gives him a long look, as if trying to decide who this apparition could be, and then a polite nod. "I believe that we dead die several times until we finally disappear forever," she whispers. His brow furled in thought, Uncle Santiago agrees. "I feel certain that my son, your first-born, must have died twice, just as you say, and disappeared like time into eternity." With tedious effort, as if she were preaching to the deaf, our mother replies. "I tell you that I will never know if that child was your son. But I assure you that he did not vanish. I feel him very near and can almost swear that he's eavesdropping on us." Not daring to contradict her, Uncle Santiago merely shrugs his shoulders.

Meanwhile the plaza fills unexpectedly with couples adorned in the young century's latest fashions. Blue-uniformed boys arrange wooden chairs around the square while a band—a few bombardons, three violins, two clarinets, a trombone and a cello—sets up at the edge of the gardens. Nervous musicians smile and wring their hands or tune their instruments for the dance to come. Elderly couples flock to the archways and sunny porticos of the adjoining houses to exchange light-hearted gossip. Young lovers weave their way among the trellised flower gardens beneath the acacias, but our mother and Uncle Santiago pay them no attention. They are lost in conversation on the stone bench when they are approached by a man dressed in hunter's garb with a sack slung over his shoulder. He has on a short leather jacket with velvet breeches tucked into high boots. His graying pointed beard reminds me of the aristocratic Vandyke goatee that my brother sometimes wore. The man smiles ambiguously as he pulls out of his moneybag two tickets, the exact color green of his malachite eyes. I shudder in recognition: I have seen him before, one remote August morning, leaning on a window sill from across the street. From his vantage point he spied on my unsuspecting parents' naked bodies as they conceived my brother. I saw him again on the freezing, overcast morning of Uncle Santiago's funeral, as Sanianayake recounted the deathbed conversation he had with the man he swore was my father. *Oh yes, there is no doubt that you are his son! I can still see you sleeping on the sofa while he made love to his sister by the window!* It seems too much to believe that he meant the uncle I now see in this mirage with a violet boutonniere in his lapel. The third time I saw the man with the malachite eyes and Vandyke goatee was in the woods, squatting on a high rock over the riverbed, trying to peep through a resisting branch that broke and fell into the stream.

"The bench will cost you the same as the dance chairs, a silver peseta for the gentleman and no charge for the lady." The voice sounds raspy and distant, as if it were called up from the past after a prolonged muteness or an interminable night. From his vest pocket, my uncle takes out a coin purse, unzips it, and hands over a peseta to the man with the sack. Meanwhile my mother, trying to get a better look at his coppery green eyes, leans over to ask, "Haven't we met before in one of our lives?" Bewildered, he shrugs and shakes his head. "Lives? I only have one and it's eternal as the world. You don't know who I am, but I know you. I saw you many years ago, in the arms of another man."

"Where was that?"

"On a balcony, just around the corner. I was leaning out a window from the other side of the street."

"But that could not have been your house. If you were a neighbor, I would remember you."

"I was sent there to witness your lovemaking. It was barely dawn and a snail crawled up your thigh."

Mother exchanges a silent glance with Uncle Santiago. It is he who now asks the bowed old man, "What about her sons? The boy she conceived that morning and the one who died the night before?" The old man loses composure, as if not expecting such a question from the specters. "I believe one sleeps while the other keeps vigil," he stammers.

Uncle Santiago persists. "Will we see them again, alive or dead?"

"I don't know. I only know the present and the past. The future does not concern me."

The man turns away to resume collecting for the dance chairs, when my mother stops him. "And my husband? The man I made love to on the balcony?" Without turning to face her, the old man answers. "You'll never see him again. He has vanished like smoke into the night."

My mother suddenly starts to weep. Surprised, I realize that this is the first time I've seen her in tears. Uncle Santiago must be thinking the same, as she had never before cried in our presence.

"He disappeared with Federico. They left only their names behind." These are the final words of the man with the malachite eyes before he disappears into the crowd. Uncle Santiago is pensive as he returns his coin purse to his vest pocket. He now takes his sister's hands but does not look her in the eye since he cannot share her grief. From across the street, I try to read my mother's face as others would read a book. Eyes downcast over her bare feet, her face pink from the crisp morning air, her temples have the purplish tinge of winter edelweiss unique to apparitions lost in thought.

The crowd applauds as a skyrocket explodes over the plaza and a flock of white doves is released from a balcony grate into the sky. To my surprise, my mind flashes back to another festival—my last one in life—that I now recall from darkest oblivion. My father had announced that we would avoid the season's vulgarity of street dances and carnivals by going to a spa where he had already made reservations. Betraying no emotion, my mother consented. If she could avoid the nastiness of an argument, she would allow her husband to control her. It was dawn when, beneath another flight of pigeons, we boarded a local train on the new platform leading from the tree-lined boulevard. The train was almost empty and the station master, doffing his striped cap, stalled the departure to chat with my father through the train window. He asked whether the uprising in Cuba would turn into a full-blown war. His son had been called up but, so far, had not seen active duty. A colonial conflict could whisk his boy off to the jungle to have his throat slit by Mambi warlords. My father shook his jowls and shouted that even Spain, with its corrupt monarchy and laissez-faire politicians, had the sense to realize that open warfare would be a lost cause from the start. Cuba would gain its freedom, because we could not go on indefinitely usurping an island at the far end of the universe simply to maintain protectionist tariffs at home. "Did you know that the Cuban creoles cannot buy their clothes from Florida, a stone's throw away? Those savages must cover their asses with rags manufactured here in Tarrasa! Is that not an outrage?" The station master cast nervous glances over the empty platform. "By Christmas, we'll be out of

Cuba without a man lost. Then we'll garrote the Queen María Cristina in the Puerta del Sol and proclaim our Republic from the gallows!" He was still raving when the station master suddenly hailed the train off. An hour later, we got off at the spa, while a heavy-set bearded blackamoor collected our suitcases and strapped them to his cart. My father stopped at a kiosk to buy a newspaper, which he used to fan himself on the way up the eucalyptus-lined boulevard. The porter sat me on top of the loaded cart he pushed up the hill to the hot springs. My mother walked at my side, holding my hand and smiling reassuringly from time to time. Her thoughts were elsewhere. I could see myself, perhaps on an imperceptible horizon reflected in her innermost being, watching her from this very same rooftop as she traced her steps along the steep path of another time.

Once my parents had bathed in the healing pools, we had lunch beneath the high casements of the almost empty dining hall. They then went to their room for a long siesta while I entertained myself by tracing the clouds in the sky. Later that afternoon, we took a stroll through the almond groves beyond the hot springs. My father said he was taking us to the landscape of his youth, part of which he spent in a nearby farmhouse, where rest and mountain air erased a wet dark spot in his left lung. He swore that there was no other place, not even in the immediate area, where the mountain ridge turned so blue as to be almost transparent. He may have been right, because I would never again see, except in a few of my brother's paintings, such translucent peaks and slopes as on that afternoon. This was the first time that my father returned to that special place of his childhood, because he grew to be strong and massive as a fighting bull. The landscape had changed over time, or perhaps his memory was playing tricks, feigning to remember what it had long forgot. He was looking for a pasture next to a pond bordered with chestnut trees, where he hunted for turtles toward the end of his convalescence. He finally found the field after many false starts and wrong turns onto overgrown paths that led nowhere. The pond was at the foot of the chestnut grove bordering an upland meadow covered with hollyhock. But my father let out a scream in amazement, because in the middle of the clearing stood a crumbling Romanesque monastery that he never mentioned when describing his former haunt.

"The ruins were there all along. You just forgot them," said my normally reticent mother in the exasperated tone she used to pinpoint the obvious.

"None of this was here before! I swear I am seeing this monastery for the first time!"

My mother, ignoring the oath of an atheist, responded icily. "I don't see how these time-corroded walls could have risen and then tumbled down by themselves."

"And I don't see any turtles either." Feeling cheated, too young to understand what was happening, I sided with my mother. "No, there are no turtles," she agreed, stabbing at an anthill with the tip of her parasol. My father was too absorbed in the ruins to listen. Scattered over the ground were stone slabs with blurred inscriptions, decapitated statues, altars split in two as if by a colossus with the slice of his hand. He kneeled before a stele and used a fistful of weeds to dust off its inscription. The letters were large and legible, although partially covered by dried moss.

"*Aegle, Erytheis, Hespera, atque Arethusa,*" my father read aloud. Suddenly, as if awaiting her cue, my mother chimed in with a dialogue overheard solely by the mute heavens: "These are the four Hesperides and this must be their garden, the one with the golden apples."

"The Hesperides?" my father asked in a hesitant voice. "How do you know that?" She shrugged her shoulders, her hands clasped and leaning on her parasol. "I don't know how I know it. It's as if someone forced me to recite it."

They said no more and I had my attention turned elsewhere. I stopped in front of a niche in an ivy-covered altar where, staring straight at me, was perched an owl. But for its huge, coppery green eyes, I would have mistaken it for one more statue, gray and motionless. Neither did I so much as blink. I submerged myself in its stare as if, completely detached from the world around me, I had dived into a pond that took me back to the forgotten glow of my mother's womb. I felt my father's hand on my shoulder and heard him call my name, bringing me back to the realm of reality: to a flock of bleating sheep with bells jangling on their necks and to the pungent smell of basil in the enclosing dusk air. "Let's get out of here," I heard my mother say. "I'm afraid."

Now, so many years later, while white doves fly into the sky and a skyrocket explodes in a panoply of sparks falling over the plaza, my mother's apparition repeats these same words to her brother's shadow: "Let's get out of here. I'm afraid." Perplexed, Uncle Santiago shakes his head. A lively waltz opens the dance and, although I can make out her every whisper, perhaps he does not hear my mother's words over the music. Watching her brother search the crowd for her husband, she cautions him: "My husband has been erased for good. We'll never find the old man with the green eyes either. I don't know who he is, but I immediately recognized the look he gave me." The music softens, the cadence slows, and the young couples begin to dance. Girls with roses pinned to their bodices and young men, their hair parted down the middle of the forehead, swirl in front of the stone bench.

"How can you recognize his look if you don't know who he is?"

"He had the eyes of the owl in the Garden of the Hesperides."

"The Garden of the Hesperides?"

"There are four Hesperides, who at times are mistaken for clouds in the western sky but who tend the tree with the golden apples. It's guarded by a dragon with his tail twisted seven times around its trunk." Her brother interrupts to add: "The garden is at the western edge of the world, where the ocean ends at the strait. You have never been that far. You never even went as far as my house in Croydon, England."

"Everything must shrink as it passes from myth into life," my mother speculates. "When I was there, the tree had disappeared, but the site was only an hour by train from our house. I found the place with my husband and my older boy, the son you always thought was yours."

"What was left of the garden?"

"The garden? Nothing. A monastery had been built on the site. We found it in ruins, but on a broken slab of stone, we read the names of the four Hesperides."

"If at the dawn of time, the garden was at the edge of the world where the sun sets, it must be very far away. It's barely dawn here in the plaza and it will take an entire day for night to fall." My mother does not reply. She has once again retreated to the depths of her soul and, entranced, follows the dancers and the musicians. The waltz is almost a murmur: the sound of water splashing over a clouded mirror or the soft chirp of birds in a nameless forest. My mother quietly picks up a rose that has fallen at her feet and places it in her lap. Watching the silent couples waltz by, she whispers to my uncle: "They've forgotten that, like us, they are dead. They dance because this is the Festival of Fondora."

Older people now come up and sit near the stone bench, their backs turned from the plaza. They are wealthy cattle owners in crinkling jackets with watch fobs dangling over their waist sashes. The wives, their hair held high with combs and their breasts trussed up under lace ruffles, look like a gaggle of broody hens.

The men greet our uncle: "Pleased to see you, it's been a long time. Did you come all the way from London for our festival?" "Where are your husband and your sons?" the women ask our mother. "Will they be along later?" Without taking her eyes off the rose she has shredded in her lap, my mother replies in a low voice: "They won't be coming. All three are dead, just like us." Knowing her younger son is still alive, she lies to keep her answer curt. The ensuing silence is broken when you, sir, stop the waltz and everyone applauds. Hand in hand, the young couples walk to the banquet tables beneath the porticos for a glass of lemonade or sugared strawberries served on hand-painted plates depicting hunting scenes of wild ducks on a wintery afternoon. "Death? What is that?" The women exchange smiles behind their Valencia fans and chuckle as if they were telling naughty jokes behind their husbands' backs. "Death is like a dream," Uncle Santiago responds, "or like memories tucked away in a closed book." The women do not answer because the music strikes up again, and the couples join in the two-step, the polka, the Boston, the mazurka, the Polish hop, and the Blue Danube waltz. "Why aren't you dancing?" the shades of my mother's acquaintances wonder aloud, while one of the matrons flashes a smile of gold teeth that evokes memories supposedly long dead. "On Christmas Eve, when women were allowed in the casino for the winter ball, we loved to see you dance the lancers and the tango with your husband, even though he was a bit clumsy and heavy on his feet." "Yes, my dear, it's so true," chimes in a woman in a purple dress and plumed hat. "We'll never forget the year that Her Majesty Queen Victoria Eugenia stopped in Fondora on her way back from Paris and our town fathers brought her to the casino. I remember that I was seated beside her since I was the mayor's wife. *Who is that lady who dances so lightly and gracefully to everything from the cakewalk to the polka, even the stately schottische?* doña Victoria asked me, and I blushed red as a beet since it was the first time I was ever addressed by a queen. Her strange accent had me befuddled, and the look in her eyes ran shivers through me. *My Lady, she is,* I stammered as soon as I found my voice, *the wife of a solicitor.* The Queen seemed perplexed. *She dances divinely, but she is a very sad woman,* was all she said."

The woman's story is received with a strained silence. The musicians are on break between numbers and happily fanning themselves with their score sheets. Your hand, sir, has changed the sky to mother-of-pearl, crisscrossed by two clouds sailing to the mountains like birds on the wind. "Why don't you two dance?"

the women urge Mother and Uncle Santiago. "You, señora, would dance far better with your brother than with your husband," says the woman with the gold-capped teeth. "Besides, as alike as you are, you would make a handsome couple. You aren't by chance twins, are you?" Lost in thought as if in a trance, Mother makes no reply; so Uncle Santiago answers for her, saying merely that they are brother and sister but not twins. Then, at the insistence of the neighbor women, he leads my mother by the arm to the center of the plaza. The other couples retire to the porticos, the band begins to play a very slow waltz, and the crowd watches in amazement at how effortlessly my mother glides barefoot in her brother's arms.

"Do you remember this music?" Uncle Santiago asks.

"I remember it quite well. Do you know the name of it?"

"It's an old forgotten song, but it was popular in our youth. It's called 'The Garden of the Hesperides,' if I remember correctly."

"Of course not. That would be redundant."

"Then it goes by the name of another myth."

"Yes, that's it. 'The Golden Rain,' the rain that fell the morning I conceived my son." The waltz suddenly ends or slips away into silence, but my mother and Uncle Santiago continue to spin beneath the pearly sky.

"Which son are you talking about?"

"Which one do you think? The boy I conceived in the state of grace." Uncle Santiago silently gropes to makes sense of her words. Finally, looking straight into his sister's eyes, he recites: "And the pain not to be what is was I have been, / the loss of the kingdom that was mine on this earth, / the thought that for naught I could never have dreamed, / and the dream is my life since my moment of birth!"

"Who wrote that?" Her tone betrays worry or impatience.

"I forget. I'm sure that these lines foretell everything. I wonder who they refer to."

They say no more and continue to waltz while a lizard slithers across the eave of an overhanging roof. He has the same color eyes as the old man with the money sack and the Vandyke goatee: the one who vanished from the dance as if you, sir, regretted inviting him in the first place. Or perhaps he came and went on his own volition even if you wanted him to stay.

"You were the love of my life," whispers Uncle Santiago in my mother's ear.

"I loved you too, but the love of my life was my son. My second son." Not understanding her, her brother simply nods. My mother continues in a detached tone, as if she were talking about a unavoidable fact far removed from her feelings and outside her sphere of existence. "I made love to him. He was the rival lover that made you so jealous. He aroused me like no other man: not even you or my husband. In the midst of my dreams—nightmares of crowned ramparts, striped like tigers in the shadows—I would awake desiring my son." Uncle Santiago stares at his sister wide-eyed, as if trying to recognize her. "Do you know what you are saying? Can you hear what you're telling me?" They are now dancing so slowly they seem like toy figurines on a music box winding down at the decline of an entire era: the era of Freud as he lay dying in his home on Elsworth Road, of Gherardo de Sagra singing Filottete, and of my sister-in-law and the albino antique dealer in Pisa or Pistoia bargaining over the throne of the *Can Grande della Scalla*, lord of Verona: *Pago, e voglio che mi si tratti ammodo*, to which he replied that the work was priceless, *egregia amica, io parlo delle cose eterne*. It was the end of the era of the baroness of Drameille, poking at her *gâteau feuilleté à la crème* and bemoaning her deceased husband: *A-t-il aimé vraiment? A-t-il vraiment rêvé? Je ne saurais te dire;* of monsieur Archimandrite or Archi-prêtre flying over this very plaza, shouting wildly from his air balloon's basket: *Une femme est morte ou au moins évanouie là dédans, sur la balustrade!* Of Uncle Santiago driving his open carriage across the snow, followed by young Sanianayake, in turban and leggings strapped at mid-calf. Of Federico's and my father's spec-ters, blue from the cold, calmly conversing on a winter morning: *"I think back on who I used to be and I can't recognize myself." "We were surely shadows back then. We dead have no other reality than the present, even if we cannot fathom it."* And of the green-eyed old man squatting on the top of the rocks, watching the concentric waves made by the fallen branch. The music is winding to a close, and my mother and uncle have the last dance. The dying strains con-jure up paintings like *Incredible Enigma in Velázquez's Studio*. It is a portrait of the painter in the act of painting, of Damiana gazing into a mirror held by Francisquito de Asís, and of His Majesty pushing open the door to the workshop. *Don Diego*, the melody strums, echoing the words of the court jester, *you will enter a labyrinth of your own design where you'll be lost if you don't let me lead the way. In this adventure, I'll be your guide and scribe.* The monarch's voice from the doorway resounds in the cadence: *Continue, my friends. I don't mean to interrupt. I missed Mass because my cold kept me bedridden. I got up and thought I would shake off my headache by seeing what don Diego was dabbling with in the Treasure House.*

Like a sharp refrain, Uncle Santiago's shocked words can be heard over the music. "Do you know what you're saying. Can you hear what you're telling me?" But my mother continues her reveries. "One summer night, I dreamt about the sculpture of a nude boy. It was lying on the site of the medieval monastery my husband and I found but that he swears never existed. The statue had its eyes closed and its head turned as if blindly trying to look over its shoulder. A white sheep appeared from the shadows and started to run its tongue over the nude torso as if trying to lick the salt from its loins. From the statue I heard the sobbing of a child—trapped in the unflinching stone, swallowed up by the mountain, and perhaps eaten away by remorse. When the whimpers changed to sighs of pleasure, I think I dreamed that I awoke. . . ." "Stop! I can't bear to hear any more, even though I must have suspected everything while we were alive. If I think back to that time, it makes hideous sense. Say no more, I beseech you." Oblivious to her brother's presence, my mother does not seem to hear his plea. Her speech rambles as if she were talking to her reflection in the mirror. "Sleepwalking, I tiptoed out of the bedroom so as not to awake my husband. Still asleep, I went down to the beach and followed the edge of the tide across the bay to the cliffs beyond. The only light came from the far-off lanterns on the fishing boats beneath the stars. There was a boat stranded on the dunes. Nearby I found the boy, but he was not made of stone. He was lying naked, and the profile of his face was outlined against the curve of his arm. Once in a while, a wave washed against his legs without disturbing his sleep. I stretched out next to him and traced my tongue over his moist thighs. It was then I realized that I was awake and that the statue, trembling in my embrace, was my son."

In no longer than it takes a fish to dart or a voice to echo, our uncle flashed a somber glance over his sister's face before shaking his head to say: "No one has the right to judge anyone. We could condemn only if hell existed." As automatically as if she were reciting a well-known theorem, my mother replied: "But at the brink of limbo, there is only a blank page into which we vanish." Insistent, my brother repeats: "You have been the love of my life and my death. I neither condemn nor condone what you've done." In a trance, my mother ignores him to return to her reveries. "From time to time, I raised my head to see him writhe in shame, too weak to resist my caresses. Then I wrapped my arms around his hips and traced his loins with my mouth. When at last we screamed in unison, a fishing boat rowed by. Two fishermen gaped at us in bewilderment, not sure if we were real or they were hallucinating. They rowed off in silence without so much as a glance back." His face pensive, Uncle Santiago shakes his head. "Forget them. Soon we won't even be shadows. Remember only that your brother truly loved you." Forcing herself to believe him, my mother stares him in the eyes. "Perhaps I loved you too. I'm not sure. What sense does it make if we're about to be erased?" Furling his brow, my uncle darts his eyes over the plaza. Despite his sister's belief that the dead die twice before vanishing forever, he seems to be searching the crowd for the green-eyed man: the one who claimed to live one life, eternal as the world. "It may make no sense at all, but I never stopped loving you." As they dance, they begin to vanish into the morning mist. Their specters turn into outlines, the outlines into nameless shadows, and the shadows then disappear into the void.

I suddenly realize that I do not remember my mother making love to my brother on the beach. Perhaps I witnessed their abandon like a dumbfounded fisherman and blocked it from memory out of jealous shame. It is also possible that the scene was no more than the raving of my mother's lurid imagination—as the epitome of the love she felt for the beloved son conceived, not by her husband, but by the golden rain. Whatever the case, it is another rain that now distracts my thoughts from them. It begins in the form of a fine mist, falling imperceptibly as a bubble lighting on the ocean, and suddenly turns into a downpour forcing musicians and neighbors, forgetting the vanished couple who danced at their urging, to rush for shelter under the archways. The entire plaza is in turmoil as laughing partners flee from the quickly disassembled stage. Their jackets pulled like hoods over their heads, the men bump into one another; and the women, with skirts hiked high, squeal as they leap over puddles. Like a swarm of bees that forgot they were extinct, the specters huddle under the awnings. Fearful and forlorn, they stare from the porches, looking much like our early ancestors watching the rain from out their caverns. Without warning, the same hand of destiny that swept away Mother and Uncle Santiago now begins to change the specters into crude scribbles and to push them back to the line on the page where they first appeared.

You seem, sir, to be enjoy making the scene play like the preview to a destiny that I will soon share. First the musicians vanish and then entire families are blotted out, while young couples smile or kiss passionately in the shadows. Women raise handkerchiefs to dry their faces, and a few dandies take out pocket combs to rake their hair into place. The rain is now a raging storm streaked with lightning bolts. Thunder echoes off the valleys and pine-scented gusts of wet wind cut across the dark skies. Rivulets streak down the curbs and wind through the side streets. Attached to the eaves encircling the plaza, gargoyles release their downpour. They are monsters with flat expressionless faces: a conclave of stone-faced judges presiding over the living and the dead.

Once the last shadows disappear into the archway, the storm abates and the sun rises over a luminous new day. From the nearby highway can be heard the rush of morning traffic, like the crash of waves combing ancient, worn-out seas. I can sense the clangs and knocks of the city as it wakes, yawning behind its closed balconies, drawn curtains, and barred doors. Coffee pots perk and great rounds of toast are spread with sage-flavored white honey. Men and women dress in a daze and look in the mirror without seeing their face. Perhaps the light will awaken my brother. Stretched on his back in bed, he will blink and rub his eyes to try to recognize the stuccoed pattern on the ceiling. Perhaps in his semi-conscious mind, he will hum the verses clarifying *Incredible Enigma: And the pain not to be what it was I have been, / the loss of the kingdom that was mine on this earth, / the thought that for naught I could never have dreamed, / and the dream is my life since my moment of birth!* In the blurred memory of dreams, a woman may wonder: Who wrote that? And the man who recited the stanza will answer, *I forget. But I'm sure that the verses foretell everything. I wonder to whom they refer.* Meanwhile, the first crimson shadows streak over the walls and parterres. One is hurled like a javelin to split the plaza diagonally. I trace it down the overhanging eaves, across the plane trees filled with chirping birds, to the curved back of the bench where Mother sat with Uncle Santiago. Camouflaged in the mosaic of the glazed tiles, glistening in the morning rain, lurks a solitary snail: blacked-mouthed and tiger-striped.

4

I BARELY RECOGNIZED HER, AND SHE TOOK ME FOR A GHOST. WHILE *I was on Pheasant Isle arranging at our sovereign's behest the marriage of our Infanta to His Most Christian Highness, Louis XIV of France, word spread through the court that I had died. No one knows who started the rumor or whether it was done by mistake or out of malice of forethought. The whispers spread from the Palace to Caños del Peral, from the Prado to the Rastro. Only Juana refused to believe it, although she admits that she awaited my return in dread. Her passionate greeting surprised me, because ever since the death of our daughters and our sweet Inés Manuela, the older granddaughter, my wife quietly dried up like sun-scorched esparto grass. I no sooner walked into the Treasure House than she tearfully hugged and kissed me on the mouth in front of my son-in-law and his bride-to-be.*

"I never doubted that you were alive!" *she shouted turning to the others.* "If he died, then everything is a lie, including the sun in the high heavens!"

My son-in-law trembles like a rabbit as he throws his arms around my neck. I notice that he addresses me familiarly by my first name. I tell him: "Go ahead and call me Diego, in the name of the living God! We're fellow painters and, what's more, you're the father of my granddaughter!" *Couched behind Juan Bautista, his soon-to-be second wife smiles nervously and twitches as if she felt unwelcome.*

"Don Diego, I am planning on remarrying. She too is named Francisca and will love my Inés Manuela like her real mother. I pray that you and doña Juana will understand and give us your blessing." *I gave my consent and, since he bowed down on his knees, blessed him. It was then I remembered that I had never given my daughter the gift from Pope Innocent. I found it in the cedar coffer and, to Juan Bautista's amazement, offered the gold chain to him for his new bride. That his wife would replace my daughter and be stepmother to my grandchild was no cause for grief. I grieved for having outlived, as the buffoon had predicted at the Royal Hunting Lodge, both my daughters and the first Inés Manuela. I was also taken aback by the coincidence that the bride-to-be had the same name as my dead daughter. Two Franciscas and two Inés Manuelas.*

How many times must we repeat ourselves without ever learning who we are?

"Alive, yes, but exhausted," I admit, "and burning with fever. While I lie down, would you bring me up a pot of elderberry tea? Tomorrow I'll be like new again. And while you're at it, have Acedo come by. I want him to relay to His Majesty the news that I'm back and why I'm late in making my bows."

They insist that we summon Dr. Moles, the head physician, to have me auscultated and leeched. But I refuse and, keeping my reasons to myself, repeat that I must see the buffoon. Begrudgingly, they agree. Juana and Juan Bautista undress me to my breeches, which I will not take off. They sit me on the bed to slip my shirt over my shoulders and stand back gaping at the shriveled pallid skeleton I returned from my trip: the deep-sunk eyes, parchment skin, collar bone and ribs almost poking through my wasted flesh. Shaking her head, my wife declares that I cannot go on like this. In a trice, she promises, she will prepare me a hot malmsey wine and a tender parsleyed chicken.

"What have they done to you on that island!" she wails. From beneath the sheets, I shrug and briefly recount my stations of the cross: from court we made Alcalá de Henares in one day, blessed by a brisk tail wind that combed the broomsedge on our path. From Alcalá we stopped at Guadalajara, Jadraque, Berlanga, San Esteban de Gormaz, and a few villages whose names I forget, until we reached Burgos. From Burgos we went to Briviesca, from there to Pancorbo, Miranda, Tolosa, Hernani, San Sebastián and made Fuenterrabía by the first of May. The King took two weeks to catch up with us. While we were burning up the highways at full gallop, His Majesty's entourage was having a fine time fishing and attending bullfights along the way. When the King arrived on Pheasant Isle, the palace was in gleaming array for the wedding and celebrations, and I was decked out in a satin suit with silver brocade and starched ruff. On my chest was embroidered the Cross of Saint James and from my neck hung the Apostle's insignia, a gold scallop shell encrusted with diamonds and emeralds. It wasn't until the trip home that I finally succumbed to poor appetite, fatigue, and high fever. I could no longer mount horseback and, shivering and swearing, had to be carried by litter. As I had never been sick in my life, at times I wondered whether that prostrate old man wasn't someone else.

"Diego, the buffoon has arrived, but he's not alone. His Majesty, God save Him, insists on seeing you at once."

Juana had just left a pot of elderberry tea and the servant had already served the steaming goblet of mulled wine to wash down the all but untouched chicken breast when my wife returned with the news. She should have been accustomed to the monarch's frequent visits, but each *stop he makes at the Treasure House seems to her like the first. She is always taken by surprise, more put off than pleased, as if awakened in the middle of a quiet sleep by an early-breaking dawn.*

"Bring in our King and Lord, even if I only asked for the fool."

Juana ushers them in and, after making her reverences, retires. The King's blue eyes are glistening, and he appears happy to see me. But a hint of concern crosses his face. I try to sit up to kiss his rings, but he takes me by the shoulders and leans me back against the pillows. Eyebrows knitted and arms crossed behind his back, Luis de Acedo keenly observes us. In one of his eyes, I think I see a cloud that didn't used to be there.

"Who spread the word that you died on the island or in Fuenterrabía? I must find out," announces the King. "And for what purpose? Any fool can lie to his heart's content, but what I don't understand is how it spread like wildfire through all Madrid. The court is nothing but a bellows."

"That rubbish must have come from Your Majesty's first wife, may her soul rest in peace," Primo answers. "If she can convince Sister María de Agreda that she's in limbo paying for her sins of vanity, she can whisper tall tales to any lady-in-waiting just to amuse herself. Ghosts, as everyone knows, are real gossips."

"Leave the dead in peace," the King admonishes. "We'll be sharing eternity with them soon enough. Besides, the Queen suffered enough in this world because of me. Don't do disservice to her memory."

"I gladly pardon anyone who swore that I died and went to a better beyond," I tell the monarch. "Knowing his penchant for tricks, I wouldn't be surprised if it were the fool himself."

"If you believe that, Your Excellency, it's you who's the fool!" Acedo is truly incensed. "I couldn't possibly have spread that rumor. In my chronicle, the three of us are still breathing and I'm recording our words as we speak. There has to be another historian who records our lives and my tale from a different vantage ground."

All ears, the King neither speaks nor so much as twitches a muscle. He could be mistaken for a wax statue with page-boy hair and bluish wrist veins. I have done so many portraits of him that, if I close my eyes, his face appears before those of my own daughters. With a deep sigh, he shrugs and turns to me.

"Books within books!" he protests, his arms outstretched. "Records of the dwarf's every scribble! True lies lying tangled in truths! It was never so complicated when we used to separate yesterday from tomorrow and history from chivalric tales. Ever since you started painting mirrors and windows, the past intrudes into the present and human beings become brushstrokes. You'll never be forgiven for turning the world inside out."

"I merely painted it as it is and not how we see it. That's the lesson I learned from the elder Herrera."

"Our times are reflected in your paintings and that's where they will be immortalized. Unless another fire like that in the Royal Salon burns them up first, in which case we, your models, will have lived in vain."

"But, My Lord, that's all over. Your Majesty, I beg you not to torment yourself over the world I stretched on the rack, so to speak. I know I'll never paint again."

From the silent looks that the King and the fool exchange, I see that my confession comes as no surprise. Indeed, I am the one startled when don Luis scrambles off the chest and leaps onto a table by the door in order to peer into the oeil de boeuf. He seems oblivious to the affront of turning his back to His Majesty. So does King Felipe himself, even though in another court such improper behavior would be met with a lashing. In the meantime, His Sovereign, like an uncertain actor, begins to mouth lines he knows partly by heart and mostly by faith. My affliction is no more than life's fatigue compounded by the exhaustion from the trip. But to erase all doubts, he will summon his two personal physicians, don Miguel de Alba y don Pedro de Chávarri. He reminds me that no one can refuse a royal decree and, besides, autumn soon will have the Guadarrama Mountains brimming with deer. I must do another portrait of him dressed like a huntsman with a greyhound at his feet, like the one I painted when we were young.

"I don't remember the hound's name, but I recall that he died shortly thereafter from a chancre on its haunches. Every time I look at your portrait, it brings me back to the afternoon you sketched it out. I can still smell the pungent air through the oakgrove and hear the yelps of that old pack of dogs." I listen and vaguely recall the hunting party. It conjures up the picnic at the Royal Hunting Lodge when don Luis told me that I would outlive Ignacia, Francisca, and my first granddaughter. But I'll never paint that outing because I can't capture it. It would be better told in plain language that mentions us all, including our ghosts.

As if he were reading my mind, without turning around or unfolding his hands at his back, the buffoon addresses me: *"Don Diego, I too am almost finished with my work. But before I can affix the end period, I must know why you summoned me to the Palace Treasure House."*

"Just say I wanted to see you on my return from Pheasant Isle."

"I could but no one would believe it. Tell me the truth."

"The truth? Haven't you figured it out already? What is your truth except what you fantasize in your scribbles?"

"That may be so, but I'm not so sure," he says, half turning his head to look beady-eyed at His Majesty and me. *"I may be drafting my work with the inadvertent urge to translate the portrait that you did of me.*

*Maybe my chronicle and I will end up as details in another painting,
where my portrait is a miniature reflected by a magical little mirror from
the canvas back into the book. But something's missing, something you're
keeping from us."*

My fatigue is overwhelming and my soul weary. On Pheasant Isle,
His Most Christian Highness the King of France broke protocol to pull
me aside. I do not know anymore if I'm remembering or imagining what
His Majesty said to me then: "Is it true, as my father-in-law boasts,
that you met Rubens in person in your youth? What was your impression
of that monster?" Feeling weak, I replied indecorously, "My Lord, he
said that the end of the world draws near when the avenging angel will
bring time to a close. To quote Rubens, we are approaching Doomsday
in this time of decadence because of women's shriveled breasts and puny
nipples." The King burst into peals of laughter that brought tears to his
eyes, smudging his false eyelashes and tinted eyebrows. His shirt ruffles
and lace cuffs gave off the musky scent of civet, and his wig, the fumes
of Chios turpentine.

"Don't be shy, Your Excellency," the buffoon interrupts. "Confess
everything that you had in mind to tell me."

"I'll tell you another day," I answer in a wisp of voice more like a
thread of water dribbling from the roof of my mouth. "We mustn't bore
His Majesty with our problems."

Don Felipe sides against me. "I'll be offended if you don't. Your father's
dead, so you're left with me. Besides I'm your conscience by divine right."

Any other afternoon, I could have resisted their insistent entreaties
but today I am too weary. Stretched out on my side, I struggle to lift
the covers that lie heavy as stone across me. It is Acedo who pulls them
back gingerly, like a puppet whose strings are pulled by invisible fingers.
I close my eyes and feel my heart in my chest, but as the dwarf slips my
breeches off from under my shirttail, the heartbeats seem more like the
thrashing of a bird felled by a hunter's bullet. I suddenly remember the
hunting parties that don Felipe took me on to snap me out of my boredom.
I can smell the pungent air through the oakgrove and hear the yelps of
that old pack of dogs. Then my memory clouds and I look up to see the
sovereign and his buffoon examining my genitals. They are staring at
the chancre sore that erupted at the base of my foreskin the moment I
entered Fuenterrabía. No one speaks while Acedo pulls up my pants and
covers me up again. Whether in my dream or half awake, I know their
looks are pitying.

"Have you been whoring behind my back?" The discreet tone of the
King's voice betrays his concern.

"Art is my lover and has given me lovely children." Poorly quoting
Michelangelo, I answer with bravado more suitable to a gentleman of
pleasure than to a man of honor.

"*Your Excellency, answer our questions as if we were your father confessors,*" retorts Acedo. "*I never took the Hippocratic oath but, believe me, I know more than I let on. And a lot more than the butchers who pass themselves off as court physicians. Unless that chancre sore is a sugar gumdrop, you've been sporting with loose women.*"

"*Only in thought, and that was with Damiana.*" My answer shocks me since Damiana has been dead for years. In my memory she is fragile as a petal pressed in a book that, if opened to the light of day, would fly off on the first puff of wind.

"*And in deed. Now let's be serious, in the name of God,*" the King cuts me short.

"*Very serious,*" Acedo chimes in. "*This may be a mock court, but it's not the Inquisition. We're only asking for your good.*"

"*Only for your good,*" the King seconds.

The register of his voice makes me half open my eyes and peer closely at him sitting on a stool at my bedside. Normally pale, his face has turned white and his blue eyes have waxed over from worry. I distantly recall the day he stood before the equestrian portrait I did of the Count Duke of Olivares. The sky is supposed to look like that of Fuenterrabía in flames the day it falls to Olivares. But it looks to me more like a backdrop of half-woven brocade. Make-believe truth masks behind your make-believe lie. The portrait exists and it is still unfinished; but what I cannot figure out is whether the King made those statements in my studio or whether they, like ourselves, were mere words on paper. In either case, it seems a paradox that I should have painted a Fuenterrabía that Olivares would never take and that I wouldn't see until my chancre erupted.

"*Did you have a mistress, yes or no?*"

"*Although it seems incredible, I was unfaithful to Juana only in my dreams.*"

"*Tell us about those dreams.*"

I whisper that dreams are always in the past, because they fall to shreds in memory. Then unexpectedly my words drift back to my youth in Pacheco's home. I return to a long-lost Seville where I daydreamed about being the court painter before my sudden and unlikely appointment that makes my life read more like fiction than fact. I retrace my steps through the Baratillo bordellos that I frequented with the other apprentices. The whorehouses were immaculate, far better kept than anywhere I could imagine: lavender-smelling beds, geraniums in the window planters, and pictures of saints Justa and Rufina above the armoires. Everything looked freshly scrubbed and no one scrimped on hauling the water casks all the way from the Fount of the Three Shoots. The streets outside reeked of the discarded skins, guts, and blood of animals from the slaugh-

terhouse; of the sweat and blasphemy of the butchers; of chamber pots emptied from the windows into the street with shouts of "Gardyloo!"; of rats racing in packs through the maze of back alleys or fearlessly nursing their young in the archways; of gangs of street urchins rummaging through the garbage to haul off a worm-eaten lamb's head, rotten testicles, or butchered calf's eyes tossed into the gutter. Taking refuge in the bordello was like being released from hell to stroll through the Pearly Gates. I forget the whores' names, maybe because I always figured they were fake. In bits and pieces a few faces reappeared in my canvases painted from memory: a glance, black as pitch, the eyes of a pure-blooded Abencerraje beauty; the smile of a young whore, her face half hidden in a fold of her shawl; a grinning Gibraltar gypsy with a pink carnation in her teeth. Better actresses than I ever saw on the Buen Retiro stage, they were all accomplished on the tambourine, castanets, zither, pan flute, rabeck, bagpipe, jingles, and piccolo. Those with husky voices sang flamenco seguidillas and soleares. The clear-throated girls joined in the less difficult verses. Come fast now you're coming / Come fast now I feel ye / Come while I'm filling / Your lap of white lily. *From them I learned the great drama of love, especially when they faked it. They were equally convincing feigning tenderness, orgasm, ingratitude, or jealousy. Intuiting their clients' penchants and weaknesses, they could suffer spasms of passion or lie stone still as if dead. At the time I was so lazy that I could have spent my entire life in a brothel, and be spoiled like a old pimp by his tender-hearted whores. At the insistence of the Monarch and the fool, I pull these haphazard memories out of darkest oblivion while I slip over the threshold of sleep. Acedo violently shakes me awake.*

"However you care to describe her, one of those sluts or sisters of mercy gave you the French pox."

"What foolishness are you talking about?"

"Yours. His Majesty don Felipe will back me up. He knows far more than I about the wages of whoring."

I look beseechingly into the King's eyes, but he turns away and looks down to study his hands folded in his lap. Reading his thoughts, I realize that I am dying. Whoever spread the rumor that I died in Fuenterrabía did no more than predict the truth with his lie. Don Felipe has lost so many relatives that he is truly grieved to say good-by to a friend who has kept him company in his loneliness. I can barely hear him as he sobs: "Don't believe don Luis, at least not word for word. He's neither Hippocrates nor Galen. But I'm sending immediately for my physicians. Even if you did catch the French disease and it's been incubating for years, my doctors can cleanse you."

"My Lord, you do me great honor, especially since once I wished that it had been I and not Your Majesty on the couch with Damiana in my

studio. But now I only wish to sleep. You can save yourself the kindness of calling for your doctors."

"You belong to the world, and you can't abandon it. You say you've given up painting. For God's sake, I refuse to believe you!"

"I'm telling the truth. How could I knowingly lie to you? I am the man you made when you named me Portraitist and First Court Painter at the age of twenty-three. If it weren't for you, I would have been and done nothing. My time is short and my hours draw near. You can't force me nor can your physicians save me. Right up to the end, my life seems inexplicable."

"Shush, now be still, will you? I'll not have you talk or even think such thoughts. Rest and leave everything in our hands."

"I gave up my free will when you forced me out of laziness and made me your painter. My art has been my cross; it is my curse. It plagues me now, because not being able to paint makes me feel that part of me is already dead. Strangely enough, I always felt that if I weren't compelled to be an artist, I would be a free man."

"Yours is a suicide of indolence," the buffoon reproaches me sternly. "This can't be the first time that pustules, even small ones, have erupted."

"Pustules— yes, time and again— but never so painful. They disappeared as soon as I decided to see my surgeon, Dr. Moles."

"Did it never occur to you," the King presses me, "that you were infected?"

They seem to have divided their roles like actors. Don Felipe is all kindness and sorrow, because in me he is losing part of his past: his raison d'être. The dwarf is the enraged prosecutor who accuses me of the capital sins of pride and, most of all, sloth. Suddenly my mind clears and I realize his true motives for thundering and prolonging my mock trial: it will all become part of his history of our lives. In order to record it truthfully, he assumes the role of participant-observer in my bed chamber. He plays his part admirably and purposefully: so that the written word may bear us witness, as a Pope told me while I was doing his portrait in Rome. His Holiness did not want to be mistaken for Julius II, nor me for Michelangelo.

Finally, they start to leave, but not without the King turning around to promise me an immediate appointment with his doctors. I pull the covers up over the side of my face and pretend to sleep so no one will force another goblet of mulled wine on me. Then I start settling scores with myself, neither to pardon nor condemn— who am I to judge anyone?— but to find out who I was before crossing the bar.

I have no doubt that I caught the Gallic scourge in some Baratillo brothel. Part of me must have known all along and inserted hidden clues into my work. I think about my landscapes where nature is a mere *backdrop for the painting. I recall other canvases where my figures are reduced to smudges and haphazard brushstrokes, while time is captured in one fugitive instant of life. Such a view of man and his world— that of ghosts irrevocably crossing the threshold of a mirror— is the vision of a gravely ill man, even if the world applauds his lucky stars on life's stage. I remember that it was on the Feast of Saint Ignatius, the same day as today, that a girl in a Triana bordello read my cards. As if they had turned up something unimaginable, she insisted on reading the lifelines in my hand. She made a prediction that I did not believe then and put in the back of my mind until now.* It's all so confusing, because the cards and the lifelines say the same. There's royal blood in your veins and in your lineage; but you will die in the King's house believing yourself the most unfortunate of men. *She was Portuguese like my grandparents and spoke with the same accent. It was the end of July and outside the streets were scorching under the blue skies. We made love under an open window and studied the cards scattered across the floor. Her name draws a blank, but I remember her curly pubic hair the color of rose-hip honey. I don't know that she passed me the pox, but her oracle is coming true. As I lie dying in the Palace Treasure House, I am the most wretched of creatures.*

Now it is the buffoon who whispers through the mists of time. Some men are destined to be repeated; some are not. You and I have been created so exceptional—you an exceptional artist and I an exceptional runt—that we could pass for a pair of freaks. *His implacable voice is coming from the Royal Hunting Lodge where we tasted the jars of pickled celery.* The future bloodline of Kings will not pass through little Inés Manuela. It is God's will that she die before her mother, so that Francisca will give you another granddaughter identical in every way who will also be named Inés Manuela. *They say that the pox passes from one generation to the next like water slithers unnoticed from rock to rock. The sins of the father fall on his children who inherit his weaknesses as easily as his voice or his surly character. Once I think about it, I understand why my daughter Ignacia and granddaughter Inés Manuela died so young, followed by Francisca in the prime of her life after giving me my second Inés Manuela: because they inherited my curse. I conceived my daughters for them to die, in the same way that Francisca delivered her first-born. An instant of pleasure I do not remember was their undoing, in a Seville that vanished with my youth. Their death sentence is incomprehensible but it neither absolves nor frees me from my wretchedness. It is useless to say that I would give my life for theirs. I don't mean this miserable existence waning away in a bed chamber but the glorious life of a man blessed by gods and kings.*

I remember my thoughts at the Royal Hunting Lodge—that I married Juana to please Pacheco, and then fathered my daughters to placate Juana each time she hounded me for a child. As a matter of fact, I never willingly nor consciously brought them into the world and I must admit that I gave my daughters a poisoned life that they never asked for. As a father and grandfather, I was also inadvertently a hangman and assassin when, in fact, it wasn't my seed that killed them but my lack of will. I first succumbed to my father when he brought me to Herrera's studio and then I ceded to Pacheco. I painted only to wile away the boredom of my indolent life. The truth is I never wanted to make anything of myself. From the very start, I capitulated to another's will— my father's, my teacher's, Juana's, that of the adolescent apprentices who took me to the flea-market brothels when I was all but indifferent to women. I likewise relinquished my free will and very being with my first equestrian painting of His Majesty, may the Heavens help him. Many lost and squandered years followed until he sent me to Pheasant Isle to oversee the Infanta's wedding ceremonies. This is my secret and these are my credentials. I disregarded or dismissed my only valid counsel, the elder Herrera's, except for his advice in painting. I was the man that the others either saw in me or wanted me to become. I was never my own man, the man I should have been. Only now in this epilogue can I feign sleep and turn my back to the world so that it will grow accustomed to my death.

I suddenly hear voices through the sun window that Primo peered through on tiptoe. I force myself up and grope my way along the walls for support. The oeil de boeuf looks into a storage loft piled high with broken-down furniture and my daughters' old clothes. Stumbling, I pull myself up onto a chest and hold onto the window frame to witness the most incredible vision through the round hole. The loft has turned into a bedroom where I discover the old windbag in the mysterious woods in Pacheco's dream at the Royal Hunting Lodge. I could swear he is still alive, stretched out on the cushions of a high bed, but he looks like Methuselah in that loose nightgown engulfing his skin and bones. On a quilt at his feet is seated the child who was with him in that spectral mist. Yes, of course, he is a ghost— translucent in the light. He is dressed in the style of an era yet to come: all in blue with short pants and stockings up to his knees, and some sort of bib on his back.

"Perhaps you don't know that the sixth of August is not only the anniversary of my conception—you told me that yourself—but also of another calendar day fundamental to the fine arts," *says the old scarecrow.*

"I have no idea what you're talking about," *answers the boy thumbing through a date book on the night table.* "According to the calendar, it's the Feast of our Holy Savior or the Transfiguration of Christ."

"Right you are. The Transfiguration falls on the same day as the death of Velázquez in another era—to be exact—in the fateful year of 1660, and according to the records, at precisely two in the afternoon."

The portent does not surprise me, nor am I taken aback by the bell-toned voices from a long-awaited time that has not yet occurred. I know that they are not lying and I am not hallucinating. They are speaking of my death in a past as remote to them as jousts and chivalric novels are to us. I realize that I will die with all due punctuality, just like the old man's prediction in reverse.

"Tell me about the death of Velázquez," the child insists. "How do you know so much about it?"

"So much I'll have to summarize it for you. A lifetime would not be enough to tell it all. There was a time I thought about writing a book entitled *The Death and Resurrection of don Diego de Silva Velázquez.* I gave up the idea when I figured out that some-one either already wrote it or else would write it for me."

"Just tell me about his death."

"On the morning of August 6, the artist dictates his last will and testament to don Gaspar de Fuensálida, the Royal Notary and a personal friend of the buffoon who signs as witness. Veláz-quez is given the Last Rites by don Alfonso Pérez de Guzmán el Bueno, Archbishop of Tyre and Patriarch of the West Indies, who comforts him with an edifying sermon regarding life as exile. His Majesty listens with tears in his eyes. Velázquez is lucid to the end and tries to comfort those present in his bed chamber, asking them to generously forgive the sorrow he is causing them by dying. It is almost two o'clock when he begs Juan Bautista del Mazo to bring him the little girl, the second of his grandaughters named Inés Manuela, as you well know. He kisses the child and gives thanks to heaven that she is too young to remember the death of her grandfather. Smiling, he closes his eyes as his son-in-law leads the granddaughter by the hand out of the room. And with the smile still on his lips, he draws his last breath."

"That's all?"

"In his book, *The Portrait Museum: The Scala of the Visual Arts,* Antonio Palomino assures us that the soul of Velázquez was re-turned to his Maker, who created him so the world could marvel at His talent. I'll withhold my opinion since I don't encroach into the realm of the invisible, but I can tell you that his last will and testament exists and it reads magnificently."

I listen to the old man and feel certain that in precisely six days everything that he describes in his century will come to pass in mine. When I die for real, it will be as if I were performing my own death, begging forgiveness for causing such distress, calling for my granddaughter at the last moment, and smiling up to the very end. Damiana was right when she said the world was a stage. Even dying is played out, although I erroneously thought that death was the only unquestionable truth in our comedy of errors. On this stage, art is like a knife that makes a diagonal incision across a mirror, thus capturing it in both sides of the blade. Using pencils and brushes, art reflects and externalizes its slice of time.

At this very instant as I peer through the glass of the sun window, my vision clears and the scene stands out in sharp detail. On an armoire next to the window, leaning against the wall like a tiny easel, is a small painting on wood. On it are details in miniature of three of my countless paintings, finished or unfinished: The Family, *with the Infanta and her maids-in-waiting; the portrait of the buffoon and scribe, don Luis de Acedo; and the nude portrait of Damiana seen from the back. The central figure is no other than myself painting* The Family *and looking off into the void. Whoever painted this was born to copy me. It is so correct down to the minutest detail that I could not say for sure whether it was done by my hand or another's.*

"They first wrapped the cadaver in a worsted shroud to symbolize the demise of the flesh into dust, ashes, and nothing. Then they dressed it as if it were still alive. As was the habit with knights of the military orders unless otherwise requested, they then covered him in a long tunic with the cross of Saint James embroidered on the chest. They fastened on his sword, hat, boots and long spurs." *The old man gets himself so worked up talking about my funeral that he flays his arms as the boy listens enraptured.* "The wake was held in his bed chamber where he lay in state on his own bed, with two candelabra burning before a makeshift altar. Votive candles cast light on the wooden crucifix that Martínez Montañés had carved years before as a present to Velázquez."

"Is that all you know?"

"Not all. On the following day will take place the royal funeral service he was accorded. His corpse is placed in a coffin adorned with gold studs and silver sconces, lined in black velvet trimmed in Byzantine gilt, and fastened with a double set of latches. At the appointed hour, they carry him to the funeral chapel at the parish church of Saint John the Baptist. There the body is received in the Monarch's name by the Royal Marshall, the King's successor in that office. On either side of the catafalque burn the royal candelabra, the ones only lit at the death of the King or the birth of an Heir. The Palace choirs, voices and instruments such as have not been heard since the funeral service of the late Queen, sing the Requiem Mass. In the morning, the Knight of Calatrava don José Salinas, the Royal Marshall, and two other nobles whose names history omits, carry the coffin on their shoulders to the Fuensálida family pantheon."

The preview of my wake and funeral does little to impress me. It is all part of the drama where I come in at the end to play my rehearsed role. As a brief aside, since the irony is inescapable, I wonder why the King would insist on exulting me when they will shroud my body in a worsted tunic to remind us of the frail thread of life that sustains us. It seems incomprehensible that such a paradox should escape those who will survive me. I almost do not notice it myself because I am caught in realities far removed from the pomp and circumstance of my funeral pile. Even my death, so close at hand, seems remote as that of a stranger. I step back from it all as I spy on the windbag and boy through the sun window and relive the tranquility I felt upon completing The Family. *Today, like then, I feel very close to a point where time and space converge and where art takes on the glow of immutable infinity. In that canvas, I had hoped to eternalize an instant, just like another is trapped on the wood painting above the armoire: in the miniature which could pass for the work of my hand where next to the copy of my self-portrait are joined the mirror images of two more of my canvases—* the vera effigies *of the dwarf Luis Acedo and the nude of poor Damiana.*

*But I am no longer thinking; I am observing. I perceive, in the vitreous specter of the child, my friend the buffoon. Their voices even have the same register. If infinity and eternity can be inverted and caught in paint on a canvas then there is no reason why words can't be superimposed or interwoven, no matter how disparate and distant they may be. And so when the boy in white stockings says—*Thank you for telling me about Velázquez's death, because it helps me understand who we are—*I think that I hear the buffoon in my studio saying:* Leave that cloud out of my portrait. It doesn't exist. As Your Honor so often says, painting only understands truths; for farce and mockery, life will suffice.

But it is the decrepit old man I cannot take my eyes off. He looks crazed with his wild hair, jet-black eyes, and a skull that seems to have shrunk with the years. While he chats with the child's specter, he passes a quick glance up at the sun window as if he sensed my presence from his century. Although a great span of time separates us, I can almost recognize him. Either that or I am confusing him with someone he could have been. Even without the mole on his temple, the extended lower jaw, the pale blue eyes, he could pass for His Majesty the King in the masquerade of an old scarecrow some time in the far distant future. Then I look again and realize that I have forced, as only an artist can, any and all similarity. The truth lies elsewhere and, although I half wish I could avoid it, it is in the old man's true reflection wherein I see myself.

I have no idea by what name he'll go in the unknown time allotted to him on this earth. But I do know that I, Diego Rodríguez de Silva Velázquez, am also this man who does not yet exist. I could have looked like him if I too had lived to an almost unimaginable old age. To see his face is to see myself in the future. It is as if the oeil de boeuf had turned into a mirror and, racing across it through the centuries, from its dawn to its death, was time itself. "Ever since you started painting mirrors and windows into your paintings, the past intrudes into the present and men become brushstrokes. You'll never be forgiven for turning the world inside out." I look at the old windbag and smile and forgive my spineless nature and the inadvertent wrongs I committed. Whether we be portraits in a painting or characters in a novel, I hope that in the next life Francisca, Ignacia, and Inés Manuela can also absolve me. I go back to sleep and wait for my pot of tea. The portent will come true in the span of a few days. After dictating my last will and testament, I will receive Extreme Unction at the hands of the Archbishop of Tyre. By then, they will be polishing the gold-studded coffin and lining it with velvet and gilt. Don Gaspar will make a public announcement that to him I am like a brother and will be buried in his family pantheon. I will bid my adieu with a smile on my face and a kiss for my granddaughter: my only surviving heir. Then I will cross the bar thanking my good fortune for the brief glimpse of my canvases copied onto the tiny wooden easel. It makes even a disabused artist like myself pleased and proud.

Heads and Tails

1

He openly dismissed it as a minor miracle, but in his heart he knew it was an epiphany more splendid than the sum total of his singular existence: his irrevocable and unrepeatable life. On the sixth of August, the feast of the Transfiguration of Our Savior and the anniversary of the death of Velázquez—a coincidence passed unnoticed by the press releases—he awoke with the mental faculties of ten or twenty years past, restored as if by magic incantation during the night, perhaps in a long-forgotten dream.

While the nurses shaved him and untangled his long hair, he looked into a hand mirror and, recognizing the withered reflection in the glass, concluded that the portent was a manifestation of limited scope after all. Deep down, he was comforted and even pleased that his new lease on life belonged to the image, or disguise, of the same old spook with charcoal-black rings under his eyes, pallid complexion, scrawny neck, and stooped shoulders. Only his jet-black pupils, the legacy from his mother, betrayed the Faustian transformation behind the mock-tragic mask. As they finished shaving and splashing him with cologne, he began to whistle his favorite tune, a Catalonian *sardana* —the name of which remained, despite his revitalized memory, inexplicably filed away.

One year had passed since the last sixth of August when, he remembered, he described to his brother's specter the funeral services of Velázquez, recounting them like imperial honors while the Royal Choir chanted the psalm of darkness in the candle-lit chapel. There had been nothing newsworthy about the year. The brothers had spent August to August in the doldrums of shared loneliness. They either sank into interminable bouts of silence or grumbled, as Velázquez would have said, with the disdain of the disabused. The summer squalls and autumn thunderstorms were followed by an unseasonably golden winter, and a tempestuous spring preceded the drought and the summer brush fires lasting until Transfiguration. Only on the rarest of occasions did they make mention of the vanished specters: those of their parents,

Federico, Uncle Santiago, or for that matter the multitude of phantoms that gathered in the plaza for the Fondora festival to disappear in the mist like a mirage in the haze.

Neither brother felt any nostalgia for the specters released to eternity. It was as if losing them amounted to giving them up. Each spoke of his parents as if they were literary characters, remote from life and incidental to the story. They could have been, merely for sake of illustration, the young field hand mentioned on page one of *Don Quijote* who saddled the knight's hack, handled the pruning knife, and disappeared into nothingness; or the nameless servant in red livery in *War and Peace* who officiously delivered Ana Pavlova Sherer's invitation: "If my lord Prince has nothing better to do and is not horrified at the prospect of spending an evening with a sick old woman, I should be charmed to receive you between the hours of six and eight."

The artist made occasional mention to Federico's work but never alluded to what had happened between them or how enormously it had affected their careers. One warm winter afternoon, he brought up Lorca's *Poet in New York* and the posthumous collection of poetry where Federico expressed his apocalyptic vision that the industrialized world was drawing to a close, that nature would reclaim Manhattan, and that soon cobras would hiss from the rooftops of the vine-draped skyscrapers. *Like they say about those Central American rain forests, where you think you're climbing a hill looking for great green macaws through your binoculars. You dig your rubber sole into the slope to find out that it's a pyramid swallowed up by the jungle, erected in honor of an unknown and uncommon timeless deity. Do you follow me?* He saw his brother nod in answer and continued in a faltering voice fading to a sigh. In *Poet in New York*, avenging nature took on both apocalyptic and personal tones for Federico, an innocent abroad in the inferno of the Great Depression, who offered himself up as a self-imposed penance. Pederasty, to use the jargon of the time, was the archetypical sin against nature. Still in its adolescence, the world was unaware of its capacity for true evil which would be revealed in the extermination camps and over Hiroshima. Federico would not live long enough to see his vision come true. In his naive arrogance, he shouldered the blame for an entire civilization. He damned the world and himself for having sinned against nature that was going to destroy them both: the world for its injustice and him for his sodomy. It never occurred to him that it would be men, not nature, who would destroy him. He felt condemned but mistook his executioner. His envisioned demise was infinitely more noble than the one he encountered at the hands of paid assassins.

Nature, the avenging angel of his final poems, took the deliberately ambiguous image of a *"masquerón,"* which means both figurehead and face mask. *It can appear on the prow of a ship in the form of a frightening statue brought from Africa to avenge the memory of the slave trade. It can also be a huge disguise, such as in Poe's "Mask of the Red Death" that Federico had read while pretending to study English at Columbia University.* He then recounted a parable with sources traced to the medieval dance of death that Poe—an apparently deranged alcoholic, obsessed with finding the South Pole in the core of his being—resets in a Renaissance palace where nobles gather in seeming isolation from the scourge raging outside its walls. *It was a pestilence that formed scarlet stains on the face of its victims before cutting them down in their tracks. As the fugitives celebrate their good fortune with a masked ball, a shrouded figure appears in the guise of the Red Death. They shirk back instinctively, scandalized by the impudent intruder. However, they quickly regain their composure and applaud such blasphemous temerity. After all, death can only befall someone else. Let me tell you the moral to the story. The mask is the Red Death—the selfsame pest that becomes Federico's masthead—and the dance is the dance of death for those haughty masqueraders, just as nature sits in final judgment of the world in Federico's poetry.*

However, on the morning of the Transfiguration of Our Savior, the artist felt far removed from the Red Death, Federico, and Depression-era New York: a chaos of bankrupt stockholders, millionaires reduced to selling apples from broken-down carts— *Arise, children of starvation!*—and long lines of sullen men out of work circling the soup kitchens of Al Capone. *Oh Baby, you're so lovely / and you're gonna die some day. / All I want's a little lovin' / before you pass away.* On the Feast of the Transfiguration, the anniversary of Velázquez's death, the painter felt resurrected, reborn. His brother had vanished and he knew instinctively that the specter had not fallen into another dream, days or years long, from which he would reappear when least expected, yawning and stretching, He was finally free of his nemesis. The shade had slipped away the night before just as sooner or later every specter must take leave or, like his mother and Uncle Santiago at last year's festival, bow out dancing.

He was free and his freedom gave him at last a new and authentic existence. Dressed in his nightshirt and slate-gray robe, he saw that his almost translucent hands were no longer trembling. He could recreate on canvas the agate-streaked horizons across a desert wasteland, with a miniature of *Venus of the Mirror* reclining nude, or a diminutive version of the Infanta Margarita or of the Count Duke of Olivares. Beaming like the actor who wins an immortalizing role or the revolutionary who, on another stage, delivers the coup de grâce to an Empire, he began to shout and to frantically ring for his wardens to awaken. Startled by the commotion, they all came running to the bedroom and stood in amazement at his revivified temper.

They half-knew it was real and half-feared it was a living nightmare. They were even more confounded to hear him holler that there was no flesh-and-blood author nor book-qua-mirror to reflect his life. He was his own master, he wrote his own destiny in pictures that only he could interpret. By his own volition, he was free of the living and, above all, the dead. He needed only one more canvas to complete his life—one canvas to culminate his life's work—as if that were a valid distinction in his case. *It's not, but I express myself like that so you can follow me.* He also doubted the world's capacity to comprehend his purpose but was determined to broadcast it as soon as possible. *My resurrection will not last forever, and I must sketch out my painting as soon as I have announced it.* He demanded that they call a press conference that very morning.

It was a difficult order to fill and they only half-succeeded. In August, all Europe hides out on islands ignored by cartographers or in faraway lands lost in medieval maps. They trek to undiscovered continents beyond the world's horizon. They camp at underwater sites in Atlantis or leave forget-me-nots at the unknown tomb of its rediscoverer, Pierre Benoit. Or like sheltered cave bears that give birth and nurse their young in hibernation, they languorously bask on the high steppes once belonging to marauders or on tucked-away marshes and beaches. What is more to the fact, the world had all but forgotten him. While he—a skeptical and indolent Proust—took to his deathbed with only the ghost of the child he despised for company, his fame and tomfoolery were lost to an entire generation of artists indebted to his work. Museums fought for his works while customs officials authenticated fakes of the originals to sell to Franconian dukes seen playing golf on the glossy-printed fairways of movie-star magazines. American universities were swindled into buying the transplanted forgeries for their east-campus museum or behind the statue of the unknown soldier fallen in defense of slavery. These institutions of higher learning then published textbooks and monographs that included their collections, but wherein his biographical sketch was reduced to a single name, date, and place of origin. He was born in a benighted country, renowned for its artists, toreadors, aristocrats, and despots—Picasso and Dalí, Joselito and Manolete, Goya's Duchess of Alba, and don Manuel Godoy y Alvarez.

One press agency refused to distribute the news about a nobody and a has-been. At high noon—*an hour ablaze with buzzing locusts*—a telecast gave him a passing mention more like a brief publicity spot. His assorted minions dashed around for hours and finally assembled two cameramen and a handful of reporters—a Soviet journalist found with his wife in a sandy cove burning themselves to a crisp in the blazing sun; a harpy famous for her interviews, surprised between flights; the correspondent for an American weekly, catnapping on the terrace of a rented farmhouse; and a Bavarian widower, the author of two articles on *Incredible Enigma in Velázquez's Studio* and *Portrait of My Dead Only Brother*, whom they chased down at a gasoline station as he and his three young daughters strained their eyes trying to locate the ruins of The Castle of our Lord and King on the map. As the sage was telling the innocents: In the fourteenth-century, the master of the castle attempted to gorge himself with lust by beheading and devouring two of his wives. The ogre was eventually apprehended and condemned to the gallows without ever fully comprehending why they were executing him. His Most Ceremonious Majesty, King Peter of Aragon, had wanted to pardon him since the castellan was a most gifted flautist and could play bucolic madrigals on the piccolo and Pan flute. But it so happened that about the same time, the King had slapped his daughter who was three months pregnant and had the misfortune to knock her down and cause her to miscarry on the spot. The following day the princess bled to death and the King's act of contrition was to have the uxoricide's tongue cut out with a mountain knife. Naked as a caged monkey, the murderer was exhibited in the public square. Bound hand and foot to four rutting colts and, by posting mares in heat at the four corners of the plaza, he was quartered. His torso was hung from the ramparts of the castle, which was immediately sacked and set torch to by the serfs. They threw heath, tinder, and firewood into the flames while singing psalms to the only true Lord, Saint Martin of Tours on High.

The art historian agreed to attend the press conference on condition that he be allowed to bring his daughters so that one day they would tell his grandchildren they had seen the painter of *Incredible Enigma*. The condition was granted and the press conference convened. With few but highly select participants, it had already started when a shadowy man of indistinct age and appearance stepped into the chamber of experts. No one knew who he was but, surprisingly, nor did anyone stop him to ask for his credentials. Like shade spreading across a wall, he had slipped by the Praetorian guard and through the labyrinthine corridors to a room lit by an interior patio, complete with bird cage, and a fireplace ablaze in the summer heat. In nightshirt and dressing gown stood the artist, ready to edify the supreme council of his Sanhedrin.

Since opening questions from the press were explicitly forbidden, the Resurrected was on the threshold of his speech when it dawned on him that he had no title for his canvas. As luck would have it, in that instant of panic he crossed glances with the late arrival standing in the shadows at the back of the room. A ray of light dim as the stranger himself fell across the man's brow just barely revealing his eyes, but the brief glimpse was the spark needed. As if suddenly possessed by a benevolent daytime demon, the artist declaimed the title of his next and final work: *The Garden of the Hesperides.*

"*J'aime pas mes rêves, mais je les raconte.*" He spoke in his best French, with bits of Spanish, langue d'oil and d'oc thrown in, without anyone noticing that he had lifted his opening line from a verse by Paul Eluard. He did not exactly steal it; he simply got carried away and thought he was back in Paris, 1937, shivering in Nush and Eluard's apartment without electricity or heat, not even charcoal for the stove. He loaned them 3,000 francs knowing he would never see the money again, and Eluard recited the verse that was to form part of a longer poem translated and illustrated by Man Ray: "I don't like my dreams, but I relate them / I love others' dreams when they paint them." The poet asked him if he liked the rhyme and he nodded in agreement since he wanted to think of Federico and Eluard as his favorite poets. Then Eluard said something outrageous that he had forgotten until the very morning of the press conference: *One day you'll remember this verse, but by then we'll be separated by space and time for all eternity.*

"Aegle, Erytheis, Hespera, and Arethusa. These are the four Hesperides who are at times mistaken for clouds in the western sky but who tend the tree with the golden apples. It is guarded by a dragon with his tail twisted seven times around the trunk." Inadvertently, he was repeating the lines recited by his mother before he was conceived. "The garden is at the western edge of the world, where the ocean ends at the strait of Hercules." *One day you'll remember this verse, but by then we'll be separated by space and time for all eternity.* "Not only is the garden to be found at the edge of the world, it projects into the only plausible eternity: that of death." He felt quite smug, thinking he had answered the poet with an image fusing the duality of the interminable. "In the atrium of infinity, the apples illuminate the darkness. I can in all truth say that the dead must pass through that light before fading into the shadows. According to the myth, Hercules destroyed the demon dragon and stole the apples. Myth lies! Only art can reduce the demon to its own image and likeness, and that's what I plan to do as soon as I steal the golden apples. I'll rob them from my own *Garden of the Hesperides*, where I will depict the final setting sun at the threshold of eternity. I so decree. Now leave me in peace to commence my work."

They left in a buzz of whispers: the erudite Bavarian, the Soviet journalist, the little girls, the harpy, the cameramen, and the American correspondent. As if by a hidden and ancient directive, his wardens left with them, with the last one to file out meekly closing the door behind him. He was left alone with the indefinable stranger. The ray of light that had fallen on the brow of the intruder now descended across his eyes. He could have been any man or, like Ulysses, No Man. And like Ulysses returning from the shadowy realm wiser and lustier, the artist felt greedy for life as never before, not even in his youth, as he prepared to snatch the sacred apples from the most golden of dreams and to superimpose them—*montage des montages et le plus doré des rêves*—onto his painting.

He turned to the nameless stranger. "Who are you?," he demanded. "What business do you have here?"

"I'm someone who got lost and came here by mistake. Don't you remember me?"

"Perhaps," he vacillated, "but if we crossed paths before, I can't place where."

"It was at the Saint-Denis, in New York, the afternoon Kennedy was assassinated. Don't you remember? We had to shout at one another to be heard over the deafening cries and wails in the lobby. A nun, pregnant by a street mime, read the news in his sign language and miscarried on the spot. One of the chef's assistants hanged himself with a braid of garlic."

"But you don't exist! I remember the suicide, the miscarriage, and a Battery Street bus leaving a trail of tears that could shock the screeching gulls. But our interview never took place! You don't exist, now or ever, except in my dreams!"

"I am afraid that it's you who don't exist," the intruder answered in a gentle voice while from his pocket he pulled out a handful of newspaper clippings. "As you can read for yourself, people the world over tore their hair over your death, but there were no stillbirths or suicides."

His hands did not so much as tremble as he read the yellowish papers, dated almost exactly a year before. He merely stepped closer to the fireplace to take advantage of the two sources of light from the embers and patio window. According to the headlines, he died in his sleep at home, in this very house. His funeral service was as flamboyant as that of Velázquez, to whom one journalist fervently compared him. The King and Queen, whose portraits he had done, presided over the ceremony. Helicopters landed on the rooftop unloading somber statesmen who came to express their deepest condolences and then rushed back to more urgent national affairs after having munched down a salad of escarole, endives, and toadstools, like the ones the young Acedo picked at the Royal Hunting Lodge called "wolf farts." The artist was flattered by such homage but missed the plumed corsairs such as André Malraux provided in the name of France for Braque's *de profundis* and *dies irae*. He smiled at the praise from the pundits who a quarter of a century before had denounced him as the prototype of the co-opted artist, a Fascist sympathizer, a throwback to the age of the enlightened despotism, and a marginal figure in the socio-critical panorama of contemporary art. It was something to admire, he reflected, how the country buried its dead under a landfill of words or—as Federico would and indeed did say in another elegy—under a heap of silenced dogs.

"But if I died, what are we doing in this room? What happened to the press conference? How will I paint *The Garden of the Hesperides?*"

"You were buried , at your expressed wish, here in the fireplace. Look through the flames and you can read your names and dates on the tombstone. It's flameproof. On the days the house is open to tourists, they scrub it clean so the Japanese can take pictures of your epigraph. Every dead man deserves his appropriate plot. This space is all yours; you don't have to share it with your brother."

"How do you know so much about us if we only met once, and what I told you then was a pack of lies? I either made the facts up or purposefully kept them from you."

With the patient look of a man resigned to the inevitable, the visitor nodded in agreement, admitting he had not been deceived at the Saint-Denis: "I knew all along that the date of *Incredible Enigma in Velázquez's Studio* was faked—a smoke screen to conceal Federico's molesting you. This lie, so patently apparent, was ironically my first hint that you had given yourself to the poet, and to your mother as well. I followed the clue down the sinuous and imbricated mazes of your paintings and your relationship with your brother. The true nature of your dialogue with your brother's specter was finally revealed to me after I had spent hours meditating in front of *Portrait of My Dead Only Brother*, which now hangs in the Allen Museum in Oberlin, Ohio.

"As far as the relationship between your mother and uncle, I found that out from Sanianayake, in Croydon, a few months before he died. In spite of occasionally confusing you with your brother or taking you for your uncle's son, he hadn't lost his grip on the past. A case in point, he recited from memory the anonymous note: *Words fly faster than time and it is time to put an end to this chapter.*"

"Have you finished your book yet?"

It was now the author who was caught in the act. He hesitated before saying: "I was planning to write two books, your biography and one on Velázquez. But while studying an engraving of your *Incredible Enigma*, I opted for one fictional text where the two would coincide. I can't say for sure whether that decision was entirely mine, because something irrepressible overcame me and forced my hand. To satisfy that urge, I would have sacrificed everything: my life and those of my children (assuming I had any or, for that matter, that life itself belongs to the one who lives it). It goes without saying that you had one foot in the grave when I began my work, but you hadn't keeled over yet when I thought I had completed it. I had intended to finish you off in a last chapter written in cursive, where Velázquez peers through the sun window into the loft and overhears you describe his funeral ceremonies."

"I remember telling my brother about the great homage paid to Velázquez at Court and at the church of Saint John the Baptist. But the coincidence shouldn't come as any shock. The amazing match between fiction and reality didn't just happen in the last chapter of your book, but in earlier ones too. I figure it must be a recurring theme from cover to cover. When he imitated my French, my brother's ghost would call your book *mes limbres.*"

"Without realizing, that's how I quoted him."

"It wouldn't surprise me. But what I can't understand is what you're doing in my parcel of eternity or, for that matter, in this unexpected epilogue. My brother may have been right when he predicted that you, our chronicler, would end up slipping and falling into your own pages."

Unconvinced as to the humor in the joke, the author forced out a weak laugh. To the artist's dismay, the laughter reminded him of someone else's. When he finally pinned it down, he shuddered. It was the imaginary chortle of the buffoon, such as it sounded to him as he painted *Incredible Enigma* or when he witnessed the Velázquez picnic outing in the oak grove. *Don Diego, where will the blue of today have gone tomorrow? If everything gets tossed into the illusive files of memory, I wonder whether the void itself isn't an illusion.*

"I never wanted my book to be your brother's limbo. I had hoped to turn it into the vehicle for my own immortality. I don't mean as an imperishable work or a monolith to pride. I've always tried to avoid those pitfalls and, besides, I don't give a damn if I'm remembered by those who outlive me. Forgive me if I bore you with these digressions and permit me to speak familiarly to you—even though you're an icon, and I'm a scribbler."

"Please, go on."

"I used to dream about one of my books, where I could wander after I died. I supposed it to be in this novel and that I would die in its final pages. Turned into my own shade, I would meander through the text—a voyeur to all you creatures of my imagination. Invisible to your eyes, I could overhear your brother describing how your parents conceived you on a balcony overhanging the street, the same balcony Monsieur Archiprêtre or Archimandrite pointed to as he shouted: *Une femme! Une femme est morte ou au moins évanouie là-dedans, sur la balustrade!* I watched you and your uncle cross through the Tate Gallery and stop in front of your painting of *Incredible Enigma*. Still in hiding, I followed you to Hyde Park where he was to tell you: *I must say that I could never take a woman without the memory of your mother diminishing her before my very eyes as soon as I tried to make love to her. I repeat "to make love" because love, heartfelt and true, was something I could never cherish for anyone else.* In my narrative, I could step into a canvas as if through a looking glass and imagine I heard Damiana panting in the arms of Felipe IV. Like the King in exhausted pleasure, I longed to run my fingers across her body while she pressed my testicles in the palm of her hand. To smell the sweet marjoram in an upland meadow surrounded by wild teasel and rustic vineyards. To savor the sweet and sour taste of pickled Cypriot celery, the present from the Queen to the jester for making her laugh."

"But you're deceiving yourself. Your hour has not yet come. You'll outlive me and this book—which will turn to dust like the vineyards at Felipe IV's hunting lodge. It was only by mistake that you wandered into the epilogue anyway."

"You're right," the author agreed. "This meeting makes no sense whatsoever. Your world no longer belongs to me; I better let you go. Your fate is to abscond with the golden apples for your painting. Mine is to labor line by line and, I tell you, each line is a tough row to hoe. Writing is a cross to bear, while painting is a release from one's cares. But I have an irrevocable life sentence to link pauses and periods in one book after another."

"Don't go. Let me get a better look at you. You're nondescript, but there's something indefinable about you that reminds me of the vague way he resembled my brother. Or when I completed *Incredible Enigma* and obliquely saw both Velázquez and even Felipe IV in myself."

"Or the coupling of Damiana and the King fusing into yours and Federico's. Or for that matter, my novel as a metaphor for whatever Acedo was writing in his chronicle while Velázquez painted his portrait."

The outline of the author's face and figure turned indistinct as a stone in muddied waters. Startled to see his author effaced, the artist lunged at him: he would never know if he meant to embrace or to retain a hold on him. He wanted to know the book's title and the author's name, long forgotten since the interview in New York; but it was too late. Eternity did not condense time; it just allowed it to slip through its shadowy cracks. He suddenly realized he stood empty-handed, his palms outstretched before a fireplace wherein he could read his last names behind the blazing logs.

While he warmed his hands to prepare himself to sketch *The Garden of the Hesperides,* he reflected on the triviality of names and titles. In one corner of the labyrinth stood an enormous blank canvas. For lack of will and vision, he had abandoned it to squander his last surge of energy arguing with his brother. Now in death, the canvas would serve as his mirror, his life's reflection. Like Velázquez who entitled his masterpiece *The Family* without knowing that two centuries later it would be called *Ladies-in-Waiting,* he would paint himself in the foreground in the act of painting while looking into a nonexistent mirror. His parents, brother, and Uncle Santiago would stand to one side in the middle plane. Behind them in diminishing oblique perspective, he would place Federico and Freud with bicycle and snail, Oscar

Domínguez and Madame Drameille with the entire Rambouillet Ballet Company, his deceased wife, the Pomeranian photographer beneath the air balloon of Monsieur Archiprêtre or Archimandrite, Dalí among the palm trees in the Queen Alexandra, and the great Gherardo de Sagra singing *Filotette*. The vanished would never return, but he could evoke them all—even Picasso as an old man talking about his father—from memory onto his painting. He would also include, next to the young minions of the *voyant-voyeur*, the figure of the wayward writer who had stumbled across the artist's death in the epilogue. It was only fitting that the author, undefined in life, would have a place in *The Garden of the Hesperides* since the writer had found one for the artist in his novel. In the background, behind Damiana, the buffoon, Their Majesties, and the spouse, daughters and granddaughters of Velázquez, he would open a rear door as an obvious salute to *Ladies-in-Waiting*. In the threshold leaning against the jamb—just as Velázquez had painted that other Velázquez, don José Nieto Velázquez entering the studio—he would place the man with the pointy goatee and malachite eyes.

When his masterpiece was completed, he would make off with the golden apples and place them atop a fiery copper brazier before his *chef-d'oeuvre toujours inconnu*. A most fitting final resting place, all the figures on canvas could gaze upon the sacred fruit while imagining themselves in the looking glass. It would concern him little to vanish into infinity, because his master work, illumined by the gold of the Hesperides beyond the gaze of worldly eyes, would endure in the midst of eternity. He gradually came to perceive that the novel reflecting his life and death was written for only one purpose: to bring him to Velázquez. Moreover, he felt certain that don Diego had not yet disappeared because he was awaiting both him and his painting with patient indolence. Separated by centuries on earth, their lives and their works were paths that would cross in infinity before falling into the void.

As he applied the final touches and placed the flaming brazier before the canvas, the specter of Velázquez appeared. Both made a reverential bow and they possibly even shook hands. The master paused to study the intrepid homage to *The Family* wherein another artist paints a portrait of himself in the act of painting. Perhaps he said aloud that he, despite his skepticism, was proud to have lived because three hundred years after his allotted time on earth, he inspired a miracle: *The Garden of the Hesperides*. He may have even placed his hand on the dead artist's shoulder and smiled like a father who saw all his hopes and dreams fulfilled in his son.

2

I awake to find myself alone, stretched out at the foot of the bed. To die is to dream, definitively so for us ghosts, and to go stark mad. In my dream, a demented unending delirium, I was a wandering soul in a book; and I had a brother, conceived in carnal rage after I passed away. Now, my eyes open, I see that neither brother nor book ever existed. It was solely to me, my parents' first-and-last-born son, that they gave life, albeit ever so brief. Death is not a novel but a fistful of remembrances scattered by the winds into oblivion.

Wide-awake, I can sort my memories from my dreams. I recall the stormy day I feigned sleep and saw my naked mother draped over an armchair as she offered herself to Uncle Santiago. But I had to have been hallucinating when I saw her through the dim light of an August dawn grappling with my father on a ledge over the street. The sight of my mother making love to my uncle, later begging him to take her to London, made me dream that my brother was a child of the gutter. Precocious but chaste, not even a genius such as mine could have imagined my parents' lust, nor could I have witnessed the scene in Uncle Santiago's house without transforming it into a nightmare. *How is it possible that my husband hasn't noticed. One look at me should be enough for him to tell. I know he would kill me because he has the temper of a wild beast. I'm afraid of him. I want to leave everything and run away to London with you and my son. When will you take us?* I repressed what I saw that winter morning, but in sleep I transferred their embrace onto other arms. I don't mean only those of my parents giving counterfeit life to my imaginary double. In my nightmares, I saw my so-called brother seduced by my mother and by a fictitious poet named Federico. I dreamt my mother made love to my father in a theater box while a tenor named de Sagra sang *Filotette*. The texts were interspersed like metal and wood in damascened inlay. And like an hallucination in triptych, my third nightmare was about a facially grotesque, blue-eyed King ravishing a Venus, the same Venus whose color portrait hung brightly in my father's office.

More unhinged than a living dream, the dream of the dead deranges memory into infinite distortions. From the Sovereign's tryst with the goddess of nubile hips and tapered waist emerges the chimerical silhouette of the poet sodomizing my brother, and the thrusts of my unnatural sibling into his wife's buttocks. In a variation of the nightmare, his wife demands to look him in the eye, thus causing his impotence. At another intersection of the dreams, my mother—blanched by the moon to the translucence of alabaster—straddles and possesses her son. *I love you so much, my little lamb. Now be still, my child. It was all a dream, just like everything else in this world of shadows.*

Through the window, the sun is dawning with neither living nor dead to stroll through the plaza. I can see the curved bench with its glazed mosaics now free of snails. In one of the side streets stretching from the old sector of town, the postal carriage will stop at a cantina. Beneath braids of red peppers strung from the ceiling over a blue zinc counter, the postman will fortify himself with espresso and brandy before heading to the train station to pick up the mail. On warm afternoons with a breeze chasing the clouds, my father will take me to the railway gardens to discuss law briefs as if I were his clerk. The train station, the park, the saloon, and the post carriage will survive, turned to glass by a sandstorm. The entire labyrinthine dream lasted no longer than it takes to conjure up a specious brother—a nick of time, let's say, or a blink of the eye.

Soon my parents and Uncle Santiago will stroll into the plaza from a side street. I want to believe that they are still alive and will appear as solemnly as if posing for a street photographer. Contrary to the dream visions of Federico and my parents describing concentric circles in the snow beneath this window, my family won't be shades but living creatures. Dressed in white from head to foot, with Belgian lace at her neck and wrists, my mother will be walking between the men under a large sun umbrella and tapping the brilliant tip of her own parasol against the sunny pavement. Negligent as usual of his appearance, considering style to be a bourgeois fetish, my father will be dressed in a baggy suit that accentuates his portliness. Of course, he'll have his Roskoff and gold watch fob pinned to his vest and jade cufflinks displayed on his heavily starched false cuffs. In total contrast, my uncle will be wearing a fitted jacket, spats, and pointy shoes. He'll have tucked under his arm his Borneo cane with marble handle and spiral of monkeys hand-carved down the shaft.

"Give them up! You know very well that they've been gone a long time. Even their shadows have stepped into eternity. Why must you so stubbornly believe they're alive?"

I turn around to find the man with the green eyes and the graying Vandyke. He watches me, smiling and shaking his head, as if pitying my disbelief.

"Who's gone?" I demand in a high-pitched voice seeming to belong to someone else. "What business is it of yours?"

"They're twice gone. Even their specters have passed into infinity. And that brother you think you've dreamt up also vanished into the void. While you were asleep, he gave up the ghost. If you don't believe me, look around the room where you used to converse and the house constructed in the image of his madness."

"I hardly recognize it. There's a sun window in the wall that I've never seen before. Who are you, anyway?"

"First you wanted to know what business I had here. Now you ask who I am, yet you've seen me before. If you don't mind, I'll save my reply for later. But you're quite right in noticing the window that wasn't there before."

"Did you put it here? Are you the author of this tale?"

"Now you call tale what you used to call limbo. You dismiss it as another man's dream. I hate to defraud you. I never told a tale, though many have been written about and because of me. As far as the bedroom goes—with or without the oeil de boeuf, not my handiwork, naturally—you should recognize it in a single glance."

"There's no painting over the armoire!" It suddenly dawns on me that, if I accept its absence, I must admit the reality of the brother who painted it. "The *Incredible Enigma* is missing!"

"I'm pleased you noticed. Now I know you're awake and using your highly praised power of observation. It just may be that your father and his freethinking friends were not so dumb as they seemed, but I personally place no faith in those who doubt the existence of the Absolute. They paraded you like a circus monkey, but you displayed some talent. As for the painting, it was auctioned off after your brother's death. The Musée National d'Art Moderne in Paris pulled strings for its purchase by a rich American. Since the value of art is measured in its price, perhaps in its capacity to survive human neglect, I suppose they did justice to a masterpiece."

The man with the silver-streaked hair is smiling and talking to me, but heretofore unheard whispers in my ear seem to muffle his words, held at bay as if by a puff of smoke or an upraised hand. *Ever since you started painting mirrors and windows, the past intrudes into the present and human beings become brushstrokes. You'll never be forgiven for turning the world inside out.*

"How does the window figure into all of this? Did the author insert it behind my back while I was asleep?"

"My guess is that he set it in while you were awake, enthralled by your brother's account of the death and funereal honors of Velázquez."

"You'll never be forgiven for turning the world inside out." I hear myself echoing an echo.

"I never turned anything inside out, neither the universe nor a sock! I suppose it's time to tell you who I am, although I have no earthly idea what I'm doing in this epilogue of an epilogue. I've been called so many names I wish I could forget them all and just be known as No Man."

"I am No Man. Not even my name is my own. It was my father's and the world knows it as my brother's, if indeed he existed as you say and I didn't dream him up. No matter. I'll never quite believe you, because you have all the marks of an imposter."

"Skepticism must run in your family," answers the man with the verdant gaze. "A circus trick was what your brother called the meeting with his author in New York. Now you call me a fake, and you may be right. Ever since the Absolute banned me from the universe, I've been nothing but his mimic. In order to snatch his realms, stars, winds, hours, beaches, wild beasts, women's labors, and men's crimes, I had to incite you all in the name of art to create from nothing, or to snatch illusive memory from the jaws of oblivion. You used to say that my worst sin was not to make-believe that I didn't exist but to make you believe there was life after birth. Well, you lied. There are two lives: one on earth and another here in eternity, and yours are definitively winding to a close. So let's return to your questions. You asked what business I had in your book."

"If you are who you say, you can answer."

"I am who I am, but I can't tell you for certain. I've aged as eternity itself wrinkles in boundless infinity. I not only invented the theater, but I tricked visionaries into staging my parody of creation. Although a few—Velázquez and your own brother, for example—never took me or the world seriously, others gave me a role or used me as metaphor in their misguided mockeries of the universe. You and I met up three times on earth; four times, in your limbo at the author's behest. Now we are meeting on our own accord, since we're outside the domain of his book."

"But why did you search me out in the epilogue? Can anything be added to what's been written?"

Distracted, he merely shrugs. He is older than any living being and the first to die. His malachite green eyes witnessed the dawn of light, time, and the ocean floors, before earth was created, and grew livid with envy because the creation could have been his. Suddenly, he reads my thoughts and, with a touch of impatience, commands: "Don't worry yourself over my appearance. I opted for a discreet disguise and kept it so as not to confuse you. My vocation as mimic allows me to assume any role. I could play Uncle Santiago making love to your mother, or your mother dropping her boa in the theater box to expose her unadorned breasts. I could also pass for Felipe IV, complete with tumor on the forehead and failing blue eyes. Or else, the buffoon's cherub of a son—Francisquito de Asís y de la Santísima Trinidad, I believe he was called—holding the looking glass for Damiana. But I'll spare you the tricks I use to wile away my solitude."

"Why didn't you spare me this meeting. I didn't ask you to come nor do I know why you're here. If you can't call up my brother from a book lost in the shadows, you can at least leave me in peace."

"All right, all right." He throws his head back as his smile breaks into a laugh. "That's the ultimate irony of a species not always humane. When he was alive, and you dead, you were both consumed by jealous hatred. You talked your heads off, as if each wanted to exorcize himself from his other. And now you want him back! I can't ransom your brother, but I can recall a part of your past."

"No one can retrieve the past! No one can unveil the twice-shrouded dead!"

"No one can, but our words endure. They are as believable as those mirrors of the past we call paintings."

"What words do you mean? Aren't they all silenced and the book closed?"

"I'm only talking about a few pages, where your brother described Velázquez's exequies while don Diego de Silva listened through the window."

"Velázquez could overhear our words in his lifetime?"

"He could see you with his naked eye through the bull's-eye, *à l'oeil nu et à travers de ton oeil-de-boeuf.* Just like before, in the oak grove, when you spied on his picnic at the Royal Hunting Lodge but dismissed it as trivial and importune. I digress. If you'll permit me, I will return to my first text and confess that I retrieved the papers thrown away by the author."

"You have them on you?" My voice surprises me because it sounds so anxious.

"As bad luck would have it, I lost them. I have no idea where. I thought I had tucked them into my sack the evening your mother and uncle made their appearance at the spectral ball." He flashes a grin between his trimmed mustache and beard. "Can't you still see the mayor's wife, in the purple dress and plumed hat, reciting the Queen's words? *Who is the lady who dances so lightly and gracefully to everything from the cakewalk to the polka, even the stately schottisch? She dances divinely, but she is a very sad woman.* Excuse me, what were we saying? Oh yes, I lost the papers the author threw away, but I can recall them from memory."

The same sense of dread accosts me that I felt the morning on the stone balcony when my parents sired their other son in fury and lust. It shames me to remember how I longed to be both of them at once: my mother, with her bleeding lips breaking into a smirk as her contempt changed to pride, her pride to passion, her passion to completion; my father, taking his wife with the frenzy of an enraged ram in rut. To know that I am consumed by the desire to be the unborn brother already stealing my life, as he was to steal my name. To sense that now, just as in that dawn, I stand blindfolded before my destiny.

"If you remember, recite it from start to finish," I beseech him, "every word they spoke, every pause they made!"

"If I wanted to, I could do more than recite it. It's not for nothing that I invented the stage."

"What do you mean the stage? I only asked for the script."

"It would be better if I conjured up the scene for you to witness through the sun window. While you were sleeping, I pushed the Can's armchair against the wall for you to stand on. Incidentally, that throne is an obvious fake. It could never pass for a baroque copy. It was done during the reign of Carlos III, when he was King of Naples, for his initiation into the Masonic lodge of *Divina Santa Agata delle Belle Mammelle*, The Divine Saint Agatha of the Beautiful Breasts. At any rate, I doubt that it will collapse under the weight of a light sprite. Climb up and peer through the window."

At his beck and command, I obey without so much as a protest or a glance back and lift myself up to grab hold of the gilded window frame where I rest my chin. On the other side of the glass, I expect an unknown scene that will sum up my life's existence. Perhaps the revelation in store for me is in a garret dating back to the time of Velázquez before his studio was removed, by royal decree, to a wing in the Alcazar. It may also await me in a resurrected room in the house where I was born: a house that no longer exists but on whose lot my brother was to erect his labyrinth. Perhaps in my father's first law office, the one with *Venus of the Mirror* hanging next to the arched window, or in the dining room where my mother displayed her dowry of Bohemian crystal and Japanese tea cups in the breakfront buffet.

"What do you see, my child?," asks the Imposter.

"Nothing," I lie, knowing he won't believe me.

I see neither our house nor that of the Palace Treasure House, but rather the station promenade lined with maples that were later cut to widen the curb. To the astonishment of the passers-by, the full red moon lights up the rails, connections, hangars, switches, barriers, and wayward wagons on dead-end tracks. To my distress, I peer through the glass into a crystal ball of lost time, where I see me and my father strolling beneath the maple trees. Suddenly I understand that the lost pages were my forgotten childhood memories that the Mimic conjures through his magic lantern. It is an evening from my last summer on earth, before I fall sick and take to bed—with neither my father nor I realizing that I was on the verge of dying. I'll never know if the author discarded those pages thinking they were erased from my memory, or whether other events—from the life and mind of Velázquez in the second book to crisscross this limbo—forced him to abandon the writing. But no matter, it is merely a passing, Byzantine hypothesis. My interest is now fixed on the reflections of me and my father, bareheaded and in a rumpled cotton suit, as we stroll beneath the trees in the glow of the gas lamps. Other people out for a stroll—married couples walking arm in arm, or ladies in bustled skirts holding lace fans—all tinged in vermillion by the penumbra, stop occasionally to greet and chat with my father.

"Solicitor, isn't the full moon dangerous when it shines so red?" The question comes from two ladies I vaguely recall being our neighbors.

"Beneath this moon, the only ones in danger are the workers' babies. When the moon is blood red, the Queen Regent turns into a she-wolf and enters their shacks through the window to devour them."

"Oh, our dear solicitor! Why do you scandalize us with your brazen ideas?" They chuckle at his irreverence, as if it were part of a circus act renowned for its insolence, and wave good-bye with their fans.

"My, what a precious lad in the moonlight!" Another lady stops to touch my cheek with her open palm. "I am three times a grand-mother, but I've never see a more beautiful child. Tonight he looks like a celestial vision."

"A red moon portends bad luck. I see it and wonder what disasters await us," her husband interrupts. "The same moon appeared last summer over the farmhouse where I was born. The village idiot saw it and predicted that within a score of years, a student would assassinate an archduke and a war would come that would change the face of the earth."

"Nonsense!" My father cuts in. "What's coming is a workers' uprising that will spread from England across the continent. In a blink of the eye, libertarian communism will take over all of Europe. Only feudal Russia will withstand the revolution for a century to come."

Through the maples murmurs a fountain and we choose a nearby bench to sit on. My father, suddenly silent, sinks into gloomy introspection. At the foot of a tree lies a dead bird, its wings flayed. As we watch, a train whistles and a shooting star falls in the western sky. My fathers dips his hands over the foun-tain's iron spout and splashes water over his face. It runs from his bald pate down his thick jowls and into his false collar that reminds me of a starched gibbet. In the red glow of the moon, one could almost swear blood was dripping down his face. Lumi-nous, pure blood like that of a martyred innocent.

"Are you happy, my son?"

"Yes, Father. Very happy."

"My treasure, you'll never be so happy as I when I see you so beautiful and alert. A genius and an angel, I tell myself watching you sleep." He falls silent, yet his words I overhear through the sun window reawaken a thousand lost memories. He then begins to talk as if to himself, perhaps daring to do so for the first time. "I hated and cursed you when I learned your mother was in the family way, fearing that you would be born a monster if you lived. You don't know how many times I wished that she would trip on the landing and tumble down the stairs. I wanted her to miscarry but lacked the courage to give her a shove. I repeated over and over to myself: *If this child is born dead or deformed, I will be his hangman for having been his father.* You see, right after your mother became pregnant, I found out I had syphilis. I can still see myself in the doctor's office behind the Barcelona cathedral with my shirt off and my suspenders down. The doctor didn't try to mince words when he told me the diagnosis. I looked up at the gargoyles profiled in the March sky, winced and asked: *Doctor, will my son inherit this?* Strangely enough, it never crossed your mother's or my mind that you could be a girl. You had to be a boy, perhaps a deformed monster, but always a male child. *We won't know until he's born. Any way, you should've never fathered him.*

"I sensed a note of disdain in his voice. I don't think it was my misfortune that caused it, because from diseases such as mine he collected his fees and enlarged his practice. He was more disgusted by my ideals and all the anarchists I defended and got acquitted in the Queen's tribunals. Unable to get dressed or look him in the eye, I asked if there was a cure for my malady. The doctor finished washing his hands in the enamel sink. *I can't heal it, I can only contain it.* My thoughts flashed to Olympia Tower, the Fondora brothel where I must have contracted it during a student vacation. It was run by Madame de Mauleon, a bona fide Parisian procuress who went by the name of Grace. Everything about the woman fascinated me: her bleached white hair, tiny cameo watch, peacock-plumed hat, but most of all her accent so out of time and place. I had been to Barcelona brothels with floorboards reeking of lye, rat-infested patios, and filthy, blood-stained sheets. I always left downhearted, unable to touch a woman, wondering whether a demented god didn't exist and whether these were not his perverse creatures. In striking contrast, Madame de Mauleon used to recite *Les Fleurs du Mal* from a wicker armchair beneath a willow, as if Baudelaire had written *La Beauté* in dedication to her. *Je trône dans l'azur comme un sphinx incompris; / J'unis un coeur de neige à la blancheur des cygnes; / Je hais le mouvement qui déplace les lignes; / Et jamais je ne pleure et jamais je ne ris.* Dressed all in yellow and looking like an array of daffodils, the whores would receive us in the back garden where they played croquet, giggling like little girls.

"Although I have forgotten her name, I remember one with a Lisbon accent. I feel certain that it was she who passed me the disease. She was a redhead who claimed to be a card reader. Hair the color of rose hip honey curled between her thighs. One afternoon, while we sprawled naked in bed, she shuffled cards before throwing them onto the floor to read them. *How very strange,* she whispered. *The cards say I am the same woman I was in a past era. But today you are not yourself, but a man who chased after the secret point where space intersects with time.* She shrugged her shoulders and let the full deck fall with a shake of the pillow. *I*

don't understand a word I'm reading! I'd rather be born blind, my friend.
I had slept with her before, but seeing her there naked and aloof,
she seemed like a stranger. Then she blurted out: *Have you ever
been in Seville?* I answered that I had never been so far as Madrid
nor ever set foot south of Barcelona. *Then it's stranger still,* she
whispered. *I've not been to Seville either, but at times I imagine that
we sported there a long time ago.* She asked me to leave, because my
presence disturbed her and made her cross. When I returned the
following year, she had moved out and no one could give me
any news of her. She was vaguely remembered, as if she only
half-existed."

My father stops talking and presses me against his chest. He
repeats that I am his greatest joy and says he could not survive
if I died or left him. Watching him through the sun window, I
can hear his Roskoff tick in my ear as he sighs and hugs me with
all his might. Then the tick-tock of his watch begins to wind down
as our mirages grow faint. My father and I grow indistinct before
the trees, the fountain, the moon itself fade and disappear. The
red glow lights up the empty night as if awaiting the dawn of
creation. It still taints my cheeks when I turn to face the Mimic
stretched across the bed that was my brother's. He is propped
up on an elbow, grinning.

"You saw what I put on stage, but still you tell me you were
blind to such enchantment?"

"I have no idea why I was conceived, but at least I know why
I died so young. With life, my father also gave me his disease.
But I don't hate his memory. Without realizing, I suppose I ab-
solved him a long time ago."

"Your brother was wrong to call you a bastard and the fruit of
incest. They call that jealousy the envy of Cain."

"Don't tell me what they call it. If this epilogue forms part of
our book, I here refuse to forgive him."

"Can you be so harsh on one who has disappeared twice?"

"Vanished or not, his accounts are still due. For him to be born,
I had to die a young innocent. That's how my brother planned it
before we existed. Men's desires must sometimes precede them
into the world, just as the stars write our destinies before we're
conceived."

"I never imagined such a drawn-out feud." He yawns and
shrugs in bed. "The fact is, my son, you're beginning to bore me."

"Don't leave! I want to see the pages you didn't stage."

"Unpublished pages? They're aren't any that I recall. What I
gave you was the entire script."

"No, it can't be! Something's missing and I can't explain what. Without the last piece, the entire puzzle makes no sense!"

"Maybe there isn't any. I know of no other drafts. Even the words that flew faster than time ended with a period. Forget them and whoever wrote them."

He breaks into a laugh and, by degrees, turns into someone else although he promised to spare me such tricks. While his eyes turn black, his face flattens and his skin grows taut, he swaps his sardonic look for a mask of sorrow. Cinder-colored velvet clothes such as those worn in the seventeenth century cover a massive, taut body while his Vandyke goatee disappears. Over his broadened shoulders and under his jowls appears a pleated ruff. He is in the disguise of Francisco Pacheco: the father-in-law of Velázquez whom Uncle Santiago said looked like a goatherd or horse doctor. His rough tone takes me totally unaware: *As you well know, and since he wrote it all down, people think I married off my Juana to Velázquez and did everything I could to make him the court portraitist because I was overwhelmed by his untapped talent. It may be so, but it's only a half truth. Let's just say it's the head of a coin and the tail bears my cross. I never could admit it, not even to my own confessor, but I declare now that it wasn't just the genius of the young man that captivated me. I was totally smitten with him since the afternoon his father first brought him into my studio. Until then, I always thought love between men was a sin against nature and fuel for the inquisitorial flames. Let me assure you that I never laid so much as a finger on the lad's sleeve nor gave voice to the desire that burned me alive. I don't know whether he sensed it or not. You should understand me better than anyone, since at times you wished you had survived so that Federico could make love to you.* The imitation of Pacheco is anything but convincing. Even in old age, when we spied upon him through the thistles of the oak grove, he was far too manly to lose his head over his daughter's husband. On the other hand, I am startled to learn that the Imposter knows so much about me and my deepest thoughts. I have no idea how he perceived my distant fantasies. But I do know that if I hadn't died so young, I could never have given myself to Federico or to any homosexual. If I fantasized it, it was to prove my brother didn't exist. That was merely my distorted way to deny my brother his life and my name.

Meanwhile, the Great Mimic changes into a new metamorphosis. Now he is my brother's wife, sporting a suit with pointed shoulder pads and the patent leather high heels with ankle straps she wore when driving along the Hudson River, past the billboards of the armed forces. He speaks in her voice to the shy seminarians in corduroy slacks and hand-knitted sweaters. *And you, my boys, what do you do to help the American war effort and free the world?* She doesn't look at them but turns her gaze on me and seductively stares into my eyes. She says she always saw me, although my brother and I thought my specter was invisible to everyone else. She confides that I would never know how many times she wanted to bounce me on her knee like a son, knowing she could never embrace my illusive spirit. *Your brother has disappeared for the very last time. Now that he's dead, mon chou, it's like he never existed. It no longer matters whether his paintings were his or someone else's of similar talent and equal store of patience. Since the world will never know his true self, he will come down in history as someone else. On the other hand, you and I—both shades now—know him as he really was and are free from his yoke. His empty house, a hallucination in stone, is now ours.* She assures me that here we can finally find happiness, because in this labyrinth she discovered the son she never had, as I will find in her a mother. She hastens to add that she will be different from my natural mother. *You have nothing to fear in me. I'll not seduce you in the moonlight, nor will I pass on any disease, such as the one your father confessed to beneath a red moon. Far removed from morbid concerns, we will wander through this maze of corridors, vestibules, staircases, antechambers, alcoves, garrets. salons, reception rooms, butler pantries, rotundas, closets, patios, side rooms, cellars, bedrooms, and attics until we reach the center of this chaos. Perhaps there abides the meaning to this enigma, created in the image of your brother's madness.*

Before I can answer her, the unpredictable Mimic changes into another woman. My brother's wife disappears and in her place I see a much younger, naked redheaded girl. Lying still, her hands clasped behind her head, she silently stares at me. Because of her downy hair the color of pink honey curling between her thighs and the cinnamon freckles dotting her abdomen, shoulders and swelling breasts, I can guess the latest transformation of the Great Imposter. He changed into the Portuguese wench, who in different times and through ominous repetitions had passed the pox to Velázquez and to my father. The parody incarnate of the eternal mother, she is the whore who passes on death rather than life. It was she who caused the death of Francisca, Ignacia, and the elder Inés Manuela. It was because of her that I perished so young that August of tiger-striped snails. But because of her, the second Inés Manuela was born, with all her Kings for descendants. So also was my brother and his work. But I still don't understand the reason for her appearance, since in her the Great Trickster only repeats what I already know.

"What's this all about?"

He doesn't answer. A burnished light comes through the sun window. It crosses the room and gilds the nude on the bed. In order for me to see the aura, the Mimic must have needed the redhead. Her flesh would catch the glow better than that of any other woman, fair-skinned or dark. Meanwhile, she smiles enigmatically and begins to fuse into the light. Although the ray turns the sheets golden and almost blinds me with its intensity, the girl in living flesh vanishes before my very eyes. As if moved by an overpowering force, I turn again to peer into the window from my perch on the Can's throne. Through the oeil de boeuf, I hears voices whispering my name: my inalienable name, not my father's nor my brother's, though the three may sound identical. At the same time, a warm wave of joy fills and carries me away. On the other side of the pane, the moonlit vision in the park has disappeared to give way to the scene of my brother's studio in this very house. The vaulted workshop, taller than an arsenal, had been closed a few years prior to his death. There on the floor inside a copper brazier glow the golden apples that can only have come from the Hesperides' garden.

The splendor is so intense that I must squint to focus. Their brilliance lights up the studio and the bedroom as if its walls, furniture, and even myself were gilded with gold leaf and set out in the sun. It makes me proud to think that my brother, my full sibling, would in death reach the mythic garden—pursued in vain in his life time—to vanquish or beguile the dragon and steal the apples and bring them to his studio. While metamorphosed into my sister-in-law, the Imposter mentioned a hiding place wherein was either veiled or reflected my brother's reason for existence. That spot must be the pot-bellied brazier filled with the fruit of the Hesperides: a still life that not even Velázquez could have painted in his lifetime. Or perhaps, mesmerized by the golden fruit, I am mistaken and can be missing even greater wonders that the sacred apples may merely announce. If that is the case, I must make haste to discover them, because even in these indescribable moments, I can sense that my time is drawing to a close and that soon I will slip into the same void that swallowed up my entire family.

In fear and trembling, I raise my eyes and see the painting resting against the wall. It is as tall as the entire nave and aglow from the fire of the brazier. Seeing it, I shiver in delight because

I feel certain that I have reached the end of my wanderings. In the foreground, my brother has painted himself looking into a hypothetical mirror. *Why did you bring me to see* Ladies-in-Waiting *if you knew I couldn't step into the mirror to kiss the hands of Velázquez?* To his side and slightly to his back, he has grouped me with my parents and Uncle Santiago, all posing for him in his studio. In diminishing perspective, he positions Federico and Freud, the bicycle from Ellsworth Road and the snail on the mosaic park bench. Nearby I see the aerostat of Monsieur Archiprêtre or Archimandrite and, further back, the entire Rambouillet ballet troupe encircling the baroness in her Argenteuil gardens. There is even the ballerina who dived into the fountain and called to my brother: *Maître, isn't it true that at one time we were fish and our ancestors came from the sea?* Behind her, de Sagra sings, my sister-in-law walks a deserted beach, and Dalí broods among the palms of the Queen Alexandra. The picnic outing at the Royal Hunting Lodge reappears just as we saw it from the oak grove. It is inevitable and fitting that it be here, since from a frustrated book on Velázquez our chronicle was born, and fragments of his biography crisscross the story of our lives. At the very back of the room, behind the easel supporting *Incredible Enigma*, the man with malachite eyes enters through the vacuum of a diminutive open door. More serene than indecisive, he stops and rests his arm on the jamb.

The shadows are reclaiming me. I need more time to recognize all the figures in the canvas that my brother doubtlessly entitled *The Garden of Hesperides*. But the clock is running, and I'll never know the name of the stranger half-eclipsed by the naked models from the bacchanals at the Robert or Saint-Denis. There are other figures, whom I almost forgot, but now identify—the fisherman who brought my parents and young brother to their rustic hut on the cliffs, driving his mule overburdened with the champagne crate of tableware, the stack of mimosa fire wood, the double cooking range, the hat boxes, the bed linen, and the canary cage—the bare essentials for their stay. Or for that matter, the exiled Victor Hugo demanding if death knew his name during the seance at his home-in-exile enshrined in tobacco-colored clouds off the North Sea. Or the spirit of Queen Isabel, the chaste wife of Felipe IV, contritely appearing to Sister María de Agreda and beseeching prayers from purgatory, where she was expiating her sins of vanity in dress and of levity of tongue in recounting her menstrual curses and miscarriages to Castilian courtiers. I was surprised to see people my brother had never met and scenes that only I could have recounted: the spectral young couples dancing the polka, the mazurka, the Charleston, and waltzing beneath the window of the bedroom where he lay sleeping; or the chatty matrons swapping tidbits of gossip about our mother and Uncle Santiago.

Seeing them painted in such true detail, and with my account as his only reference, I begin to apprehend the ultimate meaning of *The Garden of the Hesperides*. My brother must have thought that he painted it for Velázquez on the threshold of his ultimate eternity. But if Velázquez saw it, he must have accepted it as skeptically as he regarded his own masterpieces, with the calm indifference of one who sees art as slightly more real than the illusory world. Since Velázquez was the sanest of men, he would then tell my brother that it was for me also that he inadvertently created his canvas. I could swear that at this point, and with a similar revelation, our scribe is finishing our family chronicle, where his gaze spans from *Ladies-in-Waiting* to the irretrievable yesteryear of our mortal beings. My sole regret is that only my brother, perhaps Velázquez, and myself laid eyes on the painting. I would like to believe that when the hour arrives for the chronicler to fade away, he too will vanish through this curtain of the void. I hope that he will catch a glimpse of the fruits of the sun illuminating the canvas and, thus, recognize his text in the frame that another man's hand had turned into a mirror. Perhaps the unknown author will come to share the peace I feel as I let myself go without fear or protest. It is as if I have returned to Calador Bay, where in my brief life my father taught me to swim, slowly sinking into waters that become more golden as they deepen and reach toward oblivion at the unknowable point of infinity that can only be the end period of a novel entitled *The Garden of the Hesperides*.